Panama Deception

Jennifer Haynie

Cover design by Indie Designz, http://www.indiedesignz.com

ISBN:
978-0-692-39282-9

Dedication

For all of those who labor in the shadows and walk the knife's edge between lies and truth to keep us safe.

Be alert and of sober mind. Your enemy the devil prowls around like a roaring lion looking for someone to devour.
—1 Peter 5:8 (NIV)

Prologue

He was next.

Hakim al-Husseini knew it deep within his bones, like he felt the cold that night. While the night air bit into his skin and chased away any feeling from his nose and fingers, the fear that he could die before his time chilled him all the way to his heart and soul. What else should he have expected when a dozen of his comrades had died mysterious deaths over the past two years?

He shook out a cigarette. With shaking hands, he lit it. The nicotine calmed him, and as he exhaled a stream into the frigid air, the tension in his shoulders dissipated a little.

Hakim stared into the darkness surrounding the Whispering Springs Resort. Another puff helped him shift his mind to why he stood outside of a cabin high on a mountain in West Virginia.

Lara.

A feminine silhouette paced in the lit picture window. She must have been talking to their children. An unwilling smile tipped his lips upward. Then he cast a glance at his watch.

Time to go.

1

He tossed the cigarette to the ground and squashed it out with the toe of his shoe.

Hakim shut the door behind him and laid his jacket across the back of the sofa. Before him, his wife leaned against the couch as she chatted on her cellphone. "Make sure that Yacoub and Gabriel behave themselves and don't stay up too late, okay? I don't want Nana and Papa to have to be enforcers while we're away." She caught his eye and blew him a kiss. "I love you too, Nadia. How about put Nana back on for me?"

The delicate scent of lavender teased Hakim's nose as he banked the fire for the night. He gazed at the woman clad in the little black dress that showed all of her curves. Only the few gray strands in her upswept dark hair and the fine lines around those gray eyes indicated how long they'd been married.

Twenty years.

"I love you too, Mom. We'll see you Monday. Tell Dad I love him." Lara hung up and dropped her phone into her purse.

Hakim wasted no time in drawing her close. "Is everything quiet on the home front?" He nuzzled her hair and kissed her on the fair skin revealed by the twist.

"Hmmm. Keep that up, and we might not leave." Then she sighed. "Yeah. Mom's worried."

He winced. So much for forgetting part of the reason why they'd planned this trip. "I know. So am I."

"Isn't there any way to go down in a couple of weeks or even next week and file the paperwork?"

"It's not that easy." The tightness returned to Hakim's chest. "I wish it were, but—"

"I know. I know. You're committed to the mission." Lara shook off his embrace and grabbed her jacket from its peg.

"Ed's got my back. I promise you on that. Please." He stepped closer to her and tried not to notice how she draped her jacket over her arms like it was a shield. "Let's remember why we're here."

"To get away from the stress, I know."

He lifted his hand to her cheek. "Yes, that, but if I remember correctly, exactly twenty years ago at this time, I promised to you that I would be faithful to the very end."

Tears pooled in her eyes. A trembling smile crossed her lips. "I never took you for the sentimental type."

"I am when it comes to you." He kissed her.

At first, she tried to pull back, but then she leaned into him and brushed her hand across the back of his neck.

He seriously considered canceling their reservations for seven o'clock.

"Maybe we should stay here," he murmured against her lips. "You know, call out for pizza or something."

Lara giggled. "And miss our reservations at Gregory's? I'm just as sentimental as you."

Hakim took her coat and held it for her. "Then let's go."

They stepped into the night, and he locked the front door. The lights of his Jeep Grand Cherokee flashed twice as he unlocked the doors. He held the passenger door for her. "M'lady?"

She slid inside and buckled her belt. Once he started the SUV, he backed out of the driveway and pulled onto the road. Snowflakes drifted across the windshield. "It should be good skiing weather tomorrow. How many slopes do you want to hit?"

"As many as we can." The soft glow of the dashboard lights lit Lara's face. "But, I'm also up to coming back early and being a ski bunny."

"Nadia would be jealous since she loves to ski." Hakim fell silent as they stopped where the road dead-ended at the winding two-lane highway. "Next year, when I'm retired, I'm going to go skiing with her as much as I can. It'll be good to spend time with her since she'll be a senior."

"Yacoub and Gabriel will also enjoy having you around. Gabriel wants to race BMX in the spring, you know. And summer. I guess I'll have to haul him around for just a few more months."

"Until the first of July." Hakim fell silent as the road steepened. The night before when he'd made a late-night run to the drugstore, he'd noticed ice, especially on the curve up ahead. He pressed on the brakes.

Nothing happened.

His heart began pounding.

"You might want to slow down," Lara said.

"I'm trying." He pushed the pedal harder. It went all the way to the floor. Hakim gripped the wheel tighter.

"Hakim!" Lara's husky voice rose an octave.

"The brakes are shot!"

The sharp curve to the right appeared in the headlights. He yanked on the emergency brake.

Nothing.

"We're going too fast!"

Hakim threw the SUV into first gear, but when he tried to navigate the turn, they skidded on the ice. Lara screamed as they tore through the steel guardrail and plunged into the gorge.

He thought it was a strange feeling to plummet to his death. Like being on a rollercoaster on that first big hill. His stomach dropped. An unearthly voice filled the air. Maybe his?

Then came the impact and the crunch of metal.

Then nothing.

Day 1
Sunday, June 11, 2017

1

1215 hours Central Daylight Time, Panama City, Panama

The Honda motorcycle wove in and out of traffic as it sped down the wide boulevard toward downtown with controlled fury. Salsa music blared from the small radio on the instrument cluster.

Ahead, the traffic signal flashed to yellow and red.

Jabir muttered under his breath as he came to a stop behind a pickup truck with tires stacked so high in the bed that he feared he'd be buried beneath them if the load gave way. He flipped up the visor of his helmet and stared at the clock below the radio.

He was late.

Ed didn't tolerate lateness.

Jabir scowled at the signal. One hand massaged the throttle while the other clamped onto the brake.

The light turned.

He shot forward and slipped around the lumbering pickup before darting between an old Ford minivan and a Cadillac Escalade.

The driver of the Cadillac honked and flipped him the bird.

Jabir didn't care.

Five blocks ahead of him, Hotel Panama loomed, its windows glittering in the bright sunlight like sirens luring their sailors to a rocky death. On his left, a large cathedral came into view.

At a break in the traffic, a policeman stepped into the road. He held up a white-gloved hand.

Jabir muttered under his breath. He had no choice but to stop since winding up in jail would make Ed even unhappier than he already was. Cars flooded onto the hot pavement from the cathedral, so many that he wondered how many people it held.

Finally, the policeman neatly turned on his heel ninety degrees and began waving people through.

Jabir gunned the engine and wasted no time in racing to the hotel. He cut across the path of an oncoming bus and truck, once more earning blaring horns as a reward. After parking the motorcycle under a low-spreading palm, he locked his helmet to it before running his hands through his hair. Sweat shot out in a spray.

His phone began chiming.

More sweat trickled down his back as he checked the Caller ID.

Abdel.

"Abdel, hey."

"Where are you, buddy?"

"I just got here. I'll be there as soon as I can get into the building."

"Alrighty, then." Abdel's Texan drawl did nothing to reassure him. "Ed's grumbling about kicking you off the team."

Jabir's heart almost seized.

"Just kidding. But he's getting antsy."

"I hear you." Jabir opened the side door to the hotel with his key card. "Give me two."

He hung up and dashed up the fire stairs to the fifth floor. Room 524 was eight doors down on his left. He inserted the key into the lock. The bolt clicked back, and he slipped inside. Almost total darkness greeted him.

"Good that you could join us." That comment came from the man sitting at the worktable pushed against the wall. He turned, and the pale light from the screens of the laptops reflected off his reading glasses. He popped open a bag of Cheetos and tossed one into his mouth.

As Jabir's eyes adjusted to the dimness, he recognized Abdel lounging in the easy chair under the golden glow of the one lamp on in the room. Ari sprawled on the couch in front of the window. Bright noonday sun fought to permeate the closed drapes. Stephen sat on the other end. Jabir noticed the way he slid the Beretta he held under a pillow.

"Take a load off," Ed told him. Reaching into the cooler resting at the foot of the bed, he pulled out an icy bottle and tossed it to Jabir. "What took you so long?"

"I got caught in traffic, including a mass exodus."

"A what?" Stephen frowned at him.

"A mass exodus." Jabir unscrewed the top and took a swig. The icy water cooled his worries and quenched his thirst. "The cathedral up the road five blocks let out from Mass just as I got to the intersection. I don't think it would have been too wise to try and run over a cop."

He seated himself on the cooler.

Stephen snickered. "Good one."

"Good one what?" This came from Ari.

"Pun, silly. Mass exodus. Ha!" Abdel chuckled.

"Enough of that, gentlemen. Let's do a final briefing." Ed spun around in his chair so he faced the small circle. "I'll start with an update. As you know, Samir Kamil is scheduled to come and close on the property a week from Tuesday on the twentieth."

Everyone nodded.

"It looks like things might have changed."

"What?" Jabir frowned and rested his bottle on his knee.

"Since Finch, May, and Gilbert has been preparing the contract, we've been tracking the attorney's e-mails. And it seems as if Ms. Forrest has now been requested to come and do the walkthrough rather than the local attorney."

"What are your thoughts on that?" Stephen asked.

"I think she smells a rat. Melanie Forrest is no dummy."

"Or someone tipped her off." Stephen rubbed his chin.

"Probably. And they were smart enough to keep it quiet and off the e-mail until Ms. Forrest contacted the engineer who'll be assisting her. Regardless, she's going to see that property, and she's going to realize her boy Samir has been lying to her over the past four or so months." Ed shook his head. "Knowing that, guess what? Plan B is now becoming more of a reality."

Jabir swallowed hard. He'd always hated Plan B. It made him nervous and sick to his stomach.

"With that being said, I want to go over our status and roles in this op for Plan B. Al-Omri, what do you have?"

Jabir began ticking through his duties in his head. He'd secured the safe house. Thanks to his recent efforts, he had enough nonperishable food to last for quite a while. And water—

"Al-Omri!"

The sharpness in Ed's voice told him one thing. He'd been thinking too long.

"Sorry. The safe house is ready. The only thing we need to do is to move the food and water we've collected up there tomorrow."

"Good. And your tasks for the snatch?"

"I'll keep surveillance in the lobby and make sure Melanie gets to her room."

"And you'll disguise yourself. No need in making Ms. Forrest think twice about you. And then?"

"After the closing, I'll scope her out tomorrow night in the bar."

Abdel yawned as if feigning boredom. "My money says she'll be at the outdoor bar."

"Huh?" Jabir frowned.

"Five says she's not a big fan of over air-conditioned buildings and will try to drink away her worries in a tropical setting where she can at least imagine she's on vacation." Abdel grinned. "Anyone in?"

"Pass, thanks."

Ed cleared his throat. "Moving on. You're on the snatch team with me, al-Omri. And you've got a critical piece. Ms. Forrest has a heart condition, right?"

Jabir nodded as he recalled the dossier Ed had built on their target. "Cardiomyopathy."

"Right." Ed leaned forward and pinned him in his sharp gaze. "You're to make sure we've got her medication. A dead hostage would end our ride real quick, wouldn't it?"

Jabir shuddered.

Ed sat back. "Karesh, your status."

Stephen straightened. "I've gotten her room set up in the hotel's reservation system to be Room 748. It's not next to the stairwell like we wanted, but it's close. Two doors down. And I'm going to help Abdel get the bug placed. Then assist Jabir in finalizing things at the safe house."

"Excellent." Ed nodded. "Al-Rashid?"

"Right-o. So like Stephen said, I'll be doing the bug. Then I'll head down to the pool to catch some sunbathing beauties—Ow!" Abdel scowled at Ari and rubbed his shin where his friend had kicked him. "What was that for?"

"On task." Ari eyed him with mock sternness.

"Okay. No, seriously, I'll be backup here in case anything goes down and will get the room cleaned up when we swing into action."

Ed nodded. "And you're the man in charge of the gear bag. You and Karesh will be waiting for us in the van when we come out. Rosen, you're on."

Ari leaned forward and rested his muscled forearms on his knees. "I'm following Melanie. I've got the taxi ready and a couple of disguises in case she wises up."

"Ten says she's clueless." Abdel grinned.

"What got you into a betting mood?" Jabir asked.

"Man, I'm going to Vegas when we get back. I've got to get my betting money from somewhere. Anyone in?"

"Pass," all four men chorused.

"Poopers." Abdel tossed his empty bottle at Stephen, who batted it away.

"Back on task, gentlemen." Ed's voice cut into their fun. "Rosen?"

Ari nodded. "I'm on the snatch crew with you and Jabir."

"Excellent." Ed turned and glanced at one of the laptops. "I'll be up here keeping an eye on things until we're ready to move. I imagine Ms. Forrest will be presenting a negative report, and it doesn't take a genius to realize what her client's going to do. And I'll be on the snatch crew. Good. Sounds like we're locked and loaded. Any questions?"

Jabir bit his lip. His stomach knotted as he thought about what the snatch meant.

The kidnapping of an American citizen.

He opened his mouth to protest, to say that he thought what they were planning was unethical at best, illegal at worst, and that he wasn't comfortable at all with the prospect.

"Son, is something bothering you?" Ed focused on him. The pale light from the laptops bleached his gray eyes so much that he seemed like some sort of ghost.

Jabir shivered. Then he shook his head. "No. Nothing."

"All right. Dismissed until tomorrow. Rosen, Ms. Forrest lands at eleven, so be prepared." Ed pulled up an e-mail they'd intercepted. "A Señor del Fuente will be meeting her at the airport. Get on him like stink on a dog first thing tomorrow."

"Roger that."

"I'll see you all later." Jabir jumped up.

"Hot date?" Abdel grinned.

"No. It's time for me to hit the gym. Later, guys." Jabir escaped from the room and into the stairwell. Once there, he leaned against the wall and rested his head against the slick cinderblock.

Words from Tiny, his boss at the Department of Homeland Security's Unit 28, haunted him. "Your mission is to get enough evidence to determine whether or not Ed DuBois is the killer of the CIA's senior native Arabic speakers. CIA IAD can't move unless we get something definitive. Get close to him, but watch your back. You'll be operating on your own out there."

Jabir turned, fled down the stairs, and dashed through the parking lot.

As he cranked his motorcycle and sped toward the gym, more of his conversation with Tiny echoed in his ears. "The guy you're replacing was killed along with his wife in an auto accident in West Virginia. With your background, you were a perfect candidate for the job."

"Thanks, Tiny," Jabir muttered under his breath as he thought about the leader of the snatch.

"I worked with Ed in Afghanistan," Tiny had told him that February day. "He's someone who's always operated in the gray. The question remains as to how dark a gray."

Once Jabir arrived at the gym, he jumped rope to release some nervous energy. Then he moved on to the speed bag. The look he'd seen in Ed's eyes made his fists go through the motions to the point where the bag was almost a blur. Some of the last advice Tiny gave him before he departed the office came back to him in a flash. "Whatever you do, don't ever question Ed's authority. He hates that and won't tolerate it."

Jabir muttered, cocked his fist, and rammed it into the speed bag. It came off its mooring and flew into a corner. Flushing, he glanced around. At least no one had seen his actions. He paced in a tight circle, hands on his hips, chest heaving, as both his body and his temper cooled. Jabir lifted his chin and closed his eyes as he realized the enormity of the next several hours.

If things went as planned, he would have willingly participated in the kidnapping of an American citizen.

2

Furious fists beat the punching bag in rhythm to the pounding of Pink's "So What?" screaming through the ear buds. An occasional kick punctuated the anger flowing through Alex.

All thanks to James Ray and his idiotic methods of breaking up. At the thought of him, another hot layer of anger ripped through her. She delivered a hard roundhouse kick that sent the bag twirling on its rope.

A guy caught it. He grinned and said something.

Alex yanked the ear buds out, and merciful silence descended around her. "What?"

"Nice kick." Josh Thornton, her next-down brother, held the bag and grinned at her. "I figured you'd be blowing off some steam here at Joe's."

"What makes you say that?"

"Mom says you bolted out of church like your tail was on fire. You weren't home. Diana didn't know where you were, and you didn't answer your cell. My next logical chain of thought before I called the police was that since it's so hot out, you came to Joe's."

15

Alex slid into her boxer's pose and began bouncing on her toes. This time, Josh held the bag as she delivered a flurry of jabs. She imagined it was James's face. "So?"

"What happened?"

"James Ray is what happened." She delivered a cross punch that made Josh stagger. Then she stopped and brushed back the wisps of dark hair that had slipped from the stubby ponytail of her pageboy cut. Breathing heavily, she wandered to the bench where she'd dropped her water bottle and towel. Alex collapsed onto it and began unwinding the tape from her hands. "He broke up with me. On my first day of vacation, nonetheless."

Josh settled beside her and raised an eyebrow. "Oh?"

"Yeah. By text." Alex scowled. "The jerk didn't even have the courage for a phone call, let alone a face-to-face conversation."

She took a pull on her bottle and mopped her face with a towel that had the motto "Keep calm and carry on" embroidered on it.

"Probably for the best."

"Maybe. It's just…" Unexpected tears flooded her eyes as the rejection stung again like an angry wasp.

Josh put his arm around her shoulders. "Hey, forget about him."

He gazed at her for a moment as she dabbed at the corner of her eyes and tried to pretend they stung from the sweat. "This runs deeper, doesn't it?"

Alex hated that he was right. After a moment, she blurted, "I feel like a loser."

He didn't say a word.

"I mean, I can't keep a guy. I was stupid, ran off, got married and divorced, all within three months."

"You were in crisis."

"Hah. That's one way to put it, I guess." Memories from four years ago swarmed around her. She released a shuddering breath. "And while I paid for the 'crime' of our mission, Jabir got away scot-free."

Josh pulled back and studied her. She wondered what ran through his head. Maybe something like how ungrateful she was for grousing about his taking her in when she'd retreated to her hometown or the way his then-contractor and now-wife had offered her a job working at with her to renovate his house, even when Alex had no experience. He said neither.

He stood. "Mom wanted me to tell you she's fixing supper and for you to be there at six. And I think Joe's ready to close." He nodded toward where the owner stood at the door, a ring of keys dangling from his fingers. "Clean up, and we'll see you in an hour."

Alex rose and watched him go. Suddenly tired, she heaved a sigh, gathered her bag from the locker room, and bid Joe goodbye. Maybe Josh was right. Maybe it was for the better, this cowardly breakup with James. Then the hurt rose up inside of her as she thought about his text.

It's not you. It's me.

Whatever.

She scowled, wrenched open the back door of her yellow four-door Jeep Wrangler, and tossed her gym bag onto the backseat.

As she opened her door to climb inside, her cell began chiming. She checked Caller ID. Melanie Forrest, the guest of honor for the upcoming bachelorette week in Costa Rica. "Melanie, hey."

"Hey, girl." Melanie's southern drawl conjured memories of the Fantabulous Four as youngsters sitting in the woods and feasting on the sweetness of honeysuckle blossoms. "How's it going?"

"Fair to middlin'." Before she could stop herself, Alex sighed.

"Hmmm. I'm not so sure about that. What was that sigh about?"

In short, clipped sentences, Alex explained the breakup. "I mean, I feel like such a loser."

"Why would you say that?" Melanie's concern radiated all the way from Manhattan to Weatherly.

"You know. I mean, I can't seem to keep a boyfriend. I lost a good career even though I was simply doing my job. My marriage lasted three months. And Jabir." Alex's eyes filled as she paced in small circles next to the Jeep. "I'm sorry. You'd think that four years after everything happened, I'd be over it and happy here in Weatherly."

Melanie was quiet for a moment after she let her friend wind down. "Sometimes things take longer to process than we anticipate. You haven't talked to him?"

"Don't you remember? He deserted me and tried to make nice about it." Alex narrowed her eyes as she thought back to that chilly March day two years before. "I told you about how he sent that letter. And I returned it without opening it. So no, I haven't talked to him." She leaned against the Jeep's fender. "The problem is, I still feel hollow."

"Oh, Alex."

"It was two years too late. I'm done with him. Our friendship ended when he deserted me."

Liar.

"Anyway, how are you? *Where* are you?" Alex added when she heard her friend murmur something.

"I'm at a Mexican restaurant in Manhattan waiting on Samir Kamil to show up."

"Wait. Samir, as in ex-flame-from-law-school Samir?" Alex waved as Joe locked the gym's doors and headed to a pickup truck.

"Yeah. His company is a client of my firm, and since he's general counsel and my firm's the outside counsel, I guess you could say he's my client. He's been in the Hamptons for two and a half weeks on vacation and wanted to see me." Her voice petered out. After a moment, she said, "I'm worried about him."

"How so?"

"Noor, his sister who's also COO of their company, called me about ten days ago. She wanted to meet, so we met at my condo one evening and had supper. Samir didn't know about that."

"And that's worrisome why?"

"I think he might be mixed up in something. Something bad. That's what she wanted to talk about."

"Like?"

Melanie sighed. "I don't know. And that's what bothers me. You see, my company's doing an audit on the books for Kamil International. And Kamil International's also getting ready to buy a property in Panama City."

"Which is why you're going there tomorrow." Alex reached into the small cooler she kept in the back and extracted a Gatorade.

"Right. Not to get into too many details, but apparently, someone spotted some discrepancies in their finances that were enough to request a forensic audit. And, his father, who's president of the company, wants me to do the final walkthrough as well as the closing, which isn't normal procedure. I guess I'm worried. Will you pray for me?"

Despite the heat outside, Alex felt a flush starting in her cheeks. "Um…"

"Look. I know you and God aren't exactly on speaking terms right now, but I'd appreciate it."

"Okay." Alex swallowed hard.

For her friend, she would.

Maybe.

"So long as you'll pray for me," she added with a weak attempt at levity in her voice.

"Always. Have you talked with Becca and Ellie?"

"Not yet. I'm going to call them tonight after supper."

"Look at it this way. You're the one who can flirt with the guys and have some fun. Maybe that's what you need."

"True." The barest traces of a smile lifted Alex's lips as she thought about how they'd planned this trip ever since Melanie had gotten engaged the summer before.

"He's here. Oh, and pray that I somehow figure out how to tell him I'm engaged."

"He doesn't know?"

"Not yet. It's complicated."

Alex knew all about complicated.

"Send me your flight info too," she hastily added.

"Will do. See you soon, Alex." With that, Melanie hung up.

Alex shoved her phone into her purse and climbed behind the wheel. She cranked the engine and turned the air conditioner on full blast.

As she turned her wheels toward her flat at the center of town, her thoughts roved through what she knew.

It sounded like both she and Melanie needed a vacation.

Big time.

She could only hope that days spent on pristine beaches and nights spent dancing would wipe away the feelings of failure that still stalked her.

And memories of Jabir.

If they didn't, she didn't know what she'd do

3

The sleek black Corvette cruised beneath streetlights beginning to glow in the artificial dusk created by the urban canyon of Manhattan. Techno music pulsed from the speakers, and Samir enjoyed the feel of the summer breeze whispering through his hair, the rumble of the eight-cylinder engine, and the rich aroma of freshly polished leather. It was a man's car, one that made him feel powerful and worthy.

He slowed to a stop under the Aztec portico of the Mexican restaurant. A valet met him at the curb. After cutting off the engine, Samir climbed from the seat before handing off the keys. "Take good care of it, and there might be something for you."

He strolled into the restaurant.

Melanie had said she'd be on the patio.

His gaze swung to the hostess. "I am meeting my friend on the patio. Perhaps she told you I was coming?"

She smiled. "Tall? Blonde? Last name of Forrest?"

"That's her."

"This way, please." She turned and led the way through the cool tile interior and onto a patio of slate.

Samir's heart caught when he noticed Melanie sitting at the table, her phone to her ear, a half-empty margarita in front of her. The short skirt and sleeveless blouse highlighted the tanned legs and toned arms he remembered from so long ago.

Her gaze met his, and she ended her call. She stood. "Samir, it's good to see you."

Samir pulled her into a light embrace and kissed both of her cheeks as her perfume teased his nose with the pleasant scent of lavender and many memories of her waking up in his arms. He released her. "Melanie, you are beautiful as always. A year has been too long."

"You make me blush." A smile flickered across her face. "Please, have a seat. My apologies for ordering a drink already, but I arrived early."

"And I apologize for my tardiness." Samir settled across the table from her. "Traffic was a bit heavy coming back into town."

"Where were you?"

He ordered his own margarita and set the drink menu on the burnished wood of the table. "I was in the Hamptons finishing a two-week vacation. The entire family went to a cousin's wedding there."

"When are you headed to Beirut?"

"After I leave here, I'll be flying on our private jet back to Beirut. Everyone else decided to linger a little longer on the coast and will meet me at the airport. Please. Enough of that." Samir picked up a glossy menu and studied it. "Let's decide what we want."

Once they'd ordered their meals along with another margarita for Melanie, she leaned forward. "Tell me about this property of yours."

"What is there to tell?" He shrugged. "It is a good piece of property that is perfect for the needs of the company and our potential client."

She cocked her head. "How so?"

"You do not know?"

"I'm a lawyer, not a mind reader." She smiled, but it faded.

Unease uncurled deep in Samir's gut.

"I can make suppositions, but I'd like to hear it in your words." She sipped her drink.

Samir fell silent for a moment as he recalled the story he'd rehearsed and provided so many times over the past few months. "You know we have operations all over the world in major ports. Hong Kong. Singapore. Mumbai. New York. Marseilles. Name the port, we are there. Save for Central and South America. We have been looking for suitable property in that part of the world for a long time, you see."

Melanie nodded.

"We have found properties in Rio de Janeiro on the Atlantic side, but we are still struggling on the Pacific side."

"Nothing in Mexico?"

"Papa is leery of Mexico and for good reason." Samir leaned back and crossed his legs, anything to project an image of confidence.

"True. I'd be leery too until things calm down a bit."

"Panama City offers us a large port on one of the busiest canals in the world and on the Pacific Ocean."

"How'd you hear about the property?"

"Why all of the questions?" Samir asked.

"I'm curious. I mean, I've been working on the contract since late January, but I've never heard of how you came to know about it."

"An associate of mine informed me." He leaned forward. "It is the way we do business sometimes. Clients of ours, who either want to work with us further or know us from other ports oftentimes want us to move into another area on their behalf."

"Care to share who?"

"No." He couldn't tell her that Tarek had informed him one night shortly after the New Year about Jihad of Light's desire to have the property. "This associate is considering a renewal. Call it a trade secret. The thing that would tip it in our favor to win the renewal is for us to have operations in Panama City."

"I see. Has Noor been there?"

"No, no." Why was she asking so many questions? Samir scrambled for an answer that would make sense. "She has been very busy lately. We are considering a reorganization of our operations structure, and as COO, she has been overseeing that with no time for extraneous travel. I told her about the property and showed her photographs my associate sent me. She said it looked like a viable opportunity, and if I thought it would add another client, then I was to proceed with the purchase."

Melanie studied him for a moment. "No one from Kamil International has surveyed the property?"

"No."

"Samir." She began shaking her head.

The unease wound its way into his heart. He tried a smile. "Melanie, Melanie. I have been busy as well, you understand. Before vacation? I was in Cape Town. Then Mumbai. Then over to Singapore before heading to Beijing and back to Beirut. It has been like that ever since the New Year. You must understand that sometimes, I have to rely on the opinion of others even if they are not from my company."

Melanie remained silent for a moment. Then she sighed and shook her head. "I do. I understand that. But as a lawyer specializing in real estate transactions of very high dollar, I'd be remiss in my duties not to ask questions. Before our food arrives, let's finish our business." She reached into her briefcase and pulled out her tablet. She touched it a few times and laid it on the table to reveal photographs. "I think we've reviewed the contract *ad nauseum*, and all of your assets and debts have been properly accounted for. These are the photographs you forwarded to me. Close to a hundred. Thank you for that."

Samir pulled his chair closer so he could see them. Once more, her perfume induced heady memories of having her by his side during their law school romance. "Yes, those are what I sent you."

"From what I've been able to tell, it looks like a pretty decent property, though maybe a bit small. Why's that?"

"Because we have one potential client, not several. We could grow if need be."

Melanie raised an eyebrow as if she doubted every word he'd said. "At least Kamil International can purchase it for cash and not incur anymore debt." She slid the tablet into her handbag.

Samir stayed where he was, their shoulders almost touching. He wanted to take her hand, but he didn't dare. "They will do the walkthrough this week, and I will fly in and meet you for the closing next week. Correct?"

Melanie bit her lip. She refused to meet his gaze. Then she did. Her brow had knitted, and she surveyed him with such an intense look that he feared she could see into the dirty depths of his soul.

"I'm going to conduct the walkthrough."

Samir's heart nearly seized. "What?" He blinked. "But why? Isn't that such a long ways for you to go? And then to return the following week for the closing?"

"Not when I'm headed in that direction for vacation."

"I don't understand. Why?" His pulse hammered in his ears.

Somehow, she must have discovered the truth.

He sat straighter and leaned away from her.

"Your father asked me to do so. I accepted since he personally requested it. It's no problem. Really. I mean, I'm going to Costa Rica for vacation, and it's not that big of a deal."

"Is that normal?"

"If we have offices in the country, we let the client decide. We don't have offices in Panama, so our San Jose office contracted it out to a Panamanian firm we use when dealing with clients in that country. They did all of the legwork to prepare the contract on the Panamanian end of things. Most of the time for the walkthrough, we use the local attorneys. But sometimes, our clients specially request someone from the home office to do so. As president of Kamil International, your father requested it, so I'm going. Why is that such a big deal?"

"It is not. I guess I was…" Samir fought to maintain his composure. "I was surprised. That is all."

He gulped his margarita and winced as it stung going down.

Melanie began twisting a ring on her left ring finger. "I'll complete the walkthrough and send you, Noor, and Farouk a report the same day. Based on that report, Kamil International has the option of backing out of the contract. You'd lose your earnest money, but it'd be better than the amount it would take to purchase the property."

"True." Samir sighed. Something or someone had tipped off Papa, and Samir had no choice but to acquiesce. To protest further would have made Melanie more suspicious. "I'm sorry. It's just that usually an associate doesn't conduct the walkthrough, correct?"

"Like I said, it depends." She resumed twisting. "I promise that if your father decides to go through with the closing, I'll be there with you."

Suddenly, Samir noticed her actions. "Melanie, you...is that..."

"What?"

"Your ring. You are engaged?"

The flush began as a delicate pink at the open neck of her blouse. It began working its way up her neck. "Um, yeah."

"Since when?" His eyes widened.

"Last year. Rick proposed to me while we vacationed in Hawaii over my birthday." She spread her left hand on the table, and the solitaire sparkled in the fading sunlight.

"It is very beautiful." He choked that out.

Melanie smiled. "Thank you. We're marrying in the middle of August. I'll be with the firm through the end of July."

"You're leaving us?"

"Leaving the firm. And yes, I guess leaving Kamil International as a client. Look." Melanie sighed. "I'm sorry I didn't tell you earlier. It's been...awkward. Since we were so serious in law school, you know.

"Please, Samir." She reached out to touch him on the arm but instead almost knocked over her margarita glass. He steadied it as she continued, "Rick and I thought about what to do when we married. He could move here, which he most definitely didn't want to do. We could have two 'homes,' one here in Manhattan and one in Atlanta, but we agreed it was pointless to do something like that. Honestly, I'm fine with leaving Manhattan. It's crowded. Expensive. Cold as heck in the winter. I'm planning on starting at the first of the year with a firm down there that does real estate law and estate planning. I'm fine with that. Really."

Hurt stole his appetite. What should he have expected three years before when Melanie became their outside counsel? Especially after over five years of separation and the way she'd failed to reciprocate when he'd tried to rekindle their romance?

Once they had their food, Samir probed her with questions about her fiancé. In his mind, he surpassed Rick in every aspect of life. He was richer. More handsome. In a more important job. Melanie could do better than to marry someone involved in what she called a ministry.

Melanie remained guarded. When he brushed her hand accidentally on purpose, she withdrew it. She refused a third margarita that could help him convince her to go with him for the night. Finally, she rose and insisted that she needed to get home since she had to rise at four the next morning.

When they walked outside, Samir handed the valet his ticket. Then he shoved his hands into the pockets of his khakis. Clutching her purse, Melanie remained beside him. She offered him a tremulous smile that did nothing to comfort him.

Finally, Samir sighed. "This is it?"

"I'm afraid so." Melanie met his gaze for a second and glanced away. When she looked back at him, he thought he saw tears pooling in those blue eyes he loved. "Honestly, we were so long ago. I've changed a whole lot since then. You have too. It's just that…"

She closed her mouth.

The valet pulled up in the Corvette. He hopped out and accepted the fifty from Samir. Then he left them alone.

Samir turned to her. "So, perhaps one last kiss goodbye?"

"Um…probably not a good idea. I'm engaged, you know." Melanie took the tiniest step back.

"Then at least accept this." He took her hand, lifted it to his lips, and kissed her fingers. "Know I will always love you. And I'm happy for you. Truly."

The lie sent a bolt of pain through his heart.

"Thanks."

"Do you need a ride to your condo?"

"Thanks, but no." A tremulous smile crossed her lips and faded. "I'm going to walk. It's too nice a night not to."

"Then *adieu*." With that, he climbed into the sports car. Suddenly, he hated the rich purr of the engine and the heady aroma of the leather seats.

He eased forward. At the first break in traffic, he hit the gas. The tires chirped as he pulled in front of a Mercedes. The restaurant quickly receded in the distance.

If only Melanie's memory would do the same.

And the trouble he suddenly faced.

Because he knew that once she presented the report to the rest of his family members, her final rejection of him might be the least of his problems.

Day 2
Monday, June 12, 2017

4

Silence reigned in Room 524 of Hotel Panama. Silence and darkness.

Ed preferred it that way when on a job.

Then the noise of cellophane broke the stillness as he popped open a snack pack of Cheetos. He tossed one into his mouth as he studied the four laptops lined up like sentries along the worktable's top.

The one on the far right showed e-mails flickering to and from Melanie Forrest's work account about everyday things like her review of memos and requests for meetings when she returned. Next to that laptop, another showed the e-mails to and from Samir Kamil's e-mail account. That one remained silent save for mundane work issues. The third laptop contained four panes, each one tracking the text conversations between the cell-phones of his four-man team. And the last? An audio program glowed on the screen.

The phone clipped to his belt chirped a bird tweet.

Francesca had texted him.

He grinned when he saw the text from his longtime girlfriend. *I'm planning our trip for this summer. When will you be back?*

He tapped out a message. *By the first of July.*

31

To be safe, I'll make it for the latter half of the month. How does a trip to paradise sound? Love you.

With you, anywhere is paradise. Love you back. Ed's grin softened to a smile.

Crackling and jagged lines appearing on the audio program's oscilloscope made the smile fade. He set his personal phone on the table by his work phone.

"Testing. Testing. Can you hear me?" Al-Rashid's voice came across as if his operative were standing next to his chair.

Ed clicked on the text window for al-Rashid. *Loud and clear. Get up here.*

"On our way." Rustling told Ed that al-Rashid and Karesh were collecting their tools. The door to Melanie Forrest's room thumped softly shut. Now, Ed could hear anything in that room, from her shower running to any sighs she made while she slept. Perfect.

His gaze swung to the text screen for Rosen. A series of messages appeared. Rosen was following the subject of this op. She'd left the café where she and the engineer who'd done the walkthrough with her had dined on a late lunch. Nothing from Rosen indicated she had any idea she'd had a tail all day long. He tapped out a message to al-Omri. *Subject on the way.*

Al-Omri's quick reply told him he was waiting and would pick up the tail once Rosen and Ms. Forrest arrived at the hotel.

Ed frowned.

What was with the kid?

He was the best of the best. Tiny had indicated so when he'd called him up to say he was sending him over. Ed hadn't expected the best to look like he was barely old enough to take a drink. During the final brief the day before, al-Omri had acted like he dreaded the op. Didn't he have guts?

Ed didn't have time for formal protests.

The lock clicked in the door.

Ed snatched up the Beretta on his lap and placed his finger on the trigger guard.

Karesh and al-Rashid slipped inside and shut the door behind them.

"Welcome back, boys." Ed's gaze flicked to the screens in front of him. "The bug works fine."

Al-Rashid dumped his toolbox on one of queen-sized beds. "Good. Took us long enough to figure out how to install it without setting off the alarm."

"Be glad you didn't do that. Be very glad."

"I hear you." The tall, lanky American-born Egyptian grinned. "You mind if I turn on a lamp?"

Karesh settled at his post on the couch, and Ed handed him his gun.

"Go ahead." Ed swiveled his chair to face the computers. "And make sure we've got all of our gear in that bag."

"Roger that. After I get changed."

Another message flashed from Rosen's phone.

Ed straightened. "They're here."

"Cool." Karesh popped the top on a bottle of water.

"They made the handoff. Ms. Forrest is now being tailed by al-Omri. Meaning Rosen should be walking through that door any minute."

A moment later, the lock clicked again, admitting Rosen in his taxi driver's duds.

"Welcome, earthling," al-Rashid intoned in a nasal voice.

"You're incorrigible, Abdel." Rosen grinned and opened the cooler. Ice rattled as he fished around for a bottle of water.

"What's that?"

"Really?" Karesh rolled his eyes.

"A pain but in a pleasant way." Rosen sighed.

"How'd it go?" Ed pivoted and faced the three operatives. Rosen now sprawled on the easy chair while al-Rashid shrugged into a shirt and buttoned it.

"Like we thought it would. Our boy was a fool to think he could snow Melanie." Rosen shook his head.

A sound of a water drop splashing made Ed turn back around. "Al-Omri just got on the elevator with her."

A few moments later, the lock to the door clicked again, this time admitting al-Omri.

"So she's here." Ed's gaze darted to the computer with the audio program.

The line of the oscilloscope bounced as her door shut. A sigh reached them, as did the sound of someone heaving a suitcase onto the dresser. Then the undoing of a zipper and the murmur of clothing as Ms. Forrest changed into something that was probably more comfortable than the suit and heels he'd seen in the pictures Rosen had forwarded. A soda can popped. A muttered exclamation as her computer chimed reached them.

"Ms. Forrest wonders what Samir was smoking."

Al-Omri crossed his arms and leaned against the door. "I don't think things went well."

"You think? Get a load of this." Ed pulled up another audio file. "Rosen recorded this using the directional listening device." Voices squeaked as he fast-forwarded to a certain part of the conversation. "He got this while Ms. Forrest and the engineer were having lunch at a café."

The engineer spoke in accented English. "Señorita Forrest, I've been in practice as an engineer for over thirty years now. Eight of those in your country and the remainder here in Panama. And I have to say I was absolutely appalled by the condition of the property. Appalled. Really appalled that someone would even consider buying something in such appalling condition."

Al-Omri grinned. "Appalled. He loves that word."

Ed chuckled.

Ms. Forrest's honeyed voice replied, "I understand. Which is why I wanted an engineer to go over it with me. Thank you again for your assistance."

"What will be your recommendation? After all, I know mine. I'd do my license plus my firm a great disfavor by recommending the acquisition of the property."

"I agree. And that will be my recommendation as well."

Ed cut off the file. "Our boy's in big trouble."

"Samir?" Al-Omri pushed himself away from the door and pulled a bottle of water from the cooler. He sat down on the edge of one of the queen beds.

"Who else?" Ed shook his head. "We'll wait. She's probably writing up that report. And as soon as she does, we'll know pretty much how our next week will go."

"I'm betting it'll take her an hour to write up the report," al-Rashid said.

"What is it with you?" Karesh grinned.

"Like I said, I'm going to Vegas when we get back. I've got to earn my spending money somehow. Why not off my friends?"

"Incorrigible. Bad beyond correction or reform. Incorrigible." Rosen swung his feet onto the coffee table and took a swig of water.

"What are you, a walking dictionary?"

"Something like that."

The crew fell silent as they listened to fingers tapping on a keyboard. The sliding glass door in Ms. Forrest's room scraped. She must have stepped onto her balcony for some air. Then she cleared her throat. "Noor, it's Melanie."

"Uh, oh," Karesh muttered.

"Uh, oh's right." Ed leaned forward and stared hard at the computer recording her conversation.

A sigh greeted them next. "It's bad. I'm sorry, but the property is totally not what was in the pictures…I know. I'm sorry. But I wanted to tell you myself before I e-mailed you the report…I know…Well, let me send this. I'll be on vacation after this, but you can reach me if need be…Keep me posted." The conversation seemed to end after that.

"Looks like we found out how Melanie got tipped off." From his place on the other end of the couch, al-Rashid leaned forward, a frown on his face, his eyes narrowed. "Noor Kamil-Sultan must have seen something that worried her."

Al-Omri opened his mouth to say something, but Ed held up his hand to silence him. He switched his attention to the computer that traced e-mails from Ms. Forrest's account. Al-Omri crowded closer as a message flashed onto the screen.

Farouk, Noor, and Samir,

Attached you'll find my report of the walkthrough of the property in the Port of Panama City (Plait Number 04149320493). Based upon the condition of the property, as evidenced by the photographs within the report, I recommend against the purchase of the above-referenced property. Please notify me of your decision. I am currently booked to return to Panama City on Tuesday, June 20th and will remain available for closing if you wish. Between tomorrow and that period, I'll be on vacation and unavailable. I'll look for your reply tomorrow. Melanie.

"So the snatch is moved up," al-Omri muttered.

"Plan B. Lock and load, baby," al-Rashid added, but this time, any humor had vanished.

"You're right on that one." Ed rose and stretched. He sighed as vertebrae in his back popped. "I hate sitting like that."

He studied al-Omri.

Either it was the lights from the computer, or the kid looked like he wanted to throw up. "Get over it, son. We're doing the snatch. Your job is to go with Karesh and get the safe house set up. Then to scope out Ms. Forrest in the bar. Got it?"

"Yeah."

"Take the Land Cruiser." Ed grabbed his keys from the table and tossed them to Karesh.

Karesh rose and handed off the Beretta to Ed.

"Then get on with it. Rosen, see if you can't scare us up some supper. Al-Rashid, let's start getting stuff cleaned up. And get that gear bag ready."

As his men filed from the room, Ed turned back to the computer. His mind whirled. His three guys were in one hundred percent. And the kid? Ed wasn't sure. Not that al-Omri had a choice. Not at all.

And if he didn't like it? Tough.

5

"It's amazing how much you can stuff into a Land Cruiser." Stephen shoved a pack of bottled water through the right rear passenger's door.

Jabir picked up a large box that had Cheetos imprinted the side in bold orange letters. "I'm still mystified that Ed wanted three boxes of Cheetos packages."

"What can I say? The man likes his junk food."

"The last time I had any was when I was in elementary school." Jabir crammed it into the rear hatch and closed it.

"We're like family, right? And all family members have their quirks."

"I'll say." Jabir shook his head and lowered the door to the storage unit with a rattle of metal on metal. "That's it. Shall we?"

"You drive." Stephen slid into the passenger's seat, and they rumbled through the gate of the self-storage facility and into Panama City's rush hour. It took them another couple of hours to repeat the transfer process in reverse. By that time, darkness had fallen across the jungle, and the only remaining evidence of daylight was the glimmer of the sun's rays in deep shades of red and orange. Every night creature in the lush foliage had come to life, and their cacophony made Jabir shiver.

"You hate the jungle, don't you?" Stephen asked as Jabir started the Land Cruiser.

"I'm more of a fan of the urban ones."

"City boy, huh?"

"Born and raised in Chicago."

"Nice."

"How about you?"

"Florida. My parents immigrated there from Lebanon right before the war started. I guessed they sensed things were about to go from bad to worse."

Jabir nodded as he thought about why they made a good team for this op. Stephen, the Lebanese Christian. Ari, the Sabra Jew. Abdel, the Egyptian Muslim. All Americans who had decided to serve their country in one of the most clandestine ways possible. Jabir's stomach began twisting on itself.

"You're doing okay?" Stephen asked.

"Should I not be?" Jabir glanced over at his comrade, who studied him intently in the headlights of passing cars.

"You seem nervous."

"I've never done a snatch before."

"Never?"

"No. How about you?" Jabir refocused his gaze on the road.

"Several. When I was right out of the Farm and a green agent working in Iraq." Nothing behind Stephen's voice reflected any horror. "I was undercover at that point. You know. Working in the Red Zone. Snatches were the best way to get intelligence."

Jabir saw his opportunity to collect information for his other job. "Did you work with Ed any?"

"Sure. Lots. At least until 2007 when they pulled him and some others out of the field."

"What did you do for him?" As they came into the city, Jabir slowed behind an oil truck.

"Snatches and interrogations."

"Water boarding?"

"If we had to." Stephen shrugged. "Honestly, I hated it. Ed didn't seem to mind, though. Same with some others. I guess they got thick skins. I didn't. At least not that thick." He gripped the handhold above the window and stared into the darkness. "Don't get me wrong. Ed's good at what he does. He plans well, and he thinks through all of the contingencies. He saved my butt a couple of times out in the Red Zone too."

He might be too good at what he does, Jabir almost blurted. He took the exit into the heart of the city and toward the hotel. "When did you come back?"

"2010. When I turned thirty, I asked for an assignment at Headquarters. I'm not an eternal bachelor like Ed who can have a longtime girlfriend, you know? I wanted to find a wife. Fancy I met Jessie a month later when I took a long vacation at the beach. Speaking of which, our first anniversary is today."

"Is that so?" Jabir grinned. "Congratulations."

"Thanks. I miss her." A soft smile flickered across Stephen's face, and his hand shot up to grasp the cross dangling from a gold chain around his neck. "She's a gift from God."

"I'm sure."

"We dated for almost six years before I proposed. I wanted to be sure she knew what she was getting into by marrying me, but she doesn't scare easily."

"What does she do?"

"Trauma nurse. She'd already seen it all when she met me. I promised her we'd go out when I get back."

"Absolutely."

"We're planning on starting a family next year. Time's ticking, you know?"

Jabir nodded. He turned inward once more as he thought about the team Ed had put together. They were like family. They did everything together. Ate. Worked out. Bickered. They'd bonded too. Jabir knew he could count on any of them to watch his back.

Except Ed.

He worried Ed would put a bullet in his back rather than watch it.

"Jabir!" Stephen's voice made him blink.

"Huh?" Suddenly, Jabir realized how he'd be thinking, all the while ignoring his friend. "Sorry. I think too much."

Stephen chuckled. "I was asking if there was anyone special in your life."

"No." Jabir's reply was too quick, even for his own ears. "There's a woman I love. I was about to tell her when she dumped it on me that she'd fallen in love with another guy."

"Ouch."

"Yep." Jabir didn't feel like discussing the failed mission and his subsequent mishandling of his feelings for Alex. He cleared his throat. "Hey, here's a question."

"Shoot."

"Do you ever worry about that guy who's been wiping out agents who are native Arabic speakers?"

A short, nervous bark of laughter answered him. "Do I? All of the time. I mean, the guy's hit those of us who are in our late thirties on up. Meaning we're really seasoned. The young guys?" Stephen shook his head. "They're trying to train them up as quickly as possible, but they just don't have that field experience. It's disheartening. You know you replaced one of the guys, right?"

"Someone named Hakim?"

"Yeah. Hakim al-Husseini. A really good guy. It's torn his kids up big time. Shortly after the funerals, Abdel and I went over to their aunt's and uncle's where they're living. Not a good situation." Stephen muttered under his breath. "It's like having a target painted on my back." He cast a glance at Jabir. "I'd watch your back as well. Could be that once he's done with us, he could move on to DHS."

Jabir shivered at the thought as they pulled under the portico to the hotel. "Tell Ed I've run back to my apartment to gear up and get some rest. I'll be back by ten, okay? Then as soon as I drop my stuff, I'm headed to the bar."

"Roger that." Stephen slid out of the SUV. "See you soon, my friend."

With that, he stepped through the sliding doors.

Discouragement slammed into Jabir as he drove the short distance to his apartment. He had no information on Ed. Only suppositions and the fact that Stephen's fear was genuine and clear.

Jabir didn't know how close Ed and Stephen were, so he couldn't ask direct questions of his friend. Not now. Maybe later, when Stephen totally trusted him.

Jabir parked the Land Cruiser in the lot in front of his apartment building near the university. Even from where he stood, the blasting music reached him from the adobe structure. No classes for the students meant all-night partying. He grimaced and trotted upstairs to his apartment. Even when he shut the door, the muffled bass pulsed through the walls and almost rattled his bones. He wasted little time in stuffing his backpack with the agreed-upon uniform for their stay up at the safe house—cargo pants and T-shirts.

Jabir knelt by an outlet between the bathroom and closet doors. Using the screwdriver he kept in a drawer in his nightstand, he undid the cover. Then the socket itself, which he'd disconnected from the power the day he moved in. Behind it sat the cellphone Tiny had given him.

He needed to update his boss. It was more than that. He needed to hear Tiny's reassuring voice and understand that his real mission wasn't futile.

He checked the battery and plugged it in. Then he sat on the bed as he kicked off his businessman's shoes and tossed his fake glasses into the trash. Jabir rubbed a hand through his hair, wincing as the gel he'd used to slick it back made the curls stick up in little spikes.

"Tim Daniels." Tiny's voice came on the line. "Jabir, hey."

"Hey."

"Are you doing okay?"

"Yeah." Jabir glanced at his cellphone for the mission. It sat next to his backpack on the other side of the queen bed. "Things start tonight after midnight."

"Really?"

"Yeah. It looks like Samir Kamil fed his sister and father a bunch of baloney, so they got an outside firm to do the walkthrough. A Melanie Forrest came down, and, to put it mildly, things didn't go well."

"Interesting."

"Uh, huh." Jabir swallowed hard. "We're snatching her."

A sharp intake of breath confirmed that snatching an American was a great risk, especially if things got out of control. But all Tiny said was, "Seeing that Ed's the one planning the op, I'm not surprised."

"Speaking of Ed, I've got nothing. Nada. All I know is Stephen Karesh is really worried. He thinks he's got a target on his back."

"He probably does seeing that Hakim met his maker in February."

Jabir winced. "I'm going to find something. Promise."

"We'll shake some trees on our end too. I know you're getting ready to go active."

"Right. I'm not sure when I'll be able to report in again, so if you don't hear from me for a while, don't worry."

"Understood. Just be very careful, okay? Watch your back around Ed. And keep an eye on Melanie."

"Oh, I will." Jabir's mind flew back to when they'd been researching her and learning as much as they could. It was then that they'd discovered Melanie's heart condition.

Tiny cleared his throat. "If you get into trouble, all you need to do is send up the flare for help."

"I will."

"I'll be praying. Take care, Jabir."

Jabir hung up. Then he shoved the pack onto the floor, set his alarm for half past nine, and turned on his side to sleep. He clamped a pillow over his head and somehow managed to drift away.

His alarm woke him a two short hours later. He was tired, but he knew he would be. Jabir showered and changed into a pair of khaki cargo pants, a black T-shirt, and a long-sleeved button-down shirt for an overshirt.

Then, after shoving his feet into some sandals, he checked the charge on the emergency phone. Fully charged and ready to leave for a week if need be. He rose and stashed it in the outlet before securing the cover in place.

Jabir hauled his pack into the living area of his apartment and stared at the laptop for a moment. Should he take it? He decided against it since if Ed got curious, it could get him into trouble. Finally, after one last look, he shut and locked the door before heading into the steamy tropical night.

6

Jabir smelled it in the air. Machismo. The heady power of men who thought they had a way with women and wanted to dominate them. It swirled on the warm, silky night breeze just as much as the hibiscus and other tropical scents he couldn't begin to name.

He gazed at the clientele in the hotel's outdoor bar. Since it was a Monday night, fewer people crowded onto the tiled patio with its palm-thatched roof. Jabir didn't recognize most of them since they were likely patrons of the hotel who sought the relaxation while having a beer and watching a game of baseball. Others continued to discuss business in the conversation groups scattered along the perimeter at the edge of the artificial moat some interior designer had thought to be a good idea. A few regulars who worked at the tall office buildings downtown lined the bar and stared at the soccer matches and baseball games shown on the flat-screen televisions that hung above the liquor.

His gaze flicked to the women. All had dark hair, and none of them seemed to be alone.

Jabir lifted his phone to his ear as if he spoke to someone, but in reality, the microphone that doubled as a button on his shirt picked up his every word. "Are you sure she's in her room?"

Ed's Cajun twang filled his right ear where he'd inserted an ear piece. "Sure as the swamp's a nasty place, son. She lay down for a nap at about five or so and hasn't made a peep since. We'd have heard her if she had and followed her."

"Thanks." Jabir lowered his phone and rested his head against the high back of his faux rattan chair. He closed his eyes and tried to let the tinkling sound of water from a nearby fountain in the form of a heron relax him.

Lord, I don't want to do this. To kidnap an American. I know it's wrong. But I've got a mission. What do I do? Warn her? Stay with the mission?

"Sounds like her door just closed," Ed reported a moment later. Then came the crunch of another Cheeto meeting its maker.

Jabir winced.

Something like an electric shock rippled through the room. A rumble of male voices reached him. He caught a few words in Spanish. *Gringa.* Beautiful. Candidate for a night.

His eyes flew open, and it didn't take but a second to recognize the source of interest.

Melanie stood there.

Dressed in a pair of Capri pants and a deep blue tank top of some fine material, her eyes remained half-closed as if she'd awakened just minutes earlier. She held a tablet in one hand, and in a graceful move with the other, she skimmed hair the color of spun gold off one bare shoulder.

"Eh, she's hot, isn't she?" One of the businessmen leaning against the bar nudged his pal.

"Hot enough to take to bed. Señorita, may I buy the lady a drink?" his buddy called.

"No, thanks." Melanie offered a quick smile and shook her head.

"A margarita for you," a regular called as he slid off his bar chair.

Her eyes searched for an open seat at the bar. She turned her attention to the conversation group where Jabir sat. Their gazes met, and another electric shock ran through him.

Then she whirled. "Do you mind?"

She took a step away from the regular who must have touched her inappropriately.

"You want to spend the night with me?" He slurred his words.

Jabir tensed to stand.

"I don't think so. Now how about leaving me alone?" She turned her head and wasted no time in claiming the vacant chair.

Jabir relaxed and watched as she picked up the small binder that contained the drink menu. She flipped through a few pages. Then the bartender approached, and she chatted for a few seconds as she placed her order.

Melanie set her tablet on the bar. She stared at it, as still as a nun in prayer. Then she shook her head. Whatever her internal argument was, it occupied her full attention rather than what was on the tablet in front of her.

Jabir lowered his gaze to his phone. Somehow, he had to figure out a way to start a conversation with her. Why did it feel like he was trying to ask someone out on a date for the first time?

"Stop, will you?" Melanie's angry voice in Spanish reached him. "Stop touching me. Now."

The drunk regular had inserted himself into her personal space so close that she was almost bent double over the bar with her back pressed against the edge. He gripped her wrist in such a manner that told Jabir she'd tried to slap him. "I asked you a question earlier, and now you try to slap me?"

"You touched me, and I don't like it. Now leave me alone!"

Jabir stood. He deftly inserted himself between the two.

"Señor, I suggest you leave," he stated in Spanish.

"I'm not letting you take her. She's mine." The man tried to portray himself as a man of action, but Jabir easily read the fear that flickered in his eyes.

"Señor, you heard the man." This came from the bartender, who now stood across from Melanie. "Leave now, or I'll have you thrown out by those two gentlemen and banned from the hotel."

He nodded toward where two security personnel stood at attention near the entrance to the bar.

The man released her wrist, called her a foul name, and stomped past the guards and into the hotel.

The bartender sighed and shook his head. "My apologies, Señorita. When he drinks too much, Javier can forget how to treat a woman."

"If he ever knew," Melanie muttered.

"True. Your drink. And it's on the house for your trouble. And your appetizers as well. For you, Señor?" the bartender asked as he placed a cocktail napkin on the teak wood in front of Jabir.

"A virgin daiquiri, please, and some plantains." Jabir's glance lifted. While Melanie probably thought he checked the score of the baseball game, he really noted the placement of the security camera. It was slightly to his right, meaning that so long as he kept square to the bar and didn't turn his face to the right, the scar on his left cheek would remain hidden. That wouldn't be a problem since Melanie sat to his left.

Melanie turned to her tablet, which he noted contained an e-book of some sort. She flipped pages, but from the way she squinted and stared at it for a few minutes, he knew her mind lay elsewhere, most likely at the site she'd visited earlier that day.

Jabir leaned his right hip against the bar and rested his foot on the rail near the floor. "Someone's had a big day."

"That's not the half of it." A small sigh escaped her, and she set her tablet down.

"A rough day, maybe?" He fished a pack of cigarettes from his pocket. Using a silvery lighter, he lit it and blew a stream of smoke toward the ceiling fan. It dispersed in the humid night air.

"Your appetizer, Señor." The bartender set a plate with three items on it in front of her and placed Jabir's daiquiri in front of him. "And your daiquiri."

"Must have been a rough day for you too if you're laying off of the alcohol and going straight to the cigarettes." A hint of a smile played about her lips.

Jabir shrugged. "Not really. I partied too much in college."

"Ah. Understandable, then." Melanie sipped her drink. "Are you here on business?"

He stared at the wood as his mind raced. Suddenly, he wanted to tell her to leave. To check out of her hotel and fly out that night. He took another drag and held his breath, hoping the nicotine would calm nerves that suddenly raged. Then he released it. "Something like that. I like to mix business with pleasure."

"I hear you."

"It sounds like you're mixing business with pleasure too."

"Yeah." A smile tipped the corners of her mouth upward, but it faded shortly after that. "If I could only get excited about the pleasure part."

"You're meeting your fiancé?"

"No, no. Some girlfriends. A girls' week out."

Jabir frowned. Girlfriends. That could mean anything. But he couldn't find out, not without raising her suspicions. "That sounds like fun. Massive flirtation? Partying?" He offered his best smile.

That seemed to work. Melanie giggled. "Maybe. Where are you from?"

"Chicago. And you?"

"New York. But soon moving to Atlanta." She lowered her gaze and twisted her engagement ring around her finger.

"When you get married?" Jabir nodded as if he hadn't known that fact.

"Yeah. He's in Atlanta, and quite frankly, I'm ready to kiss Manhattan goodbye." She took a long pull on the drink, emptying the tall glass to halfway. "Too frenetic now. I guess I'm mellowing in my old age."

Her smile came easier now and lasted longer.

"I wouldn't call you old."

She laughed. "You're kind. What about you?"

"Me what?"

"Do you still live in Chicago?"

"No. I'm in the DC area. I guess I'm a city boy at heart." Impatience pushed at Jabir. He needed to get information and quickly too. "What was the sigh about?"

"What sigh?"

Jabir leaned closer as if the two of them were now good friends. He offered up what he hoped was his charming smile and said in a low voice full of intimacy, "When you were mentioning looking forward to the pleasure part of your trip."

"I'm a lawyer doing a real estate closing, and let's just say it's most likely going to fall through." She shoved the drink around in small circles, and it left a trail of water behind it.

"Oh?"

"Uh, huh. Big time." She shook her head. "But then again, I'm not the potential owner, so that's off the table for me."

Jabir's heart hammered. "I'm sorry to hear that."

"Well, I did my due diligence. All I can do is make a recommendation." She drained her glass. "Have you ever had to do that?"

"What?"

"Tell someone bad news?"

"Who hasn't?"

Melanie rested her elbows on the bar and hunched. "But professionally?" Her blue eyes beseeched him for a shred of wisdom he couldn't offer.

"Sure. I hand information to clients all of the time. Some good, some bad. It's not up to me to tell them what to do with it. This *is* good." Jabir pushed away his nearly empty glass. "Good thing there's not alcohol in it because I'm sucking it down."

"You're right. Recommendation. Got to keep that in mind. It's just hard because I also know my client personally." She slurred her words slightly, and he wondered if the piña colada had hit her harder than she expected.

"Ah, the sauce thickens. If this client of yours is professional, he or she will understand that it's not personal."

"He. And he's actually an ex-boyfriend."

Jabir smiled again. "Wow. Sounds like fun. Amicable departure?"

"I guess so. We broke up a long time ago. But it was for the better. We both agreed on it. How about you?"

"Me what?"

"Are you…involved?"

Her question made his heart hammer since through his study of her he knew who was one of her best friends.

Alex.

He shook his head and finished his drink. "Romantically? Not right now. I haven't met the right woman yet."

"Someone good-looking like you?" Then the flush began, a delicate pink quickly going red against her top. "I'm sorry. I'm…I'm…well, I don't know what."

"Tired? I noticed when you walked in." Jabir opened his mouth. It would be so easy to urge her to at least check out of that room and into another. He actually had to keep the words from forming. To do so would have been suicidal since Ed was listening to every word. "Perhaps it would be a good time for you to go to bed."

"Yes, tired is a good way of putting it. Señor, thank you. I'd better get going. Take care, okay?"

Jabir nodded as she slipped off the chair. He noticed how she remained still for a moment before shoving her way through a couple of business-men and into the restaurant. He watched to ensure she made it to the bank of elevators without being accosted.

"Good job, Jabir." Ed's voice penetrated his thoughts. "She confirmed what we suspected. Come on up when you're ready."

Jabir wasn't.

Not by a long shot.

He took a seat and ordered another daiquiri. As he waited for it, he lit another cigarette. This mission was doing nothing for his health.

He thought about his options. He could call Melanie. Or text her. Better yet, he could go directly to her room and tell her in person.

Something, anything, to get her away from the danger.

He couldn't. They had her room wired. Her phone? They'd hear her end of the conversation, and she'd be bound to ask a lot of questions. And texting? Out of the question since Ed could see all texting from his cell-phone.

He was powerless.

The best he could do would be to watch over her. Hopefully, that would be enough to help her survive.

Day 3
Tuesday, June 13, 2017

7

0730 hours local time (0030 hours CDT), Beirut, Lebanon

Samir's palms grew clammy and wet with sweat. The kind of sweat that made you know trouble of the unavoidable kind lurked nearby. There, glowing on the screen as if accusing him for thinking he could scam his father, sister, and brother-in-law, sat the message in his Inbox.

Melanie had recommended against purchasing the property.

He muttered under his breath, and the headache brought on by jetlag and a lack of sleep amped up a notch. He dropped his head into his hands and rubbed his temples. The soft noise of a gong made him open his eyes.

A meeting notification had popped up on his screen. Samir hated seven thirty meetings, but Papa had insisted since they'd been away for so long.

"Why me?" he muttered under his breath.

He didn't want to open the attachment containing the report, but he had no choice. He just wouldn't read it. As the printer whirred and spit out the sheaf of papers, he rummaged around in the top drawer of his glass-topped desk and came up with a bottle of aspirin. Maybe that would help the headache. The worry beads he pulled out would work off his nervous energy. That would be better than wringing his hands.

When the report finished, he grabbed it from the tray, stapled it, and slid it into his portfolio. Then, with portfolio and mug of thick Arabian coffee in his hand, he stepped into the suite housing the offices of the general counsel. His administrative assistant hadn't arrived yet.

Samir pushed through the door leading to the hallway and forced himself to take each step toward the suite of offices that housed his father at the opposite corner of the building. For the first time in a long time, he noticed the prints on the warm gray hallway walls that were framed in the soft glow of LED lights. Each showed Kamil International at some point in its history, from ninety years before when it was founded to present-day.

He'd dreamed about taking the helm of the company when Papa retired.

Now, he wondered if he would be lucky enough to work on the cleaning crew like he had in secondary school.

He opened the glass doors leading the spacious lobby of the executive suite. Salma, Papa's administrative assistant, smiled demurely at him. "Samir, welcome back. Your father tells me you had a lovely vacation."

"I did." Samir stopped and leaned against the counter as if the small talk could delay the thrashing that was bound to come. "It was very nice to get away and lounge on the beach. And to see family."

Suddenly, Salma glanced up. "Noor, Fadi. Good morning. Welcome back."

"Good morning, Salma." Noor's voice reached her brother.

Samir turned.

Noor smiled at the administrative assistant, but when she met Samir's eyes, the fire in her gaze almost matched the shimmery oranges and reds of the top peeking above the jacket of her business suit. "Papa is waiting on us."

Precision defined her words.

She wasted no time in turning her back on him and striding into the smaller conference room where they had their weekly status meetings.

Samir cast a glance at her husband, Fadi.

He shrugged and offered a wan smile.

Some comfort.

Samir shook his head and followed his brother-in-law. He laid his portfolio on the table and slid his hand into the pocket where he'd dropped the worry beads.

"Samir, son, good morning." Papa briefly embraced him and then put his hand over his heart in greeting. "Please, have a seat. Asa is in Alexandria finishing the upgrade of their system, so it's just us this morning. We have a lot to cover since we were out of town. My apologies for calling such an early meeting." Papa laid copies of an agenda in front of everyone. "We'll discuss the property first. Noor?"

Noor opened her folder and pulled the report from it. She stayed silent for a moment, then speared Samir in that glare again. "What were you thinking?"

The sharpness of her words startled him.

"What?"

"What were you thinking?"

"Um…"

"Answer me." Noor lifted the report. "You went behind our backs and moved ahead with acquiring a property you knew was in horrible condition."

"I—"

"You what? Thought you could get away with it? Do you think we're fools?" She bit off her words.

Samir's fingers began working the beads again. "No. I was told the property was in good condition."

"Did you read the report?"

"Uh, no."

"Then take some time." Noor flipped a few pages in her copy and tossed it onto the table.

It skittered to a stop in front of him.

Samir stared at the photographs. Melanie had done a standout job. The page contained each photo Tarek's man had doctored lined up across from the photo showing the property's true condition. He dared not reach up and flip the page. He knew he had no way out.

"Melanie reported that the seller wishes to sell this piece of…garbage for one million."

Samir tried a grin. "That's not that much. We could pay cash—"

Noor sat back and shook her head as if completely baffled by a difficult word problem. "Did you even think about how much it would cost us to refurbish it?"

"No, I—"

"If you had come to me, I would have given you an estimate." An edge sharpened her words, and she wielded each like a scalpel to cut deeper into his wounded pride. "Instead, you had to keep me in the dark and rush ahead with the sale."

"Son, what she's trying to say is that had you come to her, she could have given you an estimate of the cost of renovations needed to make the property usable. That would have determined its overall value." Papa's voice penetrated the buzz suddenly filling his ears.

Samir worked the beads harder.

"Who told you about the property?" Noor glared at him.

He kept silent.

Papa's voice reached him, and he easily read the strain in it. "Samir, answer her, please."

He couldn't tell them about Tarek. If he did and told them why Tarek wanted the property, Tarek's brother, Hashim, would probably pay him a visit in the middle of the night, and it wouldn't be pretty. He took a deep breath. "An associate."

"An associate. How very telling." Noor muttered something and hopped up. She began pacing, her stiletto heels drilling holes in the carpet like her words threatened to do to his composure. "Who is this associate?"

"I would have named him had I been allowed."

"And what did he want to do with the property?"

"He wanted us to renovate it for him and install our equipment so he could lease it back to him as a shipping terminal. Why is that such a problem?"

"It—"

"We do that all of the time, right?" Samir half-turned in his chair and faced her. "Sometimes associates don't want their names to be revealed because of the competition. This one is the same way. He—"

"It's Tarek, isn't it?"

Samir blinked.

He jumped up. "I told you, I'm not allowed to reveal his name."

"It has to be." Noor spun on her heel and approached him. "Why else would you be so reticent?"

"I have my—"

"I don't believe you." Noor got right in his face, backing him against the chair.

"Then don't believe me." Samir's voice rose to match hers.

"Who else would be interested in this dilapidated piece of garbage but someone with ties to Jihad of Light?"

"Don't you dare talk about him like that!"

Noor poked him in the chest. "I can—"

"Enough!" Papa's voice rose to a shout. He slammed both hands down onto the glass of the table.

Samir jumped. He stared at his father.

Papa leaned on his hands, anger blazing in his dark eyes. "Both of you. Sit down. Now."

Samir resumed his seat.

Noor took hers on the opposite side of the table. Fadi cast her a long look, but she refused to meet his gaze.

"I have had enough of this pointless bickering," Papa said. He sighed and shook his head. "We are in this together, are we not? This is a family business. I understand that differences can occur, but I will not tolerate both of you battling it out like when you were fighting over toys as children." He squared his copy of the report against his notepad. "I don't care who wanted us to buy the property. Samir, you should have known better than to go behind our backs regarding the purchase. Do that again, and you'll be demoted. Am I clear?"

Almost meekly, Samir nodded.

"And Noor, I understand your concerns and why you're upset. But that is no way to treat a member of the executive team. I'll not have that kind of behavior either. Do you understand?"

Noor hunched as if sulking for being reprimanded. A jerk of her chin answered his question.

"Good. I'm glad we agree on that. Regarding this particular matter, I have to concur with Melanie's findings. We will not be purchasing the property. We can afford to lose twenty thousand. We cannot afford the one million it would cost to buy it and the twenty million it would cost to renovate it. I want to take an hour's break. Each of you will go to your offices and cool off. Anymore outbursts like that, and you will deal with me one on one. We'll continue at eight forty-five sharp." With that, Papa rose.

Samir wasted no time in fleeing the conference room. He nearly knocked over one of the interns in his haste to make it to safety. As he steadied the young man, he mumbled, "So sorry."

Hanan had arrived and was going through voicemails, so he only offered a pitiful wave before closing the door behind him. He collapsed into his chair.

"That was close," he muttered so quietly that he barely heard himself.

Several deep, cleansing breaths refreshed him.

He calmed.

He'd escaped almost unscathed. If he could control how he told Tarek, maybe this would blow over.

Samir reached for the phone's receiver and dialed voicemail. Most were inconsequential, and he made notes of people he needed to call.

Then Tarek al-Hassan's voice filled his ear. "Squash at lunch? I know you're just back into town, but let me know. We need to catch up. I'm available."

Samir lowered his head into his arms. They muffled his response. "I'm not."

Finally, he raised his head and blinked. Tarek wanted more than exercise.

He wanted a report.

Panama Deception

Now he knew the truth.

Things had gone from bad to worse.

8

Jabir slid off the bar chair. He shoved his cigarette pack into his shirt pocket and pushed through the doors leading to the deserted lobby. Within moments, the elevator swished him to the fifth floor. As he approached the door, he checked the hallway around him. It was quiet, most patrons long asleep. He slid his card into the lock.

"Glad you could join us." Ed's voice held a slightly sarcastic edge.

Jabir shrugged and noted once more how Stephen laid the gun on the top of the dresser, which was now back in its original place. "I was catching up on some baseball. Braves at the Dodgers."

"And who's winning?" Abdel asked from the couch.

"Braves right now, but the Dodgers aren't but a run behind."

"My call is that they win it."

"Sorry, I'm not taking bets."

"Guys, let's get back to business." Ed slipped his reading glasses onto his face. "By now, Farouk and company should be meeting regarding the property."

A shiver rippled through Jabir. At least the darkness hid it. If he pushed away from the door, he knew he committed himself. Maybe he could manufacture some excuse to leave the room, like he'd left something in the apartment and had to run out and get it. Or he needed to ensure that Melanie hadn't wanted a midnight snack. His ploy remained as foolish as it had been when he'd fabricated it in the bar.

Jabir took a seat on the queen bed nearest the bathroom.

Ed shifted in the work chair and faced him, the glow of the laptop's screen reflecting off his glasses. "Ms. Forrest seemed stressed."

"She was." Jabir nodded. "And a bit tipsy as well. I guess she overslept because it sounded like she was starved and ordered appetizers to go along with her double piña colada."

Abdel whistled low. "Yep, the lady surely must be stressed if she's drinking that much."

"Well, she's on vacation, gentlemen, at least for another half hour or so." Ed flashed a wicked grin. "We're waiting to see what Farouk Kamil decides." He glanced at his watch. "We know Farouk scheduled a special, early status meeting since they were out of town until last night. I imagine the discussion will be a lively one and won't take long. Once they come to a conclusion, either Samir or Farouk will e-mail Ms. Forrest with their decision."

"My money's on Farouk doing that," Stephen piped up from where he now lounged on the other queen bed. A water bottle rested on his knee. "I mean, if it was Samir's idea, I doubt he'll be in the mood."

Abdel chuckled and stretched his long legs out lengthwise on the couch. "I'm with you on that one. Want to take a bet?"

"Not me." Ari grinned from where he sprawled on the easy chair. "I'm not a betting man."

"That's Abdel." Stephen rolled his eyes. "You're saving money for Vegas for what? The blackjack tables? Or was it to see the shows?"

"Abdel wants to do the shows."

"Do not." Abdel tossed his empty water bottle at his friend. "Very funny. Actually, Jabir wants to see the shows since they have pretty girls."

"Arrgh. Not me." Jabir groaned playfully.

"So what are you going to do when you get done?" Stephen peered at his comrade.

"Go back to work."

"No vacation?"

Jabir lit a cigarette. "Nope. Well, maybe I'll see my mom."

"No girl in your life?" Ari raised an eyebrow.

"No." He caught Stephen's sympathetic glance as memories of Alex flashed in his mind. He shut down that part. That was over. Done with. That much she'd made clear by returning his letter two years ago without even opening it. His budding love for her was dead on the vine, never to be revived. At least in *her* mind. Maybe he was an eternal optimist, but he still held out hope that one day, he might run into her. Or maybe he'd garner the courage to go down to Weatherly and see her. If only…

"Hey, earth to Jabir." Abdel's teasing voice brought him out of his preoccupation.

"Uh…" Jabir felt a flush starting. "Sorry. I think too much"

"Have some water." Abdel tossed a bottle to him and said, "Yep, you've got it bad over someone."

Before Jabir could open his mouth with a retort, Ed interrupted. "Guys, looks like the change in plans is confirmed."

Jabir's stomach dropped as they crowded around the screen. The e-mail intercept from Farouk to Melanie flashed across it.

Dear Melanie,

We are in receipt of your report, and I concur with your conclusions. We will not be following through with the purchase of the property in Panama City, despite Samir's insistence. Thank you for your time, and enjoy your vacation. Farouk.

Ed straightened and took off his reading glasses, revealing eyes with a gleam enhanced by the glow of the computer. "Well, gentlemen, we're on to Plan B now. Let's get to it."

Everyone nodded. Jabir swallowed hard. "I'm sorry to be a pain, but isn't there any other way to do this?"

Ed stared at him, and suddenly, Jabir could easily envision him carefully planning and executing the murders of thirteen very strong and capable men. Again, he wondered in how dark a gray Ed operated.

"You got a problem with the plan?" Ed asked.

"I'm just, um, wondering if we really have to kidnap her. I mean, she's an American. An innocent." Jabir cast a glance around the room. The rest of the guys' faces were unreadable in the dim light.

"Son, in case you didn't read the e-mail, Farouk canceled the sale. Nothing's going to get Samir over here except to hear that the woman he loves is being held by the terrorist cell that wants to occupy said property. Posing as them, we issue a simple demand. Come and conduct the closing as planned next Tuesday, and Ms. Forrest walks without a scratch."

"And if he refuses?"

Ed grinned. "He'll come."

Jabir didn't ask exactly how they'd persuade Samir.

"Now, we need to ensure Ms. Forrest extends her stay here. Karesh, time to shine."

"Yup." Stephen settled into the chair Ed vacated. His fingers flew across the keyboard. He pulled up the screen for entry into the hotel system's intranet. One password and three clicks of the mouse later, and he'd located Melanie's reservation record. He changed the departure date, saved the file, and logged out. "Now, Melanie Forrest of Room 748 will be staying not just for one night but for four. Voila! She'll hate me for the credit card charges."

"So maybe the CIA will reimburse her later," Ari suggested.

Everyone except Jabir snickered.

Ed smirked. Then it dropped away. "Let's move."

He shut the laptop and stashed it in its case.

Abdel rose. The tall man pulled on gloves and began wiping down everything.

Ari knelt in front of the large black duffel bag that served as their gear bag. He pulled a small case from it and handed Jabir and the others headsets with boom microphones so small they'd be difficult to spot with a casual glance. He offered Jabir a Beretta and clip.

Jabir rammed the clip home and checked to ensure the safety was on. He shoved it into a holster and slid that into his belt at the small of his back.

Ed tossed Stephen the keys. "Van keys. Karesh, go down and keep surveillance on the crowd we'll soon have. Al-Rashid, you've got about an hour to make sure this place is clean. Make sure you hide when the firemen come through. Then go and join Karesh. We'll see you two downstairs in a bit. With Ms. Forrest."

He pulled out a case that looked like a glasses case. He opened it and withdrew a vial as well as a needle and syringe.

Jabir stared. "Why do we need that?"

"You ever had a woman fight you?" Ed glanced at him over the tops of his reading glasses.

"Uh, no," Jabir admitted. With a sinking feeling, he realized Ed had done so, most likely on numerous occasions.

"They can fight like the dickens. Especially if they're from Manhattan." Ed chuckled, causing the rest of the crew to snigger. "But don't worry. Just for backup if need be. You saw her. What do you say her weight is?"

"Um, I'd probably say 143 pounds."

"Wow. You're precise." Sarcasm and Abdel were one as he wiped down the phone. "Want to bet she fights you guys?"

"She won't," Ari said. "She'll take one look at me and faint from fright."

He zipped the duffel closed before flexing his muscles like a weight-lifter.

"Hah. Dreamer. Twenty says she does."

"You're just getting your play money for Vegas earlier." Stephen straightened. "Good luck, guys. We'll see you downstairs. Give a shout when you're on your way."

Jabir nodded at Ari and Ed as he pulled on his gloves, thin leather ones he'd always used for ops. "I guess it's now or never."

They stepped into the silent hallway. Jabir checked his watch. One thirty. Eight thirty in Beirut. Nerves pricked him the way they always did when he began an op. The three men slipped into the stairwell leading from the fifth floor to the seventh. As they crept up the stairs, their boots barely made a sound.

They stole through the door. Jabir noted the alcove holding the vending machines and the janitor's closet.

And the fire alarm.

They went through a quick comms check. Then he glanced at Ari and Ed. Both gave a thumbs up, signaling they were ready. "Stephen?"

"I'm pulling into the street now. Wait two."

Jabir's heart pounded so loudly that he feared Ed would hear it.

"In position." Stephen's voice came across clearly.

Jabir dropped his headset to down around his neck. He inserted his earplugs.

With his gloved hand, he reached toward the fire alarm's red pull handle.

The screech of the alarm made him want to clap his hands over his ears, even with the earplugs in.

They waited.

Five minutes passed.

Then Ed tapped him on the shoulder.

Time to move.

Jabir pushed open the door to the janitor's closet and peeked around the corner. He withdrew when he noted the back of the last retreating patron. Once the door to the fire stairs bumped shut, the trio crept down the hall toward Room 748. Using the passkey they'd copied from an unsuspecting maid, Jabir released the lock. They slipped inside.

No one occupied the room.

Someone tapped him on the shoulder.

Jabir turned and found Ed standing there. His boss pointed toward the entrance to the room.

Jabir caught the meaning easily. Firefighters were already making their way into the building to check for any fire. He moved toward the bathroom.

Before shoving aside the opaque shower curtain and stepping into the tub, he noted the pill bottle containing Melanie's heart medication.

Ed followed. Then Ari, who drew the curtain closed and ensured it completely hid them.

Someone shouted in the hallway. The firemen had arrived to check the rooms on the seventh floor.

The door to Melanie's room opened, and Jabir listened as a fireman stepped inside. Then, above the din, he called in Spanish, "Room clear. Moving to the next room."

Jabir let out a breath. His tension eased further when the racket of the alarm finally ceased. He pulled out his earplugs and replaced his headset.

"I've got her in sight," Stephen said. "Do you copy?"

Beside him, Ed tapped twice on the microphone to signal his confirmation.

Jabir took several deep, cleansing breaths.

Finally, Stephen reported, "Everyone's going back in."

"Stand by," Ed whispered.

They waited.

The lock clicked, and the door opened. It shut, and metal scraped on metal as Melanie secured the chain.

"Dumb jerk," she muttered as she turned on the bathroom light.

Jabir screwed his eyes closed to preserve what little night vision he now had left.

"Stupid jerk is more like it." The lid on the toilet clunked upward. Then it flushed. "Now I'm not going to be able to get back to sleep."

Jabir shook his head.

The light turned off, sending them into darkness.

Soon, the feeling of Ed pressed close to him made Jabir think of how cows probably felt stuffed into a trailer. He listened.

In the hallway, doors continued thumping shut at a decreasing frequency. Finally, they ceased.

Jabir's night vision gradually returned.

Ed tapped him on the shoulder and pointed to the bathroom's door.

Slowly, Jabir shifted the shower curtain and stepped from the tub. He pulled the rolled up balaclava he had on his head down over his face. Whispers of air told him the others did the same.

With each foot carefully placed on the carpet, Jabir crept from the bathroom into the room proper.

Melanie lay curled up on her side, her hair spilling onto the pillow, gray in the gloom.

He eased down so he rested one knee on the mattress.

She turned onto her back. Her eyes opened. She stiffened.

"Who are—"

Jabir pounced on her.

She clapped him on the ear.

The groan escaped him before he realized it.

She pushed him.

Losing his balance, Jabir toppled off of her and hit the nightstand nearest the window. His gun slid away. His shirt rode up. A hot line of pain burned up his spine as he scraped his back against the edge on the way to the floor.

The lamp landed on top of him.

A cry told him she'd seen Ari and Ed.

Jabir leapt to his feet and tackled her as she tried to scramble away.

He rolled with her.

The lampshade crumpled underneath him.

His back slammed into a corner of the worktable.

Another lamp and a placard toppled onto him.

She clawed at his face.

He jerked away from those long nails.

She kicked at him, her foot catching him in the stomach.

Jabir groaned and struggled to breathe.

Melanie began crawling away.

Someone jumped on her.

She moaned and thrashed as Ari slapped a piece of tape over her mouth.

His air whooshed out in a gasp as she elbowed him in the ribs.

Jabir grabbed her. Using his momentum, they rolled toward the door until she lay on her back.

She struggled, her cries coming across as muted bleats.

Jabir used his body weight to immobilize her. He leaned down and whispered softly in English into her ear, "You need to calm down, and we won't hurt you. Please. Calm down."

Suddenly, Ed knelt beside them. Before Jabir could react, he jabbed a needle into Melanie's arm and pushed the syringe's plunger.

Melanie went rigid, then sagged to the floor.

Jabir slid his hand under her back and helped her sit up. She swayed like she'd had four drinks instead of the one she'd consumed. He threw one of her arms around his shoulders and eased upward until he could lay her on the bed.

His chest heaved. He wanted to rip off his balaclava, to walk away and tell Tiny how he'd hated this assignment from day one. No, moment one.

He leaned over Melanie and ripped the tape from her mouth.

She flinched and whimpered.

Again, he murmured into her ear in English, "You keep quiet, and nothing will happen to you."

Almost dumbly, she nodded.

He pulled off his balaclava and substituted a baseball cap with the bill pulled low over his eyes.

The others did the same.

Jabir pulled one over Melanie's hair. He grabbed his gun and stuffed it back into his belt.

In front of him, Ari took the lead and opened the door. His hand curled around the butt of his pistol as he peered into the hall. Then he nodded.

Ed softly reported their movement to Stephen as he took Melanie's arm and walked with her into the hall.

Jabir came last. He snagged her glasses from the nightstand and her pills from the bathroom.

With his hand resting on his pistol, he grabbed the Do Not Disturb sign from the back of the door.

It thumped shut behind him.

Jabir hung the sign from the handle.

Now, no one would check the room until Friday.

Meaning no one would miss her.

9

"I take it we're alone."

Samir opened his eyes a crack at the sound of his best friend's voice. "No one came in here before you."

He exhaled a deep sigh as the pipe at the base of the floor gurgled. Steam belched from it and filled the room with moist warmth. He took a deep breath and released it as his sore muscles loosened.

Tarek settled beside him and slouched in the same posture. "You played a good game, my friend. A hard game."

"I'm out of practice."

"Hah. You beat me on the first and came close on the other two." Tarek sprayed some eucalyptus into the air, filling it with a pleasant aroma. "You played like you were under a lot of stress."

Any relaxation Samir felt disappeared. His friend didn't miss a thing. "The deal fell through."

Tarek raised an eyebrow.

"Somehow—I don't know how—they got suspicious. Rather than use the local firm to do the walkthrough, they sent Melanie Forrest."

"Your girlfriend?"

"Ex-girlfriend. Remember? I happened to break up with her ten years ago."

"But you still love her."

"I don't."

"I happen to remember a certain conversation we had a few months ago."

"I'm not following."

Tarek expelled a deep sigh. "You were at my club. You were all excited about this deal and working with Melanie on it. You ordered several martinis."

It all came rushing back. Samir winced. "I was drunk."

"Very. So drunk that I drove you to my place until you sobered up." Tarek smiled. "You went on and on about how much you still loved Melanie."

Samir swallowed hard. He tried to chuckle, but it came out forced, even to his ears. "I thought I still had a chance with her."

"Things change, do they not?"

Samir rubbed his temples where the headache the aspirin had chased away that morning had returned. "Papa flat out refused to buy the property."

Tarek shrugged. "It's of no worry. There will be others."

Samir straightened. "It was awful."

"How so?" Tarek cocked his head.

"Noor basically attacked me. She called me a fool and an idiot." He paused as he realized his little lie. "She demanded to know who my 'associate' was."

"You didn't tell her, did you?"

"No! Of course not." A flush rose to his cheeks as he remembered her scathing words.

Tarek pumped another spray of eucalyptus into the air. "Noor wants to get her way. She always did. Even when we were dating."

"And she sulked when Papa told us to sit down."

"Typical woman."

"Hah. Agreed on that one." Samir heaved a sigh. "She knew it was you."

"Really?" Tarek chuckled. "Why? Because I broke up with her all those years ago?"

"No, because she suspects you're tied into—"

"Don't say that name here." Tarek's voice had lowered and dangerously so.

Samir clamped his jaw shut.

Steam filled the silence of the room with a soft rushing sound.

"My friend, you must understand one thing. I don't care what your sister says. She, a woman, thinks she can run the company when your father retires. She wants the job that rightfully belongs to you, and she'll do anything she must to get it. Do you see what I'm saying?"

"I do."

"Good. Then it is your job to ensure she doesn't get that opportunity, no? Regarding the property, it is of no worry. Like I said, there will be others."

"Others? Others? You don't understand. I'm surprised I still have a job. I'm really surprised I wasn't demoted, and Papa threatened to do that if I went behind their backs again."

Tarek shook his head, the condensation forming droplets on the ends of waves worn slightly long. "So the next time, we'll be more careful. Do our homework better, no?"

"I don't think you understand. There will *be* no other next time. Seriously. I'm done."

Steam puffed in a hot cloud. It obscured Tarek. A few moments passed. Then his quiet voice came as if speaking from the heavens. "Oh, there will be other times, Samir. You're involved now. Deeply involved. Right?"

Samir closed his eyes.

Tarek continued, "I know you love Melanie. Your confession in January only confirmed what I've known for years. I would hate for something to happen to her. Or to Noor since I know that despite your differences, you love her and her family very much, yes?"

71

"What do you want?"

"Merely your services again when we find another suitable property that will pass muster with your father. And this time, I promise you, we'll do our homework. We'll ensure the man we choose does the walkthrough and not some infidel woman. That, I can promise." Tarek rose. "I must be going now. Business calls. You're going back to the office?"

"No. Home. I'm still tired."

"Until later, then."

Samir remained in the steam room, slouched on the tile bench, the headache now so bad that nausea knotted his stomach. He'd call Hanan and tell her he'd be at home that afternoon. That was the easy part.

The hard part?

Tarek.

With threats regarding Melanie and Noor hanging over his head, he knew one thing.

He had no way out of this situation.

10

"Place her in there."

"Where?"

"That room. The one with the bars on the windows." Jabir pointed toward a door on the back wall of the safe house's front room.

"Roger that." Stephen held an unconscious Melanie in his arms. He eased through the doorway.

Jabir followed and watched as Stephen placed her on the bed. He brushed back some hair from her face.

"She'll be fine, son, if that's what you're so worried about." Ed's voice reached him from the doorway. "Matter of fact, I'll make sure she's more than fine."

"How so?"

"The stuff I gave her in the hotel room has an antidote." Ed perched on the edge of the bed. He shone a penlight into her eyes and checked her

73

pulse at the neck. He grunted and nodded. "Her pupils are responding well, and her pulse is good. So no worries, all right?"

Jabir nodded as he dragged the wheeled barrister's chair from the corner near the desk over to the bed.

Ed swabbed her arm with alcohol. Then he injected the antidote. "Give her ten minutes. When she's fully awake, get her into something more decent and let Ari know. And remember, Arabic unless you're speaking with her."

How could Jabir forget that? He leaned forward, elbows on his knees, his eyes on her face.

Melanie began shaking her head from side to side. She mumbled. As if fighting through several layers of dreams, her eyes fluttered, revealing a blue color that even in the dimness of the fluorescent lanterns reminded him of sapphires. She blinked. Then, with one elbow underneath her, she pushed herself upright. She toppled forward.

Jabir grabbed her arm and steadied her. "It takes time for the antidote to work."

"I...I can't see." She hung her head.

"I know. I'm sorry. Here." Jabir slid her glasses from his shirt pocket and handed them to her.

She shoved them onto her face and blinked a few times like her eyes were focusing. Then recognition flashed in her eyes. "You!"

She tried to jump up, but once more, her limbs seemed to have a mind of her own.

He caught her before she hit the floor. "Easy there. Sit back down. I promise the dizziness will go away."

"I...I don't understand. Why am I here?"

"We have need of your services." Jabir stood, stepped over to the desk and picked up a bundle. "Here. We prefer that you wear this rather than what you have on."

Suddenly, she seemed to realize that she wore only the cami top and underwear she'd worn to bed because she drew the sheet over her lap. "I'm not changing in front of you."

"I'll take you to the bathroom. This way." Jabir gestured for her to follow him through another door. From there, it was only two steps across the hallway. Once she slipped inside, he leaned against the wall.

"Abdel," he softly called in Arabic when he saw his friend in the kitchen at the stove.

"Yo."

"It's time. Tell Ari."

"Will do." Abdel stepped into the operations room at the front of the safe house.

The bathroom door opened, and Melanie stood there, this time clad in the sweats and long-sleeved T-shirt Jabir had bought the week before. Once more, he nodded at her to precede him into the room.

She stopped short when she noticed Ari, Stephen, and Abdel, all masked, striding into the room. "I—I—I don't understand,"

"You will." Abdel began unfolding the tripod.

"What do you want from me?" A tremor had crept into her voice.

"We want you to carry a message for us." Abdel attached the video camera as Ari unfolded a small camp stool in front of the bed.

"No, I'm not going to be—"

"You listen to me." Ari whirled around. "You will listen to me! You will take the statement we give you. And you will read it verbatim."

"No!"

Before Jabir could open his mouth to shout a warning, she slapped Ari.

Ari grabbed her and slammed her against the wall.

She punched him in the shoulder and darted around him, only to have Stephen push her back.

Ari grabbed her and popped her hard across the face. She staggered.

"No!" Jabir tried to grab his friend.

Ari shook him off. He drove his fist into her thigh.

Melanie groaned and crumpled to the floor.

With one hand, Ari picked her up and tossed her like a sack of flour onto the bed. Her glasses were askew on her face, and blood ran from the corner of her mouth like red ink from a leaking pen.

Ed stepped into the room. In Arabic, he demanded, "What's going on here?"

"An uncooperative hostage." Ari whirled around and glared at Melanie. "Now. Will you listen to me? Or shall I beat you some more? What will it be, Ms. Forrest?"

"Okay," she whispered. Tears turned the edge in her voice ragged.

"Good. Get her up." Ari pinned Jabir in his gaze and added in Arabic, "Sit her there."

Jabir helped her rise.

Melanie limped to the stool, and she leaned into him as she eased onto the canvas.

"When we tell you, you are to read this statement." Jabir nodded, and Stephen unfurled a message someone had scrawled on butcher paper. "Read it verbatim. That is all."

Stephen handed Jabir a rifle, and once he slid his balaclava over his face, he stood behind Melanie's right shoulder while Stephen stepped to her left.

Ari glanced at Abdel, who nodded to him. Ari said, "You may start...now."

A red light flashed on the camera.

"To Samir Kamil. I, Melanie Forrest, have become a hostage of the Jihad of Light. Why? Because you were unable to follow through with the real estate transaction in Panama City. I am being held at an undisclosed location and will remain unharmed so long as you complete the closing for the property next Tuesday, June twentieth, as scheduled." She paused as she obviously realized the import of the next sentence. "If you fail to do so, then you will..." Her voice faltered. "You will find my body delivered to your doorstep in Beirut within five days. I know you love me, Samir. I've seen it in your face. Heard it in your voice. Please. I—I don't want to die. Please come and close on the property."

The red light disappeared on the camera, and Ed shifted from where he'd stood behind Abdel. "Did you get it?"

"Every bit." Abdel nodded.

Ed stepped through the doorway.

"Very good, Ms. Forrest." Ari shut off the overhead light. "Sit there. You'll take it from here?" he asked Jabir.

Jabir nodded. Once his comrades had left, he pulled off his balaclava and wiped the sweat from his face. He tossed it on the desk and turned to find Melanie huddled on the bed. One hand rubbed her leg where Ari had hit her. He noticed how the other trembled where it rested on her lap.

"I don't want to die," she said after a minute.

With a sigh, Jabir pulled over the barrister's chair and settled in front of her, his knees almost touching hers. "If Samir Kamil follows through with the closing, you won't. I'm sorry about your lip. And your cheek. And your leg. I'm sure they hurt."

She sniffled and refused to meet his gaze.

He finally pushed back and rose. "Look. We'll take care of you. Feed you three times a day. Let you use the restroom. We're not brutes, after all."

"I'm not sure I believe that."

"I know." Jabir picked up the burlap sack resting in a corner and up-ended it. With a metallic rattle, the chain he'd bought the week before snaked onto the floor beside the bed. Bile filled his throat as he pulled two padlocks from another bag. "I'm sorry, but I have to chain you."

"What? I—I promise I'm not going to run away. Honestly, where would I go? There's bars on the windows. And I'm sure you have guards..." Melanie's voice trailed off as he looped one end around the metal bedframe between the leg and support and secured it with a padlock.

"Perhaps not. But I must." He lifted the leg of her sweats and secured the shackle with the other padlock. Both keys would go to Ed.

"I hate you."

Jabir flinched as her words seared his soul. Alex's face flashed before his eyes. He wanted to tell her so many things, like how he knew she was Alex's friend and because of that he'd take extra good care of her.

He couldn't, not without revealing his true identity.

He blew out a sigh. "Look. I'm sorry you're in this situation. Truly, I am. But when I said we'd take good care of you, I meant it. We know you have a heart condition." He stepped to the desk, picked up the bottle, and set it on the nightstand next to the bed. "Here. Here's your medication."

"How did you know?"

Could he say the CIA had studied her since February as if she were a specimen under a microscope?

"Like I said, we'll take good care of you."

With that, Jabir turned away before he could reveal on his face how he knew Alex.

11

Jabir shut the door to Melanie's room and rotated his neck to relieve the stress that had been building all morning. His head hurt, and he couldn't wait to lay it on a pillow.

"Nice work, gentlemen," Ed told them in Arabic. He placed a laptop on the table Ari and Abdel had unfolded moments before. Once he logged in, he inserted the SD card from the video camera. "Al-Omri, get those other two computers up and running, will you?"

Without a word, Jabir pulled them from their cases and laid them on the table beside Ed's. As they powered up, he turned his attention to where Ed opened the video program.

Melanie's image, bruised face and cut lip included, coalesced on the screen. The sound of her voice breaking made the Stephen's setup of the guns cease. Jabir wanted to look away, but he couldn't.

Ed played it again, Melanie's pleas ringing like accusations in Jabir's ears.

"Good job, al-Omri, in playing the good cop."

79

"It's a fine balance to Ari's bad cop," Stephen said. He settled on the other side of Jabir and opened the case containing the satellite receiver that would allow them to connect with Langley. "Hey, Ed, I'm going to go and get this going."

"Sounds good." Ed inserted a flash drive into one of the USB ports. It flashed as he copied the video. "Okay, Rosen, your turn. I know it's late for you guys. Take al-Omri home in the Land Cruiser. Then come on back up and stand guard. Al-Rashid, go and help Karesh get that dish set up. Then get some rest. Al-Omri, we'll see you for the night shift. Make sure you work it out with the embassy about your sporadic work habits."

"I've already done that." Jabir nodded. "They know I'm down here on temporary assignment and that I'm somewhat of a slacker by working odd hours."

Ari grinned. "Man, you are *such a slacker.*" He emphasized the last three words like a teenager would.

Everyone laughed.

"What was your biggest slacker moment in high school?" Stephen asked Ari.

Ari tapped his chin as if thinking hard. "I don't know about slacker, but one time, I stuffed the class nerd in a locker."

"Man, you are *cold.*" Stephen laughed. "Abdel?"

"I was an angel in high school."

"Liar." Ari wadded up a piece of paper and tossed it at him.

Ed closed the lid to the laptop. His phone beeped on his belt, and he checked it. "Guys, much as I like the chitchat, let's get a move on it."

"Before you guys go, I want my money." Abdel held out his hand.

"What?" Jabir frowned.

"Hey, don't think I didn't see your red ear. By the way, Ari, nice bad cop imitation."

"I just balanced out the good cop." Ari winked at Jabir, reached into his pocket, and pulled out his wallet. He fished out a twenty and slapped it into his friend's palm. "Play money for you."

"Much appreciated. Vegas, here I come!" Abdel whistled the opening bars from Faith Hill's "Let's Go To Vegas", which drew an amused look from Ed.

"Do Jihad of Light members know country music?"

"Only if they're educated in Texas." Abdel began undoing the cord of the fold-up satellite dish.

Jabir shook his head. "Ari, let's go."

The two men strolled to the Land Cruiser. Since Jabir would be staying in the city, Ari drove. They bumped down onto the narrow macadam road that was two lanes in definition only. Ari fiddled with the radio until a Panamanian song with a spicy Latin beat hummed from the speakers. He adjusted the volume to a low tone.

"Sorry about what happened back there," he said after a moment.

Jabir looked at him. "Come again?"

"I noticed how you got quiet, and I could see you were uncomfortable from the start. I take it you've never done a snatch before?"

Jabir leaned his head against the seat. "Can't say I have. We typically gather our intel without kidnapping."

"I understand. It's unsettling the first time it happens."

"Was it necessary to hit Melanie?"

Ari fell silent, and Jabir worried he'd offended his friend. Then the small, powerfully built man shook his head. "Some things are necessary. We've found over the years that if we come on strong, let hostages know who's boss, they're more than likely going to respect us and not try anything foolish that would endanger both them and us. It's the cost of doing business at times."

Only the samba beat from the station in Panama City filled the air.

"And I promise that outside of work, I've never, ever hit a woman. Rachel and Deborah can attest to that."

"Your wife and daughter?"

"You got it."

"How old are your kids?"

"Josiah's twenty-two. The kid just graduated college. Man, I'm glad Ed let me off long enough to go to his graduation, especially since I missed his high school one."

"How about Deborah?"

"She's a sophomore in college this year." Ari fell silent for a few minutes. Then he added, "I'm getting out, you know."

"Getting out?" Jabir cast a glance at him.

From the driver's seat, Ari smiled, the small crinkles at the corners of his eyes being the only indicator that he was in his mid-fifties. "Retiring after thirty years. This is my last mission."

Jabir blinked. "I didn't know that."

"Oh, yeah. You know I'm a Krav Maga-aholic, right?"

"How could I forget?" Jabir winced and rubbed his leg. "That first time you got me in the ring with you, I was never so terrified. I thought I was going to wind up in the ER. I had a bruise on my leg for weeks."

"Krav Maga is a tough sport. You did fine, especially when you nearly took me down. Sneaky. That's what I told Rachel that night after you surprised me in that second bout. I'm opening a gym near the house. Josiah's going to help with it, most likely teaching classes along with me. Rachel promised to keep the books."

"How about Deborah?"

"She'll probably teach too. It's funny." Ari shook his head.

"What?"

"In high school, she almost walked away from Krav Maga because some people made fun of her. But Rachel talked her into staying with it. Now she loves it. It's neat to see when your kids stop worrying so much about what other people think and start being who they are. Hah. Some people never get there."

"Politicians," they chorused.

Ari laughed.

Jabir tapped his fingers along to the beat on the radio. "Where'd you learn it?"

"Krav Maga?"

"Yeah."

"Israel. My folks were born here but had dual Israeli citizenship. And being patriotic Jews, they decided to move to Israel to set up housekeeping in one of the settlement towns. We were surrounded by angry Palestinians, so learning Krav Maga became a matter of survival."

"Interesting."

"Yeah. We wound up moving back to the States when I was in junior high. I think my parents realized that if we stayed in the settlements, chances were good my brothers and I wouldn't live through high school, let alone college." Ari slowed and stopped where the intersection formed a T. He turned left toward Panama City.

Jabir digested that one for several minutes as they sped southward toward the city.

Ari rested his arm on the sill, his driving arm relaxed along with his shoulders.

Maybe Jabir had an opening to garner more information about Ed.

"Did your experience in the settlements drive you to join the CIA?"

"That was a big part of it. I saw a lot of good people die in Israel. People who were either parents of my friends or even my friends. I knew the Palestinian side was chock full of unhappy people who were easy targets for jihadi recruiters. Matter of fact, during my earlier years with the company, I wound up spending some time working joint missions with Mossad."

Jabir saw an in, and he ran through it without hesitation. "Where did you meet up with Ed?"

"Where every other Arabic speaker seemed to. Iraq."

"How many years have you worked with him?"

"A long time." Ari paused as if calculating in his head. "I went over there as Gulf II was ramping up, so I guess that's about fifteen years or so."

"Wow. I was in high school then."

Ari laughed. "Thanks for making me feel old."

Jabir grinned. "Sorry. I guess you two know each other pretty well."

"We've socialized some. I don't know how it's like at Unit 28, but at CIA, our friends tend to be our coworkers. When Ed got sent back, I followed about a year later after Obama knocked out the black sites. You talk about a bitter man."

"Ed?"

"Yeah. When we were in Iraq at one of the black sites, we had ten insurgents in our care. He was tough on them. Real tough, but then again, we needed information and fast too. I was off duty at the time, but apparently, Ed and some others took the interrogations too far. Eight guys died that night." He shook his head. "Someone fingered Ed, and he got sent home."

How should he phrase his next question? Jabir cocked his head. "What are your thoughts on it?"

Ari sighed. "I don't know, man. Ed's a tough guy. He gets things done. I knew he had to get information in a hurry, but sometimes I wondered about his techniques. I never participated in those interrogations." He slowed as traffic thickened on the approach to the city. "He may be tough on insurgents, and yeah, he's tough on us too, but for good reason. I always know he's got my back. He plans well, and that's kept us alive over the years."

"You got back after he did?"

"About a year or so. He seemed happier. I'm sure his girlfriend has something to do with it."

Jabir's head jerked around.

Ari grinned. "I can see that surprises you."

Jabir offered a shrug and a weak smile. "I guess I never pegged Ed for a romantic."

"Yeah, me neither. Her name's Francesca Bonini. Rachel and I have gone to dinner with them a few times. They've been together for almost ten years now. I can't figure out why they don't marry. Not my business, though."

Jabir needed to steer the conversation toward his main mission. How could he do that without tipping his hand since it was clear that Ari was closer to Ed than he'd realized? "Were you and Hakim close?"

"Yeah." Ari sighed. "I guess you could say we three were of the same vintage. He and I were going down to the personnel officer together and put in our paperwork." His hands clinched on the steering wheel. "It was painful when he died. Rachel went to the funerals with me. It was awful. And I'm really worried about his kids."

"Who has custody of them?"

"Hakim's brother and his family." Ari slammed his fist into the steering wheel. "It's freaking me out, man."

"Do you have any idea who's doing this?"

"No, and I've spent a lot of sleepless nights worrying. Rachel's worried that something's going to happen between now and July. I think for the first time since we've been married, she cried when I left. I told her not to worry. Ed's got my back, and literally, the day after I return, I'm going down there. I might even do it the same day if we land early enough." Ari sighed as he pulled into Jabir's apartment complex. "Here we are. Be gone with you. I'll go to an Internet café and send this message. See you to-night?"

"Yep. After some sleep." Jabir climbed from the Land Cruiser and shut the door. He tapped the hood twice and waved as Ari drove off. Then he kicked the ground in frustration.

Stephen was scared, and Ari was worried.

But Ari trusted Ed completely.

Jabir realized one thing.

Gathering evidence to confirm Ed as the murderer of the native Arabic speakers was going to be harder than he ever anticipated.

12

1900 hours local time (1100 hours CDT), Beirut, Lebanon

Samir sipped his champagne and savored the gentle pinks and pale yellows of the dusk. Stretched out below him, the lights of Beirut began winking as if flirting with him to come into the city for a night of clubbing. The bushes surrounding the swimming pool of azure water rustled, and the mourning doves nesting within them cooed as they sang a lullaby to their young.

Samir took a deep breath, held it, and released it in a slow stream.

Tonight was for rest, not for going out on the town.

He treasured the pleasant soreness from his squash match, the rested feeling an afternoon of sleeping had provided, and the peace he'd finally gained from assuring himself over and over that Tarek finally understood his concerns. He stretched, savoring relaxation the simple motion brought him.

Samir strolled downstairs and found a plate of food prepared by his housekeeper. That, some more champagne, and supper outside would complete his meal. He settled at the glass table under an umbrella. Next door, his neighbors chatted with friends as their children splashed around in the pool. He waved to them, earning a friendly response in return.

Within seconds, the idea of simply taking in a sunset bored him. Once his laptop powered up, he popped a grape into his mouth and tapped into the Internet. He cruised several sites, including one on American hotrods and his social networking sites before finally turning to his personal e-mail. After deleting the junk mail, Samir clicked on one of the remaining messages.

The address of the sender caught his eye. It was to a personals site, the very site Tarek had set up for their use in Jihad of Light communications.

That was strange. Hadn't Tarek understood that Papa and Noor were watching him closely now?

Samir hesitated.

The mouse hovered on the link. He clicked it.

A new page flashed onto the screen, this one showing a buxom blonde with such extravagant proportions that Samir wanted to laugh.

Almost.

See more of me.

That was all the message said.

Once more, Samir moved the mouse over the link. His finger poised above the button.

Tarek, I told you I'm out of business now.

Samir eased the mouse away. Then he rose and paced along the pool's edge. He stared into the blue water.

I can't. Not now.

He had to. If he ignored the message, Tarek would keep persisting.

With a sigh, Samir returned to the table and clicked on the link.

He stared as Melanie pleaded for her life with a split lip and bruised cheek that reminded him of what would happen if he didn't comply.

Samir's cuss word echoed across the patio and the hills like a cannon blast. The mourning doves shot in startled protest from the bushes. The voices next door ceased as well. His neighbors stared at him. He raised his hand in a weak wave.

Snatching up the computer, Samir darted into the house. He collapsed into a chair at the breakfast nook's table and played the video again and again. It was short, less than a minute, but it got the point across.

The property for Melanie.

No negotiations.

None.

Twilight eased into darkness as another cuss word ricocheted throughout the room. With shaking fingers, Samir raked his hands through his hair.

He had to go and see Tarek.

Now.

He didn't even waste time changing. For this little venture, the sweats, T-shirt, and moccasins he wore would do just fine.

Samir burned rubber in his Porsche all the way into the city and the Ras Beirut district, where many of the socially elite lived. He turned off the main avenue and into a residential area. Here, imposing stone walls fronted the sidewalk, punctured sporadically with the weak amber glow of streetlights like orbs out of a fantasy novel. Some of the gates allowing access to the villas beyond had guardhouses.

Tarek's did.

Samir braked. "I'm here to see Tarek."

"He is not receiving visitors tonight," the guard said.

"Tell him Samir Kamil is here and that the matter is most urgent."

The guard remained, his stare blank. He dialed a number on his cellphone. A moment later, he stepped out of the way as the auto gate began moving inward. "He's waiting."

Samir ignored him and stomped on the gas. The Porsche spurted around to the circular drive and stopped. He practically ripped open the door as he stomped inside the mansion and paused.

Darkness enveloped the house. Only one light in the kitchen provided illumination. Another feeble light emanated from the top of the staircase that wound upward.

His friend, clad only in a silk bathrobe, waited for him at the foot of the marble steps. "May I ask what you are doing here uninvited?"

"Why did you do it?"

"Why did I do what?" Tarek cocked his head and blinked.

The heat began creeping up Samir's neck. "Why did you kidnap her?"

Tarek led the way into the kitchen, opened the refrigerator, and pulled out a chilly bottle. "I'm afraid I'm not understanding. Drink?"

Samir ignored him. His repeated question came out more like a growl. "Why did you kidnap her?"

"Who?"

"Melanie!" He reached into the pocket of his sweats and yanked out the flash drive to where he'd copied the video. He threw it onto the counter. "I got this video from that personals site we use in our communications."

Tarek poured them both glasses of wine.

Samir stood there, chest heaving, as his friend sipped his.

Without a word, Tarek picked up the offending drive and proceeded to his study.

Samir followed, almost quivering with rage. He paced as his friend played the video a few times.

Tarek, who slouched in the leather chair behind his desk, rested his chin on his hand, turned his head, and regarded him through unreadable dark eyes. He stroked his beard. Then he said, "You think Jihad of Light had something to do with this?"

"Of course. Who else would? Who else wants the property sale to go through?" Samir couldn't believe his ears.

"You think I ordered this."

Samir muttered under his breath as he shook his head. "How could I not? I know what you said in the steam room. I told you. My hands are tied. There is nothing I can do. Not without endangering my job and perhaps your ability to buy future properties."

"Samir, calm down—"

"I am *not* going to calm down!"

Samir crashed to a halt when his friend's gaze turned from flint to molten. He sighed and collapsed into a chair in front of Tarek's mahogany desk. He put his elbows on the dark wood and rested his head in his hands. He took a deep breath. "I don't want Melanie to die, and I'm stuck. There is no way this closing is going to go through. None. Which means Melanie will die."

"Samir, look at me." Tarek's command made him raise his head. "Look at me."

"What?" Resignation tinged his voice.

"I can assure you, my friend, that I never ordered such a kidnapping. I'm a smart man, Samir Kamil. You know that. I know the futility. It's like I told you today. There will be other opportunities. Other, better opportunities."

"Then who would do such a thing?"

"That, I do not know. But, I can assure you I intend to find out." Tarek sipped his wine and set his glass on the desk. "And sooner rather than later."

"But what do I do? I can't act like I didn't get the message."

"I know that." A slow, cunning smile crossed Tarek's face. "This is what you do. You go to your father. Beg and plead to do the closing."

"He'll get even more suspicious."

"No, he'll see it as sour grapes that you didn't get what you wanted. In the meantime, I'll do a bit of checking."

Samir knew the truth behind his friend's words. He should leave. Slowly, he climbed to his feet and blew out a sigh. "All right. I guess that is all I can do."

"For now, yes." Tarek offered a smile as he walked his friend into the foyer.

"Tarek? Honey?" An unfamiliar female voice reached him from the top of the stairs.

Samir glanced up, coming to a standstill when he noticed the tall woman with flowing dark hair staring at them. Suddenly, he realized why he'd been denied entry.

"Yana, I'll be up in a moment," Tarek called. He turned back to Samir. "Go home. I'll look into this."

"Let me know what you find." That was all Samir could think of to say. With that, he stepped onto the wide portico. The heavy front door thumped shut behind him without even a good-bye from Tarek. He shrugged.

Tarek had to get to the bottom of this.

If not, Melanie would die.

2130 hours local time (1330 hours CDT), Beirut, Lebanon

The custom-made motorcycle sped along the Beirut streets and wove in and out of traffic. The glow of the streetlights reflected off the shiny gas tank and the rider's bald head in drops of liquid light that slithered along metal and skin alike before vanishing.

Ahead, the light turned yellow, then red.

Bike and rider blew through untarnished, despite the presence of a National Police cruiser at the intersection. The man's hand tightened on the throttle, which made the chopper emit a raucous blast of exhaust.

Hashim al-Hassan didn't care, not when most of the cops were in the al-Hassan family's pocket. He enjoyed the feeling of power brought on by the bike and the whisper of the hot night air on the bare skin of his arms. The way he slipped through the fingers of the law with ease emboldened him.

At the next light, he made a left and entered the residential area where his brother lived. The chopper's loud growl echoed off the walls of the villas. A smile curled his lips as he envisioned little children waking up to its roar, convinced that a monster waited outside for them.

He slowed as he approached the auto gate. The guard stood aside with the barrier already open.

Hashim nodded to the man. He rumbled up the circular drive and parked behind a small Fiat that had been pulled into a shadowy alcove. Once the noise of the engine disappeared, silence draped over the area. He lowered the skydiver's clear goggles he wore so they dangled around his neck. Five strides later, he arrived at the foot of the portico's steps.

The door flew open.

Yana stepped through, clad in a trench coat even on this hot night, her purse dangling by its strap from her fingers. Platform heels added several centimeters to her height. For a moment, she stopped and glared at him, her lips drawn, brows knitted, in what he was sure was her most ferocious look.

He wanted to laugh, and his lips twitched upward.

Her posture went rigid. "Thanks for ruining my night."

"Oh?"

"He asked me to leave. Apparently, you're more important than I."

Now Hashim laughed. "There will always be other nights, Yana. When my brother calls me, I answer. Good evening."

She sniffed and continued on her way.

His humor simmered. Who cared that his brother's mistress was angry with him? He certainly didn't. He dropped his keys into an outer pocket of his cargo pants and strode inside.

Tarek joined him at the foot of the stairs.

Hashim grinned at the chinos and black T-shirt he wore. "Is this how you ruined Yana's romantic night?"

Tarek snorted. "Hardly. No, Samir Kamil did that."

"Samir?" Hashim followed his brother into the kitchen.

"Yes, Samir." Tarek opened the refrigerator and handed his brother a bottle of water before pulling out the wine bottle. He poured himself a glass. "He showed up about an hour and a half ago all in a rage."

"And that would be because?"

Tarek led the way into his study and slouched in his desk chair. "He accused Jihad of Light of kidnapping Melanie Forrest."

"I'm not following." Hashim settled his large frame onto the couch across the room.

"Now I realize we haven't talked today." Tarek shook his head. "Samir and I played squash at lunch. Then in the steam room afterwards, he told me how his sister and father discovered the deplorable state of the property in Panama City. They said no."

Hashim popped the top on the bottle and took a swig. "I'm disappointed but not surprised. There will be others."

"Exactly. Which is what I told him. He started squawking, of course, saying that he couldn't do anything more, that he was lucky he hadn't been fired for that one incident. I only mentioned how much he cared for both Melanie and Noor. That is all."

"And that's what sent him over here in a panic?" Hashim cocked an eyebrow.

"No. This was." Tarek tapped his monitor.

Hashim rose and came around the desk where he could see what glowed on the monitor. Melanie Forrest pleading for her life didn't faze him a bit. Not even his pulse picked up. "Play it again."

Tarek did.

Hashim took another swig and set the bottle on the desk. He paced, his hand stroking his beard. Thoughts flew through his head, but he couldn't place any of them.

At least not yet.

"My brother, I think someone is using our good name for their own purposes." Tarek's voice reached through the cacophony of ideas and brought him back to the present. "The question is, who."

"We are certain she's in Panama?"

"Perhaps not one hundred percent, but from what Samir told me, she was the lawyer representing Kamil International for the walkthrough."

"Not our local lawyer." Hashim shook his head. "How did that happen?"

"Someone at Kamil International got suspicious, most likely Noor. Her father requested that Melanie conduct the walkthrough."

"Interesting." Hashim picked up his water again.

"What are your thoughts?" Tarek sipped his wine as he eyed his brother.

Hashim returned to the couch. "None of our rivals here have the sophistication to pull off something like this. Nor the reach to do it all the way in Panama. I suspect the CIA is involved. They have the reach and the resources as well as the desire to shut down Jihad of Light."

Tarek began nodding.

"More than that. Our mole."

"The one who has most graciously leveled the playing field for us?" Tarek leaned forward, his elbows now resting on his desk.

"Exactly." Hashim finished his water. "How did this come to Samir?"

"The personals site we use. A message was there with the video."

"Tell him to forward you the message. Then send it to me. The video had to be uploaded from somewhere." Hashim crushed his water bottle. "Most likely, that somewhere is in Panama. Once I'm ready, I'll take the private jet with some of our men and do some investigating."

"Send the jet back when you arrive and report to me what you find."

"I'll do that." Hashim strode into the foyer. As he opened the door, he stopped and turned. "In the meantime, keep Samir contained."

"Already done."

"Good." Hashim climbed onto the chopper. As he started the motor and waved to his brother, his mind churned with possibilities.

He would get to the bottom of whoever had chosen to besmirch the good name of Jihad of Light.

And then?

They would pay.

13

1845 hours Mountain Daylight Time (1945 hours CDT),
San Jose, Costa Rica

"What do we want to do when Melanie gets here?" Alex asked.

"Clubbing?" Becca Alvarez suggested. She winked.

"What?" Ellie Watkins, the fourth member of the Fantabulous Four, stared at them.

Alex grinned. "That's a thought. Though I haven't been clubbing in years."

She sipped her drink, sighed blissfully, and stretched.

"Yeah, me neither. Hey, how about we could go to the hotel's bar for drinks? I checked it out. It's nice," Becca added.

"And she didn't tell us she was doing that," Alex said to Ellie in a stage whisper.

Her friend giggled, and Alex was grateful. In the short time she'd been with the two other members of the Fantabulous Four, she'd learned one thing. Her supposed boy problems and perceived life issues were nothing compared to the marital struggles Ellie endured or the strain in parental relationships that Becca faced. Her problems seemed petty in comparison.

If only she could completely shake her regrets over Jabir. Automatically, she sighed.

"Hey, what was that about?" Becca's teasing words brought her back to the present.

"Sorry. Nothing."

"That's not a nothing sigh," Ellie said.

"She's right. Spill it, Thornton." Becca set her drink on the airport café's table and crossed her arms.

"I miss Jabir." There. She'd said it.

A look passed between Becca and Ellie.

"Care to explain?" Becca asked.

"I regret how I ended things with him."

Neither of her friends said anything for a moment.

"Alex, remember that there's always hope for reconciliation. Sometimes it takes swallowing pride to do so," Becca took a sip of her drink and set it down. "Hmmm, mmm. Good stuff, this mango orange drink."

Right then, Alex heard an announcement for the arrival of Copa Airlines Flight 444 from Panama City. "Hey, they just announced Melanie's flight." She jumped up, more to avoid getting into the topic of Jabir than to rush with the rest of the crowd to greet their friend.

"Do you see her?" Becca stood on tiptoes to see over the heads of the gathering crowd.

"Not yet." Using her five-foot-ten-inch height, Ellie kept a watch over the passengers spilling into the terminal. "No blonde yet."

"I hate being short," Alex muttered.

"I hear you." Becca climbed onto her chair at their table and surveyed the crowd.

Gradually, it thinned.

No Melanie.

"Alex, are you sure she was on Flight 444?" Becca's question broke into her reverie.

"Yeah. Why?"

"Well, it's eight on the nose and still no Melanie."

Alex pulled out her phone and checked the message she'd received from Melanie the day before. "Yeah, that's what it says. Flight 444 at 6:50. Maybe she got hung up at customs or something." She put her phone away, then pulled it out and dialed Melanie's number. It rang and rang, and Alex kept hoping to hear her friend's voice saying hi and that she apologized but she'd gotten stuck in a long line at customs. That didn't happen. Instead, her voicemail picked up. "Hey, Mel, it's your buddies. We're wondering where you are. We're at the area right outside customs, so join us when you can."

"This is weird," Becca muttered. She paced to the status board and peered at it again.

"Maybe she went to baggage claim and we somehow missed her. Let me go check," Ellie added before either of her friends could object. When she returned ten minutes later, she shook her head. "I didn't see her. But then again, it's pretty crowded over there. I'll go back in a few minutes."

Alex checked her phone in case she'd somehow missed her friend's call. Nothing. No voicemail icon saying she had a message waiting. She watched as Ellie again returned to the baggage claim area.

She rejoined them, worry clouding her green eyes.

"She's not there. I'm getting worried," she added, voicing what Alex was feeling.

"Let's check at the ticket counter."

"I'll stay here and wait for her," Ellie told them.

Becca immediately headed to the line with Alex beside her. When their turn finally came, she asked in Spanish, "We're wondering if our friend was onboard her flight that arrived a bit ago."

The ticket agent smiled. "What flight was that?"

"444," Alex told her. "We're wondering if she missed it."

"Her name?"

"Melanie Forrest with two r's."

"Let me check." The agent typed a few things on her keyboard. A few minutes later, a frown marred her pretty face. "No. I see that Señorita Forrest was due to travel with us today on that flight, but my records show she never checked in."

Alex frowned. "Could she have changed her flight?"

"I can check." A few more taps from the agent rendered more results. "She has a return flight from here to Panama City for next week, but that's all. No other reservations. I'm sorry. Is there anything else?"

"No. Thank you." Alex drummed her fingers on the counter. She nodded at Becca, and they returned to Ellie, hoping against hope that Melanie had shown up.

Ellie sat alone at their table, chin in hand, aimlessly moving her drink in wet circles as she stared at the passenger entry area.

She glanced up. "Nothing?"

"No Melanie." Becca crossed her arms. "This is weird."

"Yeah. I agree. Let's let it be weird back at the hotel. C'mon." Alex led the way to the Explorer. As she drove them to Hotel San Jose, her hands tightened on the steering wheel. Why had Melanie bagged on them and not told them?

By the time they walked into their hotel room, she'd come up with a plan. "Does anyone know where she was staying?"

"Not me," Ellie said.

Becca agreed. "Me neither. Alex, I'm worried."

"I'm just mad." Once more, Alex punched in Melanie's number. Again, her voicemail picked up. This time, she didn't leave a message.

"Look at it this way." Becca sat on the plush leather couch and put her feet on the coffee table. "Melanie's Miss Reliable, right? If she'd missed her flight, she would've called us and told us she'd rebooked."

"But she didn't rebook. Maybe she decided to stay over without telling us?"

"And you believe that?"

"Not really." Alex sighed and finished her bottle of water.

"That's why I'm worried," Becca continued. "There's no way she'd ditch us, especially for a trip in her honor. You agree?"

"Yeah, I do." Futilely, Alex dialed Melanie's number and got the same result. She set her phone on the table where she sat. Once more, she pulled up the e-mail Melanie had sent her. They'd been at the airport at the correct time, meaning her friend had missed her flight, meaning something must have happened.

Something bad.

She set the phone on the glass. "We have no idea where she's staying, so we can't call the hotel to see if she's checked out."

"I wouldn't say that." Ellie had pulled out her tablet and started tapping on it. Then she grinned. "I, ladies, have found all of the hotels where she could be staying. Why don't we call around and see if we can't find out which one she's at?"

Alex groaned when she saw the list. "But that's so many."

"We can break those out." Becca studied the list.

"How?"

"Well, she's not a B&B person by her own admission."

Ellie tapped the screen, culling the list. The other two crowded around.

Alex straightened and remained sitting on the couch's arm. "That's still really long."

"She's traveling on business, right?" Becca's sherry eyes were intent.

"Yeah." Alex nodded and opened the refrigerator to study the drinks inside. She pulled out a Coke. "She's on business until she gets here."

"Meaning she'd probably stay in some high-end hotel. Ellie, set the search criteria to be hotels that are 150 American dollars or more a night. We'll go lower if needed."

"Ah, that's better. Just fifty. I think we can do that. You two call since you know Spanish, and I'll tell you the numbers." She recited the first one, which Alex dialed. Becca took the second. And so it went until Becca dialed the eighteenth number. "Yes, I'm wondering if a Melanie Forrest stayed with you last night and checked out this morning…F-O-R-R-E-S-T. Yes? Really?" Becca listened for a few more moments. "Okay. When? Friday…Hmmm…Well, could you put me through to her room? Thanks." Becca finally hung up and turned to her friends. "Wow. That's weird."

"What?" Alex leaned forward in the chair where she'd taken a seat.

"The guy at Hotel Panama said that yes, she'd checked in yesterday, but she wasn't scheduled to check out until Friday. I had him put me through to her room. No answer."

Alex swallowed hard. Her pulse quickened, and she jumped up and paced to relieve the nervous energy that began humming through her. Her intuition, something that had kept her safe and alive during her years with Unit 28, had started ominously humming.

"This is so bizarre," Ellie muttered. "What do we do?"

"Keep calling her." Suddenly feeling a bit queasy, Alex stared at the Coke. "We keep calling until midnight. Her cell and room. And if she's not there after that, then in the morning, we call the embassy in Panama City. Maybe they can take some action."

"Sounds like a plan to me." Becca rose and stretched. "Until then, let's chill."

Every hour they called Hotel Panama and got the same result. No answer at Melanie's room. No answer on her cell.

Finally, Becca and Ellie retreated to bed.

Alex wandered into her room and sat on the edge of her bed for a moment.

"Melanie, where are you?" she whispered into the still air.

Wherever Melanie was, Alex had a growing suspicion that she was in trouble.

Deep trouble.

Day 4
Wednesday, June 14, 2017

14

Could nothing go right for him?

Something? Anything?

Sweat built up underneath the collar of Samir's Armani shirt as he stared at his calendar. He wanted to rip off his silk tie and hurl it across the room.

He settled for loosening the knot a little.

The meeting reminder dinged again as if accusing him of his tardiness.

He'd forgotten about the opening conference for the annual audit.

Samir swore under his breath, grabbed his portfolio, and snatched the worry beads from the drawer. Once more, he made the trip down the hall to the executive suites, but this time, he entered the conference room that served as the boardroom. It was large, running from his father's corner office along the narrower side of the building to the other corner. The floor-to-ceiling windows offered a sweeping panorama of the harbor below. On the sea, two container ships with the bold red and blue of the

Kamil International logo, clear even from that distance, cut white swaths through the deep blue water, one leaving port and the other arriving.

Samir turned and surveyed those who had gathered for the meeting. An older gentleman dressed in a gray suit and muted tie conversed with Fadi and Noor. His sister's intimidation for the day consisted of her stiletto heels, black suit, and white top with her hair in a tight chignon. She raked him up and down with a slow glance and returned to the conversation. He bit back his sigh and observed the others. The seven remaining team members seemed much younger than their boss.

Seven?

Samir blinked.

Normally, a team of four accomplished the annual audit. Then he shrugged. Maybe Finch, May, and Gilbert was training some new accountants. Again, he tried to catch either Noor's or Fadi's attention but to no avail.

He observed the six clustered in the corner. Three men and three women, all clad in similar business attire, chatted at the windows as they sipped coffee from delicate china cups. He stepped near them. One of the women offered a chilly smile and turned her back slightly, as if excluding him from their conversation.

Samir gave up and took a seat at the table beside the seventh analyst.

This one was young and pretty, her blond hair up in a twist. Her eyes, which were gray, were intent on the laptop in front of her where she tapped some keys. She smiled at him. With a demur flick of the mouse, she minimized the document she was reviewing and closed the lid.

They knew something they didn't want to reveal. Was it the accounts? Shafiq had hidden them so well when he'd worked with Samir to set them up.

Now, Shafiq was gone.

Not just gone. Disappeared, according to Tarek.

Under the table, Samir's fingers worked the beads harder.

"So sorry I'm late." Papa's voice in accented English from the head of the table made him raise his gaze. "I had a phone call I simply had to take. Please have a seat."

Noor settled across from Samir. She glanced at him, then broke eye contact and smiled as Fadi seated himself beside her. The older gentleman took the chair at the foot of the table.

The young analyst beside Samir placed a sign-in sheet in front of him and opened a new file on her laptop. As she typed, it quickly became clear that she would be taking minutes.

Samir frowned. Taking minutes at opening and closing conferences was strange to him.

The meeting began. It was like he expected. The team was here for the annual audit. That was nothing new.

The tension in Samir's shoulders relaxed. Audits ran two to three days.

Then Gavin Martin, the team lead, announced that they would work through the weekend and into the next week if need be.

Samir straightened.

The tension returned. His fingers once more began playing with the worry beads.

This wasn't normal at all. They had to know something about the accounts. But how could they? Melanie hadn't reported anything strange when she had been preparing the contract. Maybe this team was young and needed the extra training time. They certainly looked that way.

The meeting broke up. Fadi offered to show the team where they could set up shop. At the head of the table, Papa closed his portfolio. Noor made for the door.

"Papa," Samir called softly.

Papa paused. He studied his older child. "You're doing well? Hanan told me you called in sick yesterday afternoon."

"I was exhausted from our trip home."

"I understand. Would you like to join Noor, Fadi, and me for lunch? We're leaving in five minutes."

"You're not going out with Gavin?"

"No. They're ordering lunch to be brought in since they wanted to get started."

The tension formed tiny knots in Samir's shoulders. "Sure. Lunch sounds good."

They wound up at an elegant French restaurant in the Ras Beirut district. They had a table outside that fronted the sidewalk. An awning erected by the staff kept the strong summer sun off of them, and the local flowers perfumed the air with relaxing scents. Under other circumstances, Samir would have reveled in talking about his nieces and watching the pretty ladies as they strolled to and from the high-end shops fronting the sidewalk. He missed the way he and Noor used to laugh about Fatima and Samira, the closeness they had as associates, and the way he could make her laugh. All thanks to his bumble with the property.

Now, as the waitress cleared away their meal and brought coffee, she refused to look at him.

He cleared his throat and fixed his gaze on his father. "Papa, is there any way you would reconsider closing on the property in Panama City?"

"I can't believe—" Noor began before Fadi clamped his hand on her arm.

"Son, did you know the property was in deplorable state?"

Samir did, but he couldn't reveal that. "No, I didn't. I trusted my associate, and apparently, he fooled me."

"Are we supposed to believe that?" Noor asked. "You think we'd be so naïve?"

Fadi's hand tightened on her arm.

Papa gazed at her for a long moment.

She crossed her arms and stared into space.

Fadi leaned over and whispered something into her ear.

"You do understand why we're not interested in it, right? After Noor and I received the report, we discussed it." Farouk glanced at his daughter.

She jerked her chin in a slight nod.

Papa held up one finger. "First, it was too small to allow for growth. The properties around it are all active with healthy firms who would not sell to us even if we inquired because they are our rivals. Second..." He held up another finger. "Perhaps your associate could use the property for his own purposes. But he'd be a tenant, nothing more. What would happen if he decided to leave? We would be left with something in bad shape, something that would require us to pay more than it's worth to renovate it to meet the needs of our clients or our needs as a shipping terminal. Do you understand our concerns?"

Samir cast a glance at Noor.

She stared at the table. Her fingers, now laced together, had tightened to the point where her knuckles whitened.

Fadi rested his hand on the back of her chair. Most likely, he ran his thumb across her back the way Samir had seen him do before.

"I do." That was all Samir could think of to say.

Papa sipped his coffee. "That being said, I propose a compromise, and if you convey this to your associate, it will be acceptable."

"What would that be?"

"Tell your associate I will consider allowing the closing if he meets with the four of us in person." Papa nodded at his daughter and son-in-law. "When he does so, he is to bring a disclosure statement that fully outlines his intentions for the property's use. Then, he will be required to sign a tenant agreement with us. If he comes to us in person and signs the agreement, I'll notify Melanie, and on Monday of next week, you will fly out and conduct the closing with her as my representatives."

Hope fought with terror. Papa had no idea of what had happened to Melanie. Samir's mind darted in all directions. He glanced at Noor.

Had things not been so serious, he would have laughed at the way her jaw had dropped and her eyes had widened.

"I can do that, and even without Melanie's help, I can still do the closing. She did such a good job on the contract that it would be easy even without her presence."

"Then it's settled." Papa glanced up as the waitress approach. "*Mademoiselle*, if you could put all of our meals on one check, please."

"*Oui.*" She smiled and scurried away.

Samir returned his gaze to Noor.

She stared at him, a shaft of sunlight penetrating the awning and making her sherry eyes almost glow with a topaz light. They narrowed with feline grace. One corner of her mouth curled.

She wanted him to fail.

The problem was, if he didn't scramble and talk to Tarek in a hurry, he might very well do that.

Then Melanie would die.

0500 hours Mountain Daylight Time (0600 hours CDT), San Jose, Costa Rica

Alex's eyes snapped open. Nothing moved in the early morning air. Even the streets, where she'd heard noise through her open balcony door the night before, had fallen silent as if sleeping off a hard night of partying.

She turned onto her back and rubbed her eyes. A headache started somewhere deep in her head, one brought about by tossing and turning. She reached for her phone, hoping that somehow, she'd muted it and had missed Melanie's call.

Nothing.

Alex lay there. As dawn began painting the white of her curtains a pale pink, she tried both numbers for Melanie again.

No response.

Alex sat up. On her phone, she pulled up the website for the US embassy in Panama City and located the emergency contact number. She dialed it and listened as the phone rang on the other end.

"US Embassy, Marcie speaking," a polite feminine voice said.

"I'd like to report a friend missing in Panama City."

"One moment." A couple of clicks told her she was being transferred.

"Consular section," another female voice answered.

"I'd like to report a missing person in Panama City," Alex said. She tucked a pillow to her.

"One moment."

She rolled her eyes, tired of the runaround. Muzak played in her ears.

"This is John. I understand you have an emergency. How may I help you?"

"This is Alex Thornton, and I'm an American staying in San Jose, Costa Rica. One of my friends was supposed to join us, and she hasn't shown up."

"Where was she coming from?"

"Where you are. Panama City. We called her hotel, and she hasn't checked out. I know this may sound weird, but she should have checked out yesterday."

"Maybe she decided to stay in Panama City."

"And miss her bachelorette week at a resort in Playa Flamingo?" Alex blinked. She couldn't believe what she was hearing.

"Could be. Spell her name."

Alex did.

Tapping echoed in her ears. "Sorry about that. I was looking at the ICE records. It shows she checked through customs in Panama City on Monday."

"She had business there and was supposed to leave yesterday for here. But the hotel says she's not supposed to check out until Friday. And she never showed up for her flight yesterday from Panama City to here." Alex rose and stepped into the common room. She noticed Becca seated outside at the table on the balcony.

Instead of munching on sweetened cereal and reading her book, she stared out at the city, a mug of coffee steaming in her hands,

"Well, I honestly don't know what to tell you except that maybe she ditched her vacation."

"She'd never do that," Alex said.

"Maybe. Maybe not." John irritated her with his logic. "Look. There's nothing we can do right now. We have no indication she's in distress. Wait a couple of days, and maybe she'll show."

She wanted to grind her teeth.

"All right, then. I guess we'll do that. Thanks." She forced politeness into her voice when what she really wanted to do was tell him what she thought of his conclusions. Like they were pure baloney.

Alex tossed the phone onto the granite bar, leaned against it, and scrubbed her face with her hands. Only when she took several deep, calming breaths did she pour herself a cup of coffee and join her friend.

Becca glanced up, the weariness evident in her eyes. "You called the embassy?"

"Yeah."

"What'd they say?"

"They think I'm crazy. They told us to wait a couple of days to see if she turns up."

"So they don't see a problem." Becca shook her head.

"Nope." Alex stared over the city as it began emerging from the darkness. "I can't do that. Not when she was there for me four years ago."

Becca raised an eyebrow.

"The day I got fired from Unit 28, it was on television. She saw it, caught the shuttle from New York to DC, and spent the weekend with me. She didn't care about how that might reflect on her at work."

"You remember when we were in high school? How hard it was for me to simply get a B in something? I remember how she tutored me in trig until I finally squeaked by senior year, even when she had her own homework to do." Becca fell silent. "Alex, she's always been there for us. We need to be there for her."

"Agreed." For what seemed to be the hundredth time, Alex dialed the two numbers from memory.

Nothing.

Morning burned on, and Ellie joined them in their vigil.

Alex told housekeeping they'd be checking out by noon instead of the required eleven. Finally, she retreated to her room and started throwing what little clothes she had pulled out into her suitcase.

"Alex?" Ellie's voice came from near the door.

Alex glanced up and found both of her friends crowded in the doorway. "Girls, I think we need to go to Panama City."

No one objected.

Everyone knew Melanie was in trouble.

If they were lucky, they'd find her and be able to salvage at least some of their vacation.

2130 hours local time (1330 hours CDT), Beirut, Lebanon

"Tonight is not a night for worries, my friend, but for a celebration."

"I like it." Samir smiled, accepted the champagne flute, and gazed at the party raging around him on the al-Hassan yacht.

Tarek laughed. "I try to do it up right, do I not? So enjoy yourself. Tonight is for that. Simple enjoyment and pleasure."

It didn't take Samir long to down the champagne. He found the bar in the lounge and asked for a brandy. It burned and soothed him at the same time. When he drifted onto the lower stern deck, he perched on the railing and chatted with friends about his travels and the upcoming tennis tournament at Wimbledon. His voice was loud, but he didn't care. Samir was in his element.

Like moths attracted to a brightly burning light, the ladies flitted across the teak deck and joined him. He draped his arm around one, an attractive brunette with blond highlights who wore a short strapless dress and tons of gold around her wrists. Another, this one dressed in a bikini with a transparent cover-up over it, cozied up to him. Her arm wound around his waist. Some wore strapless frocks. Others, bikinis, cover-ups, and platform heels. He knocked back another champagne and laughed at some stupid joke his buddy made. When he set the glass down on a nearby table, he caught sight of his watch.

Close to midnight.

He needed to leave since tomorrow was a work day. Before he did, he had to talk with Tarek. "Perhaps later, ladies?"

The two socialites pouted and turned away to find other prey.

He found his friend holding court on the stern's upper deck, lounging on a leather couch the color of a fawn. Yana curled up beside him and shimmered in a transparent gold cover-up open at the front. She wore a white bikini with designs on it that reminded Samir of Greece. Tarek had slid one of her straps off her shoulder. He nibbled on her ear and murmured something to her.

Samir traced the outline of her figure. He averted his gaze. It was never good to lust after his best friend's girl.

Samir cleared his throat. "Tarek."

Tarek glanced up. A slow smile spread across his face. "Samir. Come join us. Yana has friends, you know."

"If we could chat in private for a few minutes."

A small sigh escaped Tarek, and he grimaced. It disappeared underneath another smile. "Okay. I can do that. Baby, I'll be back in a few minutes."

He kissed her again and murmured something to her. She giggled and whispered something back. Tarek tucked her strap onto her shoulder before rising.

With champagne flute in hand, he led the way up a narrow staircase onto the bridge. Since the yacht was docked in port and guests restricted from the area, it was empty. Tarek gazed at the twinkling lights of the city for a few moments. "It's beautiful, is it not?"

"It is."

"A perfect city. One with lots of mysteries as well. Didn't they used to call it the Jewel of Mediterranean?"

"I think so. When Papa was a teenager." Samir lifted his champagne to his lips and took a sip. Beirut and his whole life lay before him. He could conquer anything now.

"What is going on that you should request talking tonight?"

"Papa approached me at lunch today."

"Oh?"

"He said he was reconsidering allowing the purchase of the property."

"Really?" Surprise rippled through his friend's voice. "How did you manage to convince him?"

"I didn't do any convincing." Samir shrugged. "Perhaps he gave it some more thought."

"And he doesn't know about Melanie." Tarek fixed him in his intense blue gaze.

"No, he doesn't. He knows nothing of what happened to her. Nothing." He swallowed hard. "If he did, then he would know that Jihad of Light—"

Tarek pushed him against the wall so fast that he almost dropped his glass. His friend got in his face. "Stop." His voice was low, threatening. "You know better than to mention that name here. Or anywhere outside of my house."

"I'm sorry." Samir flushed. "He said he would be willing to go through with the deal if my 'associate' was willing to sign a long-term lease."

Tarek released him and smirked. "We would love to have a long-term lease for the property."

"And my 'associate' would have to appear in person at five Friday afternoon to sign the lease. When he does, he must have a full disclosure statement about the intent for the property. Papa wants to meet this person. So do Noor and Fadi."

At that news, Tarek's smile dropped away as he turned and swept a hand through the waves of his black hair, mussing it. "Clever. How very clever of your father."

Then he faced his friend. "But not insurmountable by us. You understand that, right?"

Samir swallowed hard. "I only want Melanie to be safe."

"I know. I'm working to determine exactly what happened." Again, Tarek fixed him in his intense blue gaze. "My friend, I can assure you we had nothing to do with it. Absolutely nothing. My man will find out if this is the work of a group of imposters. In the meantime, we'll produce an 'associate' to appease your father. Now what of the audit?"

"It's started." Samir swallowed hard. "They think they can finish by Friday, but I'm worried."

"Have they not found anything before?" Tarek's gaze bored into his as if he could see into the dirty depths of his soul.

"No. Not in the two previous audits." Samir nodded. "Shafiq did a great job in hiding the accounts."

"Then you have nothing to worry about, my friend." Tarek clapped him on the shoulder. Once more, he studied him with eyes so blue it was disorienting, almost like Samir was coming under a spell. "Nothing at all. I've also checked with my contacts in the police, and they've not heard any whispering either. So no worries, okay?"

"Right." Samir slowly nodded. "I should be going. I need to be in early because of the audit."

Tarek's grip on his shoulder tightened. "Stay. Please. Everything I have here is yours tonight. Everything. Even my girls." He nodded to down below where Yana talked with another beauty, this one with deep auburn hair and fair skin. She sipped some champagne. "See that one talking with Yana?"

"I do."

"Josette. Half French, half Lebanese, and all woman. She's yours for the night."

"Tarek…" He found himself wilting under his friend's firm gaze.

"Come. Join me." Though Tarek's words were jovial, the insinuation behind them wasn't.

You're mine. I own you, and you'll do whatever I ask.

"Okay." Samir offered a weak smile.

Tarek led him downstairs and to the upper deck on the stern.

Suddenly, Samir realized how only the four of them were present.

The two women talked on the couch. Josette wore a cover-up of deep scarlet with designs that reminded him of the Orient. When she noticed their approach, she set her wineglass on the low table beside her. She rose with the grace of a feline. As she sashayed toward him, she undid the sash. It fell open to reveal a bikini of the same color. The gold heels she wore accented her long legs.

Samir barely noticed as Tarek rejoined Yana on the couch.

Samir's eyes devoured Josette as she approached him. He finished off his champagne.

Josette wound her arms around his neck and cuddled up to him.

He inhaled her perfume.

Samir's cheeks flushed.

She kissed him.

"Take him, Josette," he thought he heard Tarek say.

As his hand snaked under her cover-up and caressed her smooth skin, Samir kissed her again.

Tarek chuckled.

Or was it the devil?

More importantly, as Josette molded her body to him, did Samir care?

No, not at the moment.

Not at all.

Day 5
Thursday, June 15, 2017

15

Enough.

Enough worry.

Enough waiting.

Alex wanted to act. Now.

The three women climbed from the Explorer and crossed the parking lot to the gates of the embassy. They wore their most appropriate clothing for the venture.

For Alex, that had meant dressing in a frock of hot tropical colors that shimmered like a flame. She'd bought it for a night of dancing at one of the resort's clubs, not for visiting the US embassy in Panama City because her friend might have gotten kidnapped and they didn't care. That wasn't right. Everyone in the government had protocols for everything. She had to let them work.

She nodded to the Panamanian soldier who guarded the gate. Once at the window of the guardhouse, she waited until the person before her had completed his business before drawing close.

"May I help you ladies?" A Marine sentry with a Boston accent leered at her through the thick glass.

"We have an appointment with the consular section." Alex pulled her passport from her purse and showed it to the guard, as did the others.

"What time?"

"Ten o'clock," Becca piped up.

"Go up to the building and enter the double doors. The receptionist will take care of you."

Alex smiled sweetly. "Thanks."

They headed down the fenced corridor and passed through the thick glass doors into a high-ceilinged lobby. A receptionist's desk sat to the right of the doors. As Becca announced their presence, Alex chose a row of chairs underneath some draping palm fronds. Ellie sat to her left.

"It'll be a few minutes," Becca said as she took a seat on Alex's right.

Ellie immediately began browsing through a glossy magazine about the natural features of Panama. Becca pulled out her iPhone, as did Alex.

The game of Spider entertained her for only a few minutes. She checked her watch. Ten thirty. This wasn't a good sign, especially when they'd been early. She sighed and murmured to Ellie, "What are you thinking?"

"I'm worried about Melanie." Ellie flipped to another page.

"How about you?" Alex asked Becca.

"Trying to figure out what happened." Becca frowned as she tapped on her phone. "What about you?"

"Just how many times they've recorded our faces on their cameras." Alex scowled at the surveillance cameras placed so they covered the entire lobby. "When I was with Unit 28, we avoided embassies whenever we could since we didn't like having our faces known."

Becca nodded.

"Roya Alexandra Thornton," a male voice suddenly called.

Alex winced at the use of her full name. Then she bit back another sigh and rose. "Here."

Becca and Ellie followed her to where a man about her age stood. While he wore a light-weight suit, he sported no tie and loafers on his feet with no socks. Casual day had reached Panama. The glasses he wore reminded Alex of her former boss, Tiny.

He extended his hand. "Jeremy Williams. I work in the consular section here."

Alex shook it, and he turned and headed down a hall with offices on the left, all of which had glass panels to let in the daylight spilling into the hallway from the floor-to-ceiling windows that made up the other wall. He turned into one of them and stepped to an adjacent office to collect a chair for Alex before shutting the door.

"I'm sorry about the wait. We've been exceptionally busy lately." He opened the folder on the desk in front of him. "From what I understand, you're Roya Thornton."

"Please. Call me Alex." She offered her best smile.

"Alex, then." Jeremy peered at Becca. "And you're Rebecca Alvarez."

"Becca." Becca shook his hand. "It's nice to meet you."

"And you as well. You must be Eleanor."

"Ellie." More handshakes went around.

"Let me get this straight." He opened the folder in front of him and scanned something that looked like an e-mail. "You contacted us yesterday morning because your friend never showed up in San Jose."

Alex nodded. "We were due to pick her up Tuesday night, but when we showed up at the airport, she wasn't there."

She outlined for what seemed like the hundredth time what exactly had happened. All the while, Jeremy maintained eye contact, breaking his gaze with her only to take copious notes. Finally, she wound down and fell silent. Jeremy examined his scribbles.

Alex crossed her arms and stared out the window. She noted how the tropical plants in the courtyard beyond the hallway's window lit up an otherwise dreary space with a rainbow of colors across the spectrum.

A motion distracted her. Someone walked down the hall. Someone who looked like…

Alex's hands gripped the arms of the chair. A bolt of adrenaline shot through her as the man slowed. For a brief, eternal second, their gazes locked. Then he broke eye contact and turned to his coworker, who walked with him.

Alex stared at Jeremy's monitor, but instead of seeing a square chunk of plastic, her mind's eye replayed the man's black curls, his dark eyes, that two-day growth of beard. Jabir was back in the States, happy in his career with DHS's elite Unit 28.

Wasn't he?

No, that wasn't Jabir. I'm seeing things. That's all.

"I understand your concern." Jeremy's voice reached her as though from a distance.

Suddenly, Alex realized she'd tuned him out. "I'm sorry?"

"I said I understand your concern." Jeremy linked his fingers on top of the file and fixed her in his gaze. "Honestly, I do, and quite frankly, if I were in your shoes, I'd be doing the same thing. But we have protocols we have to follow, which are similar to missing persons in the States. They need to be gone for seventy-two hours, which would be tomorrow."

"But sir," Becca protested. "You don't understand how unlike this is of Melanie. She's always been dependable. Seeing that this is her bachelorette trip, why would she miss it?'

"Like I said, I understand." Jeremy shrugged. "Sometimes people are strange when placed under stress. Your profile says you're a cop, so you should know that."

"I do."

"If she's getting married, maybe she's been under enough stress to run away or something."

"Bull hockey," Ellie muttered.

"I'm just trying to say that sometimes, we humans are unpredictable." Jeremy sighed. "Look. If she doesn't show by tomorrow afternoon, come back and see me, okay?"

He reached out and pulled a business card from a holder. "My number is here." He flipped it over and scribbled something. "My cell's on the back in case you can't get me here. If something pops, no need for an appointment. Just tell Samantha up front that I told you to call if something happened."

Alex knew when she was politely being told she needed to let protocols take their course. She rose, and the others followed suit. "Well, thank you. We appreciate your time."

With that, she was out the door with her friends. She lagged behind as her mind churned.

Had she seen Jabir?

Or simply someone who looked like him?

A thought made her pause.

If the man was Jabir, was he somehow involved with Melanie's disappearance?

She didn't know.

1145 hours Central Daylight Time, Panama City, Panama

Jabir pressed his back against the wall of the hallway that ran perpendicular to the main hall. He'd waited there since he'd walked past Jeremy's office and seen Alex.

He would have recognized those sea green eyes and the determined set of her shoulders anywhere, even with her dark hair now cut so it curled underneath her chin. The heat had rocketed to his cheeks, and it'd taken all of his training not to react.

Feminine voices jerked him to the present.

Alex's two friends passed him. Where was Alex?

Jabir sucked in a breath.

She wandered by, oblivious to his presence.

Sweat dampened his palms.

Once the door leading to the lobby shut, he slowly released the breath he hadn't realized he'd been holding. At least she hadn't seen the scar on his left cheek.

Why was she there?

He strolled to Jeremy's office and tapped on the doorframe.

Jeremy grinned. "Hey, man. Come on in."

Jabir quickly framed his approach. He slipped inside and shut the door. "Hey, who were those ladies?"

"They called the embassy because they're worried about their friend." Jeremy hit a key on his computer to save his document. Then he laced his hands behind his head as he leaned back in his chair. "Yeah, they're definitely cute."

"Well, hot, really." Jabir chuckled. "Especially that one in the dress."

"Oh?" Jeremy grinned. "She's a little fireball."

That's one way of describing her. Jabir fought his own smile. "What was her name?"

"You want to look her up?"

"I might." Jabir flashed an easy smile.

"Let me see." Jeremy picked up a sheet of paper. "Alex Thornton. She's staying at Hotel Panama."

Behind his back, Jabir's hands clawed the door. "What's the story?"

"She and her friends had gone to Costa Rica for a bachelorette party for their friend at Playa Flamingo."

"That's on the west coast, right?"

"Uh, huh. Wonderful place, by the way. Anyway, they flew into San Jose on Monday and were going to pick up their friend on Tuesday, but she never showed at the airport. Never checked in for the flight."

"Their friend was flying from?"

"Here. And the hotel records showed she wasn't due to check out until tomorrow, when in reality, Alex swears she was coming to meet them Tuesday night."

"Wow. The sauce thickens. What's the lady's name who's missing?"

Jeremy picked up the file folder and opened it. "A Melanie Forrest. Apparently, she was down here on business, which was why she was connecting from here to San Jose."

Jabir's eyes widened, but his friend was so engrossed in the folder's information that he didn't notice it.

Jabir took a deep breath. His heart pounded in his ears, and suddenly, the office with its closed door grew too hot. He needed to get out of there. "What's your take?"

"My take is that she might be in trouble. Like maybe run into some bad characters." Jeremy closed the folder with a sigh. "But you know how it goes. We can't take action for seventy-two hours unless the local authorities notify us. They didn't like hearing that."

"I'm sure." Jabir opened the door. "That's interesting."

"Yeah. Guess I'd better go and get my next appointment."

Alex's face flashed before him. Not from today but from four years before. Back then tears had run down her cheeks as she'd hidden from the press after their failed mission. He'd left the next day and betrayed her in the worst way possible. An idea popped into his head. "Hey, if this Alex person shows up again, will you let me know?"

"You want to ask her out." Jeremy grinned.

Hope began ballooning within him. He forced a smile to his face. "Is it that obvious?"

"Uh, huh. Will do, my friend." Jeremy followed Jabir into the hall. But while he headed toward the reception area, Jabir turned left and took the stairs leading to his own office on the second floor.

So Alex was here. In Panama City. And preparing to go on the warpath if he'd read her expression correctly.

Jabir crossed the mezzanine above the main lobby. Two turns brought him to his office. He shut the door and eased into his chair. He spread his hands out on the blotter. They trembled from the close call.

"How did we miss that?" His question, uttered barely above a whisper, seemed to resound like a gunshot in the small space.

He had to tell Ed that things had taken a sudden turn.

Jabir knew one thing.

Alex Thornton never gave up on anything. She'd get her question of his identity answered.

The sooner he informed Ed, the better.

16

"That is so strange," Alex muttered as she stared at her mostly untouched salad.

"What?" Becca thanked the waitress, who cleared away her plate.

"A guy walked by when we were at the embassy."

Ellie set her fork down. "Shouldn't we be focused on Melanie and not cute guys?"

"I am. The guy looked like Jabir."

"Huh?" Becca stared at her. "You're sure?"

"Yeah. Or at least his twin. I've got to find out."

"How?"

Alex sipped her water. "I don't know. But I do know one thing. Girls, I can't just sit here. We've got to do some investigating on our own."

"I hear you." Becca nodded. "And, Alex, you need to eat."

"I can't," she muttered. "What's your plan?"

Becca called for the checks. "Finish half of your salad, and then we'll go sleuthing."

"Yes, Mom." Alex picked up her fork. "Talk while I eat."

"We go up and check out her room."

"But didn't the manager refuse to tell us her room number? And how will we get in?" Ellie asked.

Becca drained the rest of her drink and set her glass down with a thump. "Who said we had to ask permission?"

"Becca…" Worry edged Ellie's voice.

Alex shook her head. "No, she's right. I'd rather ask for forgiveness later than wait another day." She took a bite, chewed, and swallowed. "Okay. We go up there. But how do we get in?"

Becca grinned. "Just watch."

They rose and wandered to the front desk. Becca pasted on her best smile. "Señorita, I was wondering if you could call Melanie Forrest's room. I'd like to visit her, but her cellphone seems to be dead."

"One moment."

Alex stood on her tiptoes and gazed at the keypad as the woman dialed.

Regret tinged the woman's smile. "I'm sorry, Señorita. She doesn't answer."

The disappointment on Becca's face made Alex want to smile. "Thanks. I'll try back later."

"Room 748," Alex whispered as they strolled to the elevator bank.

Within minutes, they stepped onto the seventh floor. Near the elevators, the maid was busy cleaning a room.

Becca's hand shot out and swiped the maid's passkey, which was sitting in a small dish near the rail of the cart. They crept down to Room 748.

Alex noted the Do Not Disturb sign. She opened the door using the maid's pass key before returning it to Ellie, who in turn passed it to Becca. Her friend scurried to the maid's cart and left it where she'd found it.

Alex waited until her two friends were at her side. Then they slipped inside and let the door close behind them. Alex peered ahead of her, and her breath immediately caught in her throat. "Do you see what I see?"

A lamp from the work table lay on its side.

"Yeah, I do." Becca's voice tightened.

Alex took a careful step further into the room. Her stomach turned as she noted the disheveled bedcovers, the placard and television remote on the floor, and the lamp from the nightstand closest to the window on the floor, its shade squashed and bulb broken.

A struggle had taken place.

Behind her, Ellie whimpered.

"I found something like men's footprints in the shower," Becca reported. "Three sets from what I could tell."

Alex shook her head. "Not good. Not good at all."

"I'm calling the cops." Becca pulled out her phone.

Alex nodded and reached into her purse. "Meanwhile, before they get here, I want to do a search."

She pulled out a set of nitrile gloves.

"Why do you carry those?" Ellie asked.

"When I was with Unit 28, I always carried a pair. I guess old habits die hard." She pulled them on and slipped off her sandals. "Ellie, stay here with Becca."

Alex tiptoed into the room. First, she opened the dresser drawers. Nothing in them. All of Melanie's clothing appeared to be in her suitcase. She perused the top of the dresser. Melanie's engagement ring sparkled alongside a diamond necklace, a gold watch, and a pair of gold earrings. She turned to the suitcase and carefully checked it. The tops, skirts, and swimsuits were all neatly folded, and nothing substantial seemed to be missing. They indicated a woman ready to go on vacation.

Alex came to the worktable. Melanie's briefcase sat beside it, and her purse now resided on the floor. She checked the briefcase. It mainly consisted of business information in a folder, including a contract and a small jump drive. She noted the set of emergency necessities in case Melanie missed her flight or lost her luggage. Alex found a jewelry bag and opened it. Everything seemed to be there. She returned it to its place and located another folder.

Travel information.

Her breath caught in her throat when she noticed that one of the papers was her hotel's itinerary. Sure enough, Melanie had been scheduled to check in on Monday and out on Tuesday morning.

"Becca."

"What'd you find?" Her friend's voice came from near the door.

"She was supposed to check out on Tuesday." Alex crossed the room and handed it to her friend. "Let's make sure we get this to the cops."

"What if they won't share with us?" Ellie asked.

"They will. Becca will sweet-talk them."

Alex returned to the briefcase. Both a laptop and tablet were in their appropriate slots. She continued to Melanie's purse, which contained a wallet with credit cards and a goodly amount of cash, mostly in American dollars but with a few Panamanian notes mixed in.

Alex slid Melanie's cellphone from her purse and tried to turn it on. The screen remained blank. "I found her cell, and it's dead. No wonder our calls went to voicemail."

Alex pawed through the rest of the purse. She touched the phone's charger, the cord wrapped around the adaptor. Lipstick. Candy. Some gum. Her digital camera. Alex turned it on and noted pictures that most likely related to her work. She left it for the cops.

Alex left that where it was and continued to the nightstands. Nothing substantial. Just a phone book and a Gideon Bible. The closet contained a safe, which hadn't been activated, and the business suit Melanie must have worn to her meeting. The bathroom yielded a few further clues, like the three sets of footprints in the tub and matching ones on the floor. Nothing else.

Alex paused and stared at the satchel holding the bottles.

Nothing else?

"Girls, this is interesting."

"What?" Becca asked. She joined her friend.

Alex searched through the makeup case and satchel. "Her heart medication's not here, and I didn't see a bottle in her emergency supplies either."

She glanced at Becca, who frowned and rubbed her chin. "Maybe they did research on her. Found out she had a heart condition or something."

"Normal crooks wouldn't know something like that. It's almost like she was specifically targeted." Alex returned to the entry and pulled on her sandals.

"What do you think?" Becca asked.

A sick feeling started in her stomach. "Something bad has happened. Someone targeted her, but I have no idea why. But let's see what the police say."

Alex shucked her gloves and stashed them in her purse just as Becca opened the door to reveal two Panamanian uniformed patrolmen. Alex let her friend handle the cops. It didn't take them long to draw the same conclusions they had, that a kidnapping had occurred. A plainclothes detective joined them a few minutes later, and they spent the next half hour discussing what might have happened.

Finally, an evidence team arrived. Esteban Romero, the detective, led them downstairs to a small conference room the hotel must have set aside for them. Alex crossed her arms and leaned against the table as she let Becca continue to establish a rapport with the detective.

"Who do you think would do this?" Becca asked in English for the benefit of Ellie.

Esteban rubbed his chin as he leaned against the table. "My first guess would be thugs. It happens here more than you think. Young women travel alone. They let their guard down and talk with whomever. Maybe she got drunk and let the guy walk her to her room. Maybe he popped a date rape drug into her drink."

"That doesn't sound like Melanie," Alex said.

"How so?" Esteban asked.

"She travels abroad and alone frequently for her work, and she's told me herself how she never lets anyone buy her a drink and always makes sure she can watch the bartender fix hers."

"Someone could have offered to walk her to her room."

"She'd never let them do that either," Becca added. "But we think she might have been specifically targeted."

"What makes you say that?"

"Melanie has a heart condition that requires daily medication. Her bottle's missing," Alex said.

Esteban gazed at them as if assessing how sincere they were. "You said she was here on business."

"Right."

"And the pictures on the camera, at least the few I saw, showed a property at the port. Someone could have very well followed her and targeted her that way."

Alex paced. "How would they know about her heart condition unless they did research on her?"

The detective shrugged. "That I cannot say. I need to let the evidence techs finish. Maybe then we'll have some more information as to whether this was a simple robbery or something more."

Becca stepped close to him. In Spanish, she asked, "Do you mind sharing evidence with us? I mean, as a detective, I understand territorial issues, but I'd also like to be kept in the loop." She placed her hand on his arm and smiled a wide smile.

Flirt, Alex thought. She hid her grin.

He nodded. "All right. Come to the station in the morning, and I'll see what I can do."

"I can do that." Becca nodded and winked at her friends. "Thank you again, Detective Romero. We appreciate your concern."

That's more than what the embassy gave us, Alex thought. An idea came to her.

They trooped back to their room on the tenth floor.

But before she could share it, Ellie burst out, "I'm worried about her engagement ring. I mean, what if she doesn't get it back?"

"If it's not germane to the investigation, she will." Becca paused at the sliding glass door and peered over the city.

"Listen. I think we need to take a divide and conquer approach." Alex slipped from her sandals, wiggled her toes, and paced.

"What's that?" Becca picked up a water bottle and popped it open.

"Why don't you two stick around here and do your own investigation? Meanwhile, I'm going to return to the embassy and talk with them again. Maybe now they'll acknowledge something is going on."

"We can do that. Ellie, are you ready for an adventure?" Becca asked.

"Ready to find our friend."

"Agreed." Alex dug her keys from her purse and slid back into her sandals. "Wish me luck. I'll keep you posted."

She headed to the lobby and outside to the Explorer.

This time, she wouldn't leave until she saw some action.

17

"Are you sure our friend was right on his assumption of where our guest would be staying?" Hashim quietly asked in English as he sat in the lobby of the Hotel Panama. "I've seen no indication of any activity here."

"That is what he told me," Tarek replied. The line crackled slightly.

Hashim almost growled. Thanks to the concrete structure of Hotel Panama, his cellphone connection faded in and out if he moved his head so much as a centimeter or two.

"You could ask at the desk."

"I will if I don't see anything."

"Nothing this morning?" Tarek's voice faded so much that Hashim almost missed the question.

Hashim's jaw tightened. If his brother had so many questions, why hadn't he come instead? He adjusted his posture as he replied, "No. No one at the Internet café saw anything. I've been here at the hotel since eleven this morning and haven't seen anything either. No sign of her or any activity."

"Keep watching. Call me when you see something."

Hashim hung up and set his phone on the bar. He took a sip of water. Voices distracted him. Feminine voices.

Three women rose from a table in the adjacent dining room and walked his way.

For a moment, Hashim let himself forget about his useless mission as he noticed their beauty. These pretty ladies more than made up for any frustration he'd experienced since landing that morning.

The woman on the far left was tall. Very tall with light brown hair and a willowy figure clothed in a longer skirt that emphasized the sway of her hips with each step she took. Right now, worry clouded eyes that he noticed were green.

The second was shorter and dark, her eyes alert, every part of her breathing law enforcement to him. Sexy law enforcement at that in the skinny jeans and tank top she wore. He traced the muscle definition in her arms with his gaze. Her brown ponytail bobbed as she talked to the tall one.

And the other? Hashim's pulse quickened as he drank in her strong features. The aquiline nose, thick eyebrows, and skin coloring seemed so familiar to him. As did her eyes. Those were a sea green. Her hair was thick, a very dark brown, and shiny. She seemed almost familiar to him. Why? He found himself attracted to her in an organic way, maybe because her features indicated her Middle Eastern heritage.

Hashim lowered his gaze and observed them out of the corner of his eye as they passed him and disappeared into the lobby. He followed them from a distance and watched as they stepped onto an elevator. Once he returned from the restroom, he got another refill of water and strolled into the lobby with its ceiling soaring three stories.

He settled onto a rattan Panama Jack chair, partially hidden from the check-in area by potted palms, and shoved the fedora hiding his bald head down lower so no one could easily recognize him. He opened the laptop he carried. His attention remained focused on the lobby.

A noise sounded in the distance. Hashim cocked his head.

Sirens?

The noise solidified into a wail that ended with the arrival of a marked patrol car, rack lights flashing blues and reds, that stopped under the portico.

A portly, mustachioed man appeared from a hallway and rushed to the door as two uniformed officers strode inside. He gestured and pointed. The two policemen ignored him. He hurried behind them toward the elevators.

Hashim stroked the two-day growth of beard as he stared at the cop car.

Something had happened.

Something big.

He was willing to bet someone had discovered Melanie's kidnapping.

More noise drew his attention to the outside. This time, a man in plainclothes with broad shoulders and narrow waist entered the lobby along with a couple of other uniformed patrol members. The man took in the lobby with one sweep. He paused as if sensing a hunter lurking nearby.

The hair on the back of Hashim's neck rose or would have had he any hair on his head.

A detective. The wariness in the man's eyes told Hashim that.

He studied the laptop.

Only when the elevator dinged did he risk raising his gaze. Now, though he pretended to be a businessman hard at work, he focused on the situation at hand. A few minutes passed. The three women returned with the detective, two of the cops, and the manager and disappeared down a hallway.

Now, Hashim knew one thing. These pretty women were involved with why the police were there. They reappeared, this time alone without uniforms accompanying them, and returned to the elevator.

Hashim's thoughts raced. The women knew Melanie Forrest. How? Why were they there? Who were they? What had they found?

A few minutes later, the woman in the dress reappeared by herself.

She strode toward him, and he noticed how she'd narrowed her eyes and set her chin. She was determined to do something, but what remained a mystery to him. He perused the laptop as she swished past, her heels clicking on the tile near him.

Her scent tickled his nose. A clean scent that teased his memory. Again, he had that feeling he'd seen her somewhere before. *But where?* he wondered. *Where have I seen her before? Nowhere. That's where.*

Hashim doubted his thoughts.

He followed her with his gaze, tracing the outline of her figure with his eyes. Sweat built up underneath his collar.

Where were the other women?

Hashim waited some more. They stepped from the elevator. This time, they headed straight to the check-in desk. He tracked their progress to the indoor bar and restaurant where he'd been earlier and finally to the outdoor bar where they seemed to spend the most time. They returned to the hallway. When he saw them again, the taller one had a sheaf of papers in her hand.

They were doing some investigating.

He waited until they were outside and settled at the bar. Hashim dropped his laptop into its case. It was time for him to do some detective work of his own.

1515 hours Central Daylight Time, Panama City, Panama

"I need to speak with Jeremy Williams," Alex stated to the receptionist. The woman's name placard read Samantha Jenkins.

"Mr. Williams has appointments all afternoon," Samantha replied.

"He told me to contact him anytime if I saw fit. So I am. Please tell him an Alex Thornton is here to see him. It's urgent. Tell him it's regarding a Melanie Forrest."

"I said he has appointments all afternoon. I can set you up for a nine o'clock tomorrow morning."

Alex took a deep breath. She pulled Jeremy's card from her purse and laid it on the smooth glass of the counter. "Look. I spoke with him this morning. He said if I found out something more about my missing friend that I should come back and not to worry with an appointment. So that's what I'm doing."

The gatekeeper stared at her for a moment, her gaze narrowed and assessing as if doubting Alex's sincerity. Without breaking her gaze, she picked up the phone and dialed a number. "Yes, Jeremy, this is Samantha up front. I have an Alex Thornton here to see you. She said it was urgent…Okay. Thank you." She replaced the phone with a huff. "He'll be here shortly. Have a seat, please."

Alex wandered to a seat in a square of sunlight let in by the skylights overhead but shaded with a large plant she might have called a banana tree. The tinkling of a nearby fountain of water cascading from a smaller pool, down some rocks, and into a larger pool threatened to relax her, but the hard line of the chair's edge where she perched kept her alert. She picked up a magazine and tried to thumb through it. That didn't work. She set it down and fiddled with her phone.

Finally, she tossed it into her purse and gazed around the lobby. She liked the pool. It was a nice touch. Plants were everywhere as if the jungle had moved from the outdoors into this open space. She picked up another magazine, this one on Panamanian cultural events.

The sound of a familiar voice made her glance up.

Alex froze.

The guy from this morning stood at Samantha's desk, joking about something as he reached into the candy bowl. She raised the magazine to cover her face but kept him under surveillance. When he turned and headed toward the stairs leading to the second floor, he exposed the left side of his face.

Adrenaline flooded her body with an electric jolt.

Jabir.

It was him.

How could she forget that scar? The last time she'd seen him, it'd been an angry red line that stretched from the corner of his mouth, across his cheek, to slightly beyond the corner of his eye. Four years had faded it to a pale white she noticed only because she knew where to look.

Scum.

Her hands shook thanks to adrenaline replaced by anger.

What was he, a native Arabic speaker, doing at the Panamanian embassy?

"Alex?" Jeremy's voice brought her back to the present.

Jabir was gone, and the state department employee stood in front of her.

"Oh, sorry." Alex tossed the magazine down and rose. "We've got a problem."

"Sounds like it. C'mon." Jeremy led the way to his office, and Alex followed.

Now, she could impress upon him the urgency of her situation.

Later, she'd find out just why Jabir al-Omri was in Panama.

1600 hours Central Daylight Time, Panama City, Panama

Hashim needed to move, both to do some checking of his own and to avoid becoming too obvious. He rose and strolled outside. Though the sun rushed toward the horizon, the temperatures remained hot, the humidity instantly making sweat pop up all over his body.

He stopped at the Land Rover he'd rented and slid behind the wheel. As he waited for the air conditioning to go to work, he reached into the duffel he'd left behind the seat. His fingers brushed the cold, hard metal of his Beretta. He wouldn't need that now. Deception would be his weapon this afternoon.

Hashim thumbed through the packet and pulled out both a wallet and a gold badge. He clipped the forged shield to his belt and flipped open the wallet. It showed an image of his face, snapped and prepared before he left Beirut, this one with him clean shaven with a head full of hair. The flavor of the day? Interpol agent. With the addition of a different blazer and a wig of messy black hair a bit shaggy around the ears, he was ready to go.

Hashim strode into the hotel, head up, broad shoulders squared.

He owned the place now.

At least he strutted like he did. He stopped at the check-in desk and peered at the woman behind a counter of bamboo. "I'm here to see the manager."

"Um…" The attendant seemed overwhelmed by the events of that day.

Hashim stuck his ID under her nose. "I'm with Interpol, Señorita. I understand a crime involving an American occurred here."

"One…one moment." She picked up a phone. After she hung up, a strained smile appeared on her face. "Sir, the manager is on his way."

Hashim nodded.

True to her word, the portly man he'd seen earlier approached him. He mopped his forehead with a handkerchief and then extended his right hand. "Nando Ochoa. I'm the general manager here at Hotel Panama. Please, come with me. Cristina, thank you."

Nando's hand was so wet and limp that Hashim wanted to jerk his own away.

Nando scurried toward the hall. They wound up in his office a moment later. "I'm so sorry. Today has been horrendous. Never in the world did I expect…this."

Hashim tore his gaze away from staring at all of the hotel chain's properties featured in full-color posters on the wall. "This as in?"

"I'm sorry. Your name again?"

"Hashim Fadel. Interpol." Hashim flashed his fake ID with authority.

The manager barely glanced at it. Instead, he pulled out his handkerchief and patted his forehead again. "It's been a terrible, terrible day."

"And why is that?" Hashim asked in perfect Spanish.

"A kidnapping of one of our guests occurred. An American. That is why you're here, right?" Nando paused as if considering the man in his presence for the first time.

"It is. I'm so sorry to make you rehash this like you did with the police, but it would give me more of an understanding of what happened."

"Like I did to Señorita Forrest's friends."

"Friends?" Hashim played dumb.

"Yes." Nando shook his head. He fiddled with a pen. "They came all the way here from Costa Rica because they were worried about their friend. And I ignored them and thought they were thieves wanting access to someone's room to rob." He fell silent and stared at the blotter as he inhaled a deep, shuddering breath. "How much do you know?"

Hashim's mind flashed to his observations from the lobby and what Tarek had told him. "Someone kidnapped her. Someone who was obviously clever enough for it to take three days and three concerned friends to discover it. The Panamanian National Police contacted our office because of the international issues associated with this. I will be getting more information from the police, but I wanted to get your side of the story."

Nando shrugged. "There's not much to tell. Señorita Forrest checked in late Monday afternoon. Room 748, if I remember correctly. Then nothing until her friends showed. There was a Do Not Disturb sign on her door, and our records indicated she was due to check out tomorrow. However, her friends insisted it was Tuesday. The detective, a Detective Romero, showed me an itinerary proving that she was due to stay with us only one night."

That was interesting. Hashim nodded as he digested that information. "Continue if you would."

"I went up there when the police arrived. The crime scene is in their hands now, sir."

"These three friends. I would like to talk with them, perhaps to see if they could share what led them to their conclusions. Do you have information about them?"

"I do. I have their names and passport information since they had to show them when they checked in."

"And their room numbers?"

"I'm sorry, sir, but the best I can offer is to connect you to their room." Nando sighed. "I feel so badly for doubting them. So much so that I had them moved to the penthouse, which is on us for the duration of their stay."

Hashim mentally filed that for later. "I understand. Please. If you could put their passport information on this." He handed him a jump drive. "And you said their names were?" He pulled out a notepad as if he were sincerely concerned for Melanie.

"Hmmm. Señora Rebecca Miller Alvarez of San Antonio, Texas. Señora Eleanor Denton Watkins of Durango, Colorado. And Señorita Roya Alexandra Thornton of Weatherly, North Carolina."

The pen froze above Hashim's notepad. He didn't notice the flash drive the manager laid on the desk.

"Señor?"

"My apologies. I had a thought," Hashim lied. He noticed the drive and palmed it. "Thank you, Señor."

"Would you like me to contact them?"

"I will do that later. First, I want to talk with the police," he fibbed again. "Señor, thank you for your time." He rose. "I appreciate it very much."

Hashim retreated to the Land Rover. He yanked the wig from his head and dropped it into the bag. As the air conditioning once more cooled the interior, he wiped his bald pate with a rag. He leaned his head against the leather seat and closed his eyes.

Roya Alexandra Thornton.

How many times had his father uttered the name of his half-sister while he was growing up?

Many times. Father had wanted his sons to remember it.

He swore under his breath. Hashim wanted to return to the safe house for a rest. He couldn't. Not until he gathered more information.

He saw only one way to do it.

Hashim shrugged into the blazer he'd worn almost the entire day. He stowed the shield and ID badge in the bag and picked up his laptop case. As he climbed from the SUV, his gaze shot to the sky. Gray had overtaken the blue. A drop of rain hit him on the cheek.

If he hurried, he'd make it into the hotel before he got soaked to the skin. Then maybe he could get close enough to the two women at the outdoor bar to discover what they'd found.

1630 hours Central Daylight Time, Panama City, Panama

Jabir gazed at the e-mail glowing on his screen. He blinked, suddenly realizing he'd been staring at the same thing for the past several minutes. He sighed, reread the e-mail to his coworker, and hit the Send button.

Someone knocked on his open door, and he glanced up to find Jeremy standing there. He smiled and leaned back in his chair. "Hey, man. What's up?"

Jeremy propped himself against the doorframe, tie loose around his neck, sleeves rolled up to just below his elbows. "Did you see your crush downstairs?"

"I did when I caved into my sweet tooth. I kind of wimped out about talking to her," he lied.

Jeremy shifted and stuck his hands in his pockets. "Probably for the better."

"Why?"

"She and her friends went back to the hotel and somehow checked out their friend's room. Sounds like something bad went down. They called the cops."

"Really?" Jabir's toes curled inside of his shoes. On his lap, his fingers tightened into fists. "What happened?"

"Her friends think she was kidnapped." Rather than leave like Jabir hoped, Jeremy sank into his chair. He sighed and pushed weary fingers under his glasses. They rose off his nose as he rubbed his eyes. "Man, I need a drink."

"That bad, huh?"

"Yeah. The cops think the motive was robbery, but Alex swears Melanie was targeted."

Oh, boy. Jabir tried to keep the shiver from coming. "What's your take?"

"I'm not sure what to think. She was rather insistent."

Jabir bit his lip to keep from agreeing.

"Anyway." Jeremy rose. "I'm headed home. I've handed everything to our FBI attaché. You know Mitch, right?"

Jabir nodded.

"It's out of my hands now. He'll be conversing with Detective Romero."

"Who's he?" Jabir asked through the pounding in his heart.

"The National Police detective. Their best if I believe Mitch. Between them, I'm sure they'll get to the bottom of things. Well, have a good evening." Jeremy waved and headed down the hall, toward his office, and to the safety of home.

And Jabir?

Suddenly, he felt like a scared rabbit hiding from a fox. He was trapped.

He groaned aloud and put his head in his arms. "Great. Just great."

Jabir sat like that for a few minutes. Finally, he lifted his head and stared at the cellphone he'd dropped on his desk.

He needed to talk to Ed and badly too. The problem was, he couldn't call him up and talk. After all, Ed and the rest of the crew weren't even supposed to be in the country. Just Jabir on temporary assignment for DHS to help with security checks on visa applications. That meant he needed to see him in person, and he had night shift as guard beginning at six.

Jabir rose and shut the door. He picked up his phone. No one would know.

Would they?

He set it down on his desk.

Probably best to handle this in person.

Jabir grabbed his motorcycle helmet, shut off his office lights, and headed downstairs. He pushed through the door into an afternoon suddenly darkened by clouds. He glanced up. Rain was coming. He needed to move quickly unless he wanted to get drenched

"Hey, Jabir!"

Jabir grinned when he noticed George, one of the Marines he'd befriended during his short stay at the embassy. They bumped fists.

"Hey. What's up?" He rested his helmet on the saddle of the motorcycle.

"Nothing much. You heading out?"

"Uh, huh. Got to get some rest, you know? How about you?" Jabir glanced through the gate.

Across the parking lot, through the fence surrounding it, and across the adjacent street, he noticed a familiar figure.

The foxy fox.

Alex still wore the dress that cut such a becoming figure and betrayed her at the same time.

Double the feeling trapped part.

"Oh, me and the boys are going out for some R&R tonight."

"Huh?"

"You asked what we were doing, man. I'm telling you."

"Sorry." An idea popped into Jabir's head. "You and Hoss and Markie?"

"Oh, yeah, man." George tossed his keys from hand to hand.

"Maybe you can help me out. You see that lady at the café across the street?"

A smile added a streak of white across George's dark face. "Oh, yeah. Heard about her. That she raised a ruckus today. That she's a looker."

"She, uh…" Jabir's mind raced. "Well, she's an ex-girlfriend."

"Get out of here. No way!"

"Yep."

"She must be pretty mad at you if she came all the way down here to find you. Uh, huh."

"Could you help me out?"

"Name it."

"You and Hoss and Markie distract her while I leave? I really don't want her following me to my apartment," he fibbed.

"That we can do. Just watch the masters in action." George chuckled. "Maybe you can learn something. Like how to keep a girlfriend happy for a change."

"Maybe so." Jabir flashed another grin to hide his anxiety.

George called to Hoss and Markie. They paused a moment as George explained Jabir's request. Hoss took one look at Alex, turned, and gave Jabir the thumbs up. They strutted through the gate, their Marine confidence oozing over Jabir and boosting his waning calmness.

Jabir pulled out his phone and changed to camera mode. He located Alex and focused on her. She sat at a bistro table, a cup of coffee and a book beside her, the pocket camera on the table with its lens pointed toward him. Suddenly, the three guys were there. She started, then sat back as George turned a chair around and straddled it. Reluctantly, she shook their hands.

Jabir dropped his phone into his pocket and pulled on his helmet. He started the motorcycle and eased through the narrow parking lot and to the embassy's gate. He stopped at the stop sign as it slid open.

Now, Alex was closer. Though she appeared in conversation with his friends, her eyes kept darting toward the motorcycle and focused like sea green lasers on him. Feeling brave all of the sudden, he revved the motor.

Alex's head jerked toward him.

He flipped her a salute as he made the turn.

He was on his way, knowing that at least this time, he'd escaped.

His smugness faded.

No matter what, Alex would hunt him down. When she did, she wouldn't stop until she wrung the truth from him.

18

"I can't believe this," Alex muttered as she pulled into the hotel parking lot and shut off the engine. "Out of all things…stupid jerk." She rapped her hand on the steering wheel. "Jabir, you are in such big trouble when I get my hands on you."

Alex shoved the driver's door open, hopped out, and slammed it. Who cared if she broke a window or something? She certainly didn't. Not right then.

She began marching through the thickening drizzle toward the hotel.

Her phone chimed. "Hello?"

"Hey, where are you?" Becca's voice floated across the line along with something that sounded like samba music.

"I just got here. Where are *you?*"

"At the outdoor bar. Sounds like things didn't go too well."

"Don't ask."

"You want me to order you something?"

"How about a double?"

Becca laughed. "Of what?"

"I don't know. You pick. I'll be in there soon." Alex hung up without another word and shoved her phone into her small purse. Muttering, she paused to let the sliding doors swish open with a hiss of cool, dry air behind them. She shivered in the coldness of the lobby and escaped to the outdoor bar.

For a moment, Alex hesitated. Patrons already crowded around the long hunk of wood like animals who'd spent another hot day on the African savannah. A samba tune pumped from hidden speakers. The music, meant to liven her up, grated on her nerves. She wanted to find the stereo and rip the wires from it. For a brief, wild moment, she imagined doing just that and being arrested by this Detective Romero. Maybe then she could get her answers.

Finally, she found her friends and hurried toward where they sat at the corner of the bar. At a nearby conversation group, she noticed a man sitting on a rattan couch with a laptop on his lap.

Alex slowed.

Something about his broad shoulders barely contained within his suit jacket and strong jaw with a two-day growth of beard appealed to her, as did his strong features that were so much like her own.

And his eyes.

They were a mesmerizing aquamarine that reminded her of the Caribbean and threatened to bind her to him.

"There you are." Ellie's voice broke the spell he'd cast upon her.

"Hey." Alex pulled out a bar chair and hopped up. "Sorry I took forever and a day."

"What happened?"

"Jabir."

"Huh?"

"Jabir's here."

Becca rested her elbows on the bar. "Come again?"

Alex rolled her eyes. "Jabir's here. I saw him."

"How do you know?"

"Because I saw the left side of his face. He's got a scar running from here to here." She pointed to the corner of her mouth and then to the corner of her eye. "He had it when I awakened in the hospital four years ago. Except back then, it was a nasty red."

Ellie's eyes widened. "How did he get that?"

"From hitting a stop sign while riding his bike." Alex scowled. "The scumbag sent three Marines to distract me while he made his escape." She heaved a deep sigh. "So, girls, like it or not, we've got dinner plans for tonight. They're meeting us here at seven."

For a moment, Becca stared at her. A smile twitched at the corners of her mouth. "Alrighty, then. I guess we need to talk. But first, your drink." She shoved a tall glass of a dark liquid toward her. "Captain and Coke. Your favorite. And a double per your request."

"How much do I owe you?"

"Nothing. Sounds like you had a rough time of it. How did it go at the embassy?"

"Progress there. Jeremy took me seriously, and now we've got a meeting with a Mitch Gordon tomorrow at two. It sounds like he's going to talk with Detective Romero before then."

"Good. That's something." Becca finished her piña colada. "We had our own bit of fun here."

"Oh?" Alex sighed as she sipped her drink, which was the perfect combination of sweet and spicy.

"Yeah." Becca set the empty glass aside. "We walked through what we thought was her day. Ellie, you want to start?"

Ellie drummed her fingers on the teak as she bit her lip. "We know she checked in. The clerk remembered her and how tired she looked."

"Right." Becca nodded as she looked at a notepad of hotel stationery. "She must have taken a long nap. We know that because no one at the restaurant remembers her."

"And the surveillance videos don't show her until about a half past ten or so when she showed up here."

"She came here?" Alex frowned.

"Yeah. We talked to the bartender, who remembered when she came in." She nodded in the direction of the man, who was preparing a drink for a patron at the other end of the bar. "He said a man joined her."

"What? A man?" Alex straightened and shoved her drink aside.

"Apparently, they talked for a while."

"What did he look like?" Alex asked.

"Melanie's height. Olive tones like maybe he was from here or somewhere else warm." Becca took a deep breath. "And guess what?"

"I'm afraid to ask."

"He had a scar on the left side of his face that ran from the corner of his mouth to near the corner of his eye."

Alex froze. "Come again?"

Becca repeated herself and added, "Based on what you said, I think he was Jabir."

The heat rushed to Alex's neck, then her face. Jabir had been here? With Melanie? She felt like a tea kettle about to blow its lid.

"The *rat!* The stinking rat!" Her words exploded across the bar, causing several people to peer her way, including the man with the dazzling Caribbean eyes.

"Hey, pipe down." Ellie weakly waved to their sudden audience.

"Sorry." Alex sucked down a huge swallow of her drink. She shook her head. "I can't believe it."

"Well, believe it." Becca picked up Ellie's tablet and started messing around with it.

"How long did he stay?"

"After she left? The bartender said until about one o'clock. He was watching baseball on television as well as fiddling with his phone."

"Did he drink anything?"

"Two virgin daiquiris."

Alex stared at her drink. "That's weird."

"What?" Ellie asked.

"That he'd be drinking virgin daiquiris. Jabir's never shied away from alcohol. Not that he's a partier, but he doesn't mind the occasional drink or two." Her gaze flicked upward, and she noticed how Caribbean Eyes stared at her with open interest. The flush returned.

"The manager handed over some video surveillance footage," Becca said. She laid the tablet on the bar.

"How'd you manage that?" Alex asked.

"Guilt trips work wonders on occasion."

"Especially when they comp us in the penthouse." Ellie grinned and demurely sipped her drink.

"Wow. You guys rock. Okay. Let's look at the video."

The trio huddled over it as they traced Jabir's movements from the bar, into the lobby, and then to the fifth floor.

"Maybe that's where he must have been staying." Becca bent over it. "We lose him here since they don't have cameras in the hall."

Something didn't seem right to Alex. "Go back to the bar."

A couple of flicks of Becca's fingers sent them to the appropriate file.

Alex's heart caught as she noticed the way her friend seemed to chat with him like they'd known each other for a while. "She looks like she's tipsy."

"How do you know that?" Ellie asked.

"He's a stranger to her, and she's acting a little too familiar with him," Becca replied. "Look how he's keeping his face away from the camera. He doesn't want to show that scar. He's good, Alex."

"Or so he thinks." *You've erred, you jerk.* The tiniest smile of satisfaction teased her lips.

"Something's not adding up here." Becca glanced at the time again when the man stepped off the elevator on the fifth floor. "Ellie, let's look at the room key records again."

Ellie thumbed through a printout lying on the dark wood beside the tablet. "Okay. We have an entry into her room at ten fifty-nine. Then another after two. And another at two thirty-three."

"Two thirty-three in the morning?" Alex blinked.

"And get this. There were two guest entries. Those happened at ten fifty-nine and then at two thirty-three. Shortly after two was a maid's pass-key."

"Oh, wow. Surely Melanie didn't go for ice or something." Alex put her chin in her hand.

Becca set the tablet down. "Here's what I think happened. Melanie checked in early afternoon. Alex, you said she got up at four that morning, so most likely, she was exhausted by that point and decided to take a nap. Maybe she did. Maybe she overslept because it sounded like from the bartender that she missed supper and came here to get at least something."

"I can see that." Alex nodded.

"Then Jabir showed up. He chatted her up. She left around eleven, then at one, which is an hour before the entry happened to her room with the passkey, he left the bar."

Ellie twisted a lock of light brown hair around her finger. "Do you think that was him? The passkey entry?"

"I'm betting on it." Becca paused and bit her lip before continuing, "Then there's the key entry from her at two-thirty-three. Something's not making sense here."

Coldness settled over Alex, but it wasn't from her drink. It was from her perception. "Did the manager give us anything else?"

"Yeah. Event records." Becca nodded. "Things that happened that were out of the ordinary. Ellie?"

Ellie located the stapled set of papers and thumbed through it. "Wow."

"What?"

"There was a fire alarm just before two o'clock."

"Where?" Alex peered over Ellie's shoulder at the printout.

"The pull was on the seventh floor."

"Her floor." Alex's face flushed as it all snapped into place. "Okay. The alarm got pulled right before two. Everyone left. Then the kidnappers used a maid's passkey to get into her room, which was simple since the deadbolt and chain were off. She came in half an hour later. They grabbed her, but she fought. She was obviously overpowered, and at some point, they left. Do we have anymore footage after that? Like at the entrances?"

"We do." Becca shifted files. "I think it's a safe assumption that they went out a side or back entrance. Let's check."

Time in the surveillance files ticked forward as if everyone had imbibed too much caffeine.

"There!" Alex clamped her hand on Becca's arm. "Check out that side entrance."

Becca slowed the footage and went back a few minutes.

Shaking started deep within Alex. She felt like a Peeping Tom as she watched four figures emerge from a dimly lit side entrance. The forms jerked forward in pale black and white. All of them wore baseball caps, which hid their faces. How clever. Still, the one on the woman didn't hide the lightness of her hair.

She craned her neck. "I'm sure that's Melanie. Look how her arm's around one of the guys. She's leaning into him like she's drugged. Then they're gone." She sat back. "Anything else?"

Becca sat there for a moment. She took a deep breath. "Not much. Somehow, the hotel's reservation system was altered to show her not checking out until Friday, and the kidnappers left a Do Not Disturb sign on the door so the maid wouldn't touch her room. "

"Geniuses," Alex muttered.

"I agree with you. This was well planned, and for some reason, they specifically targeted her."

"But why?" Ellie's question penetrated the thoughts buzzing through Alex's head.

"Good question."

Suddenly, Alex felt the hair on the back of her neck stand up. A shiver made her shudder. Her gaze flew upward just in time to see Caribbean Eyes making for the lobby as if his tail were on fire.

Like maybe he'd been eavesdropping on their conversation.

"I think I'm feeling sick." Ellie's voice drew her back to her friends.

"I hear you." Becca picked up her phone and dialed. "I think we need to talk with Detective Romero. Like now."

19

Hashim buttoned his black cargo pants and pulled on a black T-shirt. He stared at himself in the mirror as he rubbed his chin. It itched. Of course it would since his beard was growing back. If only his hair would do the same thing. Not one strand had returned. At least his beard had stayed put.

In bare feet and with his laptop case slung over his shoulder, Hashim thumped down the hallway to the living area. The three men who weren't on guard duty lounged on the couch and chairs, limbs carelessly flung like lions lounging after feasting on a kill. One lifted a can of soda to his lips. When they saw him, they tensed.

Hashim ignored them and pushed through the swinging door into the kitchen. Once he'd put some water on the stove to heat for tea, he settled at the table and powered up his laptop.

His brow knitted as he started thinking about the woman he'd seen at the hotel. Why did she seem so familiar to him? He envisioned her and those sea green eyes, that dark, glossy hair. Her bold features floated onto the movie screen of his mind. Then she disappeared as he considered the information he'd gleaned.

During his brief stay at the bar, he'd risked everything by remaining close to the woman and her friends as they chatted. It had paid off. They suspected exactly what he did, that someone had targeted Melanie, planned her kidnapping, and carried it out with precision.

Should he return to the hotel and follow the three women? Doing so would most likely yield no further clues. Not to mention, he'd heard enough to know they had plans with three US Marines, not a good combination with his intentions.

It didn't matter, not when he knew something they didn't.

He had a pretty good idea of the perpetrator.

Hashim's attention returned to the woman in the dress. Her clean scent remained in his nostrils and teased his memory with featherlike caresses. He'd seen her somewhere before. But where? He tried to figure that one out until the kettle whistled.

With mug in hand, he returned to the table and slid the jump drive into a USB port. Hashim accessed the three passport files the manager had supplied to him. He opened the first one. The willowy woman was named Eleanor Watkins. The sexy cop? Rebecca Alvarez, apparently codenamed Becca. Based on the conversation he'd overheard, she was a homicide detective. He made a mental note of that for future reference.

He opened the last file of the woman in the dress.

Shock choked off Hashim's breath. He blinked as he stared at her.

He studied the picture. It was a headshot. In this particular one, she wore her hair in the same style she currently had. A slightly beguiling smile curved her lips upward.

Just like the one she'd flashed at him in a nightclub in Baghdad almost ten years before, the night hell began.

"This can't be," he muttered.

His half-sister was the very woman who had lured him into a trap.

Hashim blinked. He gazed into those sea green eyes, which pulsed in the bright glow of his screen. They were vivid, just like his. Their shape?

Almost identical. And their noses? Close as well. The same with just about every other facial feature. Once more, his eyes slid to the name.

Roya Alexandra Thornton. Known as Alex to her friends. The name Father had ground into his and Tarek's skulls during their youth. His half-sister.

Now a name to be associated with the vixen who'd deceived him and handed him over to the CIA.

Someone in the living area cranked the volume on the television. They must have been watching music videos because a throbbing dance tune reached him.

The very same song that had played that fateful night in Baghdad.

The music assaulted Hashim's ears to the point where he clamped his hands over them. In the depths of his soul, anger began humming. He closed his eyes, his mind carrying him back to that night. The images wormed their way from his subconscious to the forefront.

He laughed with some buddies as they shared drinks and noted all of the pretty ladies on the dance floor and at the bar. Two caught his attention, one especially. He drank in the short skirt, low-cut top, and heels. She wore her dark, glossy hair so that it curled over her shoulders, almost inviting him to come and play.

She smiled, her lips daring him to make a move. Hashim strutted to the bar, took her hand, and led her onto the floor for several fast dances. He bought her a drink afterward. They laughed and chatted. Her friend and everyone else faded away. For him, it was just the two of them.

They flirted.

Drank.

Flirted some more.

He took her onto the floor for a slow dance. She laid her head against his shoulder, and the clean scent of her shampoo wafted above the layers of perfume she wore. Her palms slowly rubbed his back, conjuring images in his mind of what might happen later. He threaded those silky strands of hair through his fingers and imagined how it would be to kiss her.

When the dance ended, she stood on tiptoe. Her lips tickled his ear as she murmured into his ear in Arabic, "I know where we can go to be alone."

He smiled at her words and let her take him by the hand. The woman led him down a hall. She opened a door. Hot night air filled his lungs, and the noise of the club faded and vanished as the door thumped softly shut behind him.

Someone grabbed him, wrestling him to the ground before he could even react.

"Sweet dreams," the woman said in English as a needle stung his neck.

Everything faded to black.

Hashim's eyes snapped open. In the other room, the dance tune had shifted to a woman singing a ballad about betrayal in love.

Hashim shook, the rage bubbling to the surface of his wounded soul. He took a deep, shuddering breath, but he couldn't move from his chair. His heart raced, and his sides heaved. He rested his forehead on clenched fists as more memories assaulted him.

Hashim awakened in hot darkness with his wrists secured in ropes so that he practically dangled.

His tormentor, those gray eyes almost glowing from behind his ski mask, his accented English difficult to understand, told him what he faced if he didn't give them what they wanted.

Hashim endured it all.

Slaps. Waterboarding. Constant light and music chasing away any notion of sleep.

His tormenter's laughter echoed in his ears. The man grabbed his hair and pulled. Clumps came out. He held it before Hashim and told him how he was losing his manhood. The man opened his fist, and those strands floated to the floor like chaff. Then the man shaved off his beard and even his eyebrows.

Hashim passed out.

His chin jerked up, and his eyes flew open. He was in the safe house, surrounded by walls of a cheery yellow and the noise of the jungle, not trapped in his own version of a stinking, private hell. Now, shaking permeated every bit of his being as he stared at the image of Alex Thornton on the laptop. She was the reason for his utter humiliation. Had it not been for her—

A red haze of fury filled his vision.

A growl escaped him.

He hurled the mug of tea at the wall.

It shattered, the pieces of ceramic tinkling to the tile.

Tan liquid dribbled down the painted yellow walls.

He threw the chair at the same place.

Next door, the voices ceased.

Hashim stood there, trembling, fingers in claws. He stared at nothing now.

Gradually, his pulse settled from its rocket pace, leaving him weak and shaken.

He righted the chair and practically fell into it. His gaze once more fixated on Alex's image. He reached for his phone and dialed. By the time Tarek answered, he had a plan.

"Brother, we have an interesting twist that needs resolution."

20

1830 hours Central Daylight Time, east of Panama City, Panama

Ed stood in the doorway of the safe house and dug into his Cheetos bag. His gaze remained focused on the dark, wet of the jungle as the rain poured down in a thick curtain. He popped a Cheeto into his mouth and crunched on it as he glanced at his watch.

Al-Omri was late.

Where was the kid? Was he in trouble? Had he gotten into an accident? In this rain and in the dark, coming up the narrow mountain roads increased that likelihood by a hundredfold.

"Have you heard from Jabir?" Karesh's voice from the kitchen made him turn.

"Nope. Have you guys?"

"Not yet," Rosen replied from where he sat at the table in the operations room. "I'm getting a little worried."

"You're not the only one," Ed muttered. He turned back to the blackness.

Over the patter of the rain on the neighboring jungle, he thought he heard the bee buzz of a motorcycle engine. He pulled back into the dimness of the operations room. "Company's coming."

"Finally, our boy." Rosen joined him.

"We're not sure yet." Ed jerked his head toward the row of guns they'd lined up along the wall. "Just as a precaution."

Rosen picked up the AK-47 and held it at a relaxed ready position cradled in front of him with the muzzle pointed at the floor.

Ed closed his hand around the pistol grip of the Beretta in its shoulder holster.

A headlight bounced across the house, making him withdraw even further. The hum grew louder until finally, the motorcycle parked under the roof of the porch. The light shut off.

"It's me, guys," al-Omri called softly in Arabic.

Ed lowered his hand. Out of the corner of his eye, he noticed how Rosen set the rifle against the wall. "'Bout time you showed up."

Al-Omri stepped into the pale glow of the three fluorescent lanterns they'd set up in the operations room. "I know. I'm sorry I'm late, but the rain caused three accidents on the way up."

From the doorway to the kitchen came a guffaw.

Ed's gaze swung to al-Rashid, who started laughing. "I've heard of getting soaked, but you, my friend, look like the cat who fell into the fish tank while going after a meal."

"Thanks, I think." Al-Omri wrung a stream of water out of the front of his shirt. "At least I have some dry clothing here."

"Well, get changed. Karesh is slopping out supper right now."

Al-Omri wandered through the kitchen.

Ed listened as he exchanged greetings with Karesh and Rosen. He followed him. "What's the vittles for tonight?"

"Stew. Top Secret, Need to Know Only," Karesh replied as he ladled the thick liquid into bowls. "It's a recipe Jessie and I cooked up together one night when we wanted to experiment."

Al-Omri rejoined them, this time dressed in a dry pair of cargo pants and a T-shirt. He sighed as he pulled out a chair and sank onto it. He yawned and pulled out a cigarette. "Everything's quiet?"

Ed leaned against the counter as he dug out the last Cheeto from his bag. "Oh, yeah. Quieter than a tomb. The hostage hasn't moved around much all day."

"Has she been taking her heart medication?"

"I've been giving her a pill with her supper each night." Karesh set a bowl in front of al-Omri. "Eat before you faint or something."

"Sorry. It's been a long few days."

"I hear you." Ed tossed the empty bag into the garbage bag tied to the hook they'd drilled into the wall. "I don't think it's going to be much longer, though."

"Huh?" Al-Rashid ladled some stew into another bowl. "What makes you say that?"

"I've got an asset who works in the executive suites of Kamil International. It seems like Samir went to Papa Kamil and begged. Papa reneged on his stance and told him the closing could go through if he could produce an associate."

"You trust this asset?" Karesh asked as he plopped onto a chair in the corner.

"Yeah, since we've been cultivating them for years. They know what to look for. It seems our boy set up a meeting with his sister, brother-in-law, and father for tomorrow afternoon late. You know he's going to produce that associate."

"My money says he fails." Al-Rashid pulled out a chair of sparkly vinyl.

"You think?" Rosen joined them and popped open a bottle of water. "What makes you say that?"

"He's not a careful person. He certainly wasn't with the pics of the property."

Ed took a bottle of water from Rosen and settled at the table. "Oh, I think he can be when properly motivated. What's your thoughts, Karesh?"

"Abdel, I wouldn't bet your Vegas play money on him failing." Karesh broke some crackers into his stew.

"Hey, I know when to avoid taking risks."

Al-Omri's stomach loudly growled, causing everyone to stare.

Ed grinned. "Well, eat, boy."

"Someone's hungry." Al-Rashid crossed his arms and leaned his chair back on two legs.

"I barely had lunch." Al-Omri only bit his lip and gazed at the stew.

"You feeling okay?" Ed asked.

"No, he's thinking again." Al-Rashid smirked. "Is it about hot girls, Jabir?"

"You *do* want to go to Vegas." Even in the harsh glow of the lantern on the table, a flush stained al-Omri's cheeks.

"Hey, what happens in Vegas stays in Vegas, right?" Karesh said.

"Something like that. Or what happens in Panama stays in Panama?" al-Omri replied. "Hmmm. This *is* good, Stephen,"

"Home-made all the way."

Al-Rashid chuckled. "Are you still chasing your culinary dream?"

"Oh, yeah. If I can stay in one place long enough. How about you, Ed? Do you cook?"

"When I'm in Washington. Or visiting Francesca. She's a much better cook than I. And if I'm on a long-term assignment. Otherwise, what's the point?" Ed nodded approvingly. "Good stuff, Karesh."

"Thanks. Not when you have an expense account." Karesh scraped the bottom of the bowl with his spoon. He rose, took Rosen's bowl, and rinsed them. "I'm headed to bed. I'll even leave the light on for you, Ari."

That elicited another weary chuckle from the crew.

Ed turned his attention to al-Omri. "Anything exciting happen today?"

"Um…" Al-Omri shifted his gaze to the cigarette, which he'd laid on top of its pack.

"Care to share?" Al-Rashid grinned.

"It's nothing big."

"Then why do you look like you're dying to smoke while you eat?" Ed studied the kid's expression. "Son, if something happened, you need to tell us."

"Okay. Okay." Al-Omri's cheeks puffed as he let out a breath. "People are worried about Melanie."

"How so?"

"Three of her friends showed up."

"Huh?" His spoon halfway to his mouth, al-Rashid leaned forward. "Say again?"

"Three of her friends." Al-Omri set his spoon down in the mostly empty bowl. "Apparently, she was meeting them in Costa Rica, and they were to pick her up at the airport on Tuesday. When she didn't show? Naturally, they were worried."

"How did we miss that?" al-Rashid muttered.

"And what happened?" Rosen asked. He leaned both elbows on the table.

Al-Omri picked up his cigarette and lit it. He took a puff before continuing, "They called the embassy here. The emergency number. They got handed the line that they had to wait a bit. You know, in case Melanie had gone off the deep end or something."

He paused.

Al-Rashid blurted, "So what happened?"

"They showed up at the embassy."

"*At* the embassy?" Rosen frowned.

Ed's mind began clicking through everything al-Omri had shared. Melanie was missing, and someone finally had noticed. To him, that wasn't too surprising. What did surprise him was that someone being three friends. "They filed a report in person. Big deal. You know the embassy won't act unless the three days have passed."

"Or if they had overwhelming evidence that something happened." Al-Omri took another drag. He blew out the smoke, and it hung in the air above the lantern like a toxic fog. He kept his gaze on the scarred Formica table. "Apparently, they took matters into their own hands, figured out where Melanie was staying, and got into her room."

Rosen muttered something under his breath.

"And?" Ed leaned back and crossed his arms.

"They went to the cops."

Was that a game changer? No, not if things continued playing out the way they were.

Ed shrugged. "You and I both know the cops aren't the best in these parts."

"I know. Most aren't. But some are."

"Oh?" Ed narrowed his eyes. "What else are you holding back on us?"

"I'm not, okay?" Al-Omri's fingers shook as he tapped some ashes into his bowl. "I found out about it by talking with one of the guys who's in the consular section. He's handed everything over to the FBI."

"Oh, great." Rosen cast a glance at Ed. "We're blown."

Ed gestured with his hand for Rosen to keep it calm. "So what? The investigation belongs to the Panamanians."

"And they've got their best detective on the case. An Esteban Romero."

"You're just full of good news today." Sarcasm and al-Rashid were one.

Ed narrowed his eyes. "Like I said, we can handle it. Got it? We've got less than a week before Samir Kamil shows up to do that closing. We keep calm, carry out our plan, and don't panic, we'll be fine."

"That's not all."

"Then what, al-Omri? What's next?"

"I'm sorry, all right?" Al-Omri's eyes widened as if he were a trapped animal. "Jeremy, the guy in the consular section who talked with Melanie's—"

"The hostage."

"Jeremy, who talked with them, is friends with me. He probably told me more than he should have."

"Which is your *job*, al-Omri. It's to get us information."

"I know. What concerns me is that I know one of Melanie's friends."

"What?" Al-Rashid gaped.

Ed shot him a look. "Keep it down, will you? And that would be who?"

"Alex Thornton." Al-Omri tossed the cigarette into his bowl. "She and I worked together at DHS in Unit 28 until four years ago."

"I see." Ed leaned back in his chair and studied the kid. Al-Omri wasn't lying. No, he was worried, more worried than he should have been. "You know her. And how so?"

"We were coworkers and friends. Believe me when I say she's one of the most tenacious people I know. She showed at the embassy again this afternoon and then staked out the employee entrance, waiting on me to come out." Al-Omri paused.

"So she saw you."

"Uh, yeah. I ran into her. I went to the lobby, and she spotted me."

"Oh, joy." Rosen put his head in his hands.

"I made sure I got away without her being able to follow me."

"You're sure?"

"Very."

"When was the last time you talked to her?" Ed asked.

"Four years ago." Al-Omri fiddled with his spoon.

Ed remained silent for a moment. He didn't know much about Unit 28, only that they were tasked with gathering recon information to protect the homeland. Often, their field agents and research staffs were pimped out to other agencies to help them on projects. How did a former Unit 28 agent seeing Jabir in Panama impact their mission? It didn't. What did that mean to their mission? Nothing, in his mind.

Maybe.

"Okay. What do you think will happen?"

"She's going to pursue this matter into the ground, at least until she gets answers." Al-Omri hunched on his chair and fell silent.

Something screamed in the nearby jungle, making everyone, including Ed, cringe.

Then al-Omri said, "I'm wondering if we need to call things off. It's getting too hot for my comfort. If Alex—"

Hot anger flashed through Ed. The kid should know better than to question his direction. Questioning his direction led to questioning not only Ed's wisdom but authority in this matter. He couldn't have that.

No way could he have that.

"I don't care about your *friend*." Ed hardened his voice as he glared at al-Omri. He leaned forward, elbows on the table. "Let me tell you something, al-Omri. Who's in charge here?"

"You are," al-Omri muttered. He kept his gaze on the table.

"Look at me!"

Al-Omri finally raised his gaze.

"Who. Is. In. Charge?" Ed bit off each word of his question.

"You."

Ed sat back. "Precisely. And as the one in charge, *I* make the decisions. Not you. Got it?"

"Yeah." Al-Omri cast a glance at Rosen and al-Rashid.

Both men stared at their bowls.

Then al-Omri spoke up again. "I'm afraid that Samir, when he hears of what happened, will go to ground because he thinks he's next."

"Oh, *au contraire*, my friend." Ed smirked. "Not at all. You see, that fancy equipment next door isn't for nothing. You understand? I've got assets in Kamil International right next to Papa Kamil. They tell me Samir is doing everything he can to produce that associate his daddy requires. And he will. I know he will. Anything to save his ex-girlfriend."

Ed rose. He leaned on his hands and glared at al-Omri, who shrank down in his chair. "You do your *job*. Which is to guard our hostage here tonight. And then tomorrow, you report to the embassy like you're on temporary assignment as a slacker employee. I want you to keep this Alex Thornton friend of yours close. Keep your friends close and your enemies closer, right? And report to me when you return tomorrow night."

"Okay," al-Omri almost whispered.

"Then I'm glad we have an understanding. Now you take the hostage some food, and I'm going to finish up and head to bed. Al-Rashid, you're on with al-Omri."

"Right." Al-Rashid nodded and picked up the remaining bowls.

Ed stomped to his room. He took a deep breath and slowly released it. For the first time, the kid unwittingly had revealed something to him. He wasn't a team player as much as Tiny had said. Did he have ulterior motives? Motives related to this Alex person? Something told Ed that Alex posed a threat, one that might need to be eliminated or at least neutralized.

Tomorrow, Ed would find out just which it was.

21

Jabir leaned against the wall next to the bathroom door. On the other
side of the flimsy wood, the shower ran. Sniffles and quiet sobs reached
him.

Melanie.

His eyes darted to the two bedroom doors, one at the end of the hall
and the other between the end of the hall and the door to Melanie's room.
No light shone under the door at the end, meaning both Stephen and Ari
had sacked out pretty quickly. A dim glow emanated from beneath Ed's
door. The team leader was still awake, reading or staring at the ceiling, Jabir
didn't know.

Maybe he should take Melanie and run. They could make it to the bor-
der with Costa Rica by midnight, into San Jose in the wee hours of the
morning. Then she'd be safe. The idea was so tantalizing that his gaze wandered in the other direction toward the kitchen. Abdel whistled a happy
tune as he filled the coffeemaker sitting by the stove with water.

He couldn't. He wouldn't.

To do so would unnecessarily endanger Melanie, and it would blow his cover to shreds.

Jabir had no choice.

He had to continue with the mission.

Regardless of whether or not Samir Kamil showed his face in Panama City in five days, Melanie would walk, and staying put could reveal possible evidence linking Ed to the thirteen killings of the CIA's senior Arabic speakers.

The water ceased.

Jabir pushed away from the door as it opened to reveal Melanie. Her hair hung in damp strands the color of flax. Her eyes were red. She'd lie and say it was from the shampoo, but he knew better.

He tried to lighten her mood with a smile. "Feel better?"

A rise and fall of her shoulders answered him. Melanie crossed the hall and dropped her towel on the back of the barrister's chair.

Jabir nodded toward the water and pill bottle on the table at the head of the bed. "Take your pill."

"Why? So I don't die on you?"

"I think you have much to live for."

"If I do, then why haven't you covered your face like the others?"

That caught Jabir up short. He smiled and shrugged. "You saw my face in the bar, yes? What good would it do?"

"I could ID you with the police."

"And by the time they got around to finding me, I'd be long gone with my comrades. Lie down."

Melanie obeyed. "Samir's not going to come. He's got too many layers of authority above him."

"He cares about you enough to save you. Of that, I have no doubt."

"And if he doesn't? What then? Will you kill me?"

Jabir hesitated. He cast a long glance at her. Now, her head rested on the pillow, and her eyes had narrowed. She'd challenged him and surprised him.

She knew it too.

Jabir forced himself to slide the shackle around her ankle. Once the lock clicked into place, he removed the key. "Have you ever been to Afghanistan, Ms. Forrest?"

"No."

"Think about what life would be like married to one of our men. Living life in a burqa. Being expected to birth a son. You had best hope Samir comes to save you." With that, he turned and switched off the lantern.

In the dark, Melanie hissed something, a word that showed how she truly felt about him and the rest of the crew. Though not unexpected, it hit Jabir in the heart and stung.

He shut the door retreated to the kitchen.

Abdel was no longer there.

Jabir wasted no time. He poured himself a cup of coffee and headed to the operations room. He pulled out one of the chairs and leaned against the wall next to where they'd stacked the guns. His gaze wandered to one of the laptops. He was dying to get online and find out all about Alex since he knew Tiny had kept tabs on her since her departure from Unit 28. He didn't dare, lest he be seen as a rogue who refused to be part of a team. The last thing he wanted was any more suspicion cast in his direction.

Something scrambled across the roof. Jabir shivered as once more, a shriek filled the air outside and made its way through the open window. He hated the jungle and earnestly hoped the shriek hadn't come from Abdel as he did a round on the perimeter of the property.

Footsteps approached the door.

The chair came down on all four legs, and Jabir reached for the Beretta he'd placed earlier on the small table next to the chair. Then the person on the other side whistled a country tune.

Abdel.

Jabir blew out a breath and replaced the gun.

"You had me going there for a second," he said as his comrade stepped through.

"Sorry, man. That's why I whistled. I didn't want to get shot through the door. How's Melanie?" Abdel swung the chair at the computer table around and stretched out his long legs. He pulled out his phone.

"Wondering what's going to happen to her." Jabir shook out a cigarette and lit it. "She asked me if there was an alternative."

Abdel raised his gaze. "Like if he doesn't come through?"

"Yeah. I mean, I don't think we can kill her."

"Hey, no way, man. I draw the line at killing innocents. I always have, even in Iraq."

"You served there?"

"Who didn't?" Abdel reached over and turned on another lantern, this one filling the room with the same pale glow as in the kitchen. "Yeah, I did. But in the later years. Afghanistan too, though I have to admit my Pashto just isn't there."

"You worked with Ed?"

"In Iraq some before he got sent home. Then on special missions. Man, you were pushing it tonight."

"Oh?" Jabir raised an eyebrow. "How so?"

"He absolutely hates having people question his authority. We're his worker bees. Got that? Our job is to take orders from him, not to question his decisions." Abdel checked his phone again, then cast a glance in the direction of the door leading to the kitchen.

"Seriously," he continued in a low voice, "the guy scares me some-times."

"Why?" Jabir straightened, hoping he could gather something—any-thing—to pass on to Tiny the next morning when he checked in.

But Abdel must have been scared Ed would walk in on them because he clamped his jaw shut and shook his head. He glanced upward as rain began hammering down on the roof. "Storm's coming again."

Jabir bit his lip.

All three of his comrades were worried. Ari seemed close to Ed. Ste-phen and Abdel? Not so much. None of them seemed eager to talk about the murders, more especially whether or not Ed was capable of such a thing. He'd have to let it rest for a bit longer.

"What's the deal with you and this Alex person? She sounds like a vixen."

Jabir grinned. "That's one way to describe her."

"You worked with her at Unit 28?"

"We were partners. Matter of fact, when I first found out her name was Alex, I was envisioning some sort of ex Special Forces guy. You know. Buff. Big."

"Hah. I'll bet she took you to task for that."

"Sort of. She barely scrapes five-three. But I'd never want to run into her in a dark alley."

"She's that tough?"

"Oh, yeah. Right after I started, I had a run-in with my father. We've been estranged. She was with me, and he made some sort of a comment in Arabic about my hanging out with a whore. When she smart-mouthed him back in Arabic, my brother took a swing at her. He wound up on the floor. She could've broken his wrist if she'd wanted."

Abdel whistled low. "Sounds like quite a lady."

Jabir swallowed against the lump in his throat. "She is. Very much so."

"Were you two an item?" Abdel leaned forward, elbows on knees, phone cradled in his hands.

"No." An image of an unconscious and broken Alex lying in his arms flashed through his mind. Sudden tears pushed at his eyes as he remembered the pain he'd felt when he'd gotten that unopened letter returned to him. "We...parted on bad terms."

"I see." Abdel studied him for a few moments. Then he messed with his phone, most likely checking something on the Internet. He raised his gaze. "Maybe you two will have a chance to talk it out."

"Maybe." Jabir could only hope. He cleared his throat to sweep away any emotion. "What about you?"

"Me?"

"Yeah. You got a girl at home?"

Abdel flashed a quick grin. "Something like that. At the gym, I ran into a girl I knew from high school. Rosita Melendez. Man, she was a looker then. So anyway, turns out she's also up in northern Virginia now. I had a date with her and learned she's still quite a looker and more so."

"Is she going to Vegas with you?"

"Nah. Guys weekend. I'm meeting some of my buddies from college there. But you can bet that as soon as I get back, I'm calling her. I'm tired of this single life, you know? I want to see if she'd be someone I could settle down with."

"I hear you."

They fell silent and let the rain pattering on the roof speak for them. Gradually, it slackened until Jabir could pick up the staccato noises of frogs and insects running counter to the steady noise of the storm.

His thoughts roamed to Alex. "You're right."

Abdel glanced up from his phone. "Huh?"

"I admit that I care for Alex. Maybe more than I should. But I don't know how to go there, not when she returned a letter I wrote explaining what happened. She didn't even open it."

Abdel didn't ask for details, and for that, he was grateful. His friend studied his phone some more before setting it on the table with a sigh. "Maybe Ed's directive comes at a good time."

"How's that?"

"You need to talk it out with her, right?"

"Yeah. I'm still not following."

"Think about it." Abdel grinned in the dim light. Then he rose and stepped into the kitchen.

Jabir blinked and shook his head. For the first time in a long time, hope peeked through the gloom regarding his situation with Alex. Abdel was right. When he and Alex met—it was when and not if—he could use that opportunity to talk.

Not just to find out any information regarding the investigation into Melanie's disappearance.

But to make amends.

2320 hours Central Daylight Time, west of Panama City, Panama

Blackness pressed close to Hashim as he lay on the bed. With each breath, it entered his soul, its tentacles entwining with his mind and body. The thrumming of the nighttime insects pulsed with every beat of his heart. He felt himself floating, as if being ferried from the living world into a darker one where anger and a need for revenge were the lifeblood of its inhabitants. It whispered to him, egging him on in his quest to find Alex and take his vengeance upon her.

His eyes snapped open.

On the nightstand, his phone chirped. He picked it up and noted the text from Tarek.

The message was short and simple.

It rocked his world.

Find our sister. And our friend. I will join you tomorrow morning your time. Be at the airport at 0630 hours. We will implement the plan together.

Hashim sat up, the light sheet he'd pulled up falling onto his lap. He listened. Nothing. The three men who weren't on guard duty slept.

He rose and felt his way through the dark into the kitchen. One flip of the switch sent the room into light. He stared at the floor as he waited for his eyes to adjust to the dim brightness. The shards of the mug and the tea stain on the wall remained, almost like his men were afraid of his rage if they cleaned it up.

He shrugged.

So be it.

He had more important things on his mind right then.

A plan formulated to kidnap Alex and still accomplish their original objective of gaining the property.

It all hinged on finding Ed DuBois.

Hashim began going through the photo files on his computer. Thanks to Jihad of Light's newfound influence, he now had assets all over the world.

Even in New Orleans where Ed's longtime girlfriend lived.

He located the photos he'd had his asset send him when Hashim had begun making deals with the CIA devil three years before. He smiled.

Doctor Francesca Bonini was a beautiful woman. One who had caught and held Ed's heart in her hands for several years, it seemed. She captured Hashim's attention with her black hair worn long and amazing blue eyes. He smirked when he noticed a picture of the couple dining at an outdoor restaurant. Even an untrained observer would notice how in love they were even as recently as this past spring. Hashim was willing to bet money that the sapphire ring she wore on her left ring finger had been given to her by Ed. Maybe not an engagement ring but a symbol of commitment.

Hashim began chuckling.

It would be enough.

Enough to bring Ed back under his thumb.

Day 6
Friday, June 16, 2017

22

The white Land Rover with darkened windows made the turn off of the main highway and wound its way up the narrow ribbon of blacktop into the tangled green jungle of the mountains. Hashim rested his arm on the sill of the open window and inhaled the rich scents left over from the rain. A smile crossed his face. It didn't matter where he was. Lebanon, Panama, or somewhere in between, so long as he was free, he was at home.

His passenger didn't seem to feel the same way. In expensive linen pants and shirt as well as a pair of Italian loafers, Tarek looked about as comfortable in Panama as Hashim had been locked in that hellish cell with Ed.

Tarek gripped the handhold above the door and muttered under his breath. With his other hand, he fished a handkerchief from his pants pocket and mopped his face. "How much further?"

"Not much." The smile shifted to a smirk as Hashim slowed to make the turn to the left.

They jounced over a huge bump, which drew a cuss word from Tarek.

"We're here." Hashim tapped out a code phrase on the horn to alert Asa and the others that friendlies had arrived. "The safe house is plenty big for all of us." He climbed from the Land Rover. "Asa, take the others and brief them on our security procedures. Then work them into what needs to be done."

Asa nodded and stepped to the panel van that had pulled to a stop behind them. Hashim counted nine men who climbed out and stretched. Greetings went around, and Asa led them to the back.

"Where are the occupants?" Tarek asked as he shut the door and followed his brother into the kitchen.

Hashim put some water on for tea as he replied, "We cleaned house. The Panamanians won't miss a couple of Colombian drug runners."

"One can hope." Tarek grimaced and fanned himself. "How do you manage in this weather?"

"You get used to it. Perhaps if you change, you'll be more comfortable. Tea, brother?"

Tarek nodded. Without a word, he disappeared down a hallway.

Hashim narrowed his eyes as he listened to him ordering around the men. It seemed as if he were claiming one of the bedrooms as his own. With a shake of his head, he dismissed the petty grievance. Finding Ed was paramount, not bickering over small things. He powered up his computer. The kettle whistled, and he poured them both stout mugs of water and added the black tea. He checked e-mail and grunted in satisfaction when he noted the photographs his man on surveillance at Hotel Panama had sent him.

"The sooner we return to Beirut, the better." Those words from Tarek made him glance up.

For the first time, annoyance flashed inside of Hashim. They had better things to do than go after their half-sister, but if Father wanted her, then they would bring her to Lebanon. He could even put aside his vengeance upon her until Jihad of Light was fully functional with secure footing in the western hemisphere. "I do too, but you and I both know we have business to do."

"I agree. What do you have?" Tarek pulled out a chair and sat down.

"I've had someone keeping surveillance on the hotel since sunrise this morning. So far, he's sent me these." Hashim pulled up the photos. They showed Alex returning from a run. He tried not to notice how toned her legs were in her shorts or the way the sweat made her shirt stick to her in patches. She'd worked out hard, but it hadn't erased the lines worry for her friend had etched into her forehead. "At last check, she and her friends were at the hotel. The manager let it slip that they are staying in the penthouse. A guilt upgrade is what I call it."

Tarek rubbed his chin. "What of Ed?"

"We still don't know where he's staying."

"We need that."

"I know. As of one o'clock today, that will change."

Tarek frowned. "How so?"

"Because I made a call early this morning to his mother." The way his brother's eyes widened filled Hashim with satisfaction. "Ms. DuBois was so kind when I called about the broken pipe in Ed's townhouse. She even gave me his personal cell number, which she promised he carries around. I'll text him. He'll meet us. Then we present our demands."

"I see." Tarek drummed is fingers on the table and squinted as if he could see the far-reaching consequences of the plan. "You forgot one thing, my brother. Ed DuBois is an experienced CIA agent. He can disappear if he wants."

"Ah, but that's where you err."

"I don't follow."

"We have a hook, something that I know will keep him close." Hashim opened another folder and pulled up the photos of Francesca. "You see this woman? She's Ed's one love."

His brother stared at the screen. "Where is this?"

"New Orleans. One of our assets lives there, and when we first started dealing with Ed three years ago, I had him take pictures of her for me. You see, he has made a fatal mistake. He now cares for someone deeply, so deeply that he'll do anything to save her. Don't you agree?"

Tarek stroked his beard as he leaned back in his chair. Gradually, his lips curled in a smile. He started chuckling. "Excellent work, Hashim. Very excellent."

"These came from my asset not an hour ago."

His mirth disappeared. "Do it. Send a text. Then we'll see what Mr. DuBois has to say."

Hashim nodded. He dug into the box of burner phones he'd collected from all over Panama City. Without another word, he fished Ed's number from his pocket. With his thick fingers, he punched in the message and hit the Send button.

0745 hours Central Daylight Time, east of Panama City, Panama

Ed scowled as he rubbed the back of his neck and stared at the computer screen. E-mail messages between Samir and this "associate" he had to produce flashed back and forth. It was clear that Samir was too nervous. If he got anymore uptight, he'd have a breakdown.

You keep it up, Samir. Play it cool. Then you'll show up here and be in our hands faster than you can blink.

He shook his head. They'd planned well for this mission. Covered all possibilities.

Almost.

How could they have missed Melanie's friends meeting her in Costa Rica? All it would take would be one misstep to have the whole thing come down on their heads. Then what would he do with the hostage?

His mind raced back to the conversation he'd overheard between al-Omri and her. If Samir balked, what *would* they do? Beat her up some, then dump her in an alley. So what if the kid thought the cops knew about their research on her?

He muttered and wandered into the kitchen for a cup of coffee. He paused, listening through the open door to Karesh conversing with the hostage. Annoyance flared and made his head hurt. Ed located the bottle of aspirin they'd stashed on the counter and popped a couple into his mouth. He washed it down with coffee. Maybe that would take care of the headache a night of poor sleep had produced.

Karesh stepped into the room and shut the door behind him.

"She's good?" Ed asked in Arabic

"As good as can be expected." Karesh picked up the bowls that had held the morning's oatmeal. He set them in the sink and grabbed an orange. As he began peeling it, he cast a glance in his boss's direction. "Any progress from Beirut?"

"Oh, yeah. Our boy's busily having a meltdown. But it seems as if this meeting between his 'associate' and family is going to happen."

"Well, it'd better happen soon." Karesh separated a wedge from the rest of the fruit.

"You're concerned?"

Karesh shrugged. "Uneasy, I guess. I mean, we're operating in a friendly country. Or at least a neutral one."

Ed clapped him on the shoulder. "It'll all be over soon. Promise that. Where's Rosen?"

"Outside sparring with Abdel. Guess who's winning?"

"Rosen."

Karesh grinned. "Right. I'll clean up here, then make sure Melanie gets a bathroom break."

A hot streak of irritation flashed through Ed. "Our hostage." He glared at him. "I told you that we aren't to refer to her by her name."

Karesh met his gaze with a defiant one of his own for a moment. Then he lowered it. "Sorry. That's just hard to do."

"And that's because?"

Karesh shook his head. "I don't know." He shrugged.

"Well, you'd better find out. Got that? I set up rules for a reason. You know something? Forget about cleaning up right now. Go check the generator and see if we'll need fuel for it soon."

"But—"

"*Now*, Karesh."

Karesh shot him another look.

"And while you're at it, check the perimeter." Ed muttered under his breath as he snagged another bag of Cheetos from the case. What was it with Karesh all of a sudden? It was like the kid's objections last night had stoked a rebellious fire in him.

Al-Omri.

Ed's expression darkened further as he thought about the DHS hand-me-down. At first, he'd thought al-Omri was the total package. A tough team player who was also an independent thinker. Someone who could hold his own. What he hadn't expected was the kid's whininess. What did they do at DHS? Raise them to be crybabies at the first sign of difficulty?

He blew out a breath as he retreated to his room and stared at the patch of yard that was more mud than grass. Rosen sparred with al-Rashid, and it was clear by the streaks of brown all over al-Rashid's shirt and pants who was winning.

Ed's personal cellphone chirped, signaling he had a text. He grinned when he noted it.

Francesca.

Headed into clinic and wanted to say hi and that I love you.

He tapped out a reply. *I miss you too, beautiful.*

I RSVP'd to Rachel about Ari's retirement party. I'll come up to DC for the weekend. Then we can leave on our trip from there.

The thought filled Ed with pleasure. He smiled. *I love you. Will call when I return.*

Love you back.

Ed clipped the phone to his belt.

Outside, the sparring match had stopped. Karesh conversed with the other two. Al-Rashid clapped Rosen on the shoulder and headed toward the front of the house. Ed drifted to the operations room as al-Rashid opened the screened door.

"Ari five, Abdel zero," he reported.

"Yep. Looks like he got the best of you. Again."

"Call me an eternal optimist, but one day, I'll win. At least I didn't take any bets on my winning."

"Hah. Good one." Ed grinned as he lifted the screen on the work laptop. His mood simmered down, and he thought about all al-Omri had told them the night before. This Alex Thornton woman warranted some investigation. Lots of investigation.

He accessed the CIA mainframe. From there, it was a quick hop over to the DHS side of life where, thanks to his high clearance, he was able to access her personnel jacket.

Behind him, al-Rashid whistled. "Whooee, she's a looker."

Ed had to agree. Though it was the typical mug shot for a government ID, he could tell she was quite beautiful with her olive tones, dark brown hair hedging on black, and sea green eyes, especially if you liked the type from the Near East. "That, she is. Makes you wonder how many hearts she's gotten into. And how many sets of pants."

Both men laughed.

Al-Rashid added, "Jabir told me she's a handful."

"He tell you anything else?"

Suddenly, al-Rashid pulled back and bit his lip, almost as if he realized he'd divulged too much. "Uh, not really. Hey, I'm tired. I'm going to get cleaned up and hit the hay."

"Have a good rest. I'll try to keep it down in here."

Abdel waved and shambled into the kitchen. A moment later, the shower started.

Ed stared after him with narrowed eyes. Then he turned back to the personnel jacket. He began reading. When he got to the last mission that shot down her rising star, he smirked. Poor girl. He knew what it felt like to be wrongly blamed and publicly humiliated.

"What are you looking at?" Rosen's question made him turn to find his friend stepping through the door as he wiped his face with a towel.

"Alex Thornton's personnel jacket. I saw you beating up on al-Rashid out there." Ed grinned.

"He's getting better. I only beat him in ten minutes instead of one." Rosen chuckled. "So back to Alex. What's your read on her?"

"She's a smart cookie."

"A good-looking cookie." Rosen studied the screen.

"Yeah. I knew her daddy. Old Davie Thornton and I served together in Afghanistan right before the Wall fell. But not even having a congressman for a daddy saved her."

"Nor did all of those commendations." Rosen studied the screen and noted the long list of classified commendations that had been given to her over her eight-year career. "Looks like the boys at DHS thought a lot of her."

"Her boss did too. I served with Tiny."

"Tiny?"

"Tim Daniels. He's short. Like five-four short. That's how he got his nickname."

"Hah. Good one. What else do you know about Alex?"

"We have a faint connection with her."

Rosen raised an eyebrow. "How's that?"

Ed popped a Cheeto into his mouth and crunched for a moment. "Do you remember how we reeled in those ten guys, including Hashim al-Hassan?"

"Oh, yeah. I remember that was an impressive dragnet. Ten guys in one night."

"We were tapped out doing that many at once, so we contracted with Unit 28 for Hashim's takedown."

Rosen's eyes lit up as if he understood what Ed was saying. "Alex took down Hashim?"

"Yep. He always did have a weakness for pretty faces."

"What else do we know about her?"

"She got publicly booted out of DHS. I think she was fired by press conference."

"Ouch."

"Then she ran back home. Tiny's kept tabs on her, it seems, and she's now back in Weatherly, North Carolina, working as a contractor."

"Maybe she can redo our bathroom here." Rosen grinned.

Ed chuckled. "Maybe. Unit 28 habits never die. That's why I want al-Omri to keep an eye on her. I'm worried she might become a threat."

"Agreed there." Rosen smothered a yawn. He glanced up. "Looks like Abdel's out of the shower. I'm headed to clean up before he crashes."

An idea popped into Ed's mind. Rosen was more than a comrade. He was a friend, one who'd served many years with Ed and saved his skin on more than one occasion. "Hey, Rosen—"

Ed's personal phone trumpeted the arrival of another text. Ed frowned. Surely Francesca was with a patient now. His mother didn't know how to text. Then who… He read the message.

I know you are in Panama. H.

Ed muttered under his breath.

"Is everything okay?" Rosen's voice came from somewhere far away from the thoughts that now raced through Ed's head.

He stammered, "Um, uh, yeah, I think."

He quickly keyed in a message. *How do I know it's really you?*

Francesca is a beautiful woman. My man took great pictures of her as she left her house this morning.

Ed's blood chilled as he stared at the picture of Francesca beside her Mercedes sports car. She wore that cute scarlet number of a dress that had quickly wound up on the floor of her bedroom during a night of romancing Valentine's Day weekend. She had a purse slung over her shoulder and her sunglasses in her hand.

He shivered.

"You're sure?" Rosen again.

"Yeah. Just, um, a message about my mom. She's getting up there, you know." Ed flashed a weak grin. "Let me know when you're done with your shower."

"Sure." Rosen disappeared into the kitchen.

Ed's phone vibrated again. He turned back to the text message.

It was short and sweet, but carried a breath of threat on it. *Meet today at 1 pm at Jardín Hermoso. Be there, or Dr. Bonini will have a most unfortunate accident in that sports car of hers.*

Ed's headache kicked up with a ferocity that made him wince. His hands shook as he laid the phone on the table.

His handlers were here.

In Panama.

Why?

Karesh opened the screened door.

Ed whipped around, his hand going for the gun that wasn't in its holster.

"I checked the generator and the perimeter." Karesh's voice was neutral, and his eyes remained devoid of any emotion. "Is there anything else you need me to get?"

"Whatever else is on the inventory that you guys generated." Ed held out his hand. "I'll take it. I need to go into town."

"Is everything okay?"

"Actually, no. I need to make a call to my mom, so why don't I make the supply run?" Who cared if he lied?

"Sure." Karesh pulled off a sheet of paper. "If we're transferring to town on Monday, it's not a lot. I hope your mom's okay."

"Thanks." Ed briefly scanned it. "It's enough. Thanks. You and Rosen keep a close watch on things. I'll be back tonight."

Ed retreated to his room. Once safely behind his closed door, he sank onto the bed, whose springs creaked under his weight. He groaned softly, put his head in his hands, and rubbed his temples in an effort to make the headache go away.

It didn't work.

He stared at the dirty, scarred floor.

He had no choice. If he didn't show up, Francesca would die. Knowing Hashim, it wouldn't be a pretty death.

Ed shuddered.

Like it or not, deeds he'd committed in the past had crept up on him.

Now it was time to pay his dues.

23

"Mr. Shah, we thank you for taking the time to come visit with us and explain your reasons for leasing the Panama City property," Papa stated as the five participants of the meeting rose from the table.

Samir wanted to take a deep breath and shout for joy.

He'd succeeded.

"I appreciate the chance to come and visit." A smile crossed "Mr. Shah's" face. He cast a look at Samir as he snapped his briefcase closed. "If there is anything else I can do to clarify matters, please contact me."

"We'll do that," Samir said. He took Mr. Shah's arm and escorted him from the receptionist's area into the lobby of the twentieth floor. Under his breath, he muttered, "You did great in there."

"I did as I was told." The man pressed the Down button. "If you need anything else, call me."

"I'll do that." Samir released him. "Again, thank you."

Once the elevator doors closed behind his guest, Samir returned to the small conference room adjoining Papa's office. Salma picked up the cups and saucers of coffee they'd shared as part of the meeting. She nodded at Samir and slipped from the room. He glanced at Noor.

Her face remained expressionless, but all of the anger and mistrust from earlier that week had faded. She was now neutral in the issue. The thought made Samir uneasy. He'd rather have had her be openly hostile or openly receptive. Now, it was almost like she hid something from him.

"Son, I can see where we were remiss when we hastily came to conclusions." Papa's words made him glance up.

"What's next?"

"Go to Panama on Monday and conduct the closing as originally planned. I'll send Melanie an e-mail so she'll know to expect you." Papa took the lease agreement, already signed by Mr. Shah, and placed it in his portfolio. "Then, when you return, we'll sign and notarize the agreement as we discussed."

Samir wanted to sag to the ground. Now he was free to go to Panama. Then his heart caught. Melanie was still hostage, meaning he had to deal with these mysterious kidnappers. Tarek could help with that.

He had to get out of there.

"Papa, I'm going to my office for a few minutes before I leave."

"I need to go as well." Noor's words startled Samir. "Kate is at home with the children. She has a date tonight, and I promised to be home by seven."

Fadi took her arm. He whispered something in her ear. She whispered back, and he strode through the door.

Samir wandered down the hall to his office on the opposite corner. Hanan had already left for the day, so he was alone. He eased into his black leather desk chair with a sigh and placed his phone on the glass of the desk. For a moment, he stared at it. Then he picked it up and dialed Tarek's number.

The butler answered. Upon Samir's request to speak with Tarek, he replied, "Sir, Mr. al-Hassan is out of the country and will be so until midweek next week. May I take a message?"

"No, no. I'll call him later on his cellphone." Samir hung up and stared at the phone. Was it so urgent? No, he was headed to Panama on Monday.

He rested his head against the soft leather of the chair as he thought about all that had happened. For some reason, a memory of playing with

Fatima, his older niece, came to mind. They'd built a tower out of blocks. Finally, it got to be so tall that each block they added made it sway. Finally, it collapsed, sending both of them into laughter. This week was like that. Deception had built upon deception until the whole thing threatened to crumble under the weight of so many lies.

But it was almost over.

Only a couple of more days.

From somewhere in the hall, a door banged open, making him jump. Footsteps rushed across the carpeted floor. Noor burst into his office.

Samir started when he noticed the way several strands of hair had fallen from its twist. Her sherry eyes were wide, and he thought he saw faint mascara stains around them. "Noor, what happened?"

"I…" Her voice faded. She stood there, trembling visibly, her mouth working as if she tried to form words too horrible to contemplate. "Did you…did you see the news?"

"What? No. I was getting ready to go home."

"Check CNN." She pointed to his monitor.

Samir accessed the Internet site. There, front and center on the home page, a picture of a smiling Melanie Forrest glowed. The headline assaulted him.

American Lawyer Kidnapped in Panama.

The blood drained from his face as he read the first few paragraphs. He clenched his head between his hands. "Oh, no."

"Is this…is this why you've been so upset?" Noor's quiet question penetrated the roar in his head. "Samir, is someone pressuring you to do the closing and using her as leverage?"

Suddenly, panic washed over Samir. "Is Papa here?"

"No, he's with Fadi. Why—Samir, what is it?" she added as he leapt to his feet.

He shut the door to his office and leaned against it. His heart pounded against his rib cage with such ferocity that he feared it would leap from his chest and hop across the floor. His mind darted in all directions in a frenzy. "Noor, please. They—they've been squeezing me all week about this. I couldn't stop. Not when Melanie's life is on the line. Please let this closing go through by not telling Papa about this."

A sickening thought made his stomach plunge.

"He doesn't know, does he?"

Noor shook her head. "No. He was leaving for home after talking with Fadi."

"I *need* to go to Panama on Monday."

She bit her lip, then whispered, "I know."

Noor began pacing.

"I still love her."

"I know you do. Oh, Samir."

"I'll do anything to save her. Anything!"

"I know." Noor stopped and faced her brother. Tears had filled her eyes, and one trickled down her cheek, tracking more mascara. "She's my friend too. No, she's more than that. She's almost like a sister to me."

Samir reached out and took her hands. "Then please don't say a word to Papa."

Her gaze strayed to the article on the screen. She closed her eyes. Her hands tightened around his. "This will be old news soon. Especially here. I won't. Just…get Melanie away from her kidnappers."

"I will." Samir swallowed hard. Something else pulled at him and threatened to shatter any semblance of peace from earlier. He had to know. "What of the audit?"

"Gavin had some questions. You know. It's a new audit team he's training, and he wanted Fadi to explain some things to them." She glanced at him.

That neutral expression had slid back into place.

"Anyway, Fadi's going straight home." She broke her gaze with him and headed to the door. Noor put her hand on the knob. She turned. "I won't breathe a word of this to anyone. I promise."

"Thank you," he almost whispered.

Once Noor had gone, Samir collapsed onto his chair. The groan that escaped his lips surprised him.

196

His house of cards, so carefully constructed, had begun tumbling down.

He only had to hold on until Monday.

Then Melanie would be safe because he would do anything to protect her.

That was all that mattered to him.

24

The elevator doors to the rooftop restaurant, El Jardín, opened to reveal a small lobby with a smiling hostess in a white sheath that outlined her curvaceous figure standing behind a Plexiglas podium. Latticework with delicate vines growing from large pots concealed the dining area from Ed's view.

Her eyes lit with recognition. "You must be Señor DuBois."

He tried and failed at a smile of his own. "You know me?"

"Gray hair in a crew cut. Gray eyes. Yes, I was told to expect you. Please, follow me." She inclined her head toward the opening between the latticework.

Ed stepped through. Instantly, the breeze produced by being thirty stories up cooled his face. He took a deep breath and tugged down the hem of the blazer he'd pulled on for this visit.

Instantly, he picked out his foes. The al-Hassan brothers sat under a portico at the far end of the restaurant. Its isolation at the corner of the roof was the perfect place for their meeting. They seemed to be conversing in low voices. Upon Ed's arrival, they ceased. Tarek rose. "Welcome, my friend."

Ed narrowed his eyes. The devil came dressed in white pants and a deep blue shirt with a Rolex on his wrist.

Hashim, in black cargo pants and black T-shirt, remained seated. His elbows rested on the arms of his chair, his fingers steepled, his vivid aquamarine eyes narrowed as he assessed his opponent.

Ed tried not to notice the way the man's biceps bulged against the sleeves of his shirt. He didn't say a word, instead preferring to let the silence lengthen from cordial to awkward.

"Please. Have a seat. We just arrived ourselves." Tarek's words barely penetrated the buzzing suddenly filling Ed's head.

"It's been a long time."

"Too long. Which is why we need to catch up. Please." Tarek gestured to the menu. "It's on me today. Order, and we'll do just that."

Ed wanted to grind his teeth. He knew how this game would go. They'd dine on exquisitely prepared food placed on china of the highest caliber until Ed was ready to hit something. Then Tarek would begin his little games.

The problem?

Ed had no choice but to go along with it.

The only satisfaction he got was ordering some swordfish that far exceeded his daily per diem.

Tarek prattled on and on about Panama and how much he'd already seen in the short time he'd been there.

He lied.

Ed answered in short, clipped replies.

The waitress placed their desserts in front of them, refreshed their Colombian coffee, and left them alone.

Tarek ran off at the mouth about one of the national parks.

Finally, Ed blew out a sigh. "Enough of that already. I'm sick of your chitchat about places you obviously haven't visited."

"You don't want to hear about the zip line tour I have planned?"

"No, I don't want to hear about that. Or the snorkeling expedition a tour guide wants to take you on. Or the birds you'll see when you go bird-watching. Why am I here? Because if you're just going to act like a ditzy tour guide, I'm gone." Ed pushed his chair back and rose.

"Sit down, Mr. DuBois." Tarek's voice lowered, turning to flint.

"Good. I'm glad I finally got your attention."

"I had my reasons on acting like I swallowed a tour book." Tarek added some sugar to his coffee and stirred. Then he set the silver spoon on the saucer. "You see, I know you're very familiar with Panama." He leaned forward. "When I hear that an American woman has been kidnapped by people using our good name and when I know certain things I know, I start to wonder."

Ed blinked, trying to stay focused on why they were meeting.

They knew. They knew about Melanie and the mission objective.

"Okay. So you heard. Stop keeping me in suspense and tell me why you happened to fly all the way from Lebanon just to tell me the obvious."

Tarek leaned forward and fixed him in his intense blue gaze that felt like a laser being trained on him. "I want the truth from you. You see, Samir Kamil came running to me on Tuesday evening. Imagine my surprise when he accuses me—me!—of kidnapping his beloved Melanie Forrest. Naturally, I started to wonder who would dare use the name of Jihad of Light. And when Hashim suggested it could be you? I simply had to find out for myself. Now why were you so brazen?"

"Who said I had anything to do with her disappearance? So far as I know, she's not in Panama."

Tarek only shook his head. "Tsk. Tsk. Tsk. Wrong answer. We know she's here."

"You got proof of that?"

"Enough." Tarek brushed some imaginary crumbs from the white tablecloth.

Ed leaned forward. "There's something your precious tour books haven't told you about this country. There's drugs everywhere. Thugs too. Men who target women traveling alone for business. Maybe that's how she disappeared."

"I think not, Mr. DuBois. You see, Samir showed us the video."

Ed swallowed hard, his mind racing in all directions like cockroaches scattering at the first show of light. "Okay. You got me. You know I can't talk about that."

"And why not?"

"It's classified."

The smile dropped from Tarek's face. For a moment, he didn't say anything. Then he started chuckling and sliced off a sliver of cheesecake. "You, Ed DuBois, are an interesting man, are you not? Do you think I care about this mission being classified?"

"All I can tell you is that I got handed this assignment. You see, my bosses think Samir's mixed up with you guys, which, apparently, he is."

Tarek shrugged. "What were your orders?" he asked. "What do you have planned for Mr. Kamil?"

"I can't tell you."

Tarek winked. "Your secret is safe with us."

"About as safe as handing the keys to Fort Knox to crooks." Ed grinned, glad to have sparred at least a little with Tarek.

Tarek hissed something. He took a sip, but the cup shook. He set it on the saucer with the clatter of porcelain on porcelain. "You have some nerve. Some nerve to blather on about a classified mission when you know very well that you worked for us not too long ago. Like as recently as February, yes?"

"You've made a mess of things." For the first time, Hashim spoke.

Startled, Ed's gaze flew to Tarek's younger brother. "Me? Look, I'm just doing my job, all right?"

"I don't care about the specifics of your so-called mission. Your job has changed." Hashim leaned forward, his gaze never wavering from Ed's as he studied him, most likely assessing Ed's weaknesses.

"Oh? You want to tell me you received an e-mail from my boss?" Ed glared at him.

"We're your bosses as well, right?" Hashim picked up his fork, which looked too small in his big hand. He pointed it at him. "Listen to me, Ed DuBois, and listen to me good. We know one of Melanie's friends is named Alex Thornton."

"Just how did…" Ed stared at him. His heart began hammering.

Hashim chuckled, the sound like gravel rolling around in a barrel. "Surprised you, didn't we?"

"I have to admit, yes."

"When we found that out, our priorities shifted. The property and Samir no longer matter to us," he continued.

"But—"

"We want Alex."

"You want her? Why involve me? Why not kidnap her?"

"Because we want to take our time and plan well. Unlike you…" Hashim examined the silver as if checking for any defects. He switched his gaze to Ed. "And unlike you, we don't want to botch a kidnapping. You see, not three hours ago, CNN broke the story of how Melanie Forrest was kidnapped from her hotel room in the middle of the night on Monday."

Ed's jaw clinched. He'd heard the radio report, which had rattled him only slightly. He'd been so confident he had things under control.

Until now.

How was he supposed to have known about Alex's friends? Or Samir's actions?

"You forget something, my *friend.*" He nearly spat out the last word. "I've got a mission I'm running. I've got people I answer to, and if Samir doesn't come over here for that closing—"

"You're going to help us get Alex." Hashim kept his words low, measured.

"I don't see—"

"Oh, I think you see it quite well. It's that your other job is blinding you right now." Hashim leaned forward almost to the point where Ed had the desire to lean back to get him out of his personal space. "We'll take Melanie off your hands. Then it will be her for Alex."

"Why do you want her?"

"That's for us to know and us alone." Hashim smirked, "You know. Top Secret and Need to Know and all of that junk you CIA devils like to toss around. But guess what? I have a way to help you get out of this predicament of yours."

"What? You're going to leave the country as soon as lunch is over?"

"You amuse me, Ed DuBois." Hashim stared at him.

Ed returned the look, never wavering in his own gaze.

The waitress appeared with a small black book bearing the check. She placed it before Tarek without a word. She stood there for a moment. Then, sensing the testosterone floating on the air like a sick scent, she retreated.

Ed blinked. He sighed. "What do you propose?"

"Simple. You were found out by the cops. You run, leaving Melanie behind. Then we come and take care of her." Hashim eased back. For a moment, only the bubbly laughter from a nearby table full of women reached them.

Tarek leaned over and murmured something. The brothers whispered together.

Ed sat there, staring at his plate. Finally, he muttered, "I've got—"

"Orders? Yes, I know all about orders." Hashim smiled again, chilling him. "Perhaps you think, in your all-American loyalty, that you'll get away with reporting us. You know. Two for the price of one? But, you see, I have no desire to spend more quality time with you. The last time I did, I lost all of my hair." His hand rubbed his bald head. "This time? What would I lose?"

"Maybe your manhood." Ed smiled at his jab.

Hashim tensed to jump up, but Tarek put his hand on his arm. "Enough. This is foolishness. Listen to Hashim, Mr. DuBois. It might save Dr. Bonini's life."

Ed's pulse skipped up several notches as he remembered the photo attached to the text. Sweat broke out on his hands, his forehead.

How had they found out about his relationship with Francesca?

"You have a team down here, yes?" Hashim asked.

"I can't—"

Hashim reached down.

For a brief moment, Ed feared he'd bring out a pistol.

Hashim tossed a manila envelope onto the table. "Take a look at these. Look very closely."

Ed could barely keep his fingers from trembling as he popped the clasp and pulled the papers from the envelope. They felt like photo paper. He found himself gazing at pictures of Francesca. The one he'd received in the text. Another of them together at the last romantic dinner they'd had in April to celebrate Francesca's birthday. Another of her with a patient at the hospital where she worked. Nausea from the rich meal and rising fear made his stomach churn. He closed his eyes.

Hashim's words came as if he spoke them from far away. "I know you love her. You see, years ago, when you first wanted to work for us, I had you followed. You were foolish enough to not look for tails in your home country. You led us to New Orleans and straight to Dr. Bonini. I have my asset watching her right now. She's at the hospital seeing patients in her clinic. I'd hate to see her have an accident tonight on the way home."

"What do you want?" Ed's voice sounded all of a sudden thin to his ears.

"I want to know who is on your team."

"Three CIA and a hand-me-down from DHS."

"I assume, from the fact that you're posing as a Jihad of Light cell that they all are seasoned Arabic speakers. The remaining three."

Ed jerked his chin in a nod.

"We'll pay you well for each man you take down."

"What?" Ed gaped. "I—I—I can't do that! You've got to understand. They're comrades of mine. We've fought together. Bled together."

"So?"

"I've served with all of them for years. Ari, for fifteen. No way could I kill them. Not when they've got family. Stephen's newlywed. And Ari…He's retiring when we get back and no way—"

Hashim placed his fork on the table. "Dr. Bonini is a very beautiful woman. I would hate for your decisions to hurt her."

"Look, it's not that easy. They're—"

Hashim started chuckling. Then he shook his head as his mirth disappeared. "How strange. You didn't seem to have any qualms murdering

Hakim al-Husseini, now did you? Even though—how did you put it—he saved your life in Iraq several times? Seems that five hundred thousand overrode any semblance of loyalty."

"These men have families."

"So did Hakim. A wife who died with him on their anniversary night. And three children who are now orphans. Did you forget that?"

Ed winced as fresh guilt for cutting his friend's brake lines washed over him again. How was he supposed to know they'd give out on the mountain rather than in town where he would've had a non-life-threatening accident? "I…"

"It seems as if you don't care to cooperate. Let me call my asset. He'll pay Dr. Bonini a visit at her house. Have his way with her before he kills her." Hashim held up his phone with a number clearly displayed on it. "All I have to do is hit the Send button. I do that, and I unleash my wolf."

"Look, I only sought you out because I wanted to get back at the CIA for stalling out my career."

"And make a nice six and a half million." Hashim set his phone on the table. "Yes, I know all about how you grew up poor, how your papa hit you and your mother. You've worked hard, haven't you, but it wasn't enough. You have a great fear of starving, of not having any money. The money we paid you will ensure that you live well for the rest of your life."

"Hashim—"

"Is there something wrong, Mr. DuBois?" Hashim asked.

Ed closed his eyes. "I want more than five hundred per."

"Name your price."

"Three per."

"We can do that."

Ed's mind raced. Somehow, he'd need to call Francesca and tell her to leave town right then. To go on that vacation now rather than later. He'd join her after the mission and explain everything.

Somehow.

"We'll even pay you a bonus." Tarek's voice penetrated the cacophony of questions screaming through his head.

That jerked Ed back to the present. "And what would that be?"

"You help us in the kidnapping, and I'll add another five million to that. Then I can promise safe haven in Afghanistan. Your Pashto is very good from what I remember."

Ed swallowed hard.

He was trapped.

Trapped at his own game.

But he'd be okay. So would Francesca.

"I guess I have no choice."

Hashim chuckled.

Ed knew what he was thinking. Hashim al-Hassan now had his former captor and tormentor at his mercy with no way out.

What sweet revenge.

Bile threatened to spew upward as Ed realized the enormity of his decision.

Once again, the brothers glanced at one another. Then Tarek nodded. "Deal."

He held out his hand.

Ed accepted it. "Deal."

25

With hands shoved into the back pockets of her jeans, Alex paced. Her eyes darted from the candy bowl on Samantha's desk to the mezzanine stairs where Jabir had headed to the second floor. The gold foil of the Reese's mini-cups, meant as a peace offering for Samantha, glimmered under the overhead lights. She dared him to come downstairs to indulge his sweet tooth. Thanks to the e-mail the receptionist had sent to all staff, several gazelle had already visited the lioness's watering hole.

But no Jabir.

"What's the game plan?" Becca asked from where she leaned against a column as they waited for FBI Special Agent Mitch Gordon to show up.

"I figured that when we start to meet with him, I'll pretend like I have to go to the bathroom. Then I'll go and find Jabir since he's not taking the bait."

"Um, question?"

Alex couldn't help it. She cracked a grin. "Did you expect me to go in there and listen to what Mitch had to say? You're the cop, not me."

"Right. Boy, if you're caught..." Becca shook her head.

"If I'm caught, I'll play dumb. Or claim I was there to see George. I mean, I feel like we're buds now."

Becca nodded. "He did seem to take a shine to you. Okay. I'll cover for you, but I'm not sure how good of an actress I am."

"Recall your undercover days. That's all you need to do." Alex sighed and sank onto a nearby chair. "Why do you think Ellie decided to stay behind?"

"I think Ellie's way of dealing with crises is by withdrawing." Becca crossed her arms. "I guess I'm worried about her. You know, what with everything going on with their business and marriage and all."

"I know. Me too. But I wasn't going to push her. And besides, since they released the crime scene this morning, I guess someone had to clean out the room so the hotel could rent it."

"You're right." Becca swept a hand through her hair. "Well, we'll try to do something tonight to cheer her up. You think we could get the guys to come over?"

"George, Markie, and Hoss?"

"Yeah. I mean, they were nice enough last night."

"True. Maybe." Alex rose when a man dressed in a khaki suit with a deep blue tie knotted around his neck approached them.

"Alex Thornton?" the man demanded. He removed his glasses and polished them with his tie.

"That's me."

"FBI Special Agent Mitch Gordon." He stuck out his hand.

"Becca Alvarez." Becca shook his hand as well.

"This way." Mitch turned on his heel and led them up the stairs to the mezzanine. They turned right and headed to the set of offices over the consular section. Once they were inside, he closed the door and pointed to a couple of chairs. "Have a seat."

"What's the status?" Alex asked as she set her purse on the floor beside her chair.

"Of the case?"

Alex wanted to roll her eyes. "Our friend was kidnapped, Special Agent Gordon."

"I'm very well aware of that." Mitch poured himself a cup of coffee from the small carafe on a side table. "Coffee?"

"No, thanks."

"Our embassy released an official statement this morning saying that Melanie Forrest was kidnapped and that the local cops are investigating. If you've looked at CNN or Fox, it hit around eleven this morning. Don't worry. We're keeping your names out of the press, and the Panamanians are keeping a tight lid on the investigation too." He pulled a small bottle of creamer from the mini-fridge and dumped some into the dark liquid.

"And?"

Mitch glanced up as he ripped open a couple of sugar packets. "That's all."

Alex's eyes narrowed. "I'm not so sure of that."

He shrugged. "What else can I say? We've got it now. Thanks for letting Jeremy know yesterday."

"No, wait." Becca held up her hand. "Special Agent Gordon, let's get one thing straight here. We're not going to be dismissed on this. You got that? Melanie's our friend. One of our best friends."

"Yeah, I get that." He blew on the brew and took a sip.

"We were the ones who made the discovery, who came to some pretty good conclusions that you can't ignore."

"Like we think Melanie was specifically targeted," Alex added.

"We don't know that," Mitch replied.

Becca raised an eyebrow. "Oh? You think casual thieves would know about her need to take heart medication? Look. I'm a cop. Homicide detective with the San Antonio PD. I've been around law enforcement for over ten years, and I know enough to say that this whole situation stinks. If you're not going to give us any help here, then I'll gladly talk with Esteban Romero again. He was very helpful yesterday."

Mitch remained silent as he stared her down.

Becca didn't blink.

Then he sighed. "Okay. Okay. If you're going to be that way, then let's try to play nice and talk about this."

Alex glanced at her friend. At her barely perceptible nod, she began squirming a little. "Um, Special Agent Gordon, where's the restroom? I have to go. Sorry. Late lunch and too much water."

"Oh, uh, out in the hall." He glanced at his computer. "To the left, and then to the right."

"Thanks." Alex flashed a bright smile. "I'll be back in a few."

Alex located the restroom and slipped inside. A few moments later, she poked her head out the door. She knew they were on the second floor, but she didn't know where Jabir's office was. She solved that problem pretty quickly by wandering down the hall as if she were lost.

An employee stopped. "May I help you?"

In Spanish, she blurted, "I had to go to the restroom, but I got lost trying to get back to where I was."

The woman smiled. "It happens all of the time. Who were you visiting?"

"Oh." Alex grinned. "Jabir al-Omri. He's doing my visa for me."

"Boy, you really did wander off the reservation. Cross the mezzanine. Then turn right and then left. Third office on your left."

"Thank you."

The woman shrugged. "I work a few doors down from him. When he's in, that is. I'm headed sort of in that direction."

"Do you know him?" Alex asked.

"In passing." The woman offered a brief, tense smile. "He's here with DHS, but he's not here too, if you get my drift."

Alex tucked away that nugget of information for future reference.

They entered the mezzanine, and the woman pointed to a hall. "That's where you go. Right and then left."

Alex continued on her way. She traversed the mezzanine. Then, she muttered under her breath, "Turn right. Then left."

The third office on the left was dark. The woman's words came rushing back to her. Without wasting another moment, Alex tried the knob. Unlocked. She slipped inside, then winced as the motion sensor turned on the light. Somehow, she needed to cut that light off. She opened the top right drawer, which had been the drawer when Jabir was at Unit 28 where he'd kept all things office.

Bingo.

Alex nabbed a bit of scotch tape, tore a corner from a sticky note, and taped it over the sensor. Then she switched the light off. It stayed dark. For a moment, she stood there, her heart hammering in her chest, as she heard someone approach. They passed the office without even noticing her presence.

Good. Her ruse had worked.

She glanced down at the papers sitting on the chair. They seemed to be documents asking for comment. She set those on the blotter, sat down, and began trying drawers. Only the top drawers were open. The two drawers where he kept files were locked. She surveyed his desk. Unlike his workstation when he'd been at Unit 28, no photographs littered the desk and bulletin board. No college pennants. No screensaver full of pictures of his mother and friends. Instead, US Embassy Panama scrolled across the screen in glowing red letters.

Her eyes narrowed.

A sticky note posted to the speaker bar across the bottom of the monitor caught her attention.

Alex lifted it and read the neat, cursive writing. *Jabir, it has come to my attention that you have not been putting in hours considered to be fulltime. Please come to my office and discuss this with me. Karen.*

Alex smirked. Her mind flew back to the woman's offhand remark.

Slacker.

Then she replaced the papers on the chair, ripped the paper off the sensor, and leaned against the wall.

Did the lack of hours onsite mean he was up to something else? Possibly.

She'd have to wait to find out.

Voices in the hall shot a bolt of adrenaline through her. One of them was Jabir, and he joked with someone. Someone vaguely familiar. One of the Marines from the night before, maybe? She couldn't be sure.

Jabir's words became clear. "You bet. Hey, on Monday after work, let's shoot some hoops."

"Will do, brother. Later, man."

"Yeah. I'll…" They faded away as he turned into his office. He froze. "Alex?"

Alex seated herself on the edge of the desk and primly crossed one leg over the other.

"Well, hello, Jabir. It's been a long time," she drawled in her finest southern accent. She offered a smile tinged with poison.

"What are you doing here?" He dropped his satchel onto the desk.

"Waiting for you."

"May I ask why?"

She stood, dropped the smile, and glared at him. "Why are you in Panama?"

Jabir shut the door and leaned against it with arms crossed. "Have you ever considered that DHS assigned me here? They were short on visa reviewers, so they asked me to come down and help out on temporary assignment."

She appraised him for a moment. "You're not with Unit 28?"

He shrugged and continued to his desk.

"What's that supposed to mean?" Her eyes narrowed. "I don't believe you sometimes."

Alex resumed her perch on the edge of the desk like she'd done when they'd worked together. "You're a native Arabic speaker and one with a solid grip on the Saudi dialect. For every native Arabic speaker, there's something like ten native Spanish speakers, and thanks for your knowledge of Saudi dialect, I'd say that's more like a hundred native Spanish speakers per someone with your talents. So it befuddles me why you're down here."

"Got me." He tossed the papers from his chair onto the blotter and sat down. "Sorry to be so brash, but I've got work to do." His fingers tapped on the keyboard as he logged into the system.

Alex caught his wrist, making him stop. "My friend, who we were supposed to meet in Costa Rica, was kidnapped. You understand what I'm saying? And you're down here at the same time, which leads me to believe that you're somehow involved."

Jabir only shook her off and cocked an eyebrow at her conclusion.

Her frustration mounted. Tears filled her eyes. "You know something? I think you don't care." One escaped the corner of her eye and slid down her cheek. "Melanie is probably in mortal danger, and the only thing you seem to care about is work. When you're here, that is."

That earned a twitch in his jaw. "What's that supposed to mean?"

"I saw that note from your supervisor. What's her name? Karen?"

"That's none of your business. Look, I've got to get some stuff done since I'm obviously a little behind. Maybe we can get together later." Jabir entered another password.

Alex stood there, her fists clenching. Her mind raced. He seemed unshakable, as if anything she threw at him wouldn't stick. Except for maybe one thing. It was a long shot, but maybe it would work.

She resumed her seat on the edge of the desk.

Jabir squinted at the screen and rubbed the day-old stubble on his jaw.

Alex leaned forward. In a low voice, she asked, "What were you doing at the hotel the night of Melanie's disappearance?"

Jabir's gaze flicked to her. Those dark depths remained blank. "Huh? I'm not following you."

"Hotel Panama?"

He shrugged. "Sometimes I go there for a drink. Lots of people from the embassy do since it's got one of the nicest bars in town."

"And Monday?"

"You know that's a long time for guy memory."

"Oh, no need to worry. You see, the hotel's got evidence you were there. You were followed on video the entire time, from when you bellied up to the bar beside Melanie to when you stepped off the elevator on the fifth floor." She stared him down, noting with satisfaction at how he'd stilled, his fingers frozen over the keyboard. "Oh, and by the way, that tape now resides with the police. Since the FBI is coordinating investigations with them, I'm sure it's just a matter of time before Special Agent Gordon receives it."

"Alex—"

"Have fun explaining that one to Special Agent Gordon, especially why you deliberately kept the left side of your face away from the camera." With that, she rose and opened the door to leave.

"Alex, wait!"

A satisfied smile crept across her face. Finally, she'd rattled him.

"Stop, will you?" His words came from behind her.

She turned and examined his face.

He'd stood, and now, he regarded her with dark eyes wide, almost pleading.

"Why should I?"

"Because we need to talk. Please," he softly added. "Hear me out."

"Okay." She shut the door and leaned against it.

"You mind sitting down?"

"I'm fine right here."

Jabir sighed, seated himself, and crossed his arms. "Okay. Yes, you were right. I was deliberately in the bar with Melanie."

"Why?"

"Do you know what Melanie does?"

"She's a corporate lawyer who works for a legal and accounting firm. She does lots of things from settling disputes to real estate transactions."

"Right. She does real estate transactions. And one of her clients is a shipping firm called Kamil International. In February, we received information that Kamil International, more specifically, Samir Kamil, their general counsel, was desirous of purchasing a property here in Panama City. It caught our attention because Samir Kamil has been rumored to be mixing it up with some not-so-nice types."

"You came down here for that?"

"Yeah. DHS wanted to know why Samir was interested in the property. I did some research and conducted a survey of it myself. Then I was assigned down here until the closing occurs."

"Why is Samir interested in it?"

"I was wondering the same thing." Jabir shifted in his chair. "Honestly, it's not much to look at. Then it clicked into place when we discovered that Samir's connection with Jihad of Light was stronger than we'd anticipated. You know the group, right?"

"I know the name. But that's all since I don't work for Unit 28 anymore."

Jabir continued, "It makes sense from JOL's point of view. It's a nondescript property. They could occupy it, and most people either wouldn't know or wouldn't care. It has perfect facilities to offload goods and people, and it's in such deplorable condition that no one would ever think that anyone occupied it."

Alex pulled over a chair and perched on the edge. "Why not just scuttle the deal?"

"Because of Samir's involvement. It's most likely a lot more than just being their contact to buy a piece of dilapidated property. We suspect he's much more involved. We want to talk with him. Doing a snatch in Beirut was too dangerous, so we decided to do it here in Panama."

"Melanie would never recommend the purchase of the property if it was in deplorable condition."

"Oh, I agree. For most transactions, her firm uses attorneys from a local office to do everything that requires an onsite presence, including the walkthrough. We found out who was doing the legwork on this property. It didn't take long to figure out how to get him to fake pictures for us and paint a positive picture that Samir fed to Melanie."

Alex shook her head in disgust.

Jabir grinned. "Oh, come on. It's not like you never did anything like that when you were with Unit 28."

"Maybe I've been out of things too long."

Jabir leaned forward on his elbows. "We'd planned for our local guy to do the final walkthrough, but for some reason, Melanie's boss decided to send her instead. She took care of the contract and came down to do that the day before her vacation. She planned to return to seal the deal afterward."

"Why'd you show up at the bar?" Alex scooted her chair closer and rested her elbows on the desk.

"I wanted to gain an understanding of her reaction to the property. And it was like we thought. She busted us for doctoring the photos. She didn't say as much, but I knew enough to glean from context what she was saying."

"And you were set up in a hotel room on the fifth floor?"

"I was staying there to be close to her. I knew we needed to regroup. Then the fire alarm went off, and then the next thing we heard was that some woman and her friends were concerned because Melanie never showed in San José."

"Who is we?"

"My comrades."

"Who are?"

"Sorry. No clearance means no more information. I probably shouldn't have told you as much as I did."

She scowled. "What are your theories?"

"None that I can share."

"Jabir, look. You need to give me something here."

"Why?"

"We know someone did some research on her, enough to realize she has a heart condition." Alex watched his face for further signs of reaction.

Nothing.

"And?"

"They took her medication. It's obvious from what they didn't take that it wasn't a burglary gone bad."

"What didn't they take?"

"Her engagement ring. The diamond in that thing is huge. Diamond necklace. Technological goodies like her tablet, laptop, and camera."

Jabir assessed her for a moment through narrowed eyes. Then he broke his gaze and pulled the sticky note from the sound bar. "Okay. I'll give you one more thing. My mission changed to trying to figure out where JOL is holding her." Jabir lowered his gaze to the blotter in front of him. He smoothed the top of the sticky note so it stuck. "It's been hard. Narco traffickers are all over the place here, and it's been difficult to sort out the trash from treasure when it comes to the information we're receiving."

Alex sighed and hung her head.

"Do you believe me?"

She raised it. "Do I have a choice?"

"I don't know. You tell me."

Slowly, she nodded. "Yeah. I do. But why haven't you contacted the police?"

"You're asking me that?" Jabir cocked his head. "You *are* out of practice. I don't think the Panamanians would like us conducting an operation on their turf. We wanted to keep this on the down-low."

"We kind of blew that up, didn't we?" Alex swallowed hard.

"Not necessarily. It may not seem like it, but I care about your friend." Jabir leaned closer.

For some reason, Alex found herself doing the same so their faces were inches apart. "Oh?"

"I care about her because I care about you," he softly added. Those brown depths were deep, like she could drown in his reassurances if she let herself.

His words sailed into her soul and struck somewhere deep in her heart. No, she didn't want to think about four years ago. Not now. The moment she started thinking about it, the pain would come, pain she thought she'd vanquished.

Jabir lowered his gaze and placed his hand on her arm, startling her so much that she knocked over the pen holder. He righted it and murmured, "Alex, can we...can we perhaps talk about what happened? Please?"

She bit her lip. Hot tears filled her eyes as memories from four years before stung afresh.

How Jabir had said goodbye to her after bringing Rocky, her coonhound mutt, as a way to help her look beyond herself.

How she'd desperately dialed his number an unknown amount of times the afternoon after she'd been publicly fired.

How she'd talked with Tiny, only to have him reveal that Jabir had left on a long-term assignment without saying goodbye to her.

"I—I—"

"Look." Jabir sighed and withdrew a little. "I know you want me to go and clear the air with Mitch—Special Agent Gordon. If I do that, can we go somewhere afterward? Just the two of us to talk?"

Slowly, Alex nodded. "All right."

He smiled, and Alex thought she saw tears pooling in his eyes. "Thanks."

He rose, came around the desk, and stepped to the door. He put his hand on the knob to open it but turned. "Please know I do have Melanie's best interests at heart."

For some reason, she had to admit that he was right. "I know."

"Good." He opened the door and stepped aside for her to lead the way. "I promise we'll get to the bottom of this."

26

"What were you thinking? Are you nuts? You mean you held out on me?" Mitch's questions whistled around Jabir like shells seeking a target.

Jabir wanted nothing more than to take cover. "I had no choice. You understand that, right?"

"What? Classified? For Your Eyes Only? We discuss things like that in our weekly security status meetings, you know."

"Yeah, I know."

"And why haven't you been coming?" The FBI agent almost vibrated like he'd had too many cups of coffee.

"How many cups of coffee have you had today?"

"Four, okay? I don't see what that has to do with anything."

Jabir cast a glance at Alex. She smirked at him, clearly enjoying watching him deal with a Type-A-plus personality.

"If you'd *told* me, we could have handled this quietly."

"And like I've said, I didn't have a choice on the matter. We were to have radio silence, and that included not reading the local embassy personnel into this operation. Now, can we leave it at that?"

"What am I going to do? DHS operating here without my knowledge? Panamanian police suspicious? What's the ambassador going to say? Great.

This is just great." Mitch swept a hand through his hair, making it stand up in dark spikes. He straightened his tie and cleared his throat.

Jabir blew out a sigh. "We've got it under control on our end," he lied. "I'd suggest that you leave it be. Talk with Detective Romero and stall him. I'm working on some leads, and with any luck, we'll find Melanie."

Again, he glanced at Alex. Her eyes had narrowed as if she doubted him.

And Becca? She stared at him as if she saw right through the smokescreen he'd desperately concocted to sidetrack Mitch.

"Okay, fine." Mitch shook his head. "I'll do what I can to convince Detective Romero not to worry with the video. But you've got until Monday, and that's it."

"I hear you." Jabir held up his hands. "Thanks."

"Well, I hate to run, but there's that formal function here tonight, and I need to get home so I can take care of some stuff. You going?"

"Nope. Other plans." He offered his best smile. "Well, thanks."

Jabir rose, leading the charge to escape. They stepped into the hallway. Behind him, Alex murmured to Becca. Turning, he noticed how Alex slipped Becca some keys. He slowed.

Alex squared her shoulders. "If you can take me back to the hotel when we're done, I'll go."

"Oh, that's easy." He led the way down the stairs from the mezzanine to the main lobby and watched as Becca and Alex continued conferring.

Jabir's mind raged. He worked in a world where lies based on half-truths were better than outright lies. That had worked so far. The story he'd fed to Alex was a half-truth. Instead, he was working for the CIA on a mission where they had Melanie in their hands. He'd confessed not knowing where Melanie was, when, in fact, he knew—

"Jabir!" Alex's voice cut into his thoughts. She stood there, one hand on her hip, her sandaled foot tapping impatiently. Becca grinned at him.

He flushed when he realized she must have called his name more than once. "Sorry. I was thinking."

Oh, yeah. I was thinking. I was thinking about how to keep my butt out of a Panamanian jail.

He shook his head to dispel that thought.

"I figured." Alex smiled, but it didn't reach her eyes. "Where are we headed?"

"To this restaurant I found. It's out of town a bit but on the ocean. I know it's mid-afternoon, but we could at least have a drink or something." He led the way back upstairs to his office so he could log off.

"You're not going to talk to your supervisor about being a slacker employee?"

"Not right now. Got to keep up the image, you know." He picked up a helmet. "Here."

"What about you?"

"I'll be fine. Let's go." He led her down the hall, and within minutes they were in the employee parking lot. He climbed onto the motorcycle first, and she swung behind him. He started the engine.

As they pulled through the gate and onto the street, George waved from the guardhouse. They headed into the city. Thanks to the way he sat on the motorcycle, Alex had to lean into him and wrap her arms around his waist to hold on. Not that he minded.

Not at all.

Alex was close.

Closer than he'd dreamed two years ago when he'd received the returned letter. He couldn't—no, wouldn't—let this opportunity pass.

The city faded away, the jungle marching up to the edge of the pavement in a blaze of Technicolor green. He delighted in watching the macaws swoop into and out of the trees. Here and there, luscious tropical blooms provided sharp relief to the green as they wove along a black ribbon of highway toward their destination. Combined with Alex's touch, the cacophony of color and the warm breeze sent goose bumps up and down his arms.

The main road curved inland. They took a two-lane road toward the coast and followed it. Thanks to the way it hugged the shoreline, the jungle parted enough to show tantalizing peeks of calm water.

A cinderblock building next to the water came into view. He pulled to the side and led Alex to the back where tables sat both in the open and under a portico. Thanks to the time of day, only a few patrons occupied the bar.

"Table for two?" the hostess asked in Spanish.

"Two. Thanks," Jabir replied in the same language. "Señorita, could we have that table under the tree?" He nodded toward a small bistro table sitting next to the parking lot under the low, spreading limbs of a banyan tree. There, he knew they'd have absolute privacy.

"What will you have? Just drinks?"

"A Coke for me," Alex said before Jabir could open his mouth.

"And for you, sir?"

"The same. Thanks." Jabir held the chair for Alex before settling on one across from her. He added in English, "It's nice to get out of the city."

"Agreed. Do you manage that often?"

"Sometimes." Jabir cleared his throat, not wanting to talk about how he'd found this place while scoping out potential safe houses where they could hold Samir—or Melanie.

The waitress saved them by bringing out some icy cold drinks. "Your drinks. And please, if you so desire anything else, let me know."

"Thanks." Jabir smiled at her.

Alex took a sip of her drink and sighed. "How'd you find this place?"

"It was on one of my trips out of the city. I was exploring." He inwardly grimaced. "Anyway, I kind of stumbled upon it, happened to be hungry, and decided to go ahead and grab a bite. They won me over."

"That's nice." Alex returned her gaze to the water.

The ocean sparkled before them, and the breeze made the shadows over them dance in time with the tree's leaves.

Seconds stretched into minutes as Jabir wondered how to broach the topic. He rehearsed lines in his head.

Alex, I'm sorry for the way I ran off four years ago. It was a hard time for both of us.

Too trite. She'd scorn him.

I was a jerk. I'm sorry.

Too humble. She'd see it as false humility.

I'm sorry. I realize that I should have stayed by your side. I was wrong to leave you when I knew you needed me most.

Too prepared.

Finally, he blurted, "I like your haircut."

Way to go, Jabir.

He wanted to kick himself.

Her hand shot up to the ends of her bob. "You do?"

"Yeah, I do. It's very becoming on you. When did you cut it?"

"Four years ago right after I returned to Weatherly."

"Why?"

Sadness pinched her features. "I knew you liked long hair. I mean, you told me so yourself."

Having remembered the times he complimented her on her glossy, thick, dark brown locks, he nodded.

"I cut it to get back at you. Twisted, huh?" A smile crossed her face and faded. She toyed with her straw wrapper.

Jabir swallowed hard. Fear clamped his mouth shut almost as much as wire would have. He observed her.

She sat back in her chair, crossing her arms and legs, almost as if she wanted to shield herself from whatever he might say.

The waitress zoomed in, brought them fresh drinks, and scurried back to the shelter of the portico.

Lord, give me the words. Help me to say what I need to say without hurting her more. Please!

He leaned forward and took another sip of his drink, followed by a deep breath. "Alex, I wanted to…I wanted…no, I owe you a huge apology. A *huge* apology for what happened four years ago. I was wrong, and it took a returned letter from you for me to realize just how wrong I was."

"You *hurt* me." She stared hard at him for a moment. Then she looked away, blinking fast as her eyes filled.

"I know." Jabir swallowed hard as memories from that horrible month four years ago surfaced. "After everything happened—I didn't know how to handle things. We were under fire. Not literally, of course, but

225

figuratively. I had a hard time processing everything. When an out came, I took it, if only to get from underneath all of the stress."

"You left me to suffer by myself." She glared at him. Then she scooted to the edge of her chair and leaned forward so her elbows rested on the table. "Do you understand how much I suffered? Do you?"

He couldn't answer that, so he kept silent.

"It was awful. You were there when I began my physical recovery, but what about afterward? What about then? After DHS hung me out to dry? Tiny tried to save me, but he couldn't. He even offered to resign or retire early.

"You got to keep your job. Your pride. Your life as you knew it. And me? I lost everything. Everything! It took me a full year to completely recover from my injuries, and in the span of one press conference, I lost my job. My future. My best friend.

"Who thought only of himself."

Jabir swallowed hard.

Every word she'd said was true.

Alex took another sip of her drink, and it shook as she set it on the metal table with a loud clunk. "I didn't have direction anymore, so I drifted a bit. I didn't know how to process anything. When Eric offered to take me to Vegas for the weekend to shake the blues, it sounded like a good idea. And after I drank myself silly that Saturday night, getting hitched to him at an all-night Elvis chapel seemed even better."

Jabir lowered his gaze. If he'd been there—if he'd been more of a man and faced everything—perhaps he could have spared her a lot of pain.

She laughed, but it was without humor. "Imagine Mom's and Dad's surprise when I showed up after my weekend and announced to them that I was moving down to Woodbridge to live with Eric because we'd eloped. I think it took Mom a bit longer than Dad to have it sink in. I could tell she was really upset, but I didn't care. I thought I was right. Hah! Was I ever wrong."

She swiped at a tear and touched the spot where her wedding band must have rested. "It took only three months for him to start running around on me. We had it out, and I told him I was leaving. He didn't even have the grace to help me pack. He didn't protest when I filed for divorce."

"Alex—"

She rambled on as if she were unburdening herself. "After that? I got depressed. Really depressed. I stopped eating. Stopped working out. Essentially stopped taking care of myself. Everything I knew was poison. Mom finally convinced me that moving back to Weatherly was a good idea, like maybe a change in scenery would help.

"It took some doing, but when Diana, who Josh had contracted with to renovate his house, offered to hire me, I couldn't say no. I moved. And I vowed to forget you." She lowered her face, her shoulders trembling as she wiped at her tears. More slid down her cheeks, and when she met his gaze, he noticed how her red eyes made the sea green in them almost glow. "I got so angry when I got your letter. How dare you act as if nothing happened when *everything* happened? How dare you?"

Jabir's heart pounded as he listened. Seconds ticked into a minute. Finally, he reached out and cupped her chin. He brushed away her tears with his thumb.

"Alex, I'm sorry." He swallowed hard, surprised at the way the rush of emotion choked his voice. "I'm so very sorry. I realize…" The lump in his throat made him stop speaking. "I realize how I was selfish. I was foolish not to stay by your side, especially when everyone, including Tiny, advised me to do so. I hurt you. I hurt Mama. I even hurt your parents. It took getting the returned letter and a long conversation with your mother and father for me to realize that."

He took her hand in both of his and rubbed his thumbs across her palm. "Ever since I got that letter back unopened, I prayed. I prayed for a chance to see you again. To be able to explain to you what had happened. I promised God that if I saw you again, I'd apologize and set things right. I guess He wanted that to happen as well. Will you forgive me? Please?"

Alex's mouth pressed into a thin line. She jerked her hand away, turned her head, and again stared at the ocean.

Her chin trembled.

Jabir's heart pounded.

Lord, please. Please. Please!

Softly, he added, "I'd like to try another friendship with you. I know…I know things won't be the same. They can never go back to the way they were before the mission. We're way past innocence now."

"I forgive you," she said so softly that at first her words were barely a whisper above the rustle of the banyan tree's leaves. She took a deep, shuddering breath. "But I'm not sure I trust you."

More silence followed.

She rose, swiped at her tears, and rushed toward the restroom.

Jabir slowly released his sigh and stared after her.

1545 hours Central Daylight Time, east of Panama City, Panama

Hashim placed the crosshairs squarely on the man's head and pressed the button. The camera clicked as he noted the way Alex fled to the building. The man slouched in the metal chair, his arms folded across his chest, his head hung. Hashim recorded two more images and lowered the camera. "Who is this man?"

"He's obviously friends with Alex." Tarek gazed at him through a pair of binoculars.

"It seems like he wants it to be more, but she doesn't." Hashim raised the camera again.

Alex emerged, but her hunched shoulders and crossed arms screamed her lack of trust.

"That's interesting to know." Hashim finally lowered the camera, set it aside, and started the engine. "I've seen enough."

He eased onto the asphalt and turned around in the parking lot of the grocery store across the road.

"How can we work this to our advantage?" Tarek asked.

In Hashim's mind, an idea snapped into place. "We'll find out."

He picked up his cellphone and dialed Ed. When the CIA agent came onto the line, he said, "A young man is with Alex. Do you know who he is?"

"Describe him."

Hashim did.

Ed chuckled. "He's one of my operatives and apparently a good friend of Alex's. His name's Jabir al-Omri, and he's the hand-me-down from DHS I was talking about."

An idea germinated in Hashim's mind and flourished. "Set up a meeting. Tell him the game is up, and that you understand how things have gone bad. He's to bring a squad up there to rescue Melanie. But instead, you're to take out your men. We'll take Melanie off your hands and also kidnap Alex's friends."

"And what about me?" Ed asked.

Hashim grinned. "You're one of us, are you not? You call us when you've completed your task, and we join you. Until then."

He hung up.

"Why don't we kidnap Alex?" Tarek asked as the first signs of the city began appearing.

"We try that first. But if we don't succeed, we take away options for her. She loves her friends, yes? After all, their loyalty to one another is admirable." Hashim stared out the window as he considered his plan. It would work.

Hit them hard.

Hit them fast.

Leave Alex with no options.

"We need to divide the men. We know where they are staying. Most likely, they'll separate since it seems that Ellie is more timid than her friend, Becca. You catch her at the hotel. I assume Becca and Alex will be clamoring to be a part of whatever rescue Jabir sets up. We'll catch them up at the house. But in case the two of them separate, then Ed can be of assistance to us."

Tarek nodded.

Hashim fell silent as his mind raced to formulate the plan.

Soon, Alex would be in his hands.

Then she'd pay for humiliating him.

27

"Ed, hey." Jabir rested his elbows on the table.

"Jabir." His boss's voice came across strong and clear. "Where are you?"

"Out with a friend. I'm headed back at five."

"Don't bother."

"What?" Surprised, Jabir frowned.

"I'm in town. I had to talk to my mom, and we needed supplies."

"Is she okay?"

Ed sighed. "Yeah. Just getting old. Bothers me, you know?"

"I'm sure."

"We need to meet in our normal spot."

Jabir winced.

"Okay." He glanced at his watch. "I can be there at four thirty."

"That works. I'll text you about where I'll be."

"Thanks." Jabir dropped his phone into his shirt pocket as he noticed Alex sliding into her chair.

She must have splashed water on her face since there were faint mascara smears around her eyes. The redness had receded, and the lines between them had vanished.

"Alex?"

"I'm fine." She sighed and sipped her drink. Her eyes met his. "I wish you could understand how hard this has been for me to talk with you. Right now, I'd like nothing more than to hold on to my anger and resentment toward you and walk away."

His hand clenched around his glass.

"But I know I can't." She began shredding her napkin. "Can you bear with me on this? I'm having a hard time processing it."

"I can."

"Thanks." Her shoulders rose and fell in a little shrug. "I know that God calls us to forgive. Maybe there's still a shred of my faith left."

The sacred space in his heart reserved for her affection tightened. He wanted to stay there, to explore her statement, to ask how her tailspin had impacted something she'd valued so highly.

Jabir glanced at his watch. No more time. "I wish I could stay. I really do. I want to stay and talk not just for minutes but for hours."

"Would you…would you want to come to the hotel tonight?"

"Becca and Ellie won't kill me?" Jabir pulled out his wallet and tossed down a few bills.

Finally, a genuine smile crossed her face. "No. So long as they know you're on our side."

If things spin out of control like I fear, then you won't be thinking that.

He managed a weak smile. "Maybe I will. And if you're lucky, I might have some information."

The smile turned to a grin. "If *I'm* lucky? What about if *you're* lucky?"

"Ah, true. C'mon. Let me get you back to the hotel." With that, they wandered to the motorcycle.

Alex once more curled her arms around him. He forced himself to focus on the road, lest they wind up a wet spot on the highway because he was too distracted by her presence.

God, I know You're a God of second chances. Are You granting that to me? To us?

Jabir stopped under the hotel's portico and ignored the stare from the bellman.

Alex pulled off her helmet, mussing her hair. She dismounted, handed it to him, and smoothed her short locks. "Thanks for being patient with me. It's been a long, hard road, and quite honestly, I did miss you. Very much so. Hearing your apology has helped enormously."

"Thanks."

"I'm sorry if I was a jerk earlier. It's just that Melanie is one of my closest and oldest friends. When everything happened, she was a lifeline for me. She kept me sane, and losing her would devastate me."

"I know." Jabir chilled a little. "Let me get your number."

She recited it, and he entered it into his cellphone.

"I'll call you later."

"Sure. Jabir, thanks." With that, she headed toward the doors, which swished open. Before entering the relative coolness of the hotel, she turned and smiled one last time.

Jabir managed a weak one of his own. Oh, boy.

Things had gotten complicated.

Too complicated.

1630 hours Central Daylight Time, Panama City, Panama

Jabir checked around him for tails as he approached the theater. Nothing. No signs of Mitch and no signs that someone in the Panamanian National Police had followed him. No embassy personnel either. Then again, no one from his embassy job would dare be seen at a theater like this, at least not during the daylight hours.

Only Jabir.

He cringed as he bought a ticket from the bored attendant who leaned on his elbow and smoked a cigarette.

With a deep breath, Jabir opened the door and stepped into a lobby smelling of stale popcorn, butter, and dirt. The place may have been grand in its heyday, but now, the carpet was a little too worn, the concession stand too antiquated with its gold paint down to bare wood in places. Posters on the walls advertised the porn films that would be coming soon.

Jabir glanced at the text message Ed had sent.

Theater 2.

Jabir glanced at the concession attendant. The man seemed more interested in looking at his phone than ensuring that patrons went to the correct theater.

Jabir squared his shoulders and strolled down the hall leading to his meeting spot. He pulled open the door and cringed at the music playing.

The warm, moist air in the theater that heightened the stench of cigarettes and something else he couldn't or didn't want to place made him recoil. It clung to his skin and tried to permeate his soul.

With one hand shielding his eyes from the screen, he made his way up the aisle and found Ed slouched in the last row. His hand dipped into a bucket of popcorn as he stared at the movie.

They were alone.

Jabir settled beside him and averted his gaze to his lap. Anything to avoid the images on the screen. "What's going on? Why don't you want me up at the house?"

"Change in plans."

"Okay," Jabir drawled. His curiosity rose.

"You're so funny." Ed chuckled.

"Why is that?"

"You never watched porn?"

Jabir wished he could tune out the noises emanating from the screen. "Sure, in college."

Before I came to know Christ and when I was angry at my father.

Jabir wanted to jump up and leave, and he found his feet actually shifting to do just that. "What's up?"

"I've given your concerns a lot of thought."

Finally feeling justified, Jabir asked, "And?"

"You're right. It's getting too risky to continue."

"Especially since they got me on video cozying up to Melanie," Jabir muttered. He filled Ed in on what had transpired, first with Alex and then with Mitch. He left out his conversation with Alex at the restaurant.

Ed nodded. "Thanks for letting me know. It seems like it's only a matter of time before they figure things out. Okay. It's a bust. Karesh, al-Rashid, Rosen, and I will beat feet and leave Melanie there. You know. Kidnappers get scared and leave the hostage."

"How would I start things?" Jabir began wrestling with the idea in his mind.

"Call up your FBI pal. What's his name again?"

"Mitch. Special Agent Gordon. What got you thinking?" A tornado of confusion swirled inside Jabir.

Ed ignored his question. "Call up this Special Agent Gordon, tell him you've got a lead. Then help organize the rescue."

"Good, because I need to stay close to Alex." Jabir shifted in his seat.

"So which is she?" Ed's gaze flicked to the screen.

Jabir frowned. "What?"

"Is she a friend or enemy? Or something else?" Ed grinned, obviously enjoying Jabir's discomfort.

"I'm not sure I follow."

Ed shrugged. "Just echoing what you said earlier, son. Anyway, since your assignment ends at the end of the month, you can keep an eye on Melanie's rescue." He set the popcorn bucket on the floor. "I guess this is it. Good work. I'll take it from here. Nice working with you."

He extended his hand.

Baffled, Jabir automatically responded.

Ed shook it. "I'll tell Tiny to give you a commendation for your assistance."

With that, he rose and disappeared from the theater.

Jabir waited another eternity longer as he tried to figure out what had changed Ed's mind.

Then, as if he were escaping a doctor's office after an exam, he fled into the humid afternoon.

2100 hours Central Daylight Time, Panama City, Panama

"I want to be more than a mere observer," Alex muttered as she carried the empty plates to the kitchen. Cups, napkins, and a pizza box from that night's meeting to plan the rescue remained on the table.

Becca gathered the cups and filled the top rack. "Yeah, me too. I'm up on my shooting, and I've even been competing."

Alex added some detergent and leaned against the counter after starting the dishwasher. "I'm up on my shooting as well since Jake takes me to the range when he goes."

"I know." Jabir collected the pizza boxes and opened the door to leave them in the hallway. "I'd like to be the first in as well, but this is their territory. Not ours. We'd do the same thing to them."

Alex sighed, hating to admit he was right. Once she'd wiped down the counter, she settled onto the couch and tucked a pillow to herself. "I trust Esteban Romero one hundred percent on this. If he says his boys are good, I believe him."

Becca joined her and picked up the remote. "When he and I were talking yesterday, he said he'd always wanted to be a cop. I think his daddy was one. It seems like he's done some of the same training I have. Matter of fact, he was at the same conference I was when I met Rodrigo."

"No way." Alex grinned. "How cool is that?"

"It's a small world. Hey, where's Ellie?" Becca suddenly asked.

"I think she went to the bedroom."

"Is she okay?" Jabir's voice remained low as he shut off the lights in the kitchen and sat beside Alex.

Becca bit her lip and stared at the closed door leading to the second bedroom. "I don't know. Her way of dealing with conflict is to withdraw."

"I hear you." Alex picked up the placard listing the television channels available. "What time do you want us up again?"

Jabir looped one arm over the back of the couch. "I'll be here at five, so be down front. And be discreet."

Alex grinned. "We're the queens of discrete. Right, Becca?"

"You got that right." Becca glanced at Jabir. Then she hopped up and made a show of stretching that made Alex want to laugh. "I'm pooped, you two. See you in the AM. Jabir, it was good to meet you finally."

"Nice to meet you too." Jabir watched as she strolled into the bedroom.

Alex hugged the pillow tighter and stared at the television. As Jabir began flipping through channels, she thought about all that had transpired that day. Her hard work and patience had paid off. She'd outed Jabir. They'd planned well for the rescue. By this point tomorrow, Melanie would be with them. Maybe they'd stay in Panama City. Or maybe they could recover at least part of their vacation at Playa Flamingo. Regardless, she almost vibrated with an energy she hadn't felt in a while.

Why?

Alex straightened and cocked her head as if trying to listen to that faint echo.

"What's on your mind?" Jabir's question made her blink.

"Huh?"

"You look like you just had an inspirational thought."

It clicked into place. "Tonight was fun."

"Really?"

"Not a dance-the-night-away kind of fun. More like a stimulating kind of fun." She bit her lip as she tried to define her feelings. "It made me remember everything I loved about being in Unit 28. Sure, we'd stay up almost all night planning a mission and beating it into the ground. Knowing our mission, knowing that what we did would save lives, and seeing the lives we saved made it all worth it. As did the comradery. Do you see what I mean?"

Jabir leaned forward, elbows on knees. The pale light of the television reflected off his face. "I do."

"I miss it." There. She'd said it. "I miss that feeling. I miss being with others who have a common purpose."

"You don't feel like that in your work now? Your mom told me you were working with your sister-in-law as a contractor."

"Helping someone choose the perfect design for their house or the perfect paint color doesn't compare to collecting intelligence that will foil a bomb plot." She sighed, her fingers kneading the stuffing of the pillow.

"Don't you like your life in Weatherly?"

"Oh, I do." Alex smiled. "Honestly, I do. Weatherly's home for me now. It took a couple of years, but it's where I belong. With my family. I guess I wish I could have both worlds."

"Maybe God wanted you to be in Weatherly."

Alex shrugged as she thought about where her Bible rested on a high shelf in her study. "Honestly, I haven't touched my Bible in a long time."

Jabir cocked his head. "Do you go to church?"

"Sometimes." They were straying into dangerous territory, a place Alex didn't want to study in depth. She tried deflection. "I wish I had your faith."

Jabir stayed silent.

Her fingers probed faster as she tried to put her tangled thoughts regarding her faith into words. "I remember when we confronted your dad and how afterwards we wound up at that hole-in-the-wall bar around the corner from Mom's and Dad's townhouse. You told me about why you became a Christian."

"Because I couldn't stand the way Papa treated Mama." Jabir bobbed his head. "I do remember. You seemed surprised."

"More like delighted. It was comforting knowing that I had someone as my partner who understood the value of prayer. It made all of those hellacious situations we found ourselves in easier to endure."

"Like when we were trapped in that building in Mexico when the cartels decided to mix it up?"

Alex shuddered as she remembered the way they'd huddled under the thick wooden table of the stone hut while two rival cartels had duked it out with automatic rifles and a few rocket propelled grenades. Caught in the crossfire, their only defense had been prayer. "Yeah. That was something else."

"What happened?"

She stalled. "What happened what?"

"With your faith? You were the one who always inspired me."

"Try life?" Alex hated the way that sounded. "I really don't want to talk about it now."

Jabir stayed quiet and didn't push the issue. They sat in silence, letting the low sounds of the late-night show filled the void. Finally, he sighed and switched off the television. He rose. "I wish I could stay. Honestly, I do, but four is going to come early tomorrow. Mitch won't like it if I'm late."

She followed him to the door, the words she wanted to say so badly tangled somewhere in her heart. Like how, while her physical wounds healed, she couldn't understand why God had let things happen or how she'd exchanged the loneliness brought about by Jabir's abandonment for isolation from God. Sadness gripped her.

Jabir turned. In the dim light, she noticed the gentle smile on his face.

Alex's cheeks warmed. Her heart skittered.

Why?

"Listen." Jabir's words pulled her from her ruminations. "If you want, when things down here are over and I'm up in DC, I'd like to come and visit you in Weatherly."

The flush intensified. "I'd like that. I really would."

Then, her feet got a mind of their own, and she stepped to him.

Jabir wrapped his arms around her.

Alex laid her head against his chest, her eyes tightly shut as sudden tears filled them. "Thank you for pushing past my anger. For persisting and apologizing. It's been hard trusting you again, and your kindness helped that tonight."

He pulled back. "We'll talk about everything later when we have time."

"That's all I could ask for."

"See you at five?" He sent a smile in her direction.

"Five. Be gone with you."

Once he'd left, Alex locked both locks and leaned against the door, her arms crossed. Suddenly, she yearned for everything to be done.

Not just to get Melanie back.

But to explore the overture Jabir had made.

Day 7
Saturday, June 17, 2017

28

Ed's eyes snapped open. For a second, he lay there, shrouded in inky black darkness so complete that he couldn't see his hand when he held it up to illuminate his watch face. The darkness permeated his pores and soul until he felt like he'd become one with it.

His eyes drooped closed.

Outside, the last of the nighttime insects peeped here and there, as if singing a drunken tune brought on by a night of partying. It lulled him into a false sense of security.

A scream sent a dull shock down Ed's spine. He shivered as the horrid sound faded to a low moan and then a gurgle. Foliage rustled and quieted.

A breeze rattled the leaves of the nearby banana trees and hummed through the open screen.

It's time.

Those words, whether from his mind or somewhere else, slithered across his bare skin like the dank, hot breeze stirred by the ceiling fan.

Ed didn't budge.

A puff of air through the screen licked his face.

Do it. Now.

He gritted his teeth.

Ed eased onto his elbow, then all the way upright. It took him only a minute to pull on his clothes.

He reached over.

His hand brushed the cold, hard steel of the Beretta where he'd set it on the nightstand. His fingers curled around the grip, and he knelt beside his duffel.

He located the smooth metal of the silencer's narrow barrel and pulled it out. With quick, precise motions, he attached it to the pistol.

Ed opened his bedroom door.

Blackness blanketed the hallway. At the very end, he noticed the sickly white glow of one of the fluorescent lanterns in the kitchen.

He slipped into the bathroom, shut the door, and felt for the lantern they kept there. It flared to life.

Ed placed the gun on the counter and stared at himself in the mirror. The pale light bleached out his skin and hair, making him look like some twisted spirit.

His lips twitched in a grim smile.

Ed hesitated.

Francesca.

Her face floated before him, and her laughter echoed in his ears.

He knew what he had to do.

He opened the door.

Karesh's tall, lean form loomed over him.

Ed jumped as if stung by the shock of adrenaline that shot through him.

Karesh smothered a yawn with his hand. "Sorry. I didn't mean to startle you. Too much water last night."

"I hear you. I'm done here." Ed surreptitiously stashed his gun at the small of his back and made as if to tuck in his shirt.

He squeezed past his comrade.

Karesh yawned again as he raised the toilet lid.

Ed pivoted so he faced him.

He grabbed the Beretta and whipped it out.

Karesh glanced up.

His eyes widened.

His mouth opened to shout a warning.

Ed leveled the gun and shot him in the forehead.

Karesh stumbled backwards. His hand grasped the shower curtain. He collapsed, partly in the tub and partly on the floor, pulling the rod and curtain down with a loud clatter.

Ed sent another round into his forehead.

Heart pounding, he lowered the gun to his side.

The moist darkness intensified and clung to his skin. A bead of sweat slid from his hairline and trickled down his neck.

He breathed deeply and evenly as he carefully placed each foot on his journey to the kitchen.

Where was al-Rashid?

A movement at the end of the hall increased the pounding of his heart so it thundered in his ears.

Al-Rashid poured himself a cup of coffee and added some creamer. His spoon clinked against ceramic as he stirred.

Ed took another step.

A floorboard creaked.

Al-Rashid glanced up.

Ed's pace increased, and he raised the Beretta.

Al-Rashid hurled the mug at him.

Ed ducked, and it shattered against the wall above him. Hot liquid burned his scalp and neck.

His finger tightened on the trigger.

The Beretta coughed once, and a patch of dark appeared on al-Rashid's chest.

He stumbled against the stove. Al-Rashid tried to catch himself on something—anything—to stay upright. The only purchase he found was the handle of a saucepan.

It clanged to the floor.

Al-Rashid slid after it, leaving a streak of blood in an almost black trail along the stove's door. He remained upright for a brief second before slumping onto his side.

He lay still.

Ed crept forward, his finger tightening on the trigger to deliver a final kill shot to al-Rashid's head.

"What's going on?"

Ed whipped around at the shouted question in English from Rosen. His eyes widened.

His friend charged toward him.

In what seemed to be slow motion, Ed brought the gun up and fired. He launched himself toward the table and chairs. His hip hit the seat of a chair. He groaned and tumbled to the floor. His feet caught the chair. It clattered on top of him.

A thud reached him.

Ed turned onto his side.

Dark bloomed on Rosen's neck. He lay on his front, his legs and arms splayed in a manner that told Ed the shot had severed the man's spine. The blood began pooling under his neck in a dark liquid.

A hot jolt blazed down Ed's back.

Ari's gaze met his, accusing him. His mouth worked, but only blood spilled from it.

For the briefest of seconds, Ed hesitated. Then he finished him off with a headshot.

Pain in his shoulder made time jerk back to normal.

Ed groaned. Grasping a chair, he hauled himself upright, first to his knees, then to his feet. Chest heaving, he grasped the table and surveyed the damage.

His shoulder hurt. He rotated it, and the pain lessened. His hip hurt. Yeah, he'd have a bruise there. And his back. He began trembling as the adrenaline drained away.

His comrades? Karesh was dead for sure. Rosen too. And al-Rashid?

Ed stared at him, unable to make himself go and check his pulse. The man hadn't moved, and the stain on his chest had spread.

Ed opted for stepping over his body and heading into the operations room. Two lanterns glowed there, and he noticed al-Rashid's phone resting on the table next to one of the laptops. He picked it up and toggled it on. A code screen appeared. He set it down, then closed each laptop and disconnected them from the router. They'd go with him along with the rest of the equipment and their guns.

Ed paused and listened. On the other side of the thin plywood wall, a chain rattled. The hostage must have heard the shouts and begun pacing. Maybe she thought rescue had come.

He pushed open the door leading to the hostage's room.

She now huddled on the bed, the thin sheet drawn up to her neck. Her eyes flew from his face to his gun. The chain clinked as she drew her knees to her chest and shrank away from him.

A smiled curled Ed's lips.

He shoved the Beretta into his belt at the small of his back and unclipped his personal phone from his waist. He punched in a number.

A smile crossed his face when Hashim answered.

"Come on over. The pool's open."

29

A headache pulsed in her head as Alex peered out the window of the embassy's Ford Escape that Jabir drove. She closed her eyes and rubbed her temples. That didn't help. Neither did the sudden need to find a restroom brought on by drinking two cups of coffee. Strong coffee. Like put-in-three-times-the-needed-amount-of-grains kind of coffee.

"Are you okay?" Becca asked her.

"I hardly slept, I have a headache, and I have to go to the bathroom."

"I hear you." Her friend offered a small smile.

The four-lane highway narrowed to two lanes, a sure indication they were in the middle of nowhere now.

Alex leaned forward and touched Jabir on the shoulder. "Are we on the right track?"

"This is it. What the guy who called it in said." His muscles bunched beneath the cotton fabric of his T-shirt and her fingers. Tension made him sit erect with both hands on the wheel with such force that the veins and tendons bulged in them.

"It makes sense. This area has been used in the past for narco safe houses," Mitch said from the passenger seat. "The Panamanians have been trying to eradicate them for years, but it seems that once they get one, another pops up."

"Like weeds." She shook her head and contemplated the highway ahead of them as they slowed.

Jabir put on his blinker as they approached a turn to the right.

In front of them, a panel van whizzed from the side road into the path of an oncoming truck. The truck's horn blared. Hand gestures followed.

Alex winced at the near-collision.

Becca clapped a hand over her eyes.

A maroon Suburban waited and then safely turned left after the van.

"Yeah. Like weeds." Mitch seemed unfazed by the crazy driving.

"You're sure the tipster was right?" Becca asked from beside her as they wound away from the main highway into the mountains.

"Promise on that one." The words nearly tumbled out of Jabir's mouth.

Alex frowned.

Too fast, even for Jabir in a high state of alert. What was going on with him?

The road wound higher into the jungle, which made her already agitated stomach start a new series of gyrations.

Jabir slowed and pulled to the side of the road. "We're about a half mile from the site. It's probably best to go on foot from here."

"The Panamanians will take point." Mitch slid from the vehicle and stepped to the convoy of Suburbans stopping behind them.

Without hesitation, Alex hopped down and followed him with her gaze. The squad leader had pulled together a dozen men, all clothed alike in jungle camouflage, face paint, and bush hats. They got locked and loaded while listening to final instructions.

Mitch conferred with Esteban. Even now, the FBI agent practically vibrated from the thermos of coffee he'd consumed on the way up.

Jabir came to stand next to her. She sensed rather than felt the touch of his presence. Maybe that was what happened after working so closely with him for four years.

Alex crossed her arms and leaned against the Escape. "I hate being an observer." She kicked at one of the tires.

"Me too, but we are, so gussy up." Jabir handed her an armored vest, which she reluctantly slid over her T-shirt.

Mitch rejoined them. "We're to stay back until Detective Romero gives the all clear."

"Can we have a sidearm?" she asked.

"What?" Mitch stared at her.

Alex shrugged. "I don't like being unarmed out here."

Mitch ran his fingers through his hair, mussing it like he had the day before. "No. You're a foreigner, all right?"

"Fine." She grimaced.

Esteban strode over to them.

She eyed the Glock in the holster at his waist with envy.

"We walk from here," the detective reported. He briefly fixed each of them in his gaze. "Keep with me. Then stay back when I tell you until we assess the situation."

"Roger that." Mitch nodded at the trio as if to emphasize that the others needed to behave.

Alex scowled.

Esteban murmured into the team leader's ear.

Upon the leader's hand signals, the assault team fanned out. They slipped into the jungle, fading into it thanks to their camouflage until they disappeared like ghosts.

Esteban handed them a small radio and whispered, "Channel Nine."

He climbed partially up the hill and went down on one knee at the edge of the pocked road.

The Americans remained at the bottom and huddled together.

Mitch switched to the appropriate frequency and turned the volume up only loud enough so they could catch the whispered conversation between team members.

"No activity," the team lead reported from his forward observation post.

Jabir frowned. "None?"

"Should there be?" Alex asked.

He shrugged. "Maybe a guard?"

She nodded. "They could have gotten wise and abandoned the place."

"That would be nice."

"Why do you say that?"

"Shhh." Mitch glared at them as if their whispered conversation had raised a ruckus at an art gallery.

"Go! Go! Go!"

Alex jumped.

"*Borrar!*" Clear!

She listened as they cleared each room. Then the chatter started too fast for even her seasoned ear to grasp.

Esteban's voice came across the radio. "Mitch, bring everyone up here. Now!"

She glanced at Jabir.

His eyes widened.

He darted toward the building

Taken aback, Alex ran to catch up.

The detective stood on the porch, his mouth pressed in a thin line. "Bodies in the kitchen and bathroom."

Her heart caught in her throat. "Melanie..."

"All male."

Jabir brushed past them and rushed inside.

"No!"

Alex jumped at the anguish in his voice.

She followed him. A room stood in front of her, a bare room save for empty folding tables.

"No. Stephen! Not you. No!" Jabir's voice came from somewhere toward the back of the house.

Alex whipped around and dashed into the kitchen. Her foot hit something, and she tumbled to her hands and knees. Her eyes remained fixated on the body in front of her.

A man with arms and legs bent at awkward angles stared vacantly at her. She gaped at the two ugly holes in his neck and forehead and the pool of dark red liquid that was turning brown under his neck.

Alex whipped around. She'd tripped over another body, this one clad in black cargo pants and an olive T-shirt. He bore a brown stain on his chest.

Becca now knelt beside him. "Hey, this one's alive,"

Alex crawled on her knees to him.

Suddenly, a strong hand gripped her shoulder and shoved her aside. She tumbled backwards.

Jabir fell to his knees next to the man. "Abdel! What happened?"

She pulled herself to a kneeling position beside Jabir.

The man's chest rose and fell in short, frantic breaths.

Jabir grabbed Abdel's hand.

Abdel's mouth moved like he tried to say something.

Alex cringed.

Abdel was dying. He trembled, the shaking extending to where Jabir held on. "Ed."

Jabir's grip tightened. "Ed? What about him? Where is he?"

"He...he's..."

His head sagged to one side. His breath rattled out one last time, and the light faded from his eyes, which remained open.

Jabir started shaking his head. "No. Abdel, no! We'll get you to a hospital. We'll—"

He moved as if to start CPR.

Becca grasped his arm. "He's gone."

Melanie.

Her name crossed Alex's mind. She bolted to her feet, leapt the other body, and tore down the hall.

She ripped open the first door on her left.

A man's body sprawled awkwardly across the rim of a tub, the shower curtain partially covering him like a burial shroud.

She moaned, backed out, and shut the door.

Alex darted toward the end and into a bedroom. No Melanie.

No Melanie in the second bedroom either.

She pushed open the door to the third and rushed inside.

Shock rooted her to the spot. This room had iron bars over the window to the outside and the ones that led to the front room and other bedroom.

Alex whirled and stared at the bed against the wall.

Something that looked like splatters dotted the white sheets.

She knelt for a closer look.

The splatters were crimson fast fading to rust.

Blood.

"Oh, no…" Her pulse thundered in her ears. "Melanie."

She shifted, and her arm came into contact with cold metal. She glanced down. Someone had locked a length of chain to the bedframe. But instead of a person in the shackle, it was empty.

She cringed and put her hand down to propel herself to her feet.

It brushed something.

A cylinder.

Alex grabbed it.

Melanie's bottle of heart medication.

Fear paralyzed Alex. She couldn't move, couldn't make her muscles contract and release so she could rise.

"Alex." Esteban's voice reached her through the fog of her sudden panic. "Alex!"

He bodily lifted her to her feet.

She blinked.

"We need to get outside. This is a crime scene, and a forensics unit is on the way."

Numbly, she let him take her arm and lead her into the gathering dawn. She slid the bottle into a pocket of her cargo pants.

Outside, serenity had morphed into chaos. The strike team leader issued orders to form a perimeter. Mitch was on his phone, pacing and mussing his hair as he talked at a rapid-fire pace to someone. Becca had her arms crossed and wore her own path in the dirt in front of a white Toyota Land Cruiser. Jabir slumped against it, his head in his hands.

Jabir.

Esteban pointed at him. "You! You come with me and show me everything. Now."

What was bothering her? While he was gone, Alex's mind ticked through all she knew.

Jabir had seemed stressed beyond imagination. He knew the layout of the house. He knew those men, knew them well judging from his reaction.

He'd known all along where Melanie was.

Jabir al-Omri had lied to her.

A noise made her glance up.

Jabir preceded the detective through the front door and into the building heat and humidity.

Her pulse thudded out of control. Rage consumed Alex.

"You *liar!*" She charged him.

"What the—" Mitch's words faded into the buzzing filling her head.

She tackled Jabir, earning an oomph as the breath whooshed out of him.

He threw his arms up in an effort to defend himself. Alex drove a hard right at him, which he blocked. Then she threw a hard left uppercut and a right that broke through.

Jabir groaned when it connected with his cheek.

Pain shot through her hand.

Only then did someone yank her back.

She landed hard on her tailbone. A jolt of electricity blazed up her spine.

"Alex, no." Becca hauled her the rest of the way up and kept her in a half nelson.

Alex struggled against her. "I can't believe you. You lied to me. You lied! You knew all along."

"What are you talking about?" Esteban's voice reached her.

Jabir's image shimmered through her tears. "Why, Jabir? Why did you lie to me like that?"

She tried to yank loose.

"Alex, you'll make things worse." Becca attempted to soothe her. Those words poured acid into the wound of her betrayal.

Jabir pulled himself upright so he leaned against the bumper, this time with a red mark on his face where her fist had caught him. "I didn't lie."

"Oh, I'm not sure about that," Becca said.

Jabir braced himself and hung his head.

"I'm *so* not hearing this," Mitch muttered from behind her.

Becca said, "My suggestion is that since I'm not exactly sure if you're for or against us that you get on your knees and put your hands on your head until we can search you. Sorry," she muttered to Esteban. "I got carried away."

"Do as the señora says." Esteban crossed his arms and nodded at Becca.

Jabir placed his hands on his head. With his gaze fixated on the ground, he eased to his knees.

Esteban searched him. "Nothing. He's clean."

"Start talking," Becca ordered.

"The original plan had been for us to snatch Samir Kamil. He was supposed to come over and close on a piece of property in the port of Panama City."

"Who is us?" Becca asked.

"The CIA," he admitted.

"What?" Esteban blurted.

"Oh, great! Just what we needed to hear," Mitch said at the same time.

Alex's mind flew back to the conversation the day before. "But I thought you were working for DHS."

"I'm on loan to the CIA." Jabir kept his hands on his head. "Thanks to someone murdering their native Arabic speakers, they had only three left who weren't under deep cover. At least they did until this morning. Tiny loaned me out to them."

"Who's Tiny?" Mitch asked.

"My former boss," Alex replied. She relaxed, and Becca released her. "I worked with Jabir."

"And what were you to do?" Esteban had pulled out his notepad.

"It's classified."

Alex hissed at that.

Esteban's pen paused above the notepad. When he spoke, the anger burbled beneath the surface of his words. "Señor, let me tell you how this will work. If you're lucky, I will only arrest you and take you to our jail in the city, where we can continue this discussion. If you pull this classified garbage on me, then I'll have no choice but to take this matter to our president, which will, of course, result in an international incident."

"Hey, we can work on this together, okay? Work something—" Worry had Mitch pacing.

"What will it be, Señor?" Esteban raised his voice to override Mitch's.

Slowly, anguish tingeing his words, Jabir outlined the mission and added, "Only something must have gone wrong because Melanie did the walkthrough and presented a negative report."

"Don't you blame her for this!" Again, a rage built inside of Alex.

Before Becca could move, she jumped him.

Off balance, he toppled backward, but this time, he was ready for her. She threw her punches.

He blocked her.

She tried to knee him.

Again, he blocked her.

He jerked to one side.

Because of her grip on his shirt, Alex rolled with him and found herself on her back. Jabir pinned her wrists.

Chest heaving, his glare softened. "I'm not blaming her for this, okay?"

She tried to jerk free, but he only tightened his hold. "I'm not, Alex. Please understand."

How could she? She wouldn't fall for that dark gaze that pleaded for understanding and sympathy.

"Let me up." Alex yanked her wrists, but suddenly, it was like all of her strength had deserted her. She sagged to the ground.

Only then did Jabir loosen his grip.

He remained on his knees and returned his hands to his head. "All I'm saying is that our backup plan was to snatch her. We knew Samir still loved her and would do anything to keep her from harm. And when Farouk, his father, saw the negative report, he gave the thumbs down on the property purchase. Meaning we had to snatch her."

"Which is what happened at the hotel." Trembling overcame Alex, and she found herself rising and staggering to the bumper of the Land Cruiser. She leaned against it.

"Right. Our orders were simply to hold her here until Samir showed up for the closing. Once we grabbed him, we were going to release her. May I lower my hands?"

A terse nod from Esteban gave him that permission.

Jabir lowered them and rubbed his arms. "Only we didn't expect you three to show up. Ed had me keep tabs on you."

"Keep your friends close, your enemies closer, huh?" She stiffened and scowled at him. "You used me. I was nothing more than a source of information."

"Alex, I knew I was running a dangerous game. I did." Jabir gazed at her like everyone else had faded away. "I hated what I had to do. I was telling half-truths."

"You were lying."

"Okay. I was lying, and I knew things were going to spin out of control. Ed didn't think so. But I did."

"Who's Ed?" Mitch demanded.

"Ed DuBois. The team lead for this mission."

"Oh, no!" Mitch's groan barely reached her.

Jabir remained focused on her. "Ed didn't think things were about to blow up, even once I told him about what had happened at the hotel and the embassy. I was confused when he agreed that we needed to release Melanie by making it look like we'd abandoned her here." He swallowed hard and lowered his head for a moment. He gripped the back of his neck.

Alex wondered if he struggled not to cry.

"This wasn't supposed to happen. It wasn't. No one should have died. I was only supposed to lead you here, where Melanie should have been found."

"Who were those men in there?" Esteban demanded.

"My associates." Jabir had begun sweating under the detective's scathing glare.

"Their names?"

"I—"

"We can do this here or at the police station."

Jabir stared at the ground once more, and his shoulders sagged. "The one in the bathroom was Stephen Karesh. The one who was still alive was Abdel al-Rashid. And the other was Ari Rosen. All CIA." Jabir's gaze turned to her. "Alex, I promise. That's all I have."

"Is it? Is it really?" Anguish for Melanie overwhelmed her. Suddenly, Alex realized how tears poured down her cheeks. "How can I trust you?"

He spread his arms, palms up, as if to say, "I don't know."

"Do you know what could happen?" Temper built inside of her. "Do you know what could happen if we don't find her soon?"

Alex reached into her pocket and pulled out the pill bottle. "She could die because she doesn't have her heart medication."

She hurled the pill bottle at him. It hit him in the face, scoring one square in the strike zone.

Jabir cried out. "Ow! Alex!"

She didn't care.

Alex whirled and faced Mitch. "Take me home. Now."

The FBI agent blanched, obviously not wanting to deal with her. "I, uh, need to stay here," Mitch spluttered. "You know. See if I can get some more clues."

Esteban pulled out his cuffs. "Hold out your hands, Jabir."

He shackled Jabir's hands in front of him. "You're going to the station. Jorge."

When his comrade had joined them, he continued, "Drive their Escape to the station and put Jabir in a holding cell by himself."

He handed the cuff keys to Jorge, who dropped them into his shirt pocket. "Mitch, when we get back, you and I are going to continue our chat with him. Then I'll decide which charges fit this crime. Alex, I need to ask you a few more questions. Jorge can take you to the hotel, or you can stay at the station."

She bit her lip. She didn't want to be in the same car with Jabir.

But then again, she didn't want to stick around crime scene either, especially not with the weariness suddenly surging over her.

"I'll go with them." Alex stooped and picked up the pill bottle. Then, she looked daggers at Jabir one last time before turning to go down the hill to the Escape.

Her walk turned into a run as she thought about Jabir's pleading expression.

The traitor.

He could rot in jail for all she cared.

Regardless, when they got back to town, she'd tell him to get out of her life.

Just get out and stay out.

Forever would be soon enough to see him.

30

"Alex, I want to explain things."

"I'm done talking about it."

"Please hear me out."

"Why should I?"

"Because it's important for you to know I lost three friends today."

"I don't care."

"Alex—"

"Can't you be quiet for a change?"

Jabir swallowed hard. He reached up and lowered the visor to look in the small mirror.

Alex sat behind him, and he noticed her narrowed eyes and her mouth in a tight line as she stared out the window.

Misery cloaked him as he thought about her totally justified anger.

No sniffles reached him.

No more tears.

"Melanie could die because of you." A chill filled her low voice.

He stared at his cuffed hands.

She continued, "For as long as I've known her, she's had a heart condition and has to have her medication. If she doesn't take it each day, she could wind up in the hospital. And if she misses two days…"

She let the implied result hang in the air.

"You don't think we didn't know that?" Jabir blurted. "Why else would we be sure to—"

"I don't care!" She kicked his seat.

"Hey!"

"Shut up, Jabir. I'm tired of talking to you."

Jabir swallowed hard and glanced at Jorge.

The man kept his gaze on the road as if he hadn't heard anything.

They passed a gas station with a maroon Suburban waiting to turn onto the highway.

Jabir noted it as his mind turned inward.

Abdel's easy laugh echoed in his ears. Remembering Ari's grace in the Krav Maga ring and the way Stephen's eyes had lit up when talking about Jessie made the lump return to his throat.

"Stephen had been married barely a year. He said Jessie had been a gift given to him by God. And he could cook some of the best meals out of practically nothing."

Silence.

"Ari was getting out after this mission. He was so excited because he was going to open a Krav Maga gym with his wife and children." The gruesome scene flashed before him. "And Abdel. He was from Texas. Carefree on the surface, but he was ready to settle down."

He clinched his jaw as the lump choked away any other statement.

"When we get to the police station, I don't ever want to see you again. Understand?"

"I lost three comrades today. Three friends." His mind darted back to Abdel's last word. Then it dawned on him.

Ed.

His boss hadn't been among the dead. Jabir ripped through the conversation at the movie theater the day before. Anger boiled up inside of him, and he slammed his hands against the dashboard.

Jorge only glanced at him before returning his gaze forward.

Jabir resumed his internal contemplation. Nothing had remained at the house, not even Ed's belongings. No guns. No computers. No radios. Meaning...

He shivered. "I need to call Tiny."

"No calls," Jorge grunted.

"It's okay, Jorge." Alex's words surprised him. "I know him, and he's cool."

A short nod answered her.

"I need to use your phone, Alex," Jabir told her. He turned in his seat, and he noticed how the maroon Suburban was directly behind them on the two-lane road.

"Use your own."

"I'm scared to do that."

"And why's that?"

"I think Ed's the killer, and he can track who I call on my phone. Please."

With a sigh, she tossed it onto his lap. He punched in Tiny's mobile number. When his boss answered, he said, "Tiny, Jabir here. Am I ever glad to hear your voice."

"Jabir, what's going on? Is the job finished? I thought it wasn't supposed to wrap up until Tuesday."

"It wasn't." Jabir swallowed hard as the horrid scene up at the house unfolded before him. "I'm in over my head."

In thirty seconds, he outlined everything that had happened with the exception of his talk with Alex at the restaurant. He concluded by stating, "I'm, uh, destined for a Panamanian jail cell right now."

"Oh, wow. Listen. I'm on my way, okay? Who should I contact down there?"

"FBI Special Agent Mitch Gordon. He's handling the case with a National Police Detective Esteban Romero."

"Okay. I'll be there later this afternoon." Tiny cleared his throat. "Hopefully, I'll get you sprung later today. If so, get your other phone. I'll text you some coordinates. If not, then I'll see you at the station. Where's Alex?"

"She's going to get dropped off at the hotel." Jabir cringed as she muttered under her breath.

"If you get sprung, take her with you, okay? I'm not sure how much danger there is right now. This is her phone?"

"Yep."

"You'll probably want to dump it and get her a new phone if you talked to her with your CIA one. We'll make it through this." Tiny's voice reassured him.

"Okay," he whispered before hanging up.

Alex snatched her phone out of his hands.

"Tiny's coming down."

"Then you can figure this out without me."

Jabir winced and stared out the windshield.

Up ahead, the highway divided into a four-lane road.

Jorge muttered something about crazy drivers.

Bullets shattered the window.

Blood splattered everywhere. Across Jabir, the windshield, and even Alex if her cry meant anything.

The policeman crumpled toward the steering wheel.

Jabir didn't have time to think.

Only act.

He grabbed the wheel with his cuffed hands and kicked Jorge's feet away from the pedals.

"Alex, hold him back!"

The Escape had slowed, and the maroon Suburban, gun muzzle hanging out the window, shot ahead of them.

With his left foot, Jabir stomped on the gas and sped past where the Suburban had pulled to the side of the road.

"Are you okay?" he shouted above the wind. He kept his foot down.

"Fine." Alex had wrapped her hands around Jorge's arms.

Again, the Suburban stayed on their tail. The exit for Corredor Norte, the shortest route to the embassy, appeared. He took it as fast as he dared.

The SUV tried to jump off the road, and he had to use both hands to keep it on track.

The Suburban stuck right with them, this time drawing so close that they slammed into the back.

Jabir fought to keep the Escape on the road.

At the rate they were going, they couldn't make it to the embassy.

He swore under his breath.

"Jabir?"

"Hold on!" He took the exit onto one of the large avenues, and the big SUV relentlessly pursued them.

He flinched as more gunfire popped, puncturing the side and tailgate.

Alex cried out, and she released Jorge's body.

"Alex!" Fear filled Jabir.

"I—I'm…fine. I think." She grunted. Then she resumed her place holding Jorge.

Jabir noted his surroundings as they sped down the wide road. He swung a hard right onto one of the major boulevards, which led into the heart of the city. They came to a large intersection where the left turn light had just turned yellow.

Jabir floored it.

Alex screeched as the light turned red.

He slipped through, holding the Escape on course with all of his strength from his awkward position.

Horns blared.

They'd made it.

And the Suburban?

Stuck.

Jabir slowed a bit and took several deep breaths to drop his heart rate. They needed new wheels—and fast.

After a quick series of turns, they wound up in a quieter, more residential neighborhood dotted with occasional shops. Finally, they stopped in an alley.

Jabir sagged against his seat as the shakes got the better of him.

Alex immediately jumped out.

He searched Jorge's shirt pocket and came up with the handcuff keys. They released, and he let them fall to the floor.

The sound of retching reached him.

He popped his door open.

Alex leaned over, hands braced on her knees, head hanging, a puddle of vomit on the ground below her.

Instantly, he was at her side. "Alex?"

"I…I'm fine." She wiped her mouth with the back of her hand, then winced and cupped her left side as she straightened.

"Let's get that vest off." He tossed hers onto the ground. "Let me look at your side."

"Jabir."

"Alex, please. I want to make sure it didn't penetrate."

Almost reluctantly, she lifted her T-shirt. He whistled at the size of the red mark already forming. "You'll have a good bruise, but that's it." Relief filled him. "Praise God for bulletproof vests."

"Jorge…"

"He's gone." He assessed her. Tiny flecks of blood dotted her face and T-shirt sleeves where the vest hadn't covered her.

He didn't even want to know what he looked like.

Her hand shot to her mouth.

"Alex." He held her face between his hands. He gazed into her eyes.

They were wide, that sea green color wild, reflecting the panic surging within her. She trembled, and it almost reverberated through him.

"We're going to make it, okay?"

She nodded.

"All right, then." Automatically, he smoothed her hair before releasing her. "Let me see your phone again. Did George give you his number?"

She handed it to him.

"Good." Jabir called up the contacts menu. He found what he was looking for and dialed.

George answered, "Hey, girl! Miss me?"

"George?"

"Jabir?"

"It's me. Can you do me a huge favor?"

"Name it."

"My motorcycle's at the embassy. Could you drive it to Las Tiendas near the hospital? Leave it behind the grocery store?"

"Sure. Can do. You okay, man?"

"I'm not sure. Just keep your eyes and ears open, okay? Things went down this morning in a bad way. Then someone shot up the Escape we're in and killed a cop."

"Whoa. Is that why you're near the hospital?"

"We're fine. Just a bit shaken. We need to change up our wheels."

"Roger that. You let us know if you need any more help."

"Will do." Jabir slid the phone into his pocket. "I've got a test I want to do."

"What about Jorge?"

"We've got to leave him. The cops will be here soon, I'm sure. Especially when he doesn't show." Jabir opened the driver's door. He tossed his own vest into the passenger's seat and unclipped his CIA phone from his waist.

"What are you doing?" Alex joined him.

"This will tell me a lot." He peered around, trying to gauge where they could hide. They were in the back of a drugstore.

He took her phone and dialed his number. When it rang, he answered and laid his phone on the floor where it wasn't immediately visible. "C'mon. We're beating feet out of here. Getting to someplace reasonably safe. Then waiting."

He took her hand, and they scurried behind a neighboring office building and then to a nearby gas station that was open. "Buy me a T-shirt and meet me in the men's room."

He crept to the back. After one last check, he slipped inside.

Alex joined him a moment later with a tacky tourist's T-shirt that was white with I Love Panama scrawled on the front. It showed a parakeet lounging on a hammock between two palms with a margarita in its hand.

He locked the door, changed, and stuffed the splattered one deep into the garbage can.

Jabir put the cellphone on speaker and muted it. A few minutes later, a car door slammed on the other end.

A voice spoke, one with a Cajun accent.

Ed.

"Looks like my trusty device worked. And surprise, surprise, they're not here." Cussing followed. "And looks like a cop bought it. Great. This is just great."

"It is of no matter," an unknown voice said, this one deep with a distinct accent.

Jabir frowned.

"We wait. Most likely, he'll show up at the embassy or his apartment. Right now, we have other tasks, do we not?"

"Yeah. But you've got to understand. The kid's smart. He's going to start putting two and two together."

"It's of no concern. We have other options." The call ended.

Jabir stared at where Alex's phone reported the duration of the call. His hands began shaking. From anger, fear, or adrenaline, he didn't know. "I can't believe this."

"What?"

"Ed's teamed up with the kidnappers. From the other guy's accent, I'm afraid it's Jihad of Light."

"Huh?"

He ignored her. "We need to get going," he muttered. "We've got to get to the bike and then to my apartment."

"I want to go to the hotel."

A headache began kicking at his eyes. "Alex…"

"Take me back, Jabir."

"And then what? Let them get to you to get to me? I'm not letting that happen. Not after this morning."

"They're not after me. They're after you."

"Didn't you just hear me? These guys killed three people in cold blood. You think a fourth would matter to them?"

Alex opened her mouth to say more, but then she closed it before protesting, "They're going to be staking out your apartment."

"I know, but it's a risk we've got to take. Let me call Tiny. Then I want you to call Becca and get a status. Be quick about it. Tell her we're going to ground until we can find Ed. Then toss your phone. They're going to connect the dots between my phone and yours. C'mon. We've got a hike to the hospital."

Jabir stared at the mirror. Blood and gore from Jorge speckled both his face and hair. He turned on the sink and soaked his face. He'd clean up completely later.

"How far?" Alex had slipped into the lone stall.

"A couple of kilometers." When she returned, he added, "The sooner we go to ground and collect ourselves, the better."

Jabir undid the bolt to the door and came face to face with a man.

The man took one look at Alex and began scolding them for taking advantage of restrooms for such dishonorable activities.

Jabir took Alex's hand. With profuse apologies, he led her from the restroom.

At least they'd live to see another day.

Hopefully.

★ ★ ★

0745 hours Central Daylight Time, Panama City, Panama

Anger nipped at Ed. They'd been close to taking down Jabir and snatching his pretty friend.

Once more, the kid had outsmarted them, which was like pouring salt into the wound of Ed's frustration.

Jabir had left him with one dead cop, a shattered Escape, and a whole lot of blood. The only thing he'd left behind was his phone. Maybe that would supply some information.

Ed popped the Suburban's rear doors and pulled out one of the laptops they'd used at the safe house. He returned to the backseat.

He half-listened to Hashim's phone conversation coming from the front passenger's seat. "My brother, she escaped. Implement your plan and call me when you have Ellie."

Ed powered on the computer and pulled out a USB cable.

"How long to break it?" Hashim softly asked. He muttered something to his driver, and the Suburban pulled into traffic.

"Not long. Not long at all," Ed muttered as he plugged in the USB cable and connected the phone to the laptop. He opened the program that would crack the phone's passcode.

"You know you almost killed the very one we want." Hashim's voice was low, threatening, with his anger rumbling barely below the surface.

Ed glanced over the rims of his reading glasses. "I want Jabir dead."

"Oh, he'll be dead if we find him with Alex. But, you see, I'm under orders, and those orders are that we take Alex alive and well, if perhaps a bit banged up, but alive and well nonetheless. If you kill her or hurt her, then it will be your life for hers. Understand?"

Ed froze. "I do."

Hashim's phone chimed. He answered it.

As he talked in low Pashto, Ed focused on the program. It busily pulled apart Jabir's numeric passcode, and a second later, it beeped. He grunted in satisfaction and entered it into the phone. Once the home screen flashed up, he located Jabir's contacts and scrolled through them. There weren't many, but one in particular caught his attention.

Alex Thornton.

Perfect.

Using another program in the laptop, he placed its location on a map and announced, "I've got a lock on Alex's phone. It looks like they might be on foot."

"Where?"

Ed read off the directions.

Three minutes of driving brought them to the entrance of a park. "Let me go check."

"We both will." Hashim opened his door.

A moment later, Ed peered around him. "I don't see them. But the program said they're here."

"They were." Hashim nodded toward a newspaper lying face down on a bench. He tossed it aside, revealing a cellphone.

Ed dialed the number from Jabir's, and it rang.

"They think they're so smart." He muttered under his breath.

Hashim turned on his heel and strode toward the Suburban. "We have other options. You see, we have Ellie Watkins in our hands. We'll have Becca Alvarez shortly. Trust me, my friend. We'll have plenty of options. And soon, Alex will have none."

31

"You think Ed's behind this?"

"Yeah, I do."

"Why?"

"Didn't you hear what Becca said?" Jabir asked as he stopped the motorcycle behind a small strip mall near his apartment complex.

"She said that one bedroom looked like it slept three people who'd not bothered to pack while the other was picked clean."

"Right. And then there was nothing in the operations room either except for two tables. Do you think Ed would bother to pack and strip out all of the CIA's equipment if he'd been under fire?"

"I get it, okay?" Alex slid off the back and pulled off her helmet. "What's next?"

Once Jabir set the kickstand and locked the helmets onto the motorcycle, he peered around him. They were alone. "We're about three or so blocks from the complex. You got the stuff we bought?"

She nodded and hefted the new backpack. "Binoculars, ball caps, duct tape, cable ties, pocket knives. Everything a Unit 28 agent might need."

"Except for guns, real knives, and radios." Jabir reached inside and pulled out an Orioles cap. "Put this on."

"No problem there." Alex did so and stuffed her hands into the denim jacket she'd bought.

He donned a Dodgers cap before taking the backpack and shouldering it. "Wait here for thirty minutes. If I don't come back, go into the café and call George. Then go into one of the stalls in the ladies room and wait for him. Be sure to tell him to bring at least four guys with him. I don't think even the three of them would deter Ed. It certainly didn't this morning."

"Unh, unh." Alex shook her head.

"What?"

"I'm coming with you."

"Alex…"

"I'm coming with you, all right? I'm not letting you fly solo." Her jaw clenched. "Don't argue with me on this."

"Okay, then. So be it. I take it you're in decent shape."

"Better than decent."

He began walking toward the complex. "Then here's the plan. We check out front and back. Most likely, they've got both staked out. Let's hope one's less covered than the other. Depending, I go in, grab the laptop and my phone, and get out."

"I'll be your backup down here."

"Hold on." Jabir held out an arm to stop her. They leaned against the wall of a bank a block away. From their position, they had had a good view of the parking lot for his apartment complex.

"Where are all of the cars?" Alex asked in a low voice.

"It's break between sessions." He assessed each one. Then he noticed a ratty Ford Escort, rust all over it, with two men in it. "Looks like they've got the front staked out."

He sucked in a tense breath.

"Around back," he murmured.

Alex turned on her heel.

Jabir led the way around the bank, to the café again, and then down another street that brought them to the back of the complex. They approached the drugstore he frequented and slipped through the parking lot to the fence bordering it. He nodded toward a small break.

Jabir peered through the opening.

A man leaned against one of the large boulders ringing the small, dingy courtyard of the complex.

Jabir pulled back.

"Looks like just one," he whispered. "Stay here."

Carefully placing each foot, Jabir passed through the opening. He increased his pace and slammed into the man.

His adversary staggered, but he didn't go down.

With one stroke of his leg, Jabir swept the man's ankles from under him. They grappled. Using his weight, Jabir flipped him onto his stomach and clamped his arm around his neck.

The man briefly struggled, but then he sagged against the ground.

Jabir whistled a soft owl call.

Soft footfalls told him Alex had joined him.

"Cable ties."

Alex opened the package they'd bought and handed him two.

Without his asking, she ripped off a piece of duct tape.

He slapped it over the guy's mouth. Then he searched him and came up with a pistol and spare clip. "Here. Take these."

Jabir surveyed his apartment's balcony. "Okay. I'm going in. If I'm not out in half an hour, go back to the café and do as I told you. You understand?"

This time, she nodded without arguing.

Jabir studied the dreary courtyard of more dirt than grass. No one stirred. He scurried to the supports of the balcony. One look inside the apartment below his revealed only the standard furniture supplied by the landlord, meaning those students were most likely gone for the summer. He peered upward. With a small breath of prayer, he used the intricate wrought iron pattern of the support post and his parkour skills to shimmy upward.

He dropped to the floor of the balcony and crouched as he listened.

"Hey, good move, *amigo*," a voice called from the porch next to his.

Jabir froze and glanced over. Hair mussed and bags under his eyes, his neighbor slouched against the railing.

Had he seen anything?

Jabir didn't have time to worry. He managed a weak grin and softly called, "Forgot my keys again."

"I do that all of the time, *amigo*. Too bad I can't climb like you." The man saluted him with his cigarette and wandered into his apartment.

Jabir stared through the French doors. Nothing moved in the living area. His hand shot into his pocket, and he withdrew his keys to let himself inside. Once the door shut behind him, he paused, listening for any telltale sign of someone hiding in the bedroom.

In the stillness, the refrigerator hummed. Then came silence as it switched off.

From somewhere out front, a door thumped shut.

Jabir shivered.

He darted to the desk the landlord had supplied. On top of the plain wood was the laptop specially prepared for him by Otto, Unit 28's computer specialist.

Jabir shoved both computer and power cord into the backpack.

He dashed into the bedroom, opening dresser drawers and his closet as he stuffed enough clothing into the backpack to last both him and Alex for a few days.

Jabir yanked open the drawer of the nightstand and located the screwdriver. It took him just a minute to undo the socket and retrieve the phone. He slid it into a pocket of his cargo pants and added the charger to the backpack.

A small noise made him freeze.

He listened.

Scratching, like a mongoose or some other small animal running along the roof.

The deadbolt in the front door slid back.

Jabir's blood ran cold.

His eyes darted around the room.

He had no way to the back door without being seen.

The window wouldn't work either.

Pain in his hand made him glance down. His fingers had curled around the screwdriver's handle to the point where he noticed how his tendons turned his skin white.

His jumping his attacker four years before flashed before his eyes, as did driving his knife up to the hilt into the man's neck before crawling to where Alex lay, bloody and unconscious.

A phone rang, dragging him back to the present. He realized how he shook from head to foot.

Jabir took a deep breath, praying for the tremors to dissipate so he could do something—anything—to keep from dying.

"You fool! If he's in here, you've alerted him." The words in Pashto surprised him. The male burglar paused, then replied, "No, nothing yet. But I've yet to search the bedroom. Wait. He is here. I can see the way the back door isn't locked. And footprints."

He said more, but Jabir tuned him out.

Leaving the backpack in a corner, he scrambled to his feet and into the bathroom. He cracked the door. Quietly, he opened the doors beneath the counter.

It all came together at once. He grabbed the cleanser and shook a generous amount of it into the cup he kept by the sink.

Jabir slipped behind the opaque shower curtain and eased it closed.

A board in the old hardwood floor creaked.

His attacker stood at the entrance to the bedroom.

Jabir jumped when the closet door rammed into the wall.

He took a deep breath and breathed a quiet prayer.

He braced himself.

The bathroom door slammed open.

"Nothing, eh?" the man muttered again in Pashto. He didn't move.

The attacker's heavy breathing penetrated the space, as did the smell of cheap tobacco.

"What's this?" Smugness laced the man's words.

Jabir's breath came in shallow, silent gasps as he realized how mud from the courtyard stood out in sharp relief against the clean white of the tile.

He cocked back the cup.

The curtain ripped open.

Jabir hurled the cleanser into the man's face.

His attacker screamed.

Jabir shoved him hard.

Clawing at his eyes, the man staggered backwards and slammed into the doorframe. He dropped his pistol, and it misfired.

The bullet pinged off of the tile, hit the ceramic of the tub, and embedded itself into the wooden cabinet.

Jabir flinched as pinpoints of pain hit his neck. He leapt on top of him and slammed his fist into his face.

The man moaned and fell silent. Jabir snatched another cable tie from the pocket of his cargo pants and secured his would-be attacker. He patted him down.

As he located the pistol on the floor, the man's phone began chiming.

Jabir muttered since he knew his buddy had heard the shot.

He leapt to his feet, grabbed the backpack, and bolted toward the French doors.

The front door crashed open.

Someone shouted.

Jabir ducked as the shot snapped by his ear with a supersonic crack and pierced the glass of the French doors.

He scrambled to his feet. Once on the porch, he leapt over the railing and into space. When he rolled to his feet, he shouted, "Alex!"

"Here," she called back.

"Balcony."

Her head tilted, and her gun followed. "Got it."

She fired.

Jabir sprinted toward the rock.

She paused as her clip ran out.

He leapt behind it and pulled her down beside him.

Bullets whanged off the stone.

Jabir raised his head. "We've got to get out of here. Anymore clips?"

"One." Alex rammed it home and winced as another fusillade greeted them.

It ceased.

"I've got it. Go!" Jabir popped up and fired several shots.

Alex jumped to her feet and ran. He followed, and soon they were out of sight of the other guy. They stowed their guns under their jackets. "To the café. Quickly."

"Bike?"

"Yeah." He powered on the phone and pressed his finger to the screen so it could read his thumbprint.

The home screen flashed up, and a moment later, the text icon appeared as it chirped a notification. Relief filled him when he noticed the text from Tiny containing the words "safe house," matching coordinates, and a gate code. "Perfect."

"Good news?"

"News that we can rest." Relief filled him when he saw the motorcycle.

"A safe house?"

"Yep. Take the backpack." He handed it off. Then he swung his leg over the bike.

After yanking on his helmet, he entered the coordinates into the navigation app and secured the phone to the motorcycle.

Alex wrapping her arms around his waist comforted him.

Soon, they would be safe.

Then they could figure out where Ed had taken Melanie.

32

Ed lay prone in the jungle as close to the edge of it as he dared since the Panamanian cops were still present. He pointed one of the gadgets he'd stolen at the very place he'd called home for the past several days. It picked up every single sound, from the murmured conversation on the porch between Romero and the coroner to the dismissal the detective had given the SWAT guys. Obviously, the man perceived no impending threat.

Ed's lips curled at that thought.

If you only knew.

Now, his fancy device picked up a ton of chatter from Gordon. The man hadn't stopped talking since Hashim and his crew had set up shop in the jungle twenty minutes before.

The agent paced in front of a National Police Chevy Trailblazer. "Yeah. Things went to hell in a hand basket real quick-like. Seems that the CIA was down here…Uh, huh…Uh, huh. I understand. What do you want me to do?"

Ed's eyes narrowed. How much had the kid told Gordon? He focused once more on the conversation.

Gordon now stood ramrod straight as if his supervisor were burning his ear off in a torrent of words. "Yes, sir. I understand…Okay. I'll make sure someone is there…I'm going to the station with Detective Romero to talk with him…It seems as if there's an Ed DuBois involved in all of this…Yes, sir. I know. I'll also look for a Timothy Daniels. Yes…I understand that. I'm sorry. I'll cede to you on this."

On and on he went.

Ed ground his teeth. Obviously, al-Omri had spilled his sob story to the FBI, who now knew to the upper levels that he was involved. Any hope of eliminating the kid and slipping back into his old job vanished like the morning mist in the hot summer sun. Suddenly, Ed's prone position under the camouflage netting coupled with this newfound knowledge made him want to put as much distance as possible between himself and Panama.

"We've got to get a move on it," he muttered, his voice barely audible above the humming bugs and chirping birds in the foliage around him.

The massive lump next to him stirred. From underneath what appeared to the naked eye as a mound of underbrush came Hashim's gravelly reply. "It is too soon. We wait."

"They know who I am."

"Then it's good you're one of us now, isn't it?"

Ed grimaced.

Engines started, and the armored vans carrying the SWAT team rumbled down the road.

He winced and muted the directional listening device.

Once their sound had faded, Gordon's voice again filtered back to Ed. The man yammered on and on.

Then came two technicians holding a zipped body bag. They loaded it into a van and repeated the process twice more.

Ed had thought he'd feel remorse at seeing his three comrades shuttled toward their final resting places.

Nothing came.

Romero shook hands with the coroner, and the van departed.

Since the rest of the evidence techs had left a few minutes before, three people remained. Romero. Gordon. And their target, Alvarez.

The woman leaned against a porch post and ran her hands down her dark ponytail. Her pretty features were pinched as if deep in thought.

She glanced up and smiled when Romero approached her. "Mitch is like a lovesick mockingbird."

Ed smirked.

"A what?" the detective asked.

"A lovesick mockingbird. During mating season, the males sing at all hours and never shut up."

He laughed. "Perhaps. I told him we're leaving in five minutes. A squall is coming, and I don't want to stay here any longer."

Ed cussed under his breath, then whispered, "We need to move."

"Patience. You keep talking, and you'll reveal us."

Ed fell silent at Hashim's quiet rebuke.

Alvarez had begun walking toward Gordon. "You know how it is. I just can't leave it alone."

"I understand." Romero nodded. He shoved his hands into his pants pockets. "What are your thoughts?"

Alvarez turned on her heel. "I think we might have passed the killers on our way up."

"What?"

Ed frowned.

"They hadn't been dead for long, right?"

"The coroner thinks an hour or two at most when we arrived."

Alvarez paused.

Ed could almost see the thoughts raging through her head. Most likely, she tried to play out the sequence of events.

"That van."

"What van?"

"Do you remember how it nearly got hit by a truck when turning left?"

Ed knew all too well. Hashim had shouted in alarm when Tarek's van had taken off just as a dump truck approached.

"I think so."

"I think Melanie's kidnappers were driving that. And the Suburban too since a maroon one went after Jabir and Alex." Alvarez stared at nothing as she rubbed her chin.

Ed's gaze once more shot to Hashim's position.

"That's it." Alvarez whirled and marched to the detective. "It's an older model. Dirty white like it hadn't been washed in a while. Company logo for some cleaning company or something like that. I didn't catch the name. I think it had a shirt and hanger as part of the design."

Ed muttered under his breath. Hashim had copied the logo of the laundry company used by the hotel.

"I'm calling Ellie. I've got a bad feeling about this." She punched numbers into her phone.

The detective's cell began buzzing. "Do that while I answer this."

Now, Ed grinned. Ellie wasn't there. She hadn't been for two hours since Tarek had taken her hostage.

Beside him, the lump of brush twitched. The tinkling of brass sliding into the chamber of the stolen sniper rifle reached him, followed closely by the quiet click of the bolt sliding into place.

"Esteban." Alvarez's quiet call reached Ed.

Romero turned her way, then murmured something too low for Ed to catch. He cupped his hand over the receiver. "What is it?"

"Ellie's not answering. And she promised to stay near her phone and not leave the room."

He turned his back and continued his hushed conversation.

Alvarez wandered toward the Trailblazer and stared at her comrade for a moment. Then she shook her head as Gordon kept talking and nodding like he was a Bobblehead or something.

"Becca." The cop's deep voice made Ed switch his full attention to the Panamanian.

Romero strode toward the two Americans. "The officers who were supposed to guard Ellie arrived. Ellie's gone."

"What?" She froze.

"They arrived at eight like I told them to. It looked like a table was knocked over as if in a struggle, and it appears as if one of the sheets from the master bedroom is gone. That's not all. A patrol located the Escape and confirmed everything Alex told you."

Gordon finally lowered his phone. "This stinks."

"Alex and Jabir?"

The detective shrugged. "We don't know if they're safe. That's all I've got. I want to get you back to Headquarters. Now. I'm afraid you could be next."

"What? Me? Why?"

"Yeah, why her?" Gordon slid his phone into the holster at his belt. "Sorry. That sounded bad."

"They took Ellie. Chances are they're after you. Call it a hunch."

Ed took a breath.

Around him, the buzzing, clicking, and chirping suddenly fell silent.

"We're going. Now." Romero took Alvarez's arm.

"Now? But—"

Beside Ed, the big rifle coughed once.

A red hole appeared on Gordon's head, and a pink spray erupted from behind.

The FBI man crumpled to the ground.

Alvarez's scream made Ed jump. "Sniper!"

Beside him, Hashim worked the action and squeezed the trigger.

Rather than punch a hole in the Panamanian, the shot merely punctured the window of the Trailblazer.

Romero fired toward them.

Though he knew they were out of range, Ed flinched.

A war cry shattered the air as Hashim jumped to his feet.

Gunfire chattered around them as the other two men with them unleashed a volley of bullets toward the building.

The detective and Alvarez threw themselves through the door and out of sight.

Ed knew his task.

He jerked to a crouch and grabbed the Molotov cocktail he'd prepared as well as a grenade.

Ed stumbled upright as the bruise on his hip barked at him. Using a lighter, he lit the rag on the Molotov and hurled it toward the Trailblazer. The bottle shattered when it hit and spread flaming liquid all over the roof.

Ed pulled the pin on the grenade and added some bang to the flash.

The Trailblazer exploded and merrily blazed.

Using the flames as a cover, Ed and Hashim pulled on balaclavas and advanced toward the house behind their men, who charged ahead and through the front door.

Once inside, Hashim chuckled and stepped over the inert body of the detective on the floor.

In the outer corner, one of Hashim's men moaned and lay on the floor, blood seeping between his fingers from the wound on his arm. The other was trying to pull himself upright by grasping the bed, but his ankle didn't seem to want to hold his weight.

Alvarez crowded into the back corner next to the hall, a bloody butcher's knife in her right hand. Dark wisps from her ponytail framed her face, and her eyes, a sherry color, were wide, from terror, anger, or some other emotion Ed didn't know.

"You'll not take me." She almost growled those words and slid toward the hallway door.

"Oh, I think I will." Hashim smirked as he sidestepped in the same direction and eased into a karate stance.

Alvarez had no choice but to go the other direction, away from safety.

He aimed a few probing punches in her direction and jerked back when the knife swished toward him.

Keeping his eyes on the growing fight, Ed knelt and felt the pulse of the detective.

Faint but strong.

Good. He didn't want any more deaths than necessary on his conscience.

Alvarez and Hashim kept circling. Ed ducked when Alvarez aimed the business end of the knife his way.

This was Hashim's fight, one where Ed was content to be a spectator.

Hashim charged with a front kick.

She blocked it and jabbed at him with the blade.

He whirled and aimed a roundhouse kick at her head.

Alvarez jerked back, but his downward sweep knocked the knife from her hand.

Hashim drilled a punch toward her face.

She blocked it, staggering off balance as she did so. She put her hand down.

A jab sent her all the way to the floor.

Hashim pounced. Before she could react, he grabbed her wrists and pinned them to the floor. He immobilized her legs with his weight.

She struggled against his hold. "Let me go!"

Hashim laughed. He stopped and glared at her. "You are quite skilled, Señora. What of the man?"

"Down," Ed told him. He fished in his shirt pocket for the baggie Hashim had handed him when they'd concocted their plan. "He's alive, though."

Alvarez struggled again. She cried out as Hashim ground her wrists into the floor. "You!"

Ed hid his surprise when he noticed her gaze focused on him. "I see you know who I am. That traitor, al-Omri, told you."

"I think you're the traitor here. Murdering three men in cold blood. Ow! Stop, will you?" She directed her ire toward Hashim. "They're coming, you know. We know all about you, and now the cops do."

"We're leaving shortly, Señora." Hashim smirked. "Ed, do the honors, if you will."

Ed pulled the damp rag from the baggie and shoved it over her nose and mouth,

Alvarez's struggles lasted maybe three seconds. She stilled.

"The policeman is alive?" Hashim asked.

"Knocked out."

"He was behind the door when we kicked it in," the man with the bloody arm replied.

Hashim didn't seem to hear him. Instead, he reached out and felt for a pulse at Alvarez's neck. His fingers drifted upward and smoothed some errant strands off her face. As if noticing everyone's stares, he turned his head. "Leave him. Make sure his cellphone doesn't work."

With that, Hashim swung Alvarez's unconscious form across his shoulders.

Ed unclipped Detective Romero's phone. It started ringing.

Without hesitation, he drove his heel into it, shattering it and silencing it for good. He strode after his new master.

Now, Alex would have no choice but to give herself up to save her friends' lives.

33

As they pulled into a residential neighborhood west of the city, Alex's heart still galloped like a runaway horse. Sweat flowed from underneath her helmet and ran in a river down her back, soaking her T-shirt and the denim jacket. Her arms encircled Jabir's waist, and her hands clinched around each other in a death grip to avoid falling off the back of the motorcycle.

They slowed and wound their way through a series of curves.

Toward the top, the road steepened and narrowed even further.

Jabir stopped at a closed wrought iron gate painted white.

"This is the safe house?" she asked above the purr of the motorcycle's idling engine.

"That's what the GPS says." He reached out and punched in a combination.

A motor hummed into action, and the gates slid aside.

"I guess it's right." He eased them upward.

A sharp left and a right revealed a charming stucco house painted a cheery yellow.

Alex released her grip and slid off the back of the motorcycle. She set her helmet on the seat. With her hand sliding under her jacket to grip the gun, she stepped to the pedestrian gate leading to the patio.

Beyond it, an infinity pool connected water to sky.

"Hah, some safe house," she muttered when she noted the reds and yellows of tropical flowers like exclamation points against the dark green of the foliage surrounding the pool.

The front door opened.

Alex whirled and pulled out her gun.

A man with dark hair stepped out, his hands where she could see them.

"Howdy." His Texan accent and easygoing grin told her they were among friends. "Welcome to the nicest safe house in the world."

"I'll say." Alex tucked the gun into the waistband of her cargo pants.

Jabir stuck out his hand. "Jabir al-Omri. This is Alex Thornton."

"Pleased to meet the both of you. Ryan Deal. My buddy, Parker Coats, is inside. We're with Housekeeping for DHS. Tiny said to expect you. Come on in."

Alex shoved the backpack into Jabir's arms and followed Ryan into the house.

"So sorry to hear what's happened," Ryan said. He nodded toward the man with dark blond hair who tinkered with the laptop sitting on the granite peninsula. "Alex, Jabir, this is Parker Coats."

"Pleased to meet you." Parker held out his hand.

Alex reluctantly shook it.

Ryan nodded toward the open staircase. "Tiny told us you'd probably be exhausted, and I can see you are. There's four bedrooms upstairs. Feel free to crash for a while."

Alex drew in a sharp breath. "I don't think I can. I mean, someone tried to kill us, Melanie's kidnapped, and she's in danger, and—"

"Don't worry, okay?" Parker straightened. "We're to stay here until this is resolved. The wall's topped with glass, and the drop-off has bits of concertina mixed in with the foliage. Not a good recipe for coming up the cliff. So no worries about someone sneaking up on you. We only ask that you keep the curtains pulled and stay off the verandas."

"But—"

"You're not going to do Melanie any good if you're so exhausted you can't think straight."

"You're sure?"

"Positive. There's a bathroom with each bedroom. Take a hot shower and get some sleep. We'll let you know if we hear anything from Tiny or anyone else."

"Thanks, guys. Alex, come on." Jabir took her arm and led the way upstairs.

As they reached the landing, the light dimmed. Through the open doors leading to the bedroom and the veranda beyond, she could see how black clouds had built to cover the morning sun.

Weariness surged over her. She stepped into the room as she shrugged out of her jacket. She dropped it onto the clean white comforter. Rolling her neck released the tension, but it also made the headache that had never quite disappeared surge. Her eyes burned, and all she wanted was a hot shower.

She wandered into the bathroom and found fresh towels, a terrycloth robe, and some soap in a wrapper on the sink beside two bottles of shampoo and conditioner.

Alex rubbed her temples as questions surged around her regarding Jabir. How much truth had he told her? Had he been sincere regarding his apology about four years ago? Or had he simply made nice to get her to trust him so he could feed her more lies? And what about the tale he'd told at the safe house? Was it true?

All of these questions tormented her like the winter crows cawing at each other back in Weatherly.

"Alex? Hey, where are you?"

She stiffened.

"Alex?"

"Just a minute."

She took several deep breaths in an attempt to stave off the anger boiling within her.

Alex stepped into the bedroom.

Jabir slouched against the doorjamb, a bundle of something in his arms. His eyes were closed. At the sound of her footfalls, they opened, and he offered a tired smile. "Here. I managed to grab some clothes. Sorry they're mine."

She took the bundle. "Thanks."

She tossed them onto the bed.

"I know I forgot the other necessities, but I did find some toiletries in the bathroom as well as some towels."

She turned and stared over the veranda again. Her fists clenched and unclenched, as did her jaw. She bit her lip and raised her gaze toward the ceiling.

Leave it alone, a little voice inside of her advised.

He's not telling the truth, she retorted silently.

Are you sure?

"I want the whole truth, Jabir."

"Huh?"

She whipped around. "I want the whole truth. And nothing but the truth, so help you God. Full disclosure, or as soon as we're done, I don't want to see you again. Ever."

Jabir stared, his dark eyes wide in shock. Then he blinked. "Can't it wait until we're a little more rested?"

He shoved himself away from the doorway.

"No. No, it can't."

He shut the door. With a weary sigh, he eased onto the low, modern chair across from the bed. He rubbed his stubbled chin as he assessed her.

"Start talking."

"I told you everything."

"I'm not so sure about that." Arms crossed, Alex paced in front of him.

"Everything I said when we were at my office and up at the safe house was true."

"No, I think you lied when we were at your office."

"Alex…"

"I told you. Full disclosure."

He muttered under his breath and raked his hands through his dark hair. "You know about our mission. About how we'd intended to kidnap Samir and interrogate him about his link to JOL. How I was on loan to the CIA because they'd lost so many seasoned case officers who were native Arabic speakers. All of that's true."

"Then why is Tiny involved in this? I mean you ran crying to him when things went south."

"Because I was also working a mission for him."

"I knew it." She closed her eyes and turned away. "Since we reconnected yesterday, it seems like every word you've said to me has been a lie."

He touched her on the shoulder.

Though his fingers were gentle, she shook him off and retreated to the papasan in the corner. "Don't touch me."

"I'm going to change that right now." Jabir remained where he was. He drew the filmy curtains so they covered the sliding glass doors leading to the veranda.

"How can you?"

"By reading you in fully on what I was doing for Tiny." Jabir pulled out a pack of cigarettes. "May I?"

She tersely nodded.

He lit one and seated himself on the hassock across from her. "In February, Tiny called me into his office and told me how CIA was literally bleeding senior case officers who had native Arabic skills. They suspected Ed, but they'd not been able to pull together enough evidence to bring him in for questioning. A thirteenth man, a guy named Hakim al-Husseini, had died a few days before. I'd spent 2013 to 2015 working deep undercover in Egypt, and Tiny thought those skills would make me a shoo-in for his replacement. It also meant I could get close to Ed without his getting suspicious."

"Why did they suspect him in the first place?"

"Because the guy who died way back in December 2008 had fingered Ed for taking it too far with eight guys in Iraq in late 2007. The guy died of carbon monoxide poisoning from his heating system, and the cops called it a tragic accident. The thing was, when his sister came to clean out his house in February 2009, she found maintenance records showing that the annual check had occurred in November. When the CIA started asking around, it turned out that neighbors had reported seeing a maintenance guy there in December. But there was no evidence that the company had come back."

"Maybe that was an isolated incident."

"Maybe. Except for one thing. When Ed got busted, he got pulled out of the Middle East, where he'd lived for almost twenty years. Getting re-posted to Washington was a wrist slap, but for Ed, I'm sure it was worse. He hooked up with a buddy of his from his Afghanistan days who became his supervisor. But, CIA didn't have anything on him, so, like you said, they figured it for an isolated incident. That's why they didn't start worrying until the bodies began piling up about two years ago. Hakim was the last before the mission."

"They never suspected Ed?"

"They did, but they couldn't pin anything on him. All of the murders appeared as accidents at first blush. Each time someone died, Ed was no-where near them, and by the time they called it a murder, the trail had gone cold."

"So CIA thought you could find something."

"They were desperate. And like I said, the mission Ed was running was legit." He pulled over an ashtray and tapped some ashes into it. "We worked well as a team. Ed had us work out together. Eat together. He wanted us to bond as a team…" He paused, and his dark eyes clouded.

"Didn't they worry?"

"Who?"

"Your friends."

"They did." He rested his elbows on his knees and his forehead against his clenched fists. "I knew my best bet was to talk to Ari, Abdel, and Stephen. But coming in as an outsider, it was hard."

"Didn't they trust you?"

"They did somewhat." Jabir rose and stepped to the veranda doors. He lifted the edge of the curtain as if seeking a way out. "But you know how it is. When you've worked closely with a comrade like they had with Ed, they would have trusted him more than me. Ari was very close to him. Abdel and Stephen, I'm not so sure. All were scared to a degree."

He turned, and the grief emanating from his gaze made her heart catch. "They thought that so long as they were with Ed, they were safe."

Suddenly, he muttered something, dropped his cigarette into the ashtray, and began pacing. "Something tipped Ed's hand. Made him turn abruptly."

Alex rose and leaned against one of the posts of the king-sized bed. "What?"

"I should have seen it. It was right there in my face."

"What?"

"When you were in the bathroom yesterday, Ed called me. We met, and he capitulated readily when I passed along what I knew. I should have seen it. He suggested that I finish up my assignment to keep an eye on things. Then he told me I'd done a good job and that he'd take it from there. He'd see to it that Tiny would give me a commendation. I should have seen it. Should have called Abdel, Ari, or Stephen and warned them right then and there."

"Do you think they would have believed you?"

"I don't know. I just don't know. They trusted him." He stilled and hung his head. "You know what happened."

Alex blinked as she ticked through everything he'd told her. Had he come completely clean? Her fingers curled into fists. He'd told so many lies already, so many that she wondered if his latest story was simply another pack of them to get her to trust him. Her cheeks flushed.

"Do you trust me?"

Tears flooded her eyes. Did she? She stepped to the veranda doors, then crossed her arms and squeezed her eyes shut.

I don't know. I don't know. I don't know!

Her shoulders heaved as she fought a sob brought on by stress and exhaustion.

"Alex." His voice came from near the interior door.

Hot anger swooshed through her. "Is that all?" She turned. "Is that really all?"

"It's all I've got."

"Why'd you lie to me?"

"I had to. I thought we went over that."

"How do I know yesterday at the restaurant wasn't an act? Ever since we've met, I trusted you, yet you played me *for a fool*." She wore a circle around him. "I think you were saying those words to get back into my good graces. To get me to believe you. Why should I trust you now?"

Her words echoed off the high-ceilinged room.

He grasped her arm. "I do care, Alex. I do. Yesterday wasn't an act."

"I don't believe you!" She grabbed his wrist and shoved him away. "You didn't care about me when you left. You didn't."

"You don't think I did?" His voice matched hers. "I did—and I do—care about you deeply. Very deeply."

"Oh, yeah? Am I to believe that?" She glared at him.

"Didn't you see the IAD report of what happened?"

"I don't see what that has to do with anything."

"It has *everything* to do with what happened!" Jabir's shout echoed off the plaster.

"I know what happened. I was kicked out. Forced to resign while you got to go running off to Egypt on some dandy assignment." Tears spilled down her cheeks as she made another circle around him. "Everything I knew about my life changed in the span of thirty minutes while nothing happened to you."

"Listen to yourself."

"What?"

"You're caught up in what happened to you! *Your* problems. *Your* feelings. *Your* fallout." He began untucking his shirt. "You're so concerned with your own little world that you never bothered to ask what happened to *me*."

Jabir yanked it off.

Alex's eyes widened.

Scars crisscrossed his chest and shoulders. Scars where his chest hair hadn't grown back. Scars that looked mysteriously like knife wounds.

And a lot of them.

She blinked.

Jabir jabbed a finger at the scar on his cheek. "Did you ever stop to think about where I got this?"

His quiet voice demanded respect.

"Or these?"

He gestured to his chest.

She opened her mouth to respond, but words failed her.

"That's what I thought." He pulled his shirt back on. "I *killed* for you, Alex Thornton. I killed to save your life, and I *suffered* for it."

Knees suddenly weak, she eased onto the edge of the bed.

"You didn't read the IAD report?"

"I burned it."

"You know something? You amaze me sometimes." He shook his head. "Since you never bothered to read it, I'll tell you what happened. You remember how I got that food poisoning right before the mission was supposed to start?"

She managed a nod but kept quiet when she saw the fury blazing in his eyes.

"I popped some meds and recovered enough to make it to the building. Someone else had gotten in because I noticed the door ajar. I made it up the stairs to the fifth floor in time to see your attackers leaning over you. One was about my size. The other? Huge."

Jabir put his hands on his hips and glared at her like an angry school teacher. "I took care of the smaller one first. But when I jumped the larger one, it was like jumping onto a boulder. We started fighting. I knew that if I didn't kill him, he'd kill the both of us."

He loomed over her. "I did what I had to do. I killed a man, Alex. I killed him to save your life. And it cost me. It cost me dearly, and not just with those scars you saw. During the investigation, they questioned me extensively about it and concluded that very thing. That if I hadn't sent

Jennifer Haynie

that knife into the guy's carotid, we wouldn't be sitting here talking. They concluded it was purely in self-defense, which exonerated me."

He grabbed her jacket and threw it onto the floor. "Don't think I got away unscathed. Seeing you suffer during your recovery and the investigation was almost too much to bear. I wasn't sleeping. Was having nightmares in a big way. Tiny suggested counseling, but I thought I could handle it on my own. So when that assignment in Egypt came open, I grabbed it because I thought I could work through things by myself. I was wrong."

Alex shuddered when he kicked the bedpost.

"I was so wrong. The nightmares continued, and add to that the paranoia that comes with having to blend in with a radical Islamic household. I really started praying. Started praying for healing, mostly. Somehow, some way, God healed my heart and helped me to see how the Cross covers everything. Everything! I finally got that peace I wanted. At least until I arrived home and discovered that you'd relocated to Weatherly."

Jabir whirled and grabbed her chin with so much force that she squeaked.

"So there it is. The truth, and nothing but the truth, so help me God. All that I talked about yesterday at the restaurant. That's true. All of it. I…"

He bit his lip.

"I what?" Somehow, Alex choked out those words.

He released her.

"Get some sleep." With that, he slammed through the door with such force that the house seemed to shudder.

Alex slid off the edge of the bed and down its side until she rested on the floor with her knees tucked to her chest.

She buried her face in her arms and cried.

34

Alex dozed. The ibuprofen she'd taken before her shower had finally kicked in. As she floated in the haze between deep sleep and wakefulness, an image of her with the other three Fantabulous Four members appeared before her. They were in junior high right after Ellie had arrived. Ellie wore cut-offs and a tank top in the hot summer weather, Becca much the same. Alex had on shorts as well and a T-shirt. Melanie was the only one who wore a sundress.

Melanie laughed as they jumped onto a merry-go-round. Becca ran, pushing them faster and faster as all four girls laughed with the delirious freedom brought about by summer and the feeling of almost flying. As it slowed, they jumped off.

Dizzy, Alex tumbled to the ground and lay in a heap, giggling like she couldn't stop. Above her, the trees still spun.

"Alex." Melanie appeared above her.

Alex still giggled. She closed her eyes.

"Alex." The voice had turned to a male's. She opened her eyes. Now Jabir stood above her as her world continued tilting on its axis.

"Alex." Someone gently shook her.

Her eyes finally flew open. She wasn't back at home in Weatherly in more innocent times. She lay curled up under a blanket on the papasan. Her headache had finally dissipated, leaving in its wake a weariness so profound that she couldn't move.

Jabir leaned over her, clad in a pair of clean cargo pants and a black T-shirt. His curls glistened as if he'd just gotten out of the shower. The faint ruddiness she noticed indicated it had been a steamy, hot one.

Her gaze landed on several small Band Aids on his neck. That brought her fully back to reality, and she sat up. "Jabir, your neck..."

"When I was at the apartment, the first guy's gun misfired. Some tile chips got me. No big deal. Promise."

Shame hit her. She hadn't even noticed any bleeding.

She swallowed hard as he seated himself on the hassock so their knees almost touched. She pulled the blanket around her shoulders and stared at where her hands twisted it into wrinkles on her lap. "I'm sorry."

Jabir only raised an eyebrow.

She bit the inside of her cheek so hard she tasted blood.

"I'm sorry for the way I acted." Alex raised her gaze, and his image shimmered in her tears. "I was hurting. Angry. You were a convenient target."

She sniffled.

"Forgiven." His word came almost instantly.

"What?" Alex blinked.

A sad smile flickered across his lips. He reached out and brushed away the tear at the corner of her eye with his thumb. Then he cupped her chin with his hand, this time with no anger behind the gesture. "Forgiven. As I stood under the stream of the shower, I could see why you were so angry. Had I been in your shoes and you in mine, I would have felt betrayed too."

Alex turned her face away and stared at the dark hardwood floor. "I was so foolish. So stupid to not even read the IAD report. Obviously, I didn't know the whole truth.

"I remember how you got that food poisoning from the takeout Chinese. Talk about a freak incident."

Jabir nodded. "Tell me about it."

"Then I remember picking the lock at the office building and going inside to set up. Honestly, that's the last thing that's clear. The next thing I knew, I was in the hospital in ICU and hurting all over. Family came. You came. Tiny did too." A small smile crossed her lips and faded. "Hell started when I got home. I hated the questioning we got from everyone. Congress, Tiny's bosses, the press. Like we'd done something wrong."

Jabir took her hand.

She curled her fingers around his. "It seemed like when we testified before the Intelligence Committee, they were holier-than-thou, as if they sat in judgment of us. I was barely able to stand, let alone sit for three hours."

"I know. At least you didn't pass out in front of them."

"No, I did that in Dad's office. And then, a week after that all ended, Secretary Harris fired me publicly." She bit her lip as more tears filled her eyes. "You know, you'd think that four years later, it wouldn't hurt as much. It still does. I'd heard all about the news conference. I thought Secretary Harris was going to give a public report on the mission. Instead, he fired me." She pressed her hands over her face. "Mom and Dad had offered to stay home with me. I said I didn't need them. I was so wrong. I tried to call you."

"I left for Egypt that day."

"Tiny told me when he came by the next day to receive my resignation later. He couldn't tell me hardly anything since I'd lost my clearances. Jabir, forgive me, but I was so angry at you. I felt completely abandoned. I—I guess in my hurt, I began conjuring up how you'd gotten away scot-free from everything. That made everything else worse." Alex drew her knees to her chest and wrapped her arms around them.

Jabir reached out and tucked a strand of hair behind her ear. "Again, I'm sorry."

"Don't apologize anymore. Now I know how much you were hurting." She blinked and stared at the filmy curtain over the window. "I called Melanie after that. She took the six o'clock shuttle out of LaGuardia and was there by eight. She spent the weekend with me. That Friday, while Mom and Dad went to some function, we stayed in and cooked. We broke into a couple of bottles of wine. I got pretty tipsy. I guess I was feeling sorry for myself." She bit her lip, wanting to sink back into the papasan until it swallowed her. "I went upstairs to my room, grabbed the IAD report I hadn't bothered to read, and burned it in the fire we'd lit in the fireplace, all the while trashing you. Let's leave it at that. Now I hate myself for it."

Jabir remained still, letting the seconds tick into minutes as he ruminated on everything she'd said.

Was he considering a pronouncement similar to what she'd given him? Just get through this current situation, and he never wanted to see her again?

He reached out and took her face in his hands. "I love you."

Startled, her eyes widened.

Almost as if sensing her shock, he repeated, "I love you, Alex Thornton. Have loved you for years. Only I realized it and was going to tell you when you told me how in love you were with Eric Westin."

Her mind flashed back to their closeness and the way a fast, solid friendship had sprung up between them. He'd become her confidant about everything, yet she'd foolishly believed the notion that best friends couldn't be lovers. Now, she understood the devastation that had swept over her four years before on that horrible day he'd left for Egypt when she'd listened to a mechanical voice state that his phone had been disconnected.

He began pulling back.

"Jabir, please! Please stay," she begged.

"You want me to?"

Her tired mind scrambled for words. "Yes!"

She reached out and grabbed his hands. "I do. Please, Jabir. Don't leave me. Ever."

His eyes widened at her admission. "What?"

"I *love* you, Jabir al-Omri." The words flew out of her mouth, but she realized she meant it.

"Despite everything that's happened?"

She nodded since the lump in her throat cut off any words.

He cupped her cheek, and she leaned into his hand. His next words rocked her soul. "When I got that letter back unopened, I was devastated.

I prayed to God and begged Him for another chance to see you. A chance to make things right and perhaps explore my feelings for you with you."

He swallowed hard and paused. When he spoke again, his voice shook, "When I saw you a couple of days ago at the embassy, I knew. I knew He'd answered my prayers. And in a mighty way."

With that, he kissed her.

Jabir shifted onto the papasan and held her close.

Peace draped over her, and she wanted the moment to last.

Melanie.

Alex shuddered.

He seemed to sense her distress because his arms tightened.

Alex squeezed her eyes shut and held on. Right then, that was all she could do.

35

Numb. Noor Kamil-Sultan didn't know any other way to describe herself as she stared at the report lying open on the glass of the sleek conference table in the room next to her father's office.

Gavin Martin, the leader of the audit team, summarized what they'd found.

Pain in her hands made her glance down. She'd clinched her fists so tightly that her long nails had created indentations in the tender skin of her palms. She forced her fingers loose, but they remained like claws that embedded themselves into the silk of the skirt at her knees.

"It seems that an accountant named Shafiq Rahman was the one who opened several accounts that were used to funnel the laundered money." Gavin's voice finally penetrated the buzzing in her head.

"I'm sorry?" Noor blinked. "Would you mind repeating the process used?"

"No, not at all." Gavin nodded genteelly at her.

She thought she saw pity behind the gesture.

Of course. The great Kamil International, dealer in anything shipping, especially in the maritime world, brought down by the simple actions of one if its own. Not just its own. One of the founding family.

"Take one of the transactions we traced. It started out with Shafiq opening an account. Samir himself did all of the legal work rather than handing it off to one of the regional lawyers like he did for other accounts of similar nature. Shafiq signed his name and set it up so that it ran on its own. Samir then billed work for what we determined to be a shell corporation. We don't know these owners, and they never did any real business with Kamil International."

Gavin glanced at Fadi, who nodded.

Gavin cleared his throat and continued, "When they paid the bill, your accountants simply credited a ghost account. In this particular example, the account resides in the Grand Caymans. Businesses then invoiced Kamil International, again via contracts set up exclusively by Samir, for work they didn't do for the company. These same accounts were from where the money was withdrawn. Again, we suspect that the businesses are shell corporations and that the real owner is Jihad of Light."

"And those who make 'payment?'" Papa asked. His voice was tight, thin.

Startled, Noor studied his face. He'd paled and rightly so, but his color was more light gray than anything else. Sweat had beaded on his forehead, and he ran his finger along the collar of his shirt.

"We suspect they're Jihad of Light benefactors." Gavin paused, then sighed. "Farouk, I'm so sorry to have to be the one to deliver this news. Honestly, I am. You do realize that I have no choice but report this to Interpol since this obviously crosses international boundaries. They'll coordinate closely with the National Police here, I'm sure."

"Thank you." Papa's words were a whisper.

Noor's gaze shot to her husband. His eyes were dark with worry, but she was sure it was more focused on how to handle the questions and investigation that were bound to explode on Monday than on Papa.

"I'll stay here with Chelsea, but I'm going to send the rest of my team home. They're exhausted from working eighteen-hour days. Where is your son now?" Gavin's voice came from far off.

"At home, I assume." Papa choked those words out.

"Is he planning on traveling anytime soon?"

"On Monday, he flies to Panama City to do a closing for me."

"I recommend that you cancel the trip or get someone to go in his place."

Melanie. Her friend's name flew into Noor's mind.

Involuntarily, she began shaking her head.

"Noor, do you have something to say?" Papa asked.

Suddenly, she realized her actions. "No, no. You were correct." She swallowed hard. "I—I could do the closing if you wish."

"Giselle can do it since that's her territory."

Gavin closed his folder. "I suggest you confiscate his passport so he can't leave the country. I'm sure Interpol, if not both them and the National Police, will want to speak with him. You should do that tonight."

Noor closed her eyes.

"Chelsea and I will be glad to speak on your behalf to the investigators. After all, we've seen how swiftly you've acted to counteract the damage that has been done, and I know it will go a long way with them, especially when they know how sincere you are."

He said more, but the noise once more filling Noor's head drowned out his words. Like a robot, she rose and shook Gavin's hand as the meeting broke up. Suddenly, she noticed how blackness had fallen outside during the time they'd been on the top floor of Kamil International.

"I'm still in shock," Fadi murmured.

Papa carried his folder into his office. Suddenly, he seemed more stooped than his sixty-two years. "I wish…I wish I could say I was surprised. I just didn't realize…"

"Papa?" Noor stepped closer when he dropped the folder and gripped the back of his desk chair.

Papa gasped, clutched his chest, and collapsed.

"Papa!" Noor rushed forward. "Call an ambulance!"

The evening shifted into fast forward from there. She held Papa's hand, and within minutes, the ambulance had arrived and taken Papa to the hospital.

A very mild heart attack.

At least that's what the doctor told Mama when he'd finished examining Papa. He'd been lucky this time. Allah must have been smiling at him. They'd keep him a couple of days and release him to go home with orders to rest for the week. Finally, the doctor left the three of them with Papa.

Now, Fadi had gone with Mama to get a cup of coffee from the cafeteria. That left Noor alone with Papa. She eased onto the edge of a chair and took his hand. "Papa, what do you want me to do?"

"Go to…go to Samir and get his passport."

Her mind flew to what she knew. It sat there in her mouth, like a wild creature wanting to break free of its cage. Those words clawed at her throat to reveal what she knew.

Melanie would die if Samir didn't make the closing.

"Papa, I—"

"Go and get it. He mustn't be able to leave the country." Papa's voice, though still thin, held iron strength behind it. "Giselle can handle the closing for him."

Giselle showing up would spell the end of Melanie.

How could Noor argue? She swallowed hard. "I'll…I'll do that. You'll be okay here until Mama and Fadi get back?"

He nodded.

Noor rose, bent, and kissed him gently on the forehead. Tears gathered in her eyes. "I love you, Papa."

He took her hand and fiercely gripped it. When he released her, he mouthed, "I love you."

Noor fled before she began crying. On her way to her Mercedes SUV, she tapped out a text to Fadi. *I'm headed to Samir's and then home. See you at home.*

Noor didn't remember the ride up into the suburbs overlooking the city. At least she'd driven that route so many times she could do it on autopilot. When she stopped, she found herself outside of Samir's house in an older part of the subdivision a dozen houses down from her own. She climbed from the Mercedes and shut the door.

Noor paused at the pedestrian gate. Since it was made of an ornate wrought iron pattern, she could peer at the house.

The front was dark, but she thought she saw a faint glow from the back. Maybe he was out on the town with someone. For a brief, insane moment, she wondered if Tarek had talked him into another wild night of partying.

Then she shifted her gaze to the carport. Both his Mercedes and his Porsche convertible sat in their stalls like horses content to be in the barn for the night.

She immediately sucked in the sigh of relief she'd released.

Slowly, she raised her hand to the intercom that would let her brother know he had a visitor.

Noor lowered it.

She couldn't.

She wouldn't.

Her mind raced with a dozen excuses of how she'd explain her actions. Regardless, she wouldn't be a party to Melanie's death.

36

The maroon Suburban rumbled up the steep road toward the house where Hashim and his men had holed up.

His home now too, Ed supposed as he popped a Cheetos into his mouth.

At least for the next few days.

And then?

He didn't want to think about it.

The driver jerked the wheel to the left.

Ed almost came out of his seat when they bounced over a big bump.

A low moan reached him from the cargo area. He twisted and peered over the seat. Alvarez, her hands bound in front of her, shifted a little and shook her head from side to side.

"She's coming out of it," Ed reported.

"It's of no matter. We're here." Hashim hopped out and opened the back doors. "My men will get your things. Come with me."

Ed followed him as the other three men piled out of the SUV.

Hashim carried Alvarez to the back of the house. The two men who'd been injured hobbled after him, the one with the arm wound supporting the one with the broken ankle. Obviously drawn by the noise of their arrival, others from the house joined them.

Without ceremony, Hashim dumped Alvarez into the middle of the muddy yard. He bent. With a wicked-looking knife, he cut the cable tie holding her wrists together.

Alvarez's eyes fluttered open. She must have realized where she was because she suddenly sat upright. Then she collapsed onto her side and wrapped her arms around her middle. "I—I don't feel so good."

Hashim folded his arms across his broad chest.

Ed glanced around him.

The sixteen men had formed a loose circle with her in the middle. The two injured ones babbled about how she'd hurt them. That drew some derisive laughs and teasing comments. The guy with the arm wound scowled and cussed them out. One of them stepped forward and nudged her with his foot.

Alvarez made it to her hands and knees and promptly threw up.

Everyone laughed.

She did her best to glare at them as she eased to her knees.

The comments growing rougher, the circle shifted.

Somehow, she made it to her feet.

One of the men struck. He sent a punch her way.

She blocked it, but the action made her stagger against some of the others.

They shoved her, and she fell, obviously still feeling the effects of the chloroform.

Another tried to kick her while she was down.

She barely blocked his foot, grabbed it, and shoved him away.

He staggered backward and fell onto his rear.

His pals jeered him.

With a growl, he leapt toward her. He threw a punch. This one got through and connected with her cheek.

Alvarez groaned, and her hand flew to her face.

The others began advancing, obviously wanting to take out their frustrations on this infidel woman who'd humiliated their comrades. Kicks and punches left her balled up on the ground in an obvious attempt to protect her vital organs.

One reached down to grab her shirt and rip it open.

"Enough!" Hashim's voice made everyone freeze. He jerked his head at two of the men. "You two, get her inside and mask yourselves."

They slung her arms over their shoulders and dragged her toward a nearby shed. Her feet left contrails in the mud.

"Ed, come with me." Hashim followed them.

The first thing Ed noticed was the smell.

Dank dampness. Chemicals. Just like the shed his old man had kept at the edge of the bayou.

He took a step inside.

Shelves full of cans of pesticides and other forms of nastiness lined bare cinderblock walls. A light bulb hung from the ceiling on its wire. Only two small, cobweb-infested windows let weak light penetrate.

Ed sucked in a nervous breath. Suddenly, he was a ten-year-old boy in his old man's shed. He could almost feel the sting of the buckle end of a belt across his backside for no offense other than being the son of an alcoholic.

"This makes you nervous?" Hashim's voice penetrated his memory. He shoved a worktable out of the way and slapped a chair onto the concrete under the bulb.

The present snapped into place. "No, not at all."

Alvarez's chin sagged to her chest as her two guards secured her wrists with cords and looped her arms over the back of a chair. They lashed her ankles to the legs.

Ed assessed her. Something about Alvarez had caught his attention. She was beautiful. She was tough. Resourceful. Willing to fight and sacrifice herself if need be. Then it hit him. She reminded him of Francesca in so many ways.

He shoved thoughts of his longtime girlfriend into a deep recess of his mind.

One of Hashim's men brought them the video camera Ed had so thoughtfully removed from the safe house.

"Would you like to do the honors?" Hashim held up a metal can.

Ed nodded. He took it, stepped to the sink in the corner, and filled it to the brim with cold water. He approached Alvarez and studied her face. One eye had swollen shut, and a cut had opened up across her cheek where one of Hashim's goons had punched her. Mud streaked her shirt, and he noticed a wince each time she breathed. Cracked rib, maybe? He shrugged.

Ed hurled the water in her face.

"Hey!" Alvarez startled awake. Through the eye that wasn't swollen closed, she glared at him. "Did you have to do that? I was sleeping just fine."

Ed chuckled. "Were conditions different, Ms. Alvarez, I would have considered recruiting you."

She muttered something under her breath. "What do you want?"

"Where is Alex?"

"You think I'd tell you if I knew?"

"Would you if it saved your life?"

"No."

He laughed at her forthrightness. "Somehow, I don't think you know."

"Then why am I here? To entertain you?"

"You certainly did in the yard out there." Ed nodded toward the rectangle of light where two more of Hashim's men lounged against the doorjamb. He crossed his arms and leaned against the rusty metal post in front of her. "No, you, along with Melanie and Ellie, are our insurance."

"For what?"

"To ensure Alex is in our hands."

"Even though you showed me your face?"

He shrugged. "You seem to have figured out who I am. Besides, I hate masks. So. Your life for hers, right?"

"Alex?"

"Right."

"Why do you want her?"

"That is for us to know," Hashim's voice made Ed glance up. His former prisoner approached them, his face hidden. He smirked. "Perhaps now, you've learned that respect is key."

"And maybe by now you've learned I'm not going to succumb." Alvarez's words were low, and her tone spoke more than volumes.

Oh, yeah, she was tough.

"Perhaps we can change that later. Now, you have a message to deliver." Hashim brandished the video camera. "Ed, if you would film."

He handed it to him.

"Señora Alvarez, you will read this script word for word. Deviate, try to give a clue, and we'll stay here until you read it correctly. Understand?"

"Whatever," she muttered.

Hashim tipped her chin. "I like your sass, Becca Alvarez, but be aware that too much of it can get you into trouble. Asa, turn on the light."

His man flipped the switch that made the bulb above Alvarez glow dully.

Hashim summoned another to hold the message he'd scrawled on butcher paper.

The other two got out of the way

Hashim dropped that day's newspaper onto her lap so the date showed. "Read the message. Ed, are you ready?"

"Ready. You're on, Alvarez." Ed hit the Record button.

Alvarez cleared her throat. She hesitated, her good eye obviously searching out the words. "This message is for Alex Thornton and Jabir al-Omri. As you can see, I am being held hostage by members of the Jihad of Sissies—"

Ed rolled his eyes and cut off the camera.

"Becca." Hashim, who was standing out of the picture but following the text, shook his head.

"Hey, I can't help what you write."

Ed muffled his laugh, which came out as a strangled chuckle.

"Read it verbatim, Señora Alvarez."

"Okay, okay." She nodded at Ed, and he started recording. "This message is for Alex Thornton and Jabir al-Omri. As you can see, I'm being held hostage by Jihad of Light at an undisclosed location along with Melanie Forrest. If you have any hope of seeing us, then you will show up at the embassy where the Marines will arrest—What?"

Alvarez did her best to glare at her captor when he stepped in front of the camera and crossed his arms.

"I'm warning you…"

She shrugged. "Sorry. My eyesight's a bit blurry thanks to that chloroform you guys gave me. Oh, and the way your pals decided to beat the tar out of me too."

She jerked her head toward the guards.

"She's a little vixen," one of the guards commented in Arabic. "I wonder what she's like in bed."

"Wildcat," his buddy replied and laughed.

Alvarez, who obviously hadn't understood a word they said, scowled at them. "It wasn't a fair fight," she said in Spanish. "I would have beaten them and hung their you-know-whats out to dry."

They stared blankly at her.

Ed laughed.

"Do it right." The strain had appeared in Hashim's voice. "Ed, if you would."

Ed erased the two old recordings. "Okay, Alvarez. Third time's charm."

"This message is for Alex Thornton and Jabir al-Omri. As you can see, I'm being held hostage by Jihad of Light at an undisclosed location along with Melanie Forrest. If you have any hope of seeing us, then you will show up at the property Samir Kamil wishes to purchase. You are to come with as many—"

Hashim cuffed her across the head.

"Ow!"

He grabbed her chin and went almost nose to nose with her. "We can do the easy way or the hard way. You flub this again, and the hard way will be much, much worse. Do you understand me?"

Alvarez's good eye widened. She nodded.

He released her. "Do it again. And do it *right* this time."

She did it right.

Hashim nodded. "Perhaps now you're learning that respect is the key to your survival. Tough might not mean a long survival with us." He turned to his men and said in Arabic, "Later, we'll see just exactly how tough she is. Ed, come with me."

He turned to leave.

Ed started to follow him.

"I do know who you are." Alvarez's soft words, barely audible, made him stop.

Slowly, he turned and faced her. "What?"

"I know who you are." Her attempt to smile twisted her lips into more of a grimace. "Ed DuBois. CIA senior case officer, right? Good agent gone bad, apparently."

He glared at her. "Al-Omri told you, huh?"

She ignored him. "And a murderer. Three innocent men this morning who trusted you with their lives."

He got right in her face like Hashim had. "Leave it alone."

Becca screwed up her face. "Ew! Cheetos. Gross!"

"Shut up." Ed glared at her.

"How many did you kill before that?" Her sherry eyes, or at least the one that was visible, gleamed in the dim light. "You're a traitor in the worst degree. Your mother would be so disappointed in you if she knew."

She spat in his face.

Rage flew through him. With a growl, he slapped her hard, right across her injured cheek.

Alvarez's head snapped back. She didn't cry out. Didn't even moan. It took a few seconds, but she once more gazed at him with her good eye.

No fear at all.

None.

That sent Ed into even more of a rage. He yanked out his knife and cut her bonds, then grabbed her around the waist and lifted her off the chair.

Alvarez spluttered protests. "What are you doing? Stop! You're hurting me."

She struggled as he slammed her onto the worktable.

It was a moment before she could gasp, "Let...me...go."

"No can do now."

Suddenly, Hashim stood by her other side. He drew his knife and held it to her throat.

Ed smirked as her eyes widened.

Hashim pressed the tip into her neck. "You struggle, I'll cut your throat out. Do you understand?"

Hashim handed the knife to Ed. Using more cord, he secured her wrists and ankles to the legs of the table so she lay spread-eagled. He glared at her. "I want you to think about something, Señora Alvarez, while I'm away. Respect. Respect for who we are and the sorry position you're in. You see, one word, and all of the men at this compound will have their way with you. After all, you are indeed a very attractive woman."

A smile curled his lips as he untucked her camp shirt and slid his hand underneath.

She drew in a sharp breath.

Hashim ran his fingers down her cheek. "Perhaps I'll start tonight. Think about it."

With that, he pulled back.

"Let's go, Ed." Hashim turned away. "Señora Watkins will deliver the messages for us."

They headed toward the door.

Just before they passed through, Ed paused and turned.

Alvarez lay on the table. Her chest heaved, and her hands shook.

She was scared.

He smirked.

Served her right.

Something told him she'd not draw another free breath.

37

Jabir braced his elbows on his knees and cradled the mug of hot Colombian coffee. He inhaled the steam, savoring the rich aroma and the
peace that spilled across him, peace brought on by a good, though short,
sleep and his time with Alex. He smiled, wanting the moment to last.

His phone began chiming.

As he checked Caller ID, he realized it couldn't.

Tiny.

Tension returned to his shoulders. "Tiny, hey."

"Jabir, it's good to hear your voice." His boss's baritone floated over
the airwaves. "Did I wake you?"

"No. I've been awake and am almost through my first cup of coffee."

"Good to hear. After everything that happened this morning, I'm sure
you needed to rest. I wanted to give you a heads up that I'll be at the safe
house in an hour."

"You're here?" Jabir straightened.

"In the flesh. So be ready, and have Alex ready. We've got to talk, and
I've brought along friends."

"What kind of friends?"

Tiny's voice carried a certain amount of satisfaction. "The best you could have in a situation like this."

SEAL Team Twelve.

New relief surged through Jabir. "Will do. Thanks, Tiny."

"Tell Alex I'll see her in a bit."

Jabir sat there for a moment, his phone resting on his knee. Then he rose, left it on the table, and stepped across the landing to Alex's room.

A breeze from the open sliding doors filled the room with a fresh, sweet odor as if the rain had cleansed the air and then spritzed it with tropical scents. The curtains, which Alex had left closed, billowed in the breeze, the setting sun tingeing them with oranges, reds, and pinks that shimmered like flames. He turned his attention to the bed.

Jabir's heart caught in his throat as he surveyed Alex's sleeping form. She curled on her side facing him, the sheet and comforter drawn up to the point where only her head was visible. Her dark hair spilled across the white of the pillow, and a few strands brushed her cheek.

A lump of emotion filled his throat. He reached out and brushed away those locks.

Lord, thank You for reuniting us.

Jabir tiptoed across the room and grabbed the coffee carafe. He filled it with water and added fresh grounds to the brewer. As it perked, he sat down on the edge of the bed. He ran his hand down her cheek.

Alex sighed deep in her throat and turned onto her back.

He bent and kissed her forehead. "Alex, wake up."

She mumbled something and shook her head.

"Alex."

Finally, she opened those magnificent sea green eyes. Her gaze spoke of the depths of their past friendship and the potential of that yet to come. It shook him to that secret place in his core.

Then she smiled sleepily at him. "I thought it was a dream."

"Oh?"

"You and me…our talk."

Jabir held her hand and kissed her palm as he took a deep breath to chase away the sudden lump in his throat. Remembering his reason for being in her room finished the job. "I'm no dream, beloved. Not at all."

"What time is it?"

"Just past five. Tiny called, and he's on his way here."

"On his way?" She blinked as if to dispel sleep. "As in we're meeting him at the airport?"

"No, as in he's on his way to the safe house." He ran his fingers down her hand. "I promised I'd have you ready to go."

"Big chore, huh?" She yawned and slid down so the comforter came up to her nose. Her hair stayed right where it was and stood on end.

He reached out and smoothed it down. "You have a major case of bedhead."

She giggled. It was a sleepy, contented sound, one that conjured up visions of waking up with her on a rainy Saturday morning with nothing to do but lounge in bed together. He chuckled as he forced that thought away, lest he forget why they were at the safe house in the first place.

She sat up and wrapped her arms around her knees. Her pretty features clouded. "I wish why we're here was a dream. Or a nightmare. Like I could wake up, and you and I would be on vacation, and—"

She bit her lip.

"I know." Jabir smiled gently and tucked a strand of hair behind her ear. "I love you."

Her smile answered him. "I love you too."

He rewarded her with a kiss. He started to pull back, but she wrapped her arms around him. Oh, boy. They were a match in all ways possible. Reluctantly, he withdrew.

"Coffee's perking. Be ready in twenty?" He kept his hand in hers.

"Yeah. I guess I'd better get up."

He rose and extended a helping hand.

Alex blushed. "I, uh, can't. Um, I'm, uh…well, I'm not decent."

Jabir couldn't help it. He chuckled. "I see. I'll leave you be. Twenty minutes on the landing."

Jabir stepped outside. Parker's voice as he talked to Ryan brought him fully back into the precarious reality of their situation.

Time was running out for Melanie, and he wasn't sure what they could do about it.

1730 hours Central Daylight Time, west of Panama City, Panama

Alex ran a comb through her damp hair and stared at her reflection in the mirror. Happiness from Jabir's revelation of his feelings for her competed in those sea green depths with their predicament. At least exhaustion had stunned her into sleep for five hours. Otherwise, she didn't know how she would have coped.

Jabir.

An unwilling smile tipped the corners of her mouth. Even now, she could feel his gentle kiss and smell the faint tobacco aroma and aftershave she'd always associated with him. She closed her eyes. A pop echoed in her ears, and gore from Jorge splattered everywhere. Her eyes flew open, and she whirled.

Nothing.

No blood and gore anywhere. No gunfire either, only the rustle of the palm fronds bordering the outdoor shower.

Alex slowly blew out an uneasy breath.

She stepped into the bedroom. Her gaze landed on the dresser where she'd laid her watch and the small gold earrings she'd worn. Beside them sat both Melanie's medication and her glasses. That was enough to send her emotions into a tailspin. Whatever respite she'd had was now over. Her spirits sagged to new lows. If they didn't get a move on it, Melanie stood a better than good chance of dying.

That spurred her to action. She grabbed the items and stepped onto the landing as Jabir's door opened.

"Ready to face the crowd?" he asked as he took her hand.

"Not really." She paused, took his other one, and drew him close. Tears filled her eyes, and she squeezed them shut to keep them in check.

"Are you okay?" Jabir's soft voice and his hand on her hair made her pull back.

"Melanie's dying." She held up the pill bottle.

"I know." His dark eyes clouded as he reached up and touched her cheek. "I know."

"Jabir?" Tiny's voice floated up the stairs.

"Up here." Jabir kissed her forehead and whispered, "I love you."

Footfalls echoed on the steps as their boss joined them. "Hey, you two. The first round's here. The second round's on their way."

Second round? Alex cast Jabir a glance, but he shrugged.

He didn't let go of her hand as they followed Tiny down the stairs.

Eight SEALs now occupied the great room and kitchen. Had Alex not known who they were, she would have figured them for vacationing tourists, what with the shaggy hair, stubble, T-shirts, shorts, and flip flops. Only their alert eyes and the way four had taken up sentry positions told her otherwise. The remaining four lounged on the sectional sofa.

Ryan had a laptop open on the bar and fiddled with something. He stepped to the television and inserted a wireless adaptor into one of the USB ports.

Parker dished something from a frying pan onto several plates. "Chow's up, guys. Good thing we stocked this house with lots of food. I never dreamed I'd be cooking for twelve except at a dinner party. Hey, Alex. Feeling better?"

Alex released Jabir's hand and slid onto a bar chair. "Much. Thanks for watching over us while we slept."

"Our pleasure."

"Alex, how are you?" JC Adams, the SEAL Team Twleve commander, came up and wrapped his arm around her shoulders in a friendly hug.

"Fair to middlin'," she replied.

"I hear you. I'm glad we can help out down here. Seems like we've got ourselves a bit of a challenge."

"That's one way to put it." Tiny took his plate and set it on the bar beside Alex's. "Gang, eat up while we talk. Ryan, how're we doing?"

"Good to go." Ryan hit a button, and the wallpaper of the laptop appeared on the television screen.

"Let's get to it. Gentlemen?" Tiny nodded, and all of the SEALs either settled on the couch or pulled over chairs from the dining room. All had huge piles of food on their plates.

Alex stayed where she was.

Jabir pulled up a bar chair and sat beside her.

Tiny perched on the arm of the couch nearest the television. "Okay, Alex and Jabir, I did some research on the way down here, but I want you two to explain exactly what's going on. Jabir, care to start?"

A muscle twitched in Jabir's jaw. He glanced at Alex and took a deep breath before rehashing the story from his angle.

Not that anyone blinked an eye. They were used to the twisted alliances that seemed to go on in clandestine work.

Then Alex told her side of the story in short, clipped sentences. Time was of the essence, and she felt that if she wasted even one word, they'd be that much closer to losing Melanie, this time forever. Finally, she added, "Guys, Melanie has a heart condition. Cardiomyopathy or something like that."

She held up the pill bottle. "She has to take these daily. Jabir, when was the last time she had one?"

"I assume Friday night. I think that's a safe assumption since the guys weren't killed until this morning. They would have made sure she took it."

"What time?" Doc Wilder, the medic, asked.

"Most likely at about seven in the evening."

Doc rose and took the medication from Alex. He frowned as he read the directions. "In other words, she's due for a dose in an hour or so."

Alex nodded. Not hungry, she stared at her food. Her stomach was suddenly tied in knots.

"I'll do some research on this. Hopefully, there's enough of a residual in her bloodstream to keep her for a bit. Anything else?"

"She's very near-sighted. I have her glasses as well." Alex laid them on the bar.

"Problem is, we don't know her location," Jabir muttered.

"Right, but we've got more info than you know," Tiny said. "Things went down this morning in a big way."

"I'll say." Alex muttered under her breath.

"Sometime between when you left the hotel and eight this morning, Ellie was kidnapped."

"What? How?" Alex's eyes widened.

Tiny summarized how fake policemen had ambushed Ellie at the hotel.

"How did they find out?" Jabir slowly asked.

"The guards assigned to her by Esteban Romero arrived as promised at eight o'clock sharp. They notified him."

Alex bit her lip. Hard.

"There's more."

She swallowed hard and somehow choked out, "What?"

"At approximately nine thirty this morning, Esteban Romero, Becca Alvarez, and Mitch Gordon were ambushed up at the house, most likely by the same people who took Melanie. They killed Mitch."

Alex's hand shot to her mouth.

Beside her, Jabir muttered something. He kicked the side of the bar.

Tiny paused and then added, "I'm sorry, Jabir. I know you worked with him at the embassy. Esteban survived. When their vehicle got torched, Esteban and Becca sought shelter in the house. Esteban was knocked out when they kicked the door in."

"Becca…" Alex was almost too afraid to ask.

"Kidnapped. How, we don't know, because Esteban regained consciousness right when they were leaving. He didn't see anything, not even a vehicle. Before the ambush, Becca was able to supply him with a description of the van before all hell broke loose. There's a BOLO for that. Help arrived for Esteban, and he is now under observation at the hospital."

Alex put her head in her hands.

Jabir rubbed her back.

God, no! No. No. Not Ellie and Becca. No!

She lifted her face as tears streamed down her cheeks. Alex gripped the edge of the bar as she thought about her friends, all of them now in the hands of unknown kidnappers.

"All's not lost." Tiny's quiet voice penetrated her thoughts.

"I don't see how you mean that." Her voice was hoarse. Strained.

"At about four this afternoon, a Land Rover pulled to a stop in front of the embassy. They dumped Ellie in front of the main gate and escaped before anyone saw them. She's alive," he hastily added. "Sergeant Markham and Lance Corporal O'Neill took her to the hospital. She was heavily sedated by whoever dropped her off, so they're working on bringing her out from under it."

Right on the heels of agony came relief. "Will she be okay?"

"Captain Davis flew over from the boat and checked her out with me," Doc told her from where he sat on the couch. "She's got a hurt shoulder, but beyond that, once she comes out of sedation, she'll be fine."

"How long until then?" Jabir asked. His voice was tight, the anger he must have felt against Ed simmering beneath the surface.

"Without an antidote, twenty-four hours. With an antidote, we hope in the morning because we started administering it as soon as we could. Whoever injected the sedative overdosed her a bit."

Tiny cleared his throat. "Obviously, we have security concerns, so we decided to bring her to the safe house. That's why I mentioned a second wave coming. Esteban's with them. He refused to be sidelined for this, and we need his local knowledge and coordination here." He cast a glance at Ryan, who straightened. "Guys, that's not all. Ellie was wearing a jump drive on a lanyard around her neck."

He held up a small jump drive.

Alex stared at it. "What's on it?"

Tiny nodded, and Ryan hit a button on the computer that called up a video.

Once more, Alex's hand shot to her mouth as she stared at the first video. It showed both Melanie and Ellie. Ellie read a message that had obviously been pre-prepared. The point? Alex was to show up at the gates to the property Kamil Industries was going to buy. Once there, she was to walk into the middle of the complex. Alone. At three in the morning Monday morning. They were waiting that long since Jihad of Light knew it would take time to get the message to Alex.

"Play it again," Doc ordered. He rose and studied it. "Melanie's not well."

"How so?" Tiny asked.

"She's acting out of it. See? Ellie's alert and focused. She's not."

"But why?" Alex asked.

Doc shrugged. "It could be any number of things. Maybe it's worse than we realize. Or maybe they knocked her out with something. Or she could have a concussion. Regardless, the sooner we get to her, the better. Go on."

Becca came next. She seemed to have gone down fighting, at least if the black eye, bruising on her face, and blood on her shirt meant anything. She essentially said the same thing, only adding that if Alex didn't show up, she and Melanie would disappear forever. Though she may have been beaten, the look in her eye told her friend one thing. She was still a fighter and would die that way.

Tiny clicked off the television. "Alex, are you okay?"

"No." She grabbed her napkin and dabbed at her eyes.

Deep breaths. Take deep breaths.

Tiny sighed. "That's all we know, guys. Nothing more. Only that you're supposed to be at the docks at three in the morning tomorrow night."

"Why me?" Alex slowly asked.

"I've been trying to figure that out. You never worked a Jihad of Light case, did you?"

"No. What do we know about them?"

"Not a lot, unfortunately. They may call themselves Jihad of Light, but they operate in the dark. So dark that they're one of the most secretive groups out there."

"I'll go—"

"Not going to happen, all right?" Tiny cut her off. "These guys are brutal, and I fully expect them to go back on their word. Not to mention, your mother and father would literally kill me if I let you go.

"Guys, what do we know?" he asked the rest of the group.

The SEALs began talking. Both ideas and information were in short supply. They knew that medically, Melanie was in trouble. She was nearsighted. Doc would take her glasses and pills for safekeeping. Both women were beaten up, so they had to plan on the fact that most likely, they weren't ambulatory. They had a description of the vehicle. Beyond that, no location. No numbers. No nothing, really. No ideas either.

Her headache returned full force.

Alex rose.

She wanted to be alone, to contemplate everything that had happened in solitude.

She headed toward the doors leading to the patio.

"Alex, you shouldn't go out there," Parker called.

She barely heard JC reply, "No worries. Mooch, Jeff, go out there and keep an eye on her. Make sure she doesn't run off or something."

She wandered to the pool, collapsed onto a chaise lounge, and stared at the sunset. She barely noticed the stunning display of oranges, yellows, and reds as the sun set in a glowing fireball over the ocean.

By her count, Melanie should be taking a pill in an hour, a pill that would keep her heart beating at a normal rate. Without it, her heart would slow, possibly causing her blood to clot. If a clot drifted to her lungs, heart, or brain? Sobs rose from deep within her chest and fought their way loose. Alex put her head in her hands.

A sense of weakness and helplessness filled her. She wanted to run to the property in the middle of the night the next night and give herself up so her friends could live.

She began thinking about how she could dash through the gate and hotwire one of the vehicles outside. Or jump over the edge and climb down to the road below.

All foolishness. The SEALs leaning against two of the portico columns wouldn't let her get three steps.

She had nothing left in terms of her strength.

"God, I feel so helpless." Her whispered words barely penetrated the rustling of the leaves. "So worn out. Like I've got nothing more to give because I've been bled out of all strength. Is this where You want me? At the end of my rope? I'm so scared that Melanie and Becca are going to die because of me. What do I do? What?"

She quietly wept.

The sensation of someone sitting down beside her roused her from her tears.

Alex opened her eyes and tried to get her runaway emotions under control. Tears randomly spilled down her cheeks as she dabbed at them with the sleeve of the T-shirt she wore. For a few minutes, nothing filled the air but her sniffles. Finally, she murmured, "I feel so hopeless."

"I know." Jabir sighed. A *schnick* told her he'd lit up. The acrid scent of cigarette smoke confirmed it.

"Melanie's going to die if we don't get her medication to her soon."

"I agree."

She glanced at him.

He sat hunched over like she did, except that his elbows rested on his knees while the cigarette smoldered in his fingers.

She bit her lip. "I don't know what to think. Or feel."

Jabir took a puff as he reached up with his other hand and rubbed her shoulder. Finally, he spoke. "It reminds me of when you were injured four years ago and in the CCU. Though I was released from the hospital, I refused to leave the lobby until I knew you were out of danger."

Alex remained silent.

"It was so touch and go that the pressure finally got to your dad and me. We took a walk. David told me about how he'd wound up earlier that night in the chapel praying. He said that God spoke. Maybe not audibly, but in his heart. Essentially, your dad said He told him that he would see you again no matter what, that You were in God's hands and that nothing—and that meant nothing—would ever rip you from His hands, not even death." He took a drag and exhaled a stream of smoke through his mouth.

"I don't want them to die." Alex's voice broke, and she leaned into him as another round of tears struck.

Jabir stubbed out his cigarette and wrapped his arms around her. "Me neither."

For a few minutes, only Alex's sniffles and sobs were audible. "I feel so broken." Her voice caught on a sob. "So weak. So…"

Words finally failed her.

"So crushed."

Jabir's stubble rubbed her forehead as he nodded. After a moment, he prayed. His words touched her heart and seared her soul as he prayed for peace for both of them, for healing for Ellie, and for the very real need for protection for Melanie and Becca. Gradually, like a warm comforter, peace draped over her.

Any desire Alex had to sneak away faded. She still worried for her friends and remained terrified even though she knew she had to let the fear be enough to keep her alert but not so much as to paralyze her.

The message rang loud and clear in her heart.

She would see her friends again.

If not here on earth, then most certainly in heaven.

Right then, that was all she had.

Day 8
Sunday, June 18, 2017

38

Samir lounged on the leather couch in his great room. A breeze blew across the patio and through the open French doors to shower him with all sorts of pleasant smells, including that of the sea, which was visible from where he lay. He felt as if he could sink into the soft leather and take a nap. Maybe he'd sleep away the rest of the morning. Or, he could get up, pour himself a cup of coffee, and continue his day of rest on the patio by the pool. His choices seemed endless.

He yawned and studied the news coming across his tablet. Later, he'd call Noor to see if she and Fadi wanted to bring the children over for an evening supper. After they left, he'd pack and prepare for the 7:30 flight that would take him from Beirut to Panama City. He'd not leave there until he saw with his own eyes that Melanie was safe. Samir closed his eyes and rested his head against the pillow.

A buzzing from the foyer penetrated his dozing.

Blinking, Samir rose and thumped across the cool tile into the entry-way. He pressed the intercom buzzer. "Who is it?"

"Noor."

He switched on the small monitor and smiled when he saw his sister. A press of the button on the intercom panel released the lock at the pedestrian gate. The deadbolt of the heavy front door clunked back, and he stepped onto the portico. Samir grinned as he crossed his arms and leaned against one of the Roman columns.

She shut the pedestrian gate.

"Noor, hi. What brings you over here so early?"

"I came to see you, brother." She kissed him on the cheek. Her smile trembled a little. "I hoped you would already be awake."

"I have been since seven." Samir turned and led the way inside. "Would you like a drink? Perhaps water? Or tea?"

"Water would be good." Noor nodded.

Samir stepped into the kitchen and located a glass. He filled it and handed it to her. "Where are the girls? I didn't hear a lot of racket on the intercom."

That same trembling smile appeared. "They're with Fadi for the day. He took them to see Aunt Miriam and Uncle Yacoub." It faded.

"Hah. Lucky Fadi."

"I know. He'll be ready to head back by early afternoon. What did you do last night?"

"I stayed in for a change." Samir gestured for her to precede him to the patio. "It was nice. I read for a bit, even played some video games."

"That does sound nice."

Her voice caught, which made him turn and study her face. For the first time, he noticed the small lines at the corners of her eyes and along her brow. And her eyes. Those sherry depths were sad. Something had happened.

"Is everything okay between you and Fadi?"

"Yes." That was too fast, even for her.

"You're sure?"

She nodded and raised the glass to her lips. The clear liquid quivered.

"Noor."

"I...Well, you see...we...we know about the accounts."

Samir's stomach plunged like the times he'd gone on huge rollercoasters and fallen through that first precipitous drop. His knees began shaking, and he collapsed onto a nearby chaise. "How…how did you find out?"

"The audit." Noor remained where she was. "This past spring, one of our analysts noticed some oddities, and he took it to Fadi. Fadi thought it warranted a more thorough audit. A forensic one." Noor settled beside him, their shoulders touching. "What happened?"

Samir didn't move, didn't say a word. He put his head in his hands.

"Please talk to me."

"Do you remember how, about four or so years ago, I falsified some records at Tarek's insistence?"

"I do. And from what I remembered, you stopped." Noor paused. "Didn't you?"

"I did. Promise on that one. Two years ago, Tarek approached me again. I thought about it. Honestly. I knew I shouldn't. But he sweetened the deal by offering me a cut. Ten percent as a finder's fee."

Noor remained silent, which was worse than if she'd given him a tongue-lashing for his transgressions.

"How bad is it?" Samir asked after a moment, the tremor in his body now radiating into his voice.

"Bad. We had a meeting with Gavin last night." Noor bunched some of her skirt with her fingers. Then she nervously worked to smooth out the material and repeated the process as if it could soothe her. "They uncovered the method you used as well as the amount of money funneled from Jihad of Light donors through our organization and to Jihad of Light. Almost twenty-five million or so."

Samir flinched. Even he hadn't realized the amount.

"Gavin had no choice but to go to Interpol. They'll be contacting the National Police."

He sat there as still as a cemetery at dawn, not daring to move.

"Papa collapsed last night."

"What?" Samir jumped up. "Is he okay?"

"He will be. It was a very mild heart attack brought about by stress. The doctor wants him to stay home and rest next week."

Samir muttered something and paced to the other side of the pool. He stared over the city and at the Mediterranean glittering in the distance. A cargo ship made its way toward port, most likely a Kamil International ship to be offloaded using Kamil International cranes at a dock owned by Kamil International. The heartbeat of his family's business pulsed not thirty kilometers away, and his decisions had endangered its future and the possibility of handing it down not only to his nieces but to any future children he might have.

Noor's gentle touch on his arm made him glance over.

She stood shoulder to shoulder with him.

"I'm sorry," he rasped.

"I know." She stayed quiet for a few moments. "Papa asked me to come and get your passport."

Melanie. Her name flew into his mind once more. "Noor, I've got to go to Panama City tomorrow. You know I—"

"I know. I know." Noor faced him. Her eyes glittered with unshed tears. "Don't you think I know that? I came by last night, but I couldn't bring myself to get it then even though I knew you were home. That's what…That's what Fadi and I fought about this morning. He told me that if I didn't get it from you as Papa requested, then he'd come and get it himself. I'm sorry, Samir. I truly am, but I see no way out of this, especially since both Interpol and the National Police will be talking to you tomorrow."

Samir's shoulders sagged as if the weight of decisions made years before had chained him to a fate he couldn't change now. "Are they…are they going to arrest me?"

"I don't know," she whispered.

"Melanie's lost to me now." The realization made him go weak in the knees.

Noor wrapped her arms around him and clung to him. "I know."

"I'm sorry, Noor. I've dishonored the company. My family."

"I love you."

Her statement made him cling to her.

"There may be a way out of this."

"I don't see how."

"You said Tarek put you up to this." Noor released him and gazed at him.

"He did."

"And we both know that he's the leader of Jihad of Light. Oh, his father may be the brains behind the concept, but you and I both know that Tarek and that brute of a brother of his are the real muscle and brain power." She rubbed her chin, her eyes narrowed in thought.

"I don't see where you're going with this."

"You don't?" Noor faced him. "When you talk to Interpol and the police tomorrow, you disclose that you know more about Jihad of Light than meets the eye."

"How? I committed a crime."

"I know." Noor began pacing slowly around the patio. Her fingers pressed together. "But if you agree to testify against Tarek, maybe the judge will offer leniency."

Samir shook his head. "I hate to break it to you, but Tarek is clean."

"On the surface. Yet even a good coat of paint can hide rot." Noor stopped. Her skirt floated in the breeze. Something sparked in her eyes. "If they start focusing their attention on Tarek, I imagine they'll find more. Especially the Americans. Their goal, as you know, is to eliminate Jihad of Light. With your information and an in-depth investigation, I know that will happen."

"Tarek's a friend of mine—"

"Who used you." Noor's voice hardened. "A true friend is someone who encourages you, who wants to see you succeed, not someone who will take advantage of his influence over you and ask you to commit crimes that benefit only him."

Samir fell into a miserable silence. She was right, as usual. Tarek had wielded a powerful influence over him, and he knew it. Tarek had played on Samir's greed, on his envy and jealousy of his sister, to get him to do his bidding.

It had worked.

Now, Samir would be the one to pay the price.

Unless…

"When are you talking with Interpol?"

"I—I don't know." Noor rejoined him. "Gavin was going to contact them today. Then it would follow from there. Perhaps later today or in the morning."

Abruptly, Noor turned and strode toward the house. "I'm sorry, Samir. I need to get your passport."

"Noor…"

"Please."

He had no choice but to retreat to his study. He opened the desk drawer. There, on top of some papers, sat the small booklet that would have been his key to saving Melanie.

Not anymore.

She was lost to him.

Agony gripped his heart. He took a deep breath, reached inside, and handed his sister the slender booklet.

"I'm sorry, Noor. I'm sorry for everything. I've shamed our company. Our family, especially Papa."

Tears streamed down her cheeks in two shiny tracks.

"And now Melanie. I failed her."

A small sob reached him.

When he stood, Noor flung herself into his arms.

Brother and sister held each other.

Finally, Noor pulled back. Sniffling, her eyes red, her cheeks wet, she gazed up at him. "Please, Samir. Don't talk to Tarek. Even if he calls or comes over. Ever since…ever since he hit me that one time, I've come to realize what violence he's capable of, him and his brother."

Too choked up to speak, he nodded.

"And please, go see Papa. Tell him what you want to do."

Samir swallowed hard. He knew he needed to do that.

Noor opened the door. As she was about to step into the bright morning light, she turned. A trembling smile crossed her lips and faded.

"I love you," she mouthed because anguish must have stolen her voice. She touched his cheek.

Then she was gone.

Samir shut the door. Stunned, he wandered through the foyer and great room and onto the patio. The day, ripe with such promise earlier, lay as a wasteland before him. One created by his own hand and his own foolish decisions.

He sank onto a chaise.

He'd go see Papa later.

Now?

He couldn't.

Melanie was lost to him.

His future lay shattered before him.

His family's future stood on the precipice of ruin.

All because of him.

Samir lowered his head and wept.

39

Rain pounded on the roof of the villa, providing a white noise that
would have encouraged sleep under normal circumstances, as would have
the fresh breeze and scents pouring through the window. Jabir wanted
nothing more than to laze on the couch downstairs, Alex in his arms, as
they watched old movies or simply kept the television off and listened to
nature.

Not now. Not tonight.

Rumbling reached him. Lightning flashed, and thunder emitted a low,
guttural growl like some creature that threatened to demolish them all.

Jabir shivered and leaned back against the desk chair as he tapped into
the Internet from his laptop. After logging into the Unit 28 system, he sat
there for a few moments and tried to figure out where to start. A few clicks
brought up the mug shot of Hashim al-Hassan.

"Jabir?"

Tiny's voice and a tap on the door made him pause.

"I'm awake."

His boss slipped through the door. The sleeves of his button-down
shirt were rolled up past his elbows, and his shirttails were out, a sure

indication he'd been hard at work with Esteban and JC as they tried to figure out a way to rescue Melanie without putting Alex in danger. "You snuck away."

"I had to think."

"I understand. This is a hard nut to crack." With a small sigh, Tiny eased into one of the chairs near the open window.

Jabir swiveled around. "I've been trying to figure out why Jihad of Light is so interested in her. It doesn't make sense to me."

"You haven't thought about it enough."

Jabir gave him a look.

Tiny nodded toward the screen where the mug shot of Hashim al-Hassan now glowed. "You know I worked with his father."

"Hashim's?"

"Back in the eighties in Afghanistan. He was *mujahedeen*. David, Roya, and I worked with him. Things were different back then. Alliances shifted in the nineties."

"Why did JOL suddenly demand Alex for her friends? I don't understand."

"Come over here and sit."

With a sigh, Jabir rose and seated himself on the couch of the conversation area.

"How much do you know about Alex?"

"She and I worked together for four years."

"Right. But did she talk with you about her work before you joined her?"

Jabir shrugged. "Not really. She took your advice to heart."

"Burn your past?"

"Yeah. She said it didn't make any sense to look back, only to look at the present and the future since our choices in the present impact our future."

Tiny chuckled. Then he sighed as he took off his glasses and polished them with a shirttail. "True to a certain extent. But sometimes, our actions in the past can impact the present and the future. Two years before you started, the intelligence agencies launched a joint operation that was partly an effort to find bin Laden and partly an effort to clean up al-Qaida, to de-fang them as much as we could. CIA led it, but we helped by reeling in suspects because the web they wanted to throw was so large. Alex and her partner, Monica Chapman, walked point on a lot of these round-ups."

"Why was that?"

"They were trained agents and women. Very capable women, I might add. And a lot of the suspects had one big weakness."

"Women."

Tiny nodded. "You got it. I supervised them on-site, essentially. People got to calling them Tiny's Angels."

Jabir couldn't help it. A smile broke through his somber mood. "I'm sure Alex liked that."

"Oh, she did. Very much so. During 2007, we three were barely home. It was called Operation Orb Web. The last mission of Orb Web culmi-nated in Baghdad. CIA had heard through their assets that several future leaders of al-Qaida were massing in Baghdad for a meeting with al-Qaida's senior leadership. They suspected it would be a meeting where information got passed to the next generation. And it wasn't just one meeting. It was a series."

"Didn't al-Qaida know that was risky?"

"Sure, they did. These ten guys came in gradually. They blended in with their surroundings. Our assets worked overtime trying to locate them be-cause CIA wanted to round them up all at once."

Jabir reached over and picked up his cigarette pack. He turned it over and over in his hands as he considered what Tiny was saying. "And Alex and Monica got pulled into this?"

"Uh, huh." Tiny nodded, obviously remembering that day. "It was in late November. The twenty-fifth. Because CIA wanted to do the roundup simultaneously, they called upon us to do the takedown of Hashim. You see, Hashim is a smart guy all around. Smart and brutal, but he has a major weakness. Well, two. He likes to have a good time at nightclubs, and he likes pretty girls."

"Enter Alex and Monica," Jabir mumbled.

"Right. They did themselves up. Monica wore a wig to hide her blond hair. Alex simply teased hers until she looked like a party girl. Add the right outfits and some perfume, and they looked like every other girl who wanted to go party in the re-emerging part of Baghdad. Alex wound up being the one to get Hashim's attention. According to the after-action report, they danced several numbers together and shared drinks. It seemed like he took the bait without any question. Then it was only a matter of her sweet-talking him to go out back with her. The SEALs working with her sedated him and bundled him into the back of a car."

"Where did he go from there?"

"A CIA black site."

"Where?" Jabir finally pulled one out and lit it.

"That, I don't know. Honestly. Our part was compartmentalized to grabbing Hashim and handing him off to the SEALs." Tiny leaned forward, elbows on knees. "What I can tell you, and you probably know this, is that Hashim wound up in Ed's custody."

Jabir exhaled smoke in a stream through his mouth as he nodded. "He was one of ten guys Ed had."

"Right. And your buddies who died yesterday morning were right there too."

Jabir winced as he remembered Abdel's statement about how he'd met Ed in Iraq. "They all said as much."

"What they probably didn't say is that CIA wanted information and wanted it fast. Too fast."

"Nine died, right?"

"Eight. Hashim and another guy survived. But it wasn't pretty for Hashim, as I'm sure you can imagine."

"How so?"

"He was so stressed that all of his hair fell out save for his beard and eyebrows. Those got shaved off by Ed. Apparently, his hair never grew back. And, as you know, Hashim got released in an exchange for two soldiers who got kidnapped."

Jabir nodded. He took a drag as he considered all that Tiny had said. "I still don't get how Hashim realized it was Alex."

"Think about it." Tiny gently smiled as he encouraged his protégé. "Put yourself in Hashim's shoes. You came through what was probably the worst experience of your life. You endured humiliation piled upon humiliation, which included losing your hair so that you have not one left on your head. All because some vixen you danced with schnookered you. A very pretty vixen whose face, especially her eyes, you're unable to forget."

"And you can definitely say that about Alex," Jabir added as he pulled an ashtray to him and tapped out some ashes. He leaned forward, staring at the blank white of the coffee table but seeing Alex's face. His mind began making the connections. "Ed must have told him."

"What?"

"Thursday night after I saw Alex, I reported to Ed that she was one of Melanie's friends. He must have told Hashim at some point. Though I'm still not sure what brought Hashim to Panama."

"We're working on that angle. Or at least CIA is. So there you have it." Tiny rose and stretched. "My conclusion is that somehow, Hashim found out Alex is in-country, and he saw an opportunity for revenge. What a perfect opportunity."

"Yeah." Jabir dropped the cigarette in the ashtray and followed his mentor to the door. "How's Ellie?"

"Doc says she'll be okay eventually. They're not sure if she needs surgery for the shoulder or PT. Her hometown doc can help her on that. Alex has been with her ever since they arrived."

"I know."

Tiny opened the door. "Get some sleep, okay? And make sure Alex does."

"I will." Once Tiny had gone, Jabir returned to the desk, fully intending to study Alex's personnel jacket from top to bottom to confirm Tiny's tale. It took only a second to locate it on the Unit 28 site. It popped up in a window that only partially filled the screen.

He stopped and stared. On the screen, Alex's photo glowed from the top, left corner. On the right side was the mug shot of Hashim. He cocked his head and leaned forward for a closer look.

This is weird. His eyes darted between the two photos.

He enlarged the one for Alex. Then he blinked.

No, I'm not seeing this. Am I?

They would have somewhat similar features. Alex was half-Afghan since Roya had been the daughter of an Afghan army general. And Hashim was full-blooded Afghan. Still…

Jabir leaned back in his chair and opened another program, one that would examine facial features from a purely mathematical, analytical perspective to determine if the two faces had similarities. They frequently used it to track suspects who would alter their appearances or those who were photographed while under surveillance. He selected Alex and Hashim and put it to good work.

Since it would take some time, he wandered across the room for another smoke. When he returned, the word Complete flashed in red on the screen. He cleared away the box and studied the results.

Some similarities.

Okay.

The amount seemed uncanny. Could they be related?

No.

Jabir instantly dismissed that idea. They couldn't be related since David and Roya were her parents.

Weren't they?

Doubt began swirling in his mind.

Jabir rubbed his chin as he thought about what other information might be at his disposal. Then he nodded. Both Alex and Hashim had DNA samples in a government database. Alex had given hers willingly, and it would be utilized in case of her unfortunate demise where identification by other means wasn't possible. And Hashim? His had been taken unwillingly when he'd become the CIA's guest. Jabir accessed both profiles. Then he opened up another analytical program that would evaluate the samples for any commonalities.

And I'm not going to find any, he told himself. *Nope. They just happen to look a lot alike.*

The program churned through the data.

It beeped.

346

Jabir's heart almost stopped as he stared at the results.

No, it can't be!

He blinked and ran it again.

Alex and Hashim shared fifty percent of the DNA.

He ran the program a third time to make sure.

Same result.

Nausea swelled within Jabir.

Hamid al-Hassan was Alex's biological father.

Suddenly, it clicked into place.

Hashim didn't want Alex simply for revenge. His father must have demanded that he take his half-sister.

Jabir jumped up so quickly that the desk chair rolled across the hardwood floor and banged against the bed. He ran to the door and flung it open.

He had one foot on the landing when he stopped.

Alex didn't know Hashim was her half-brother. Did she?

Jabir shook his head. No. She didn't.

She had no idea.

None.

I should tell her.

I can't. She'd hate me.

He retreated into his room, shut the door, and leaned against it. "God, why me? Why now?" His words were soft, barely audible above the patter of the rain.

He rubbed his temples as a lump formed in his throat.

If he told her, he knew what would happen. Alex would deny it and tell him to get out of her life, this time for good.

"I hate this."

Jabir opened the door again.

Downstairs, low voices of some of the SEALs talking with Esteban reached him. In the bedroom next to his, a board creaked as Tiny prepared for bed. He yearned to burst inside and confide what he'd learned, but something kept him glued to the landing. Across the way, the door to the room where Ellie rested was cracked. Only a dim light was on, but he knew

Alex sat with her friend, determined to stay up all night until Ellie awakened.

The urge to reveal the truth to Alex nagged at him. He couldn't tell her, not even when he'd vowed to be completely honest with her.

No, I've got to keep it to myself. Stuff it down inside of me. Then talk with David and Roya to get to the bottom of this. That's the only thing I know to do.

Footsteps on the stairway made him glance up. A SEAL with blond curls flopping over his forehead joined him. "I've been watching you for a minute, and you haven't moved a bit. I told you Thinker was a perfect nickname for you."

"Sorry, Romeo."

"Not a problem. You looked a million miles away, like you always are when we work together."

Jabir shrugged, unwilling to be baited into teasing. "How's Ellie?"

"She'll come out of it. Doc said it should be out of her system by morning. It'd already started dissipating by the time we checked her out to bring her up here." Romeo pushed the door open. "Hey, Alex."

Alex glanced up, her sea green eyes red-rimmed with weariness. "Hey, Romeo. No change."

"It takes time. Why don't you go get some z's? I'll let Loverboy here know if something changes."

"What?" Alex narrowed her eyes at him.

Romeo only offered a careless shrug and a grin. "Clueless women." He winked at Jabir. "Thinker, take your lady away so she can rest."

"I'll do that."

"Have your fantasies, Romeo." Alex rose and followed Jabir onto the landing.

Once she shut the door behind them, Jabir took her in his arms and held her tightly. He buried his nose in her hair, savoring its silkiness and the sweet, clean smell, one that conjured up more innocent times.

God, why me? Why did You reveal this to me? And now of all times?

"Jabir?" His shirt muffled her voice. "I, uh, can't breathe."

"Sorry." He released her.

What do You want me to do about it? What? I can't tell her. She'd hate me.

"Are you okay?" Alex reached up and touched his face.

"Just tired," he lied.

He stuffed the revelation into a deep, dark corner of his soul, the same place where he'd put his thoughts about his father. Then later, he'd pull those thoughts out, dust them off, and figure out what to do with them.

40

Alex sat on the comforter of her bed with her knees drawn up to her chest. She'd wrapped her arms around them, and now she rested her chin on top. Her eyes drooped closed, the same as they'd done ever since she'd awakened a couple of hours before.

She loosened one hand and ran it along the silky material of the comforter. How could she expect to sleep at a time like this? She certainly hadn't the night before. Alex had lain in bed from when Jabir had kissed her goodnight until the first light of dawn had begun tingeing the curtains a pale red. Now, the headache she thought she'd shaken returned.

"Alex?" Jabir's quiet voice and a tap on the door made her glance up.

"I'm awake."

He opened it and smiled as he set something on the dresser. "Good morning. Did you sleep?"

She shook her head.

Jabir seated himself on the edge of the bed beside her and ran his fingers down her hair. "Me neither."

"How can I?" Alex uncurled from her tuck and rested her head against his shoulder.

351

His hand came down and rubbed her neck. "You're tight."

"I know." She closed her eyes, comforted by his firm frame. She sighed as his fingers probed the muscles in her shoulders. "I'm so tired."

"Me too." The twittering of birds filled the silence. "I think the word exhausted is more appropriate."

"Agreed." Alex lifted her head. "This has to end. Today."

Jabir smiled as he brushed some strands from her face. "And it will, most likely."

"What?"

"Ellie's awake."

She pulled away. "Since when?"

"Dawn or so."

Alex jumped up. "Why didn't you tell me?"

"Relax. I just found out myself about fifteen minutes ago when I went downstairs. Doc said she started regaining consciousness then. They wanted to wait until she was fully coherent with some breakfast in her before beginning the debrief."

"When?"

"Like in five minutes." Jabir kissed her and rose. "Come down when you're ready. I left some coffee for you on the dresser."

"I'll be right there." Alex wasted no time. She showered and paused only to take sips from the Colombian coffee. Once robed in a clean T-shirt and pants with the cuffs rolled up, she dashed downstairs in her bare feet.

"Ellie!" she practically shrieked when she saw her friend curled up on a couch, her right arm in a sling.

"Alex!"

Alex met her halfway, and they almost fell into each other's arms. Tears of relief filled her eyes as she pulled back. "Praise God you're safe. Doc said your arm will be okay."

Ellie nodded. "Eventually."

For the first time, Alex noticed how redness rimmed Ellie's green eyes. She found Esteban Romero conferring with JC and Tiny as they ate something.

JC smiled when he saw her. "G'morning, sleepyhead."

"Hah. I hardly slept. Esteban." She turned to him. "I'm so glad you're here."

Something in the detective's eyes caught her up short. Anger. Pure and simple anger. He took her hands and squeezed them. "I promise I won't stop until we rescue Becca."

"I know."

Then he winced and rubbed the bandage above his right eyebrow. "JC, we need to get started."

"Agreed there." JC clapped his hands like a teacher would. "Gang, debrief's starting. Boys, make yourselves scarce except for Doc. Alex, grab some grub so you don't faint or something. You too, Jabir."

"I'm not hungry," Alex muttered.

"Who cares? Eat up." JC nodded to Mooch, who ladled a generous portion of eggs onto her plate plus some bacon.

Though she didn't want to admit it, Alex's stomach rumbled. It didn't take long for the eggs to disappear. She carried her cup of coffee to the den and settled beside Ellie on the couch.

Tiny seated himself on the easy chair that was closest to Ellie and perpendicular to the couch. He cleared his throat and adjusted his glasses. Then he cast a glance at JC, who had a notepad and pen in his hand and sat on the loveseat across from Alex. Esteban took the other easy chair. Doc sat on the floor, and Jabir joined them on a bar chair. The remainder of the SEALs lingered in the kitchen and dining area and talked quietly.

"How are you feeling, Ellie?" Tiny asked as he handed a steaming mug of tea to her.

Ellie shrugged. "I still feel a little sleepy."

"I'm sure. It sounds like you were given a pretty powerful sedative. How's the shoulder?" Tiny set a digital recorder on the table and turned it on. "Sorry. In case I forget a detail, which is definitely a possibility." He gave his name, date, time of day, and who was present at the debrief.

"It's hurting." Ellie winced as she shifted.

"I promise you that once you're done here, they'll give you something for the pain."

"I'm not sure I can help you. I mean, Doc told me that you want me to tell you what happened."

"You'd be surprised what you might know. Right, Alex?"

Alex nodded. "Ellie, I promise. Sometimes, bits of what you may think is incongruous actually fit together and form a complete picture. I promise you know more than you think you do."

"I…I don't know."

Alex reached out and touched her on the leg. "You do. And whatever you do know will help save Melanie and Becca."

Slowly, Ellie nodded. "Okay. Where do you want me to start?"

"What happened when you were kidnapped?" Tiny asked.

"I'd gotten up when Alex and Becca did. Once they'd gone, I tried to go back to sleep, but I couldn't. I wound up reading on my tablet. I guess it was at about seven thirty or so, someone knocked on the door."

Tiny glanced at JC, who made a notation on his notepad. "How did you know it was seven thirty?"

"I automatically checked the time on the tablet. I thought that maybe the officers Esteban had told me would come were early, but they were imposters."

Esteban nodded. "They stole uniforms from a local drycleaners."

Ellie bit her lip. "It happened so fast. I mean, one second I was undoing the deadbolt and chain and opening the door, and suddenly, I was on the floor with my shoulder on fire. They grabbed me." She swallowed hard. "They took me into the bedroom and got me with something. I guess a Taser. That hurt. Really hurt."

"I'm sure." Tiny paused, allowing her time to compose herself. "And then?"

"I came to when they were sliding me into something. I…I think it was a van or something like that because I remember hearing the sound of a side door being pulled shut. I think Melanie must have been with me."

Alex wanted to jump in and ask if her friend was okay, but a warning glance from Tiny made her close her mouth.

"What happened then?" Tiny asked.

"I remember hearing all of these sounds. City sounds. Horns. Gears grinding. People shouting. And there was a lot of starting and stopping."

"Any conversation in the van?"

"Yeah. Another language. But it wasn't a lot, and it wasn't Spanish either."

"How long do you think you were going through this city traffic?" That question came from Esteban.

Alex frowned.

Ellie shifted, wincing as if her arm protested the move. "What difference does it make?"

"It could make a big difference," Alex told her. "Remember that small chunks may form larger pictures."

"I..." Ellie squinted as if trying to see back through time. "I think my watch beeped about the time that we hit a bridge. Or, at least I thought it was a bridge."

"How did you know?" Tiny asked.

"The wheels started doing a ba-bump, ba-bump thing. You know. Like when I was living in Weatherly and we'd go to the Outer Banks. We'd go over a really long bridge. And believe me. I know my sounds."

Alex bit back a smile. "When we were growing up, we always said Ellie had dog ears because she has such great hearing."

"A bridge?" Esteban frowned and leaned forward with both elbows on his knees.

"Yeah. A pretty long one too. Then we seemed to pick up speed."

"Could you tell how long?"

"I'd gotten my wrists up to my face, so I could see pretty clearly the time. I think maybe ten or so minutes passed." Then she sighed. "Oh, I don't know. Maybe my watch beeped once we were on the bridge." A tear trickled down her cheek.

"Ellie, it's okay." Tiny offered an encouraging smile. "It's okay. We're not testing you. We just want to know what you observed."

Ellie wiped at the tear. "I do remember that after about ten minutes had passed, we turned right. It seemed like we were headed uphill or something. Then we turned left."

"Any idea of how long?" Esteban asked. His eyes narrowed, and he rubbed his unshaven jaw.

"About eight minutes or so. I do remember at the end going over this huge bump. That made my shoulder hurt."

"Was that the end?" Tiny glanced at JC, whose pen was poised above paper again.

Ellie nodded. She winced as she shifted. "The back doors opened, and someone dragged me across the floor and tossed me over their shoulder. Then I went round and round until I landed on the floor on my injured shoulder. That really hurt. Ow," she added as if her shoulder remembered what had happened. "My shoulder's killing me. Are we done?"

"Almost. Tell me about what you saw." Tiny made a mark on his tablet.

"What I saw? I don't understand."

"Everything. The room. The people. Voices you heard."

"The guy who brought me in was masked." She turned her gaze toward Jabir. "He was fairly slender but well built like Jabir. And his eyes. They were really, really blue. Intense. You know what I'm saying?"

"I do." Jabir's voice startled Alex.

Her gaze swung to him. He hunched over, his chin in his hand, his gaze focused on Ellie.

Ellie began trembling. "He scared me so much. I knew that without a doubt, he could hurt me, and it wouldn't bother him a bit. He tied me to a chair, never mind the fact that it made my arm hurt so much. Then he slapped me around. They brought Melanie in and tied her up as well. They did a ransom video. I had to read the message since Melanie couldn't see without her glasses. Then they pretty much left us alone with only a couple of guards present."

"What about the room?" Tiny asked.

"It looked like a living room. The floor was tile. There was a couch and some chairs. And at least two guards at all times." The trembling became more prominent.

Again, Alex reached out and touched her friend on the leg.

This time, Ellie gripped her hand.

"It's okay, Ellie. You're safe."

Ellie nodded. Now, it was like once she started telling her story, she couldn't stop. "They left us alone after the video. At least until another guy and his friend showed up."

"Describe them," Tiny quietly requested.

"One was really, really built."

"How so?"

"He looked like he wrestled. Tall. Muscular. His muscles bulged against shirt sleeves".

"Your guesstimate?"

"I don't know. Maybe above six feet? Two fifty or something? He also had vivid eyes, but his were aquamarine instead of blue. His voice was deep too."

"Hashim al-Hassan," Jabir muttered.

"What?" Alex blurted.

Tiny shot her another warning look.

"What about his pal?" Esteban asked.

"I think he was American."

"Describe him," Jabir commanded, which drew a similar warning look from Tiny.

"Um, gray eyes. A little shorter than the other one. In shape. He spoke with an interesting accent. Maybe Cajun."

"Ed DuBois." Tiny nodded.

"That man, Hashim. He…he gave me a sedative. The next thing I knew, I woke up here."

"Anything else?"

"I'm worried about Melanie."

He paused. "What makes you say that?"

Ellie's grip on Alex's hand tightened. "She threw up."

"Repeat that," Doc commanded.

"She threw up. And she didn't seem with it. It was like she was drunk or something. Is she going to be okay?"

Doc scribbled something before setting his notepad down on the glass of the coffee table. "She might have gotten chloroformed. Throwing up can be a byproduct of that. Since she has cardiomyopathy, that's not good."

"Why?"

"Chloroform can cause complications."

Alex swallowed hard.

"I'm scared for her." Pain laced Ellie's words. She seemed to shrink against the couch.

"Ellie, thanks." Tiny offered another comforting smile. "I promise you gave us a lot of information." He cast a glance at Esteban, who now squinted at his notepad and tapped his pen against it. "Esteban?"

The detective finally raised his gaze. "Do you have a map?"

"Yeah." JC nodded. "Romeo."

"Yo!" Romeo's voice came from the kitchen area.

"Get me our map, will you?"

"One map coming up." Romeo brought the tube to his commanding officer.

The low rumble of the others' conversations died out as if they felt the shift in the room's tension.

"Talk to me, Esteban," JC said as he spread the map out on the coffee table.

Esteban slid to his knees, and he ran his finger across the paper. "The hotel is here." He tapped the location. "Read me the times."

"About thirty minutes or so to either the bridge or on the bridge," JC reported.

Esteban moved his finger as if tracking a route. "Okay. Then?"

JC read off his notes. As he did so, Esteban traced a route that led across the bridge over the Panama Canal and then north into the mountains.

"What do we have?" Tiny asked.

Her hand still holding Ellie's, Alex leaned forward.

"They must have gone through the city to blend in. Remember that we hadn't issued the BOLO yet."

"I can see that." JC checked his notes. "It checks out with what Ellie heard."

"Then they crossed the bridge and headed into the mountains. There are many small houses up there. They're used by the cartel because of their isolation."

Tiny frowned. "How?"

"As way stops for drugs coming out of Colombia. A place for them to rest. We hit them occasionally. Arrest them when we find drugs, which we normally do. Then they go dormant for about six months because we keep them under surveillance. Once we stop, they get occupied again."

"What do you think?"

Esteban jumped up and started pacing. "I think your suspects might be holed up in one of those houses. Let me call headquarters. I'll ask them to create a map showing the route and any houses we've hit. And check to see if any bodies have showed up in our morgue. JC, come with me."

"That, I can do. Gentlemen, ladies," he added with a nod toward Alex and Ellie. "We'll be back. Doc, make sure Ellie's comfortable."

"Will do." Doc flipped his commander a salute.

Alex glanced at Jabir. He hadn't moved since his last question. His eyes remained focused on the table.

The sound of tears caught her attention. "Oh, Ellie." She carefully wrapped her arms around her friend's shoulders, which quaked under her touch. "I'm sorry."

Ellie laid her head against her. "I'm so scared."

"I know. Me too."

"My shoulder's killing me." Ellie sniffled, and a small sob escaped her.

"Let's get you upstairs." Alex nodded at Doc, who led the way.

Once he'd given Ellie a shot of morphine to take the edge off the pain, Alex resumed her seat by her friend's bed. She swallowed hard. Ellie had given them good information. No, great information. Especially if it could convert into a bona fide lead. The question remained as to whether that lead would solidify sooner rather than later.

Melanie's life depended on sooner.

"Alex?" Ellie's voice had faded.

"I'm here." Alex touched her friend's hair.

Ellie's eyes closed at that reassurance.

"Sleep, okay?" Alex murmured. Once she was sure her friend had drifted away, she rose and returned downstairs.

Tiny chatted on the phone with someone. Parker and Ryan cleaned up from breakfast. The SEALs had broken into small groups and talked amongst themselves. She noticed Jabir smoking on the patio as he talked with Mooch and Romeo.

She stepped through the glass door.

Romeo grinned, said something to Jabir, and clapped him on the shoulder. He winked at her as the pair shifted to the other side of the patio to give them a modicum of privacy.

Jabir had turned away to stare at the ocean in the distance.

"What was that all about?" Alex quietly asked.

"What?"

"Inside. You seemed to know from Ellie's description that Hashim al-Hassan was with Ed."

He took a drag.

"Talk to me. Please."

Jabir tossed the cigarette onto the flagstone and ground it out with his foot. "Tiny and I figured out their sudden shift in demands."

"What? That I go to the property tomorrow?"

A short nod answered her question. "Operation Orb Web."

Alex sucked in a breath. She closed her eyes as that final mission almost ten years before jumped out from her distant memory. "Baghdad."

"He was your target. Yours and Monica's."

"I remember." The music from that night pulsed in her ears. She remembered noticing Hashim, his build, his dark, curly hair, and those mesmerizing eyes of his. The smell of the cologne he'd worn filled her nose again. "Tiny told you?"

"Yes. I—We think Hashim remembers you from that night."

Alex's knees began shaking. She located a chaise and eased onto it. "I don't know what happened to him."

"He wound up in Ed's custody at a CIA black site along with nine of his pals. Whatever happened to him, it made his hair fall out. He wants revenge, Alex."

She shivered and screwed her eyes closed at the news.

"Alex." Warm hands on hers made her open them. Jabir knelt in front of her, protective anger flashing in his dark eyes. "I promise I'm not going to let you near him or him near you."

"How can you be so sure?"

"Because you're going to stay here."

"No, no way, Jabir." Alex jumped up. "These are my friends. I'm going to go on whatever mission the SEALs plan."

"Then strictly in an observational role and only with me by your side. If Tiny allows it, that is." Jabir glanced at Mooch and Romeo. "And as long as the SEALs agree."

A haunted look fell across his face.

"Is there something else?" Alex reached out and took his hand.

"No. Nothing." Too quick, like the day before.

"Are you sure?"

Before he could answer, the gate opened.

Both Esteban and JC stepped onto the patio. They wore satisfied smiles, almost like they'd gone to see a great movie or something. Tiny joined them. "What's up?"

"Success." JC positively grinned. "Esteban's men came through. We've finally got movement." Then he sobered. "So stay tuned. We're sending some guys up to the house now for surveillance. With any luck, we'll be ready to go guns hot soon."

41

Samir lifted his head. It pounded with a headache. His neck and back hurt as well. Even blinking wasn't pleasant.

Where was he?

Somehow, he shoved himself upright and surveyed his surroundings. He sat at the mahogany desk in his study. How he'd wound up there, he had no idea. Darkness surrounded him. He moved his hand, and it brushed a crystal tumbler.

That simple gesture recalled a day he simply wanted to forget. After Noor had left, he'd spent the next hour or so mulling over his precarious predicament. The company was possibly in ruins with Papa in the hospital, all due to his foolish actions. He grabbed his keys and sped into the city to see him. The result? Mama wept. And Papa? The man might have been weak, but he was so angry that he shouted for Samir to get out and stay out. Samir fled, only to drive aimlessly in the Lebanese countryside for the rest of the afternoon.

When he got home, his phone was ringing. Interpol agent Leila al-Kadir would pay him a visit tomorrow along with the chief inspector of the Lebanese National Police. He was to be there waiting for them. Otherwise,

363

the National Police would issue an arrest warrant. He forgot about supper; bourbon from Kentucky was his only solace. He'd poured himself a drink and wandered outside.

Now, Samir rubbed his temples in a vain effort to ease the headache forming. Using his hands, he pushed himself to his feet and stumbled into the den. Near the archway leading to the foyer, he'd stocked a small wet bar. The finest liquors from all over the world, including the Maker's Mark he'd imbibed earlier, sat on glass shelves above the rack holding an assortment of glassware. He poured himself another glass, then wandered through the open French doors and onto the patio.

He took a swallow, wincing as the liquid burned its way down his throat. A puffball of warmth formed in his stomach. He slouched on a chaise and stared at the glowing azure of the pool. It only served as a reminder of the luxuries he'd added thanks to his illicit activities.

Tarek.

The name of his best friend slipped unbidden into his mind.

Then Noor's advice.

Tell them about Tarek and Jihad of Light.

"I can't." His whispered words broke the stillness of the night air.

His thoughts flew to his past with Tarek. They'd been friends for twenty-one years, had come of age together in the new Beirut. Tarek had been there for him when his marriage had fallen apart. They'd run schemes together, been as close as brothers. How could he betray him?

Samir put his head in his hands as the headache pounded at his skull.

He knew of only one way to save himself.

Follow Noor's advice and spill all he knew about Tarek and Jihad of Light when he met with the police and Interpol tomorrow.

The thought made him sick.

He had to do something to at least warn his friend about what had transpired.

Samir jumped to his feet.

The patio tilted, and he staggered and caught himself on the back of the chaise. He made it inside only by clutching the doorway and then the post of the half-wall that separated the dinette area from the great room.

He found his cellphone on the granite bar where he'd laid it. With shaking fingers, he dialed Tarek's cell number.

1515 hours Central Daylight Time, west of Panama City, Panama

Hashim sat in the kitchen. He leaned back in his chair, one foot against the leg of the table, the other on the tile floor. An oily piece of butcher paper rested on top beside a steaming mug of tea.

Schwip.

His hunting knife slid across the sharpening stone.

Schwip.

A smile crossed his face as he touched the smooth edge. Sharp. He tore off a corner of the paper and brought it down upon it. The blade sliced the strong paper in two like a hot knife going through butter. The serrated edge was just as sharp. Perfect.

Who would be his first victim? Hashim thought about that one as he used a rag to wipe off the excess oil. Whoever tried to interfere with his kidnapping Alex Thornton. And then? Warmth spread through him as he thought about Alex. Who cared if she was his half-sister? She'd humiliated him, delivered him to his tormentor. Now, Hashim intended to finish what she'd started when she'd suggested that they slip out back for a little one-on-one, oh, so long ago.

The door to the kitchen banged open.

Hashim whirled, ready to hurl the knife.

Tarek burst through. "We need to talk, brother."

"Oh?" Hashim sheathed it and took a sip of tea. "Why is that?"

"Samir called. The fool was drunk." Tarek paced. "He said they found out about the accounts."

Hashim sat there for a moment. "Why, specifically, did he call?"

"To warn us. The police and Interpol are involved. He's meeting with them tomorrow. Of course, he promised not to say a word about Jihad of Light."

"Like I believe him." Hashim's eyes narrowed.

"We need to take care of this problem. But what of tonight?"

"Asa can handle it. And Ed."

"You trust him?"

"For now. He has no recourse if he returns to the CIA, does he? No, he doesn't. Later, we'll take care of him if he doesn't prove his loyalty." Hashim balled up the paper. "Dealing with Samir is more urgent."

"I've already called our pilots. They're preparing the plane and will return here once they drop us in Beirut."

"Good. Notify your men in Beirut." Hashim tossed the paper into the trash. "I'll inform Asa and Ed, and we can be in the air within two hours."

1600 hours Central Daylight Time, west of Panama City, Panama

"I can't see anything."

"Me, neither."

"How are we supposed to see if anyone leaves?"

"Mooch and Jarrod have it under control, okay? Now stop talking." Jabir's lips tickled Alex's ear as he whispered to her.

Alex scowled. No one could hear their low conversation above the white noise of the downpour. At least this time, what with a pistol, knife, and full camouflage, she felt like a part of the team, even though JC had put his foot down and told her to remember her Unit 28 days when she was more of an observer. She didn't care. At least she was there.

She recalled what the forward recon teams had reported. An estimated twelve men, maybe sixteen, plus Tarek and Hashim al-Hassan, plus Ed, for a possible total of nineteen very armed and trained adversaries. The orders

JC had received were clear. Take the two brothers and Ed alive and get the two hostages back.

"I see movement," Jarrod, the sniper, suddenly reported over the wire worm Alex wore.

She raised her binoculars and peered through them at the front of the house. A breezeway to the right of the porch led to a shed.

The rain intensified to a point where she could only make out two silhouettes.

"Two of them," Jarrod whispered. "Both appear to be male."

"ID?" JC's voice from his command post deeper in the jungle reached her.

"Negative. The rain's too thick. But both appear to be very ambulatory."

They couldn't be the hostages. Not with Melanie suffering from the impacts of cardiomyopathy and Becca beaten.

Alex bit her tongue as she watched the two climb into a Land Rover. The taillights flashed through the haze, and the engine barely penetrated the noise of the rain.

Hold on, Melanie and Becca. Hold on. We'll get you out soon.

1700 hours Central Daylight Time, west of Panama City, Panama

"We leave at seven."

"Shouldn't we go earlier?" Ed asked.

Asa shook his head. "No, seven will be plenty of time."

Ed watched as Hashim's man pushed through the swinging doors into the kitchen. Then a smile crossed his face. Two hours would be plenty of time to do what he wanted to do.

He strode down the hallway to the bedroom where he stayed. Forrest remained where she'd lain the night before. Only now, her wrist was in a cable tie and attached to the brass headboard. The night before, he'd spooned with her and held her in his arms. Such an act conjured up memories of Francesca, and he thought about claiming Forrest as his own. But she didn't move, even when he'd run his hand down her hair and then her side. Not even a protest. Now, her chest rose and fell sporadically.

Ed pressed his fingers to the pulse at her neck.

Her heartbeat had slowed noticeably as the residual of her medication faded from her system. He doubted she'd last through the night.

That left him with a whole lot of pent-up frustration, and he knew of only one place to go.

Alvarez.

A smile curled his lips. So what if Hashim had already claimed her as his girl?

Hashim wasn't there.

He was.

Ed crossed the breezeway and pulled on the door. It creaked open. Alvarez lay spread-eagled on the worktable, her arms and legs still bound. A damp spot on her pants told him her guards hadn't let her up for anything. One guard leaned against the post, the other against the wall near one of the windows. Both had dumped their masks and appeared bored to tears.

He grinned. "Take a break, boys. I want some one-on-one with our girl here."

The one against the wall made a cougar sound. "Maybe after you're done, we can have our turn."

"Hah. Maybe so." Who cared if their boss had staked his claim? "Now be gone with you. Come back in an hour."

Once the guards had shuffled outside, he shut the door. The room darkened, and thunder echoed dully. Then the rain came fast and loud like bullets hitting the tin roof.

Francesca.

Her name zinged into his mind. The thing was, thanks to recent events, she was lost to him. Even if she met him somewhere, she'd never be able to live with someone who'd willingly taken the lives of sixteen people.

He shoved her face into the trash bin of his memories.

Alvarez's good eye fluttered open, then closed as he approached the table.

"Oh, I know you're awake." He grinned. "I can see you're very awake."

"Let me up," she softly begged. "Please."

"Nope. No can do. Sorry. You brought my mother into this, so that's where you wound up." He reached over and checked the ropes binding her to the table. "Good. Still secure."

His fingers drifted up her arm. Ed brushed some hair off her face and ran his hand down her cheek. He noticed the dried tearstains on them. "No, you're right where I want you. Very right where I want you. You see, it's been a long time for me. You ticked me off, and I've come to collect."

His fingers wandered down her neck to her throat.

"Please. Don't."

"Don't? What? Now that you're all trussed up, you've lost that attitude?"

Alvarez sucked in a breath as his hand drifted lower.

He leaned over her, and toyed with the top button of her camp shirt. "You'll have to do better than that." He undid the rest of her buttons and shoved the material aside. "Oh, yeah. I bet you look good in a bikini." He ran his fingers along her belly as the flush intensified.

"It's you and me, Becca. Consider this a warm-up for when Hashim gets his hooks into you." He undid her belt. "Of course, I'm going to have to cut those pants of yours away."

Ed pulled his hunting knife from his belt and put point to fabric.

Popping echoed, followed by a man's scream.

He whipped around. More popping reached him, and one of the windows shattered.

They were under attack.

He cussed and used the knife to sever her bonds. Alvarez lay there, not moving. "Get up."

"I—I can't."

"Get up. Now!" He grabbed her arm, dumping her onto the ground at his feet. Ed yanked her upright, grabbed her wrists, and lashed them together in front of her with cord from the table.

Alvarez swayed.

He clamped his hand on her arm and pushed her ahead of him. "Dang it!"

He had only one way out.

A hostage.

He grabbed her ponytail and jerked back on her head. With his lips pressed to her ear, he delivered his instructions. "You're my hostage now. You stay with me, we both live. You try and get away? We both die. Got it? C'mon." Fingers digging into her arms like claws, he pushed into the rain and dragged her toward the van.

Ed tried not to notice two bodies crumpled at the other end of the breezeway or the way pieces of the jungle seemed to move as their attackers leap-frogged toward them, one pair laying down fire as the others advanced.

He yanked open the passenger door. "Get in."

"What?" Alvarez stared dumbly at him.

"Get in." He raised his hand to strike her.

Alvarez flinched. She heaved herself into the interior.

Ed shoved her into the driver's seat, thrust the keys into the ignition, and cranked the engine. He slammed his door shut. "Drive."

"Where?"

"I'll steer. Go!" Ed peeked over the edge of the dash.

Using her bound hands, Alvarez put the van into gear and stomped on the accelerator. The motor revved, and they sped toward the road.

Ed jerked the wheel hard to the right, throwing her against the door as they bounced over the bump.

Alvarez moaned as her head slammed into the side.

He jammed the wheel the other way. They wove down the mountain on the pock-marked road. The bottom of the hill came up.

"Stop," Ed ordered.

They skidded a little when Alvarez jammed on the brakes.

"Go." He turned them left onto a highway. Ed poked his head a little further above the dash. "Slow down. I'm pulling us over."

Alvarez eased up on the accelerator. The van slowed, and he steered them toward a set of shops that were closed for the day.

Ed jumped out and hustled to the driver's side. He wrenched open the door. Without hesitation, he grabbed her arm and yanked her from her seat.

She cried out as she fell to her knees on the gravel.

As he hauled her to her feet, she began kicking and screaming.

"Oh, no. We'll have none of that." Ed pushed her to the ground.

The breath whooshed out of her. As she struggled to breathe, he pulled her upright once more and dragged her toward a women's clothing store that seemed to sell sarongs, bathing suits, and other beach paraphernalia.

Using the butt of his pistol, he knocked out the glass and turned the deadbolt. Ed forced her to the back. He slammed her into the door of one of the dressing rooms.

Alvarez moaned and turned so her back rested against it. She sank to the floor.

"I should kill you now," he growled as he drew his Beretta. The muzzle shook. "Then you won't slow me down."

Alvarez's chest heaved. Most hostages would have begged for their lives at that point.

Oh, no.

Not her.

She stared at him, something akin to peace in her eyes. Or resignation.

It taunted him.

Ed hesitated.

Alvarez thrust out her legs.

Her boot-clad foot came into hard contact with his groin. Pain exploded. His vision momentarily went dark.

Off balance, he staggered backwards. His hand frantically grasped at the rack of clothing as he tried to catch himself.

Finding no purchase, he tumbled to the ground, moaning as he curled into a ball.

Deep breaths made the pain recede. Ed opened his eyes and found Alvarez crawling as best she could with bound hands to where he'd dropped his gun.

He wouldn't have any of that.

Ed staggered to his feet.

As her fingers closed around the grip, he kicked her hands, knocking the Beretta away. He got a handful of hair and yanked hard. She landed on her back with a thud. He was about to go for his gun when he heard the crunch of gravel outside.

No time now.

Ed drew back his fist. "I'll see you in hell, woman."

He slammed it into her face.

Alvarez crumpled to the ground and lay still.

Ed grabbed his gun. As footfalls on gravel approached, he darted through the back door. A wilderness shop was next door.

He dashed toward it to lay his trap.

42

From her vantage point, Alex spotted two forms sneaking from the shed. She raised her binoculars. One had a hand on the other's arm. The other, a feminine silhouette, stumbled.

The rain slackened enough for her to make positive identification.

Ed shoved Becca toward the old white van.

"Jarrod, Ed's got Becca."

"I see 'im," the sniper said. "He's using her as a shield." He muttered under his breath. "I can't take a shot. Not without running the risk of killing her."

Jabir jumped to his feet. "Jarrod, cover me."

Alex started in surprise. "Jabir…"

Heedless of gunfire zinging around him, he raced to the maroon Suburban behind the van. As the van's engine roared to life, he tried the Suburban's doors and jumped inside.

Alex ran after him, cringing as a bullet whistled by her head.

"He's got the hostage in the driver's seat," Jarrod reported. "No way can I get a shot at him."

Alex finally caught her breath. "What are you doing?"

Jabir fiddled with the wires under the dash. They sparked, and he cranked the big SUV's engine. "Going after him. I'm not letting him get away. Not this time." He glared at her. "Get in or stay here."

Alex ran around to the passenger's side and scrambled into the seat.

They tore down the road after the van. The rain nearly blinded them, even with the windshield wipers at their highest speed. The bump sent them both out of their seats.

Jabir fought to keep control and nearly slid off the road. They hurtled toward the main highway like they were on some out-of-control roller-coaster.

Alex gripped the handhold and stuffed her scream somewhere down in her throat.

When they screeched to a halt at the highway, the van had disappeared.

"Where would he go?" Jabir demanded.

"Toward town," Alex said through chattering teeth. She sucked in her breath and held it before letting it out in an effort to chase away the shakes. "Where else to disappear?"

Jabir jerked the wheel to the left, and they sped down the highway. She kept scanning through the thick rain. "There. Stop!" She pointed at a small cluster of shops.

The van sat in the small parking lot with the driver's side door hanging open.

Jabir slammed on the brakes, throwing them both forward. He jumped out.

Alex followed and reported, "We're at a cluster of shops east of the safe house along the highway. Tiendas Norte. The white van's here. Need backup."

"Any sign of unfriendlies?" That came from Tiny, who was posted slightly south of their position along with Parker, Ryan, and Esteban.

"Negative," Jabir reported through his own headset. "Looks like they're on foot."

"I'm dispatching Parker and Ryan to your position. Wait on them before proceeding," Tiny ordered.

"Roger that." Jabir lowered his headset.

She placed her hand over the mouthpiece so she wouldn't transmit her next words. "Jabir, Tiny said to wait."

"No time." He popped the hood of the van and yanked out the main fuse. Then he did the same to the Suburban, rendering Ed with no way of escape. At least not on the road. "He's here, and if we're not careful, he's going to get away with Becca or kill her."

Alex couldn't argue with that.

They crept toward the closest shop. Shattered glass lay on the stoop, and the door hung open.

Ed had come that way.

She drew her gun, every sense on high alert. She paused and brought the Glock to the ready position.

Nothing moved inside.

Thunder rumbled low and threatening. The rainfall intensified.

She stepped through the doorway, her gun following her sight.

A low moan reached her.

Becca.

At a crouch, she checked along the floor for any signs that Ed was hiding in the circular racks.

Nothing.

"Becca, where are you?"

"Help."

The soft plea sounded like it came from the back of the store. Alex glanced at Jabir.

"Go on," he whispered. "I've got you covered."

Alex's steps quickened. The dressing room area came into view. Becca lay on her side, her hands lashed in front of her. She tried to rise but fell back.

"Becca!"

Her friend turned onto her back.

Alex gasped when she saw her shirt gaping open, her belt undone. "What did he do to you?"

"Where's Ed?" Jabir demanded. Facing outward, he held his gun at ready.

"He's…gone." Becca closed her eyes.

Alex smoothed the hair off her face.

"Water," Becca rasped.

Suddenly, Alex realized how dehydrated her friend was. She pulled her hydration pack off her back and held the nozzle to Becca's mouth. "Drink."

"Alex, stay here. I'm going after Ed," Jabir told her.

"Jabir…"

"I'm not letting him get away."

"He'll kill you if he gets half a chance."

He shrugged as if to say, "So what?"

"Wait for backup. Please! They're on their way."

"I stay, and he gets away. Guard her and wait for Parker and Ryan." With that, he was gone, leaving both women staring at where some dresses swayed gently back and forth following his passage.

Alex slashed Becca's bonds.

Her hands fell uselessly at her sides.

Alex buttoned her shirt and re-cinched her belt. "Can you sit up?"

"Yeah." With Alex's help, Becca did so. She rested her head against the mirror. "He…he was going to rape me." She began trembling.

"You're safe. Parker and Ryan will be here soon. Here's an energy bar." She unwrapped it and held it to her friend's mouth, all the while keeping an ear and eye out for any telltale noises that Ed had returned.

Becca took a bite and chewed. After swallowing, she whispered, "You need to go after him."

"Jabir said—"

"He'll kill Jabir. You know that. Go." Becca offered a weak smile. "I'll be fine."

"I can't leave you."

"Help's on the way, right? I'm not dying. Just leave your water, and I'll be fine."

Alex's radio crackled.

"Hostage secured and under Doc's care," JC reported.

Relief swept over Alex. She keyed her mic. "Roger that. I need backup at Tiendas Norte." She described where Becca would be.

"Melanie's safe now. C'mon. Let's see if there's a manager's office here." She helped her friend to her feet. "If there is, then we can at least hide you there for a while." They hobbled toward an alcove. The manager's office was empty with a window overlooking a courtyard. "Stay in here and lock the door. Open it only to the SEALs or two guys named Parker and Ryan. Or Jabir and me." Alex paused long enough to report the change in plans to Tiny. Then she handed her pistol to Becca. "I'll be back. Use this if you have to."

With that, Alex made her way to the front of the store and outside. Now, maybe she could find Jabir before Ed dealt him a fatal blow.

43

Jabir tore through the rain and skidded to a stop.

His eyes darted around the courtyard.

He noticed the destroyed door at the outdoors shop and dashed toward it.

Jabir crouched and listened.

The rain beating down covered any sounds from within.

Keeping as low as he could, he stole through the gaping opening and cocked his head.

The rain lessened.

Still, nothing.

From his position against the counter, he noticed a pile of something on the floor.

Machetes.

His pulse quickened.

Something in his peripheral vision made him shift.

The single eye of a Beretta pointed at him.

Jabir threw himself onto the floor.

The bullet whizzed over him and punctured the display case holding compasses. Jabir brought his gun up and squeezed off two shots.

He scurried around the perimeter so he wouldn't become a sitting duck.

More glass shattered.

Jabir scrambled to his feet and followed.

Ed, gun in one hand and machete in the other, kicked the glass out of the door to a café.

Jabir burst into the wetness.

He pressed himself against a column, then darted so he rested against the wall beside the remains of the door.

Jabir knelt and grabbed a fist-sized rock that sat next to the walkway. After a moment's hesitation, he hurled it inside.

It crashed into the window across the restaurant.

Two gunshots rewarded him.

Jabir dove in after it and pulled down a table to shield himself.

Two bullets slammed into it. Five out of a dozen bullets spent.

Jabir popped up and got off two more shots, drilling neat holes in the display case.

A shadow caught his eye. He squeezed the trigger.

Click.

Nothing else.

The gun had jammed.

Jabir grimaced and tossed it away.

Silence ensued.

Using his foot, Jabir shoved over a chair from a nearby table.

Two more bullets.

Five left.

Jabir couldn't budge, not without knowing where Ed lay in wait for him. He reached into the outer pocket of his pants and pulled out his lighter. He set it on the ground so the shiny metal showed the counter.

A shadow reflected on the metal as Ed changed positions.

Jabir sprang forward and knocked another table over as three more shots echoed.

Two left.

Doors banged, and a cuss word reached him.

Jabir bolted to the counter and pressed himself against the floor. He climbed to his knees to peer through the glass.

Like some sort of distorted demon, Ed's face appeared the other side, the muzzle of his gun a third eye.

Jabir threw himself to the floor.

The glass exploded from two shots, which rained shards down on top of him like poisonous diamonds.

He raised his head.

Shots eleven and twelve.

Ed should be out of bullets now.

Jabir listened. No sound of a spent clip being ejected and a fresh one being rammed home reached him. He crawled to the edge of the counter and peered around the corner.

Nothing.

Ed must have fled deeper into the kitchen.

Since the swinging doors didn't reach all the way to the floor, Jabir slithered underneath. He climbed to another crouch and surveyed the wide aisle between stainless counters and the wall with its industrial sink, dishwasher, and mixer.

A war cry shattered the air.

Jabir's eyes widened.

Ed rushed toward him, machete over his head for a killing blow.

Jabir dove toward Ed but low.

His attacker's momentum carried him past, and the machete reverberated against the metal of the counter in front of the pass-through window.

Ed whipped around.

Jabir rolled away and to his feet as the machete clanged against the mixer in a screech of metal on metal with a shower of sparks.

He grabbed the sink nozzle on its retractable hose and turned the water on full blast.

It caught Ed full in the face as Jabir backed away.

"You son of—" Ed cussed loud and long.

Jabir snatched up some knives from their magnetic holders and hurled them at his former boss.

Ed ducked, and the tips embedded themselves in the wall or bounced off the doors.

Jabir scurried around the long stainless steel worktable and noticed pots, pans, and trays on a shelf underneath the work surface.

"You think because you're younger, you're going to beat me?" Ed's voice taunted Jabir. "Come out and fight like a man."

Jabir grabbed a tray and popped up just in time to see Ed cocking his arm back to hurl a knife.

Jabir threw the tray up in front of his face.

The knife clattered uselessly to the floor.

He scrambled further down the line as Ed stalked him.

Ceramic plates sat in front of him. Jabir grabbed some. As Ed rounded the corner, he launched them like Frisbees.

Ed grunted as several hit him.

The rest shattered against the walls.

Jabir dove around the corner as another knife went flying past.

"What? Are you afraid to come out and play?" Ed sneered. "You're afraid you'll lose? To lose is to lose your life, son. You see, it's a fight to the death."

"I'm not afraid to die." Jabir sucked in a breath to steady his nerves. "At least I know where I'm going."

"Straight to hell with me." Ed cackled.

Jabir frantically searched around him. Then he saw it.

Dishwashing powder.

He snatched a mixing bowl from the worktable shelf and poured as much of the powder in it as he could. Bowl in hand ready to unleash, he crept backward. "No, I'm not going to hell."

"We'll see about that." Ed's voice came from near the front of the kitchen at the pass-through window.

Jabir popped around the corner and thrust the stainless steel bowl with all of his might toward Ed.

His adversary shrieked.

Jabir turned on his heel and dashed toward the back.

Pain slammed into his right leg. Jabir collapsed onto his hands and knees before he got five steps. He wrenched around and stared in shock.

The knife Ed had thrown at him had embedded itself to the hilt in his hamstring.

He groaned and lay there for a few seconds, his chest heaving.

Fool! he raged at himself. *Fool for turning your back on someone like him!*

Moans reached him.

He turned his head.

Ed flushed his face with water from the sink's hose to rid himself of the dishwashing powder.

Jabir gritted his teeth and pulled the knife out. He tossed it toward the back to take it out of play. He gathered his feet under him, leapt upward, and charged Ed.

His foot slipped on water, and the tackle meant to knock Ed out merely sent him to the floor with Jabir on top of him.

Ed shoved him off.

Jabir lunged, trying to grab the man's arms to pin him down.

The developing suds of the dishwashing detergent made his hands slip.

Ed pushed him.

Jabir winced as his back slammed into the leg of the counter under the pass-through window. With his good leg, he launched himself again at Ed. They tumbled to the floor.

Ed got a foot on Jabir's chest. He thrust him away.

Jabir landed hard on his back and skidded through the muck. He wheezed as he tried to recover the breath knocked from him.

With a growl, Ed leapt on top of him, pinning his wrists to the wet tile. His former boss grinned, the redness in his eyes making the gray practically glow. "You thought you could win, huh? Well, son, I hate to say it, but I didn't make it this far in life by being nice."

Jabir thrashed. He reared up and clamped down on Ed's arm with his teeth.

Ed yelped. His grip slacked, and Jabir kicked at him, sending him against the leg of the worktable.

He recovered and charged Jabir.

Jabir blocked a punch and parried with a thrust of his own that caught Ed on the nose.

Ed moaned and staggered back.

Jabir rolled to his feet and jumped him, sending them both skidding on the floor and under the doors leading to behind the counter.

Ed clapped Jabir on the ear before scrambling toward the back.

He moaned and crawled after him. He tackled the CIA officer.

Ed flipped over and clawed at him, raking his fingers across his face.

Jabir grabbed his wrists. He sent Ed onto his back with a sharp jab.

A rage he hadn't known he possessed swept over Jabir.

He slammed his knee into Ed's chest and drew his combat knife. He cocked it above his head, ready to strike. "I should kill you for what you did to Abdel, Ari, and Stephen."

Ed grinned. "Go ahead. Kill me. It'll make things better, right? Like four years ago."

Jabir drew a sharp breath.

Ed sucker-punched Jabir in the face.

Though not hard, it sent Jabir off balance.

Ed got his foot on his chest and hurled him backwards.

Jabir felt himself flying through the air. He hit the floor with a grunt, rolled, and came to rest near the end of the worktable.

The knife flew out of his hands and clattered out of sight.

He eased onto his back and raised himself onto his elbows.

Ed hauled himself to his feet. He reached for something hanging from a hook.

Jabir began crab-crawling away with his good leg, leaving a trail of scarlet behind him and dragging his bad leg uselessly. His adrenaline dissipated, weakening him to the point where his limbs trembled. Pain radiated from his injury. He groaned.

Ed turned with a meat hammer in his hand. Blood streamed from his nose, and his shirt had torn during their fight. Fury blazed from those red-tinged gray eyes. Tapping the hammer in his hand, he stalked him step for step, then raised it. "I'm going to knock you out. Not kill you, mind you.

Just knock you out. Then saw you up with that machete of mine so all your girlfriend will find are pieces. And guess what? I'll start with your arms and legs so you'll feel every bit of it."

Jabir's arms gave way.

With a groan, he sank to the ground.

Lord, make it quick.

His hand frantically searched for something, anything, he could use to defend himself.

Ed grinned as if he knew his moment of triumph was at hand. "And you know what? I'm going to—"

A clang resounded. Ed's eyes rolled back in his head. His face slackened. With a moan, he collapsed in slow motion, first to his knees and then onto his front into the mess of suds, water, and blood.

Alex stood there, anger smoldering in her sea green eyes, as she brandished the frying pan. "You're what? Do tell, Mr. DuBois."

Jabir laid his head against the tile. "I thought I told you—"

"Oh, can it, Jabir." Alex cable-tied Ed's hands before kneeling beside Jabir.

With his remaining strength, he reached up and touched her cheek. "I'm so glad you're here."

He began trembling from blood loss. His vision blurred, and his heart hammered in his ears. Shouts echoed as if something pulled him down a long tunnel. They sounded like those of his comrades. Jabir gripped Alex's hand with all his remaining strength.

"You owe me," she murmured, but her smile betrayed her words. She gathered him in her arms as he passed out.

Day 9
Monday, June 19, 2017

44

"You are not to open the door to anyone. Do you understand?" Tension clipped Interpol Agent Leila al-Kadir's words as she strode to the foyer of Samir's house.

"No one?"

She stopped and faced him. "No one."

"Not even my family?"

"No. Do you not understand that your testimony puts you in grave danger?"

"Why not take me to the police station?"

Agent Mansour, who'd interviewed him along with the Interpol agent, shook his head. "Samir, you must understand that Tarek has moles everywhere. You're safest here until Agent al-Kadir can take you into protective custody."

"The Americans have offered you protective custody at an undisclosed location until Tarek is arrested," Agent al-Kadir added. "Their plane won't be here until eight thirty tonight. I'll be by with Inspector Mansour at eight o'clock. That gives you three hours to pack. I suggest you make the most of it."

"Okay." Samir hated the way his voice sounded small and thin.

"Until then, be sure to lock all of your doors. Be ready at eight. If you're not? Oh, well. You'll go with what you have on." Agent al-Kadir nodded at the inspector.

Once they'd gone, Samir rested his forehead against the heavy wooden door. After a moment's hesitation, he threw the deadbolt. Then he added the two chain locks that had come with the house. He wandered to the back. A hot breeze sifted through the open doors leading to the patio.

Already, the wind had shifted.

Samir shivered. He shut them and threw the deadbolts, grimacing at the way the glass shut out the sounds of the outdoors.

With a heavy heart, he climbed the broad staircase to the second floor. He pulled out all of his suitcases. Samir stepped into his walk-in closet and began yanking clothes from their hangars. Not even bothering to fold them properly, he stuffed them into both over-sized suitcases, closing them only by almost sitting on the lids. The smaller ones held the shoes, belts, and other accessories he wanted to take.

With a grunt, Samir lugged each downstairs. Then he grabbed an old briefcase from his study and slid his tablet and laptop into it.

A picture on his desk caught his eye. He picked it up. Noor, resplendent in her wedding finery, smiled broadly, her brother on one side, Fadi on the other. All so innocent. Tears welled in Samir's eyes as he ran his finger down the glass. He added it to the briefcase. Then he turned and found one of him and his parents on one of the bookshelves.

Papa's angry shouts and Mama's tears echoed in his ears.

He wanted to be angry at his father, but nothing came.

No, his poor decisions had led to that moment.

But Noor believed in him.

Could he redeem himself in Mama's and Papa's eyes?

Samir earnestly hoped his testimony would be a start. He pulled it off the shelf and added it to the briefcase.

He turned to leave, and his gaze accidentally landed on another photograph. Tarek posed with Samir for the camera, both holding martini glasses at Tarek's nightclub in the Ras Beirut district. Nausea knotted his stomach.

With a defiant jerk, Samir zipped the briefcase closed. He carried it to the foyer.

A drink sounded appealing at the moment. Samir wandered into the den and fixed himself a bourbon on the rocks. As he sipped, he gazed around the room as if seeing it for the first and the last time all at once.

Outside, the sun had begun its final plunge toward the sea. Its scarlet light caught the painting he'd bought with some of his finder's fee from Tarek and made the reds in it glow so much that they almost pulsed.

Noor appeared before him, her hand cupped around her belly. "Samir, I'm expecting again." Her smile lit up her face. "A girl once more. Fadi and I want to name her Samira after you."

"Noor." His sister's name escaped his lips before he realized he spoke to empty air. Emotion filled him, and he threw back his drink.

A gust of wind hit the closed doors, rattling them, making him shiver.

Samir's gaze shot to the patio. Now, the palm fronds shook in the wind. Red light fast gave way to black.

"It's easy like last time." Tarek's voice echoed off the tile and the plaster walls. They shared drinks while lounging on the leather couches and watching a football match two years before. Lubricated by alcohol, Samir's agreement to the scheme to launder money came easily. "Except this time, you get to keep ten percent of any proceeds generated. Call it a finder's fee."

"Fool," Samir now muttered. He jumped as he heard a keening produced by the wind skittering along the eaves of the house. Out of the corner of his eye, he thought he noticed a shadow flitting about the room. He shivered.

His glass was now empty.

Samir stumbled to the wet bar and picked up the bourbon bottle. His hand shook so badly that the neck tinkled against the lip of the crystal. He had to use both hands to set it down.

He gulped a swallow.

Footsteps echoed in the foyer.

Samir froze.

They were slow. Even.

He closed his eyes.

When he opened them, he gasped. The tumbler fell from his hand, the crystal shattering into a thousand pieces against the tile. He didn't notice the way the golden liquid splattered on his trousers.

"Going somewhere, are you?" Tarek's voice made reality snap into place.

"What…what are you…how…how…" Samir's voice failed.

No smile flickered across Tarek's face. The dim light of the foyer's chandelier made his blue eyes almost glitter. "I see you've packed for a long trip."

He tapped one of the suitcases with an elegant loafer. "Going someplace special?"

"N—no. Business. Papa wanted me to—"

"And where is this business?"

Samir's mind scrambled for an answer. "I…well…to Australia. We've wanted to expand to Sydney—"

"You know, Samir, you never were a good liar." Disappointment echoed in Tarek's voice. "Tell me the truth now."

Samir panicked. He turned and bolted toward the back doors.

Two men dressed in black stood on the patio.

He whipped around to try and run past Tarek, only to find Hashim now standing beside his brother.

Hashim raised a strange-looking gun and squeezed the trigger.

Something impaled itself in his clothing. Samir stared at it dumbly and tried to scream. Electricity flooded his body.

Everything went black.

A noise penetrated his gray haze. It sounded like metal on stone.

Samir slowly wagged his head from side to side. He opened his eyes.

A blurry light nearly blinded him.

Where was he?

Samir blinked, his eyes watering. Something slid down his face. A tear? Finally, his vision cleared.

He stared at a chandelier, the one that hung above his dinette table.

He moved his arm to try and rise, except that he couldn't.

Samir jerked his other arm.

Immobile.

He jerked harder, drawing the knots around his wrists tighter.

The same thing with his legs.

He began squirming and opened his mouth to shout for help.

His cry came as a muted bleat.

His movement produced a smooth feeling across the skin of his back.

Samir's eyes widened. He wore nothing except his underwear.

"Help!"

Again, something muffled his plea.

"Now, now, Samir. No need to panic." Tarek's smooth voice reached his ears.

Samir raised his head. His friend smiled at him from near his right foot. Hashim stood to his right at his head.

Tarek nodded.

Hashim ripped away the tape.

Samir moaned as the skin around his mouth burned.

Tarek stepped closer. Something glinted in his hands as he shifted it. A butcher's knife from the block in the kitchen caught the chandelier's light.

Samir's chest heaved. "Tarek, please...I told them nothing."

"Oh? And I'm to believe that?" Doubt echoed in his friend's voice. "Hashim, do you believe he's telling the truth?"

"Not at all." Hashim smirked as he ran a wicked-looking knife along a stone block. He set the block down and caressed the knife's sharp edge.

Tarek leaned his hip against the table. "I agree with my brother. You see, Samir, all throughout the years I've known you, you've been a good friend. A good friend who has, for the most part, been very trustworthy. Yet I got a little suspicious that perhaps you aren't as loyal as I assumed, and you know something? Betrayal hurts. Hurts like hell. So..." Tarek rested the flat side of the butcher knife against Samir's middle. "You're going to tell me all you know, you understand? Especially since I know time is short. Start talking."

Samir's heart hammered. He thrashed, only drawing the knots around his wrists and ankles tighter. His words came out in pants.

"I...know...nothing."

Tarek turned the butcher's knife on its edge.

Samir's scream filled the air. "No!"

Day 10
Tuesday, June 20, 2017

45

"I am so sorry for your loss, Aya," the older woman stated as she took Mama's hands.

The two women embraced.

Noor remained where she was by the window and watched the men begin disassembling the tent where prayers for Samir's soul had been given earlier that day. She'd cried so much over the past twenty-four hours that now, only her shoulders shook.

Her tear ducts had run dry.

Another woman entered the bonus room of hers and Fadi's house where she and Mama received women visitors. This woman stood tall, her dark eyes sweeping the room in one glance. Her gaze landed on Noor. She greeted Mama, kissing her on both cheeks, hugging her close, and whispering something in her ear. She stepped back and said something else.

Noor ignored her. Nothing could fill the hole in her heart left by Samir's grisly death. She closed her eyes, and the gory scene from the night before filled them. Nausea swelled, and she wrapped her arms around herself to stave off what was bound to come. As she willed her stomach to settle, she turned and resumed her contemplation of the courtyard below and the street beyond the glass-topped walls.

"Noor." A female voice said something from near her elbow.

She turned her gaze and found Leila al-Kadir next to her, a white head-scarf draped over her head as Islamic funeral custom required.

"Are you going to tell me how sorry you are?"

"Yes, and how I feel personally responsible."

"He didn't lock the doors. Of course Tarek would have gotten in."

"Actually, I know he locked the front door. I heard the deadbolt. And he was scared enough to obey me." Leila took her arm and led her toward a corner. In a low voice, she continued, "We found scratches along the pedestrian gate, indicating someone picked the lock. Then at the laundry room door, we discovered that the deadbolt hadn't been thrown."

Noor winced. Samir never would have bothered to check the door used by the household help.

"I'm—"

Voices downstairs distracted Noor.

Male voices.

A male voice that sounded too familiar.

Tarek.

Rage filled her.

Straightening and lifting her chin, she stepped into the hallway. Her feet had a life of their own. With gathering speed, she descended, barely aware of the way that the men's voices petered out.

Tarek stood in the archway separating the living room from the foyer as he talked with Fadi, Papa, and Uncle Yacoub. The devil was indeed handsome in his black suit, black shirt, and blood-red tie. He'd even trimmed the waves in his hair so they brushed his collar, and his beard hugged his jaw.

"You!" Her word echoed like a shot off the high ceiling of the foyer.

Noor came to a stop within inches of him.

"Noor, I was deeply saddened to hear of Samir's passing." He reached toward her.

"You are not sorry." She slapped his hand away.

"What?"

"You're not sorry at all."

"Noor, I'm trying to be reasonable. And when—"

"Shut up."

"Noor!" Papa's shocked voice barely registered.

"You come here and try to act like you had nothing to do with this. You are *such a liar*!" Noor charged him.

Fadi caught her before she could rake her nails across Tarek's face. "Noor."

She thrashed against him. "I know you did it, Tarek al-Hassan. You took my brother's life."

Tarek must have been aware that others stared at him. He chuckled in disbelief. "I know you are grieving, but this is ridiculous."

"He was a loyal friend and loved you like a brother." Tears streamed down her face.

Fadi's fingers felt like talons in her arms. He simply wouldn't let her go and slap their guest.

"He cared enough about your friendship to follow you, even to the point where he took the fall for your crimes." Her voice rose, but she didn't care. "And how do you repay him? You *murder* him."

That last sentence zinged around the room.

Shocked murmurs rippled through the men. A shriek and a thump told her Mama must have fainted.

Tarek only stared at her, his blue eyes piercing her soul, daring her to continue her accusations. A flush started in his neck and worked its way to his face. "Noor, I know you are sad and grieving. Perhaps strung-out as well from not sleeping. Or other things." A smile played at the corners of his mouth. "But you as well as I know your accusations are baseless and the words of a hysterical woman."

"I am *not* hysterical." She lunged at him again, but Fadi wouldn't let her go.

"Noor, go upstairs. Now." Then he added in a low voice, "Go before you make things worse."

He nudged her toward the stairs.

Her husband might as well have hurled her in that direction.

Crying now, Noor whirled and faced Tarek one last time. "I know you are guilty, Tarek al-Hassan. And I won't stop until you pay for murdering my brother."

She turned and found Leila standing halfway down the wide staircase. The Interpol agent's gaze didn't focus on her. It remained on her adversary.

"She's hysterical and grieving. I accept your apology, Fadi."

Tarek's voice taunted her as Noor ran the rest of the way up the stairs, past where two women shot her venomous looks as they fanned Mama, and into the master bedroom. She slammed the door, collapsed on the soft bed, and wept. Tears once more flowed, dampening her cheeks and wetting the comforter.

"Noor."

She raised her head.

Leila sat on the edge of the bed, her white headscarf now resting on her shoulders to reveal a pixie cut framing her face with teasing tendrils of black hair.

"What…are you doing here?"

"I heard what you said."

Noor put her face in her hands. She'd humiliated Papa and Fadi. How could she ever face them again?

"And I believe you."

"What?" Noor lowered her hands.

Leila shoved some tissues into them. "I believe you. Tarek murdered Samir. Him and his brother."

"We have no proof."

"I'll get proof." Steel strengthened Leila's words.

"How?"

"I don't know." The Interpol agent rose. She stepped to the door. "I feel responsible for what happened to your brother, and I'm going to make Tarek al-Hassan pay for his deeds. That much, I can promise."

1600 hours Mountain Daylight Time, (1700 hours CDT), near Playa Flamingo, Costa Rica

"It's good to see you haven't lost your touch." Tiny smiled as he switched off the digital recorder and surveyed the papers spread before him on the coffee table of the bungalow where Alex was staying with Melanie, Jabir, and Melanie's fiancé.

Alex had curled up in one of the veranda's chairs and sipped the mango lemonade she'd brought with her from lunch. "I couldn't let Ed hurt Becca further."

"What induced you to go after Jabir?"

"I knew Ed would kill him if he had half a chance. I have to admit that grabbing the frying pan was pure instinct."

"You saved his life, you know."

She nodded, the emotion from that day threatening to sweep over her again. She bit her lip. "I'm ready to move past that."

"I'm sure." Tiny adjusted his glasses and studied his notes.

Alex busied herself with thinking about the next move she'd spent the entire night planning. She took another sip, savoring the sweetness of the drink. "What happened to Ed?"

He shifted in his seat as he leaned back. "Let's just say he got his own trip to paradise, only his accommodations include concertina wire and lots of people he sent there."

"And then?"

"I have no idea. CIA has pretty much clammed up about it." He cleared his throat and raised his hand as if to search for the tie he normally wore. Seeming to catch his actions, he ruefully smiled. "They wanted to debrief all of you in DC. I made them an offer. If they spilled everything about the investigation into Ed DuBois's involvement with JOL, then I'd escort the lot of you to Virginia. Otherwise, I insisted that the debrief be here in Playa Flamingo. They conceded, and the debrief team for Jabir should be arriving soon."

"So I guess we girls will be going shopping tomorrow."

"Unless you want so spend all day with the CIA."

Alex grimaced. "I think I'll pass, thanks."

A boy's shout made her glance up. Below, Ellie's two children scampered down the path leading to a thin stand of palms lining the beach. Hand in hand, Ellie followed with her husband. Seeing her friend made something flit through her mind. "What about Hashim and Tarek?"

"We think they were the two who left early. Why, we can only guess. I think the CIA knows, but again, they aren't saying."

Alex swallowed hard. A ripple of unease uncurled within her as she thought about the man she'd fooled so many years before. "I guess I'm worried that I might be vulnerable to Hashim."

Tiny shook his head. "Your living in Weatherly is your best protection. He'd be a fool to risk his freedom for simple revenge."

"You're sure?"

Tiny nodded. "Absolutely. Hashim has a lot more on his mind right now too. Like staying under CIA's radar since he was the one who turned Ed."

"True."

Tiny gathered his papers into a neat stack, tapped them on the table to align them, and slid them into the folder. "So what are you plans tonight?"

"I'm meeting the rest of the Fantabulous Four at the fire pit on the beach." Alex nodded toward the glittering ocean where the sun had begun setting. "Then the guys are joining us at six. Thanks again for being willing to fly them all down here."

"It's the least I could do after everything you four endured. And I'm glad Melanie pulled through."

"Doc was awesome."

"Once we're done with the debrief tomorrow, Jabir will officially be on leave until mid-July, per my orders. I'll check in with you tomorrow before I leave." Tiny rose and turned to go.

Alex took a deep breath and blurted, "I want back in."

Tiny stopped, his hand on the knob to step into the common room of the villa. He turned, raising an eyebrow in question.

"I want back into Unit 28." Thoughts clicking like the wheels on a train screaming down the tracks, she rushed on before she lost her nerve. "I can't explain how I felt when I was trying to find Melanie. I felt...alive, if that makes any sense."

"It does." Tiny returned to his seat on the couch. "I thought you'd finally made Weatherly your home again. At least that's what your daddy said the last time I talked with him."

"Oh, it is." Alex took a deep breath. "You see, I wouldn't want to return to DC. I'd...I'd like to be a contractor, to be able to continue working with Diana in construction but also to run Unit 28 missions."

"You'd need a partner."

Her mind flashed to the bedroom nearby where Jabir slept away the afternoon thanks to the painkillers he'd taken. "I know. I'd like Jabir to be my partner."

"And you've talked with him about it?" Tiny leaned his elbows on his knees, rested his chin on his hands, and studied her with such intensity that his brow knitted.

"Not in depth," she hedged. She gripped the glass tighter and curled her toes.

Then Tiny smiled. "You always were persistent."

"Which is a good trait for Unit 28 agents—or contractors for Unit 28—to have."

"All right. You're convincing me. Talk to Jabir, and if he's agreeable, then I'll see what I can do."

"Really?" Alex jumped to her feet.

Tiny rose almost right into her hug. "Yes. Now let me take my leave. Tell Jabir I'll see him in the morning."

Alex walked him to the door. After he left, she shut it and leaned against it. A smile spread across her face.

She was in.

She knew it.

1745 hours Mountain Daylight Time (1845 hours CDT), near Playa Flamingo, Costa Rica

Waves lapped at the soft white sand. Over the water, the sun began its final descent into the ocean as it brushed the sky with delicate hues of orange, pink, and red. On the beach, a fire burned in the fire pit surrounded by small stones. The flickering of the flames highlighted the four women dressed in their finery as they leaned back in low-slung beach chairs and talked about nothing in particular.

Just like they'd planned when Melanie had announced her engagement.

"Ah, vacation at last," Melanie sighed as she sipped the piña colada she'd made at their villa.

"I hear you." Becca, dressed in white Capri pants with a red tank top, stretched and winced. "Though Hashim's 'gifts' to me still make me look like a freak."

"We don't care," Ellie told her from where she attached a camera to a Gorilla tripod clamped to another chair. "We're all together and in one piece."

"And you don't even have to worry with war paint," Alex added. She wove her toes through the soft sand.

Becca stuck out her tongue, and all four women giggled. Then the petite brunette asked, "Melanie, how are you feeling?"

"Tons better. One moment, I was in Panama feeling like I was about to die, and then, once they administered the medication, it was almost like a day-night shift. I'm just glad Doc said I could rest up at Playa Flamingo. It beats a Navy infirmary."

"By a long shot." Alex nodded. "Where are the guys? Could it be that they're running late?"

"Truer words are never spoken." Ellie grinned. "Okay, girls. We've got to get a picture before they get here. If everyone will gather around Melanie, we can do it with the frame I've got. Alex, I'll come crouch with you. On my count. One… two… three."

Laughing, they scrambled to join Melanie as the light on the camera blinked red for a few seconds. With a pop of the flash, they recorded their time together for posterity. Ellie crawled to the camera. "Perfect."

"One more!" Becca shouted.

More laughter and a click later, they heard male voices.

Ellie's children ran onto the scene. Her son grabbed her arm. "Mommy! Will you go walking on the beach with us?"

Ellie raised her gaze. Her husband took her hand and helped her to her feet. "Do you girls mind?"

"Go ahead." Becca smiled at hers as he joined her and kissed her hello.

"And where's Jabir?" Alex asked as Melanie's fiancé handed the bride-to-be an icy drink.

"He's on his way. He said something about making a stop."

"I hope not at Tiny's place." Alex scowled as she remembered how her former boss was like a father figure to Jabir. "If they get to talking, there's no telling what time he'll show."

"Our reservations aren't until seven. Thank you, sweetie." Becca took the drink from her husband's hand. In a low voice, she added, "I think Ellie and Matt patched things up this afternoon."

"Oh?" Alex raised an eyebrow.

Melanie leaned forward. "Do tell."

"She said he agreed it's time to sell the business in Durango and move back to Weatherly. I guess being apart from Ellie and then almost losing her gave him time to think."

"Wow." Alex blinked. "That's amazing." She bit her lip, not willing to share her own bit of news until she talked with Jabir.

"So what's up with you and Jabir?" The teasing tone in Becca's voice drew her back to the present.

Alex felt a blush beginning in her neck. "Um…"

"Spill it, Thornton. Are you two an item?" Melanie sipped her drink and leaned into her fiancé.

"Uh, I guess you could say that." Now, the heat had reached her cheeks. "He said he's coming down to visit as soon as he returns to DC and spends time with his mom. And—"

"And what?" That question and a drop of cold water on her arm told her Jabir had arrived.

Alex glanced up.

He stood there, dressed in a pair of chinos and a white linen shirt with the sleeves rolled up past his elbows and the shirttails out.

Her cheeks warmed as she gazed at his slender yet deceptively strong physique.

Becca grinned and replied, "And maybe you'll take your new girlfriend for a walk."

Jabir nodded and rubbed his chin as if deep in thought. "You know? That might not be such a bad idea."

Melanie laughed.

Jabir carefully set both drinks down in the sand before turning to Becca and Rodrigo. "Not for general consumption by you two." Then he faced Rick and Melanie. "Or you two."

"Yes, sir!" Becca saluted him. "Be gone with you. Just be back soon. I'm hungry."

"C'mon." Jabir extended his hand toward Alex.

She rose and took his arm.

Using the cane he'd bought in the resort's gift shop, Jabir held onto her and hobbled toward the beach.

"How's the leg?"

"Resting today helped. Doc said I could swim later this week. And hopefully stop limping within a couple of weeks as well."

"I'm glad." Alex sighed as she stared at the sunset. "This is so incredibly beautiful. Remind me to bring my camera out here tomorrow night."

"Done." Jabir held onto her hand. "How did things go with Tiny?"

"Good. He said you're talking with the CIA tomorrow."

He sighed. "Yeah. All day, probably."

"I'll go shopping."

"You would."

She laughed. "I'm just glad Tiny convinced them to do things down here."

"Me too because it gives me more time with you." He leaned over and lightly kissed her on the lips. Softly, he added, "And to be honest, I don't want it any other way."

Alex's heart tripped up a notch at that. She stepped into his embrace as he wove his hands through her hair. "I love you."

"I love you too." Those words came as a whisper. "Tiny also told me a certain someone wants back in."

She raised her face. "He told you that?"

A mysterious smile played about his lips. "The man shares no secrets if it's not classified and if it involves me."

"I know we only briefly talked about it. I wanted to talk to you more, but he showed up, and then you were sleeping and—"

Jabir silenced her with a kiss. "No need to worry. I told him I was in."

Rational thought returned with a splash. "What?"

"I'm in as a contractor. At the end of July, I'll officially separate from Unit 28. So you'd better start thinking up a name for our company."

"Oh, wow." Joy flooded her. She wrapped her arms around him and held on tightly.

"Um, that's not the best name."

"You're silly, you know that?"

He ran his hand down her back, which was left bare by the frock she'd worn to the embassy only five days before. "I try."

He fell silent for so long that Alex knew he was thinking hard.

She pulled back and ran her hand down his face, her fingers tracing the faint scar. She gazed into his eyes, which had turned almost black in the twilight. Tiny furrows had formed between them. "What is it?"

"What's what?"

She reached up and rubbed away those lines. "You seem worried. Concerned."

"Just thinking," he told her.

"As always," they chorused.

The furrows disappeared.

Alex laughed. "So nothing's really changed."

He drew her close, tipped her chin, and kissed her in a way that made any worries vanish.

"So anyway, I have this wedding to go to," she murmured against his mouth.

"Oh?" His hand slid up under her hair and rubbed the base of her neck. "And when would that be?"

"Sometime in August. I've got to wear a long, navy dress. The problem is, I have no date."

Jabir ran his hands down her arms. "So you have no date."

"Right. Um, I heard this really cute guy decided to move to Weatherly. You know him. Dark hair and eyes. Thinks way too much for his own good."

"Uh, huh."

"Will you be my date?"

"I'd be glad to." Jabir's eyes twinkled. "Matter of fact, I'd be honored."

Once more, he bent and kissed her.

Oh, how good that felt. And how good it was to know that he'd be there with her and that perhaps this one kiss would lead to something else as well.

These past ten days had been worth it.

Well worth it.

Epilogue

Jabir sipped a steaming travel mug of hot tea as he stood at the open French doors and gazed over the Juliet balcony at the people hurrying along the sidewalk below. The umbrellas created a colorful collage like mushrooms that had sprung up from the rain generated by a hurricane skirting the coast. Right then, the refreshing breeze and humidity beat the stark chilliness of the air conditioning by a long shot.

He set the mug on top of a nearby box, then rose up on his toes and stretched his arms above his head until every muscle lengthened. He released a sigh and eased onto his heels.

Reluctantly, Jabir turned and gazed at the cardboard boxes filling the living room to the level of the granite bar. Somewhere in the mess was his couch, the very couch where he yearned to nap on a rainy afternoon like this. He couldn't. Not with Alex coming at five. She'd fuss at him for being lazy.

Jabir located the small boom box he'd left unpacked. With the radio tuned to the rock station out of Raleigh, he hummed along to Van Morrison's "Brown-Eyed Girl" as he slit the tape on his dishware and began loading the dishwasher. Once he got that running, he moved on to the

409

books. By the time he'd filled the shelves, he'd knocked out five boxes and discovered his couch.

He sat down, then stretched out. Oh, yes. It felt good to lie down.

At least until a knock on the door made him jump.

Jabir sat up as it sounded again. He rose and opened the door.

Roya Thornton, Alex's mother, stood on the threshold. She smiled. "Jabir, hi."

"Hi." He grinned and stepped aside. "Come on in. What brings you to my humble abode?"

"I was going to see Mattie Hendrix. Have you met her yet?"

"Probably at the wedding, though I met so many people, I can't say." Jabir stepped into the kitchen. "Something to drink?"

"Sure. Water would be good."

"Water it is." He located a plastic cup and filled it with ice cubes. "Sorry about the plastic, but my glassware is washing right now."

"I understand. Mattie Hendrix owns Spin A Yarn, which is the store beneath Alex's flat. She got some new patterns in and wanted me to take a look. Where's Alex? I thought she'd be helping you unpack."

"She's installing some cabinetry with her crew. What do you have there?"

She hefted a gift basket onto the granite counter. "A 'Welcome to Weatherly' present for you. Check it out."

"Wow." Jabir shoved aside some of the tissue and peered at the goodies.

"Popcorn. For when you get your DVD player hooked up and can watch a movie." She pulled that out. "An application for a frequent shopper card for the Piggly Wiggly down the road. Believe me, it's worth it." Roya laid that on top of the popcorn, and a smile flitted across her face. "Alex told you about that, didn't she?"

"Uh, huh. I didn't believe her at first."

Roya laughed that deep, rich laugh that was so like her daughter's. "A gift card to the local Ace Hardware store. I'm sure you'll need that. How about some sparkling grape juice? Goes with the popcorn. And a ten-pass certificate to Joe's Gym. He was more than happy to supply me with one when I told him you were coming."

"Roya, thanks." Jabir sorted through everything, then set it back into the basket lest it get lost in his mess. "With luck, I'll be able to eat the popcorn tonight. Alex is coming over at five. I found my couch, and hopefully, I can get the DVD plugged in."

"Make sure she doesn't hog it."

He chuckled.

Alex.

The thought of her brought back memories of his discovery a couple of months before. Something told him to leave it be, to not ask Roya about it, but he'd never been good at leaving mysteries alone. "Do you have a few minutes?"

"Sure." She took her cup to the sitting area and sat down on the couch.

"Do you remember when I told you how the Jihad of Light cell had kidnapped Melanie and demanded Alex in exchange for her?"

"Of course." She shuddered. "It scared me to death."

"Me too," he admitted. "I wondered why they suddenly shifted their priorities from acquiring the property to wanting Alex. At first I thought it was because of one of the missions she had run with Monica Chapman."

Roya frowned, "Was it?"

He bit his lip and perched on the edge of the easy chair. He rested his elbows on his knees and stared at the coffee table. "Maybe, but most likely not."

"I'm not sure what you mean."

He forced himself to meet her eyes. "I started doing some research. And…" He bit his lip. Now, the brutal truth made it hard to raise his gaze. "And, I discovered that Alex's biological father is Hamid al-Hassan. Not David."

Roya's gray-brown eyes widened. Her jaw dropped, and she reeled as if he'd slapped her across the face. The cup slipped from her fingers, spilling water onto the glass of the table.

She closed her eyes and brought a trembling hand to her lips.

"She doesn't know, does she?" It came out as a statement instead of a question.

"No," Roya whispered. She put her head in her hands. "She doesn't. Not at all."

"But why?" That question exploded from Jabir's lips before he could stop it.

"David's her father. Her real father." Roya finally met his gaze.

"Why haven't you told her?"

"How can I? She doesn't need to know. All it would do would be to create anger."

"Doesn't she have a right to know? Roya, she's a curious person. She's no dummy either, and believe me, she's wondered about why all of the sudden they wanted her rather than the property."

"She probably thinks it's because of that mission."

"She knows I know something more." Jabir rose and paced along the small aisle created by the boxes.

"You haven't told her, have you?" Roya's voice came from behind him.

He turned and shook his head. "I haven't." He swallowed hard. "I think that's the kind of news only a mother should share with her daughter."

Roya closed her eyes and began shaking her head. "I can't."

"Roya..."

"I can't!"

Jabir jumped at her sharp tone. He blew out an impatient sigh. "Look. When Alex and I reunited in Panama, I'm sure you know it was a rough start."

She nodded.

"There was a lot of mistrust between us. I told her there would be no secrets. Do you understand where I'm going with this?"

"You can't tell her."

"I don't *want* to." Jabir took a deep breath and tried to bring his frustration under control. "I don't. I want *you* to tell her. Look." He shook his head, barely succeeding at patience. "I love your daughter, and it doesn't take a lot of imagination to see where our relationship is most likely headed. But I cannot, no, will not, start out a marriage with a secret like that between us. Do you understand what I'm saying?"

Roya remained silent. Her eyes narrowed, and the light suddenly glinted in them like sun flashing off glass. It didn't take much for him to imagine from where Alex had gotten at least part of her temper. When she spoke, the steel reflected in her voice. "You have some nerve, Jabir. Some nerve. I'll expect you to keep your mouth shut about this."

Jabir took an automatic step back. "Roya, please. Please tell her. Far better for you to tell her than for her to stumble across the truth."

"You'll not say a word, do you understand? Not a word. And if you do? I'll never, ever forgive you." With that, she whipped around, stalked through the boxes, and snatched her umbrella off the tile where she'd left it.

Jabir winced as the door slammed. He'd done his part. He'd put Roya on notice that such secrets couldn't be kept. Only she'd ignored him, preferring the bondage of such weighty information. He knew the truth would come out even if it never crossed his lips. And when it did? He shuddered. World War Three would start. And if he were lucky, he and Alex would still be speaking by the end of it.

Acknowledgements

Writing a novel is never an easy venture, and *Panama Deception* was almost the novel that wasn't. Thank you to all of you who have encouraged me to keep at it. For Steve, my beloved, who patiently listened as I described the difficulties I encountered and read through two drafts. I also want to thank my family and friends, including my critique group, Seven Serious Scribes, who also patiently listened and offered insights related to the content. Thank you to all for encouraging me to take the risk that became this novel.

www.ingramcontent.com/pod-product-compliance
Lightning Source LLC
Chambersburg PA
CBHW070900260626
47162CB00007B/2518